SHADOWS
OF THE
PAST

Center Point
Large Print

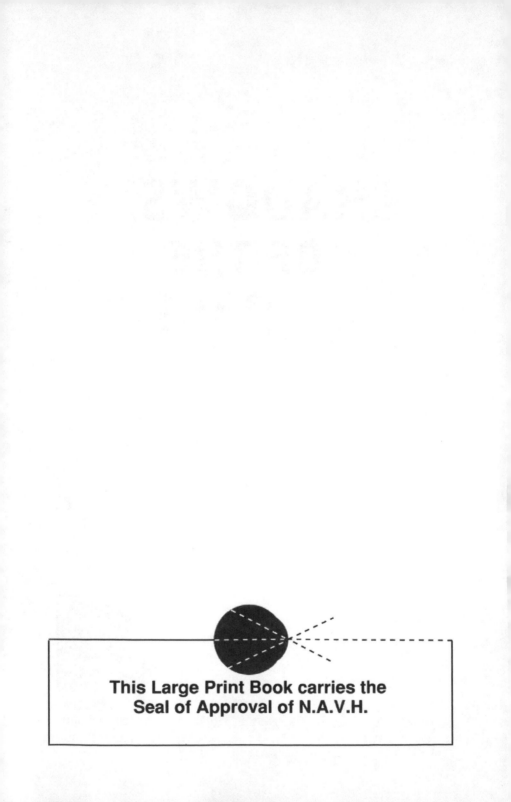

**This Large Print Book carries the
Seal of Approval of N.A.V.H.**

SHADOWS
OF THE
PAST

Patricia
Bradley

CENTER POINT LARGE PRINT
THORNDIKE, MAINE

This Center Point Large Print edition is published in
the year 2014 by arrangement with Revell,
a divison of Baker Publishing Group.

Copyright © 2014 by Patricia Bradley.

The text of this Large Print edition is unabridged.
In other aspects, this book may vary
from the original edition.
Printed in the United States of America
on permanent paper.
Set in 16-point Times New Roman type.

ISBN: 978-1-62899-019-5

Library of Congress Cataloging-in-Publication Data

Bradley, Patricia (Educator)
Shadows of the past / Patricia Bradley. —
Center Point Large Print edition.
pages ; cm
ISBN 978-1-62899-019-5 (library binding : alk. paper)
1. Large type books. I. Title.
PS3602.R34275S53 2014b
813′.6—dc23

2013041097

To Jesus, my Lord and Savior

Acknowledgments

There are so many to thank for making this book possible.

My family and friends for believing in me—my daughters, Elisa and Carole. My mom, Frances, and my sister, Barbara. Bryan for his love and encouragement. Patricia and Cheryl, who talked me off more than one ledge. My critique partners, Chandra, Johnnie, Renee, and Rob—you made this book better. And Delores, who prayed me through more than one crisis.

To Susan May Warren and Rachel Hauck—you two changed my writing life. Thank you. And thanks to the Ponderers and My Book Therapy for being one of the best writing communities out there.

To Dr. Amy Davis, my go-to for physician and hospital-related questions, and Dr. Reba Hoffman, who answered many of my questions dealing with psychology and university credentials. Any mistakes in not getting the facts straight are mine.

To my wonderful agent, Mary Sue Seymour, who loved my work.

To my amazing and gifted editors, Lonnie Hull DuPont and Kristin Kornoelje—a special thanks for your patience, kindness, and valuable input. And to the Revell art, editorial, marketing, and sales teams for your hard work—you are the best!

And most of all to my heavenly Father who loves me.

I

Death unfolds like a budding flower,
Tentatively, sweetly.
Unfurling in majestic power.
Until then, my love . . . until then.

Black roses last week, now spidery words scrawled on a scrap of paper with "Meade Funeral Home" printed across the top. Someone was stalking her, and they wanted her to know it.

Taylor Martin sucked in a sharp breath and tried to ignore the icy shiver traversing her body.

He was here.

Hair raised on the back of her neck. She turned in a circle. Heavy clouds hung low, shrouding the tall firs with their mist. An air ambulance waited in the clearing to lift off for Seattle as soon as Beth Coleman's vitals stabilized. Only a few members of the search and rescue team remained at the crime scene, packing their gear.

Whether he was one of the men who came out to comb the woods for the kidnapper and his victims, or he'd simply followed her here to this remote area southwest of Seattle, it didn't matter. What mattered was that he'd been close enough to touch her, to put the note in her pocket.

To kill her.

An artery in her temple pulsed. He had to know she volunteered her profiling skills to the Newton County Sheriff's Department.

A puff of wind brought a light fragrance. Old Spice. The scent her dad had worn. She frowned, seeking the source of the aftershave, but only encountered Dale Atkins striding toward her. The leathery-faced sheriff was her advisor and, tonight, her chauffeur. It wasn't him—Dale was a Grey Flannel man.

Perhaps the stranger with him? Her gaze flicked over him, barely registering the broad shoulders, plaid shirt, and jeans. No, too young for Old Spice. She looked past him and realized the scent had dissipated.

Had she imagined it?

The sheriff touched her arm. "You're white as a sheet."

She held up the scrap of paper. Old Spice tickled her nose again. She sniffed it and made a face. Aftershave lingered, potent. Another piece to add to the puzzle.

"Taylor, what is it?"

"This was in my coat pocket." She shoved the paper at him. "Someone wants me dead."

Dale scanned it, his eyebrows pinching together in a frown. "How did it get there?"

"I don't know." Taylor wrapped her arms across her stomach.

He tore a sheet from his notebook and folded it into a pouch before putting the note inside. "Have you worn your jacket all day?"

"Not all day." Her teeth chattered, and she ran her hands up and down her arms. "Lunchtime. I took it off then. Slipped it back on when the helicopter arrived for Beth Coleman."

Dale took off his black cap with "Newton County Sheriff" across it and smoothed his gray hair. "Could it have been in your pocket awhile?"

"No." She fisted her hands. "I haven't worn the jacket since it came from the cleaners."

"Are you sure?" He waved his hand at the expanse of Douglas firs. "We're—"

"I know where we are. In the middle of a logging road a hundred miles from nowhere." She caught her breath as heat crawled up her face. This was not like her. "I'm sorry. Can I see the note again?"

Taylor unfolded the pouch and studied the words. The cadence and the words reminded her of a student in her victim profiling class—the Goth student who'd been popping up in odd places, like the pharmacy and the jewelry store. The one she figured had left the anonymous boxes of candy on her desk and then the flowers.

The black roses were what made her zero in on him—they matched his black hoodie and black jeans and black hair—black everything—but she'd dismissed it all as a student's crush. But

9

candid photos and now this note were not things she could just dismiss. "Scott Sinclair has been following me, and a couple of his papers had notes like this doodled in the margin."

The stranger stiffened. "I don't know what's in that note, but Scott wouldn't hurt anyone."

The words shot from his mouth, his Southern accent zinging Taylor, reminding her of how syllable by syllable her ex-fiancé had hammered her drawl away. For the first time, she really looked at the man who stood shoulder to shoulder with the six-foot-one sheriff. Around her age, maybe a little older. Thirty at most. And with the saddest, most beautiful hazel eyes she'd ever seen.

Taylor took in the planes of his face and wondered whether he fought a losing battle with his beard each day or if the five o'clock shadow was deliberate. Either way, he carried it well. But he didn't look like law enforcement, which was what Taylor assumed he was when she had seen him with Atkins earlier. Up close, she realized he wore his hair too shaggy for a cop. More like a lumberjack. Probably with the search and rescue team.

She cocked her head at him. "And you know this, how?"

"I'm sorry," Dale said. "I should have already introduced you two. Nick Sinclair, Dr. Taylor Martin from Conway University. She found the link between the kidnapper and the Colemans."

The sheriff put his hand on her shoulder. "This young lady is well known in the field of victomology and teaches a pilot class at the university. She aims to be the best profiler in the country one day. Personally, I think she's already the best."

Taylor's cheeks blazed at the sheriff's high praise. But she wasn't that young. She'd be twenty-nine in exactly one month, June seventeenth. She looked away, catching sight of the air corpsman as he slammed the helicopter bay shut. She hoped Beth Coleman made it to Seattle.

Dale chuckled. "She doesn't like me bragging on her, either."

She shrugged. "It's not really about being the best, just doing my best."

He nodded toward the stranger. "Nick is a writer."

Taylor almost snorted. "Researching a book, I suppose."

"No. I'm looking for my brother. Scott Sinclair."

Maybe Nick's tough love campaign with his alcoholic brother had been all wrong. He tried to wrap his mind around the accusation this Dr. Martin had leveled at Scott. Kind of hard when the woman had taken his breath away. Not that he hadn't noticed her statuesque beauty when he first arrived at the crime scene earlier in the afternoon.

She had the kind of beauty found in high-class

fashion magazines—raven hair pulled into a silky ponytail and cheekbones most models would kill for. But it'd been the startling blue eyes that drew him in like a boy to candy. Right now, they were flashing lightning bolts at him. Just like Angie's when he'd rubbed her the wrong way. "What do you have against my brother, anyway?" The private investigator's report hadn't indicated bad blood between Scott and the professor. Only that he'd taken a couple of her courses.

"Nothing." She tapped the pouch. "This sounds like something he'd write."

His brother a stalker? No way. "Do you mind if I read it?"

"You've got to be kidding. This is evidence."

"What does it say, then?" He didn't blink under her intense scrutiny.

"It's a poem," she said finally. " 'Death unfolds like a budding flower, tentatively . . .' "

She could quit reading any time. The poem sliced through his memory with the precision of a laser. *Unfurling in majestic power* . . . "You say it's on a funeral home's letterhead?"

"Yep."

Was it possible . . . no. Scott would never hurt anyone. But he had still lived at home when the verses first appeared in one of Nick's short stories. Nick licked his lips, his conscience prodding him to reveal the words were his. "This poem—"

Three hundred yards away the helicopter

12

screamed to life, drowning out his voice, and the moment of confession passed. He turned toward the chopper, blinking against the wind that whipped his body. Less than a minute later a steady *whop-whop* filled the air as the orange chopper lifted with the victim.

When the noise abated, the sheriff cleared his throat. "Be a miracle if Beth Coleman makes it to Harborview alive."

"Yeah." Even though he wasn't from the Seattle area, Nick had heard of the level-one trauma center. He said a silent prayer as the chopper disappeared over the tree line. Taylor, he noted, said nothing, her blue eyes unreadable.

A deputy called to the sheriff, and with a nod, Atkins pocketed the note and left them.

Taylor stuffed her hands in her pockets. "So, why are you here looking for your brother?"

"Because he's the only family I have left, and I haven't seen him in almost three years." Not since he showed up drunk at Angie's funeral.

Her expression softened. "I'm sorry about that, but why here? At this crime scene?"

"Oh." He'd misunderstood her. "I didn't intend to come to the crime scene. I had a lead Scott was in Newton, and when I stopped by the sheriff's office this afternoon to discuss it, Sheriff Atkins wasn't in since he was here, but I overheard the dispatcher give directions to one of the search and rescue teams, and I sort of tagged along, thinking

I might get a chance to talk with the sheriff."

"But you stayed. And it's almost eight o'clock."

The beautiful professor had noticed him. A pang of guilt tempered the pleasure from that knowledge. Then the undercurrent of her words nailed him. "Okay, so you were right. I figured out pretty quickly the sheriff doesn't know where Scott is, but I was here, and I thought I could help . . . and I don't often get a chance to do research like this."

She rested an elbow on one hand and tapped her finger against her jaw. "Okay, that explains why you're here today, but what took you so long to look for him? You said he'd been missing for three years."

"I didn't say he was missing." He flushed. He didn't know this professor, and he certainly didn't want to air all his problems with his brother. Or that he'd been practicing tough love, hoping Scott would hit rock bottom and reach out to him. Except it hadn't worked, and recently he'd felt an urgency to locate his brother. "I . . . had cut off contact with him and lost track of where he was living. I only engaged the investigator recently." He stiffened at her questioning gaze. She was waiting for why, but why was none of her business.

"I see. Well, if you find your brother—"

"Dr. Martin!"

A man hurried toward them holding his small

daughter tight against his chest. The sheriff had identified him earlier as the victim's husband, Jim Coleman. Nick's gaze shifted to Taylor, and the naked longing in her eyes rocked him. A knife twisted in his heart. He'd seen that look before in his wife's eyes when she'd talked about wanting children.

"Thank you, Doctor." Jim grasped Taylor's hand, pumping it.

"Nothing to thank me for—just doing my job." Taylor nudged a rotted branch with the toe of her shoe. Dank spores blew over the rotting leaves, filling the air with their musty scent.

Jim hugged his daughter closer. "No. You're the only one who believed me. You saved my daughter and my wife."

Little Sarah blinked open her eyes and pulled her thumb from her puckered lips. "Will Mommy be okay?"

The child's chocolate-brown eyes stared up at Taylor, her brows knit together. Alarm darted across the professor's face. "I—"

"I told you, honey. She'll be fine." Coleman smoothed a strand of blonde hair from her eyes. "She's going to the hospital . . . I promise. They'll make her all better."

It was plain Taylor didn't want to mislead the child, but as Sarah continued her doe-eyed gaze, Taylor sucked in a breath. "I'm sure your daddy's right."

"Thank you," he mouthed, then nodded and hurried to his car.

"You did the right thing," Nick said.

Taylor exhaled a long breath. "I don't know. What if she doesn't make it?"

"She could definitely use a miracle."

This time there was no mistaking Taylor's pursed lips.

Taylor stared at the ground, seeing the image of Beth Coleman lying in the wet leaves, blood staining her cashmere sweater. Miracle? That meant she'd have to pray, and if she thought it'd do any good, she would. It wasn't that she didn't believe in God or that she didn't believe he answered prayers for some people. He just didn't answer hers.

"Sorry to have to leave you, but I have work to do." She turned to walk up the hill where Dale was wrapping up the investigation. "If you find your brother, call the sheriff, please," she called over her shoulder.

"Wait, I'd like to discuss Scott with you."

Something in his voice halted her. What was it he'd said? *He's the only family I have left.* She glanced at the third finger on his left hand. A wedding band. The sad eyes. "Your family, what happened to them?"

"What?" Nick took a step back.

Taylor rubbed the burning in her neck. She was

too tired to be standing here having this conversation with Nick Sinclair, and it wasn't like her to be so direct, but something about Nick made her want to know. Besides, it was too late to take back her question. She lightened her tone. "You said Scott was all the family you have left. What happened?"

He kicked at a dirt clump, and mud smeared across the toe of his cowboy boot. "My wife . . . died over two years ago, my parents a long time before that. I have to find Scott."

Their deaths explained his acquaintance with grief. And she understood grief. It also explained why he felt he had to find his brother. "I have to finish up here, but if you want to stop by the university tomorrow, we can talk. Just call me first."

She rattled off her cell number, then wondered if she should have. It might be an invitation to disaster, given the way her heart kicked up a notch when he looked at her with those eyes.

He jotted her number on a card and snapped a short salute. "Yes, ma'am."

As Taylor walked the short distance toward the command center, a coroner's hearse crept along the logging road with the kidnapper's body. His suicide meant no answers to some of her questions about why he kidnapped Beth Coleman and her daughter. A shadow crossed her heart. She half-halted, the skin on her neck prickling.

Someone was watching her.

She scanned to the left. One of the men who'd helped with the search ducked his head. She started toward him, noting his longish hair and camouflage hunting jacket. As she got closer, his fingers flew over his phone. Texting. Not stalking her.

Just peachy. Was she destined to suspect every scruffy male who glanced her way? Taylor retraced her steps.

"Ready to take me home?" she asked when she found Dale.

"Give me a minute with Zeke."

"Sure." As long as Taylor didn't have to deal with the prickly Zeke Thornton. Dale's chief deputy challenged her on every idea she came up with, always asking *why,* and if she was honest, he probably made her better. But he could be so irritating.

Taylor leaned against the sheriff's cruiser as the minute stretched into forty-five, and the gray twilight turned into nighttime dark. The kind of dark where you couldn't see your hand in front of your face. The kind of dark that made her think of her dad. The kind of dark she hated.

Finally, Dale returned, and Taylor slid into the passenger side and fastened her seat belt, inhaling the stale odor inside the aging patrol car that had seen too many cups of coffee and onion-topped burgers. Thoughts of her dad lingered. Tomorrow she would delve again into her search for him, but at this point, all she had was a cold trail that was getting colder.

Dale's voice cut into her thoughts as he pulled the Crown Vic onto the highway. "You did a good job today. You worked that crime scene like a pointer hunts quail. You didn't give up."

"Yeah, but with Ralph Jenkins's death, we can only guess why." Still, the sheriff's words soothed the aches in her body. At times she felt like a bird dog on the hunt, sniffing through evidence, looking for the connection between victim and assailant hidden beneath the surface 75 percent of the time. Today her instincts homed in on the father's past and scored a direct hit. Except, something bothered her about the case, but nothing she could put her finger on. She sighed. It was probably that she couldn't question the kidnapper.

"I wish Coleman had told us sooner about that wreck fifteen years ago." The kidnapping and shooting appeared to be Jenkins's revenge for the death of his wife and girls in an accident that hadn't been anyone's fault.

"Well, you were dead-on right."

Yeah, she had great instincts when it came to other people. So why was finding her father so difficult? And on more than one level. She unwrapped a lemon drop, then popped it in her mouth, the candy tart on her tongue. Her cell phone rang, and she glanced at the ID. "Do you know anyone with a 901 area code?"

"Not off hand," Dale said.

She answered, putting the phone on speaker. "Martin."

"Dr. Martin? This is Nick Sinclair. Scott's brother."

"Yes?" She should have known giving him her number would prove to be a mistake.

"I know it's late, but I'd really like to talk to you about my brother tonight."

"I'm busy right now. And I don't want to discuss him over the phone." She checked her watch. Nine-thirty. She never went to bed before midnight, anyway, and this might be an opportunity to get information on Scott. "However, I'll be home shortly, and I can give you thirty minutes."

"That'd be great. I won't stay longer than that, I promise."

After giving him her address, she hung up and turned to the sheriff. "Can you hang around?"

"Sure. I have a couple of questions for him myself."

Taylor slipped the phone in her pocket. What could be so urgent to Nick Sinclair that he couldn't wait until tomorrow? She thought of the poem. Could he have slipped it in her jacket? No, he hadn't been around for the other "presents." "What's your take on the poem? Do you think it's Scott Sinclair?"

"Possibly. What's more important is why you think it's him."

"I didn't until I received the black roses. I had no clue who was sending me candy." In late March, every week a box of Godiva chocolates had been placed on her desk. No one ever saw the gifter, but Taylor figured one of the male students had a crush on her. That happened sometimes with a student and a professor. Then in late April, the black long-stemmed roses appeared.

"Those roses sure fit that strange getup he wears," Dale said. "What do the kids call it? Goth?"

"Yeah." Scott always showed up in class wearing a black T-shirt under a black Nike jacket with a hoodie, black jeans, and black tennis shoes. And jet-black hair.

"Those photos, though. They put a different slant on the situation, and now this note really changes it. I'll bring him in for questioning again."

The photos had arrived right after the roses. Shots of her shopping, jogging, at the pharmacy, at a ball game, Taylor doing everyday tasks. Just knowing whoever took the pictures lurked that close sent a shiver through her body.

Dale had questioned Scott after the photos arrived, but the only connection to him had been the black roses, and even that had been tenuous. Several stores in the area sold the flowers, and none of the clerks identified Scott. With no concrete evidence, the sheriff couldn't hold him.

"I can usually size someone up pretty quick, and Scott Sinclair didn't strike me as dangerous," Dale said.

"Same with me. He was always somewhat shy, especially in those first classes last fall. Turned beet red when I asked him about the candy and roses. Mumbled something about not knowing what I was talking about. But then he dropped my class."

The sheriff turned his blinker on and made a right turn. "The thing is, no one saw him at the crime scene. How did he get the note in your coat?"

Taylor had asked herself that same question over and over. And came up blank. "He could've changed his look, and there were a lot of volunteers." She picked at a hangnail. "Maybe it wasn't him. Could've been anyone, even someone at the cleaners."

"I'll check that tomorrow. It also could be connected to a past case, even before you came to Newton." Dale drummed his fingers on the steering wheel. "You've helped to put away a couple of pretty bad guys, and criminals have long memories and bigger grudges."

"Sometimes I think I should have stayed in my nice, safe classroom."

"You have a cop's heart, Taylor."

She didn't know about that. Her thoughts chased around in her head. "The paper doesn't actually have my name on it. Maybe it's just a sick joke."

"We're going to check it out. Until then, you need to be extra careful."

Taylor intended to do just that. She swayed against her seat belt as the sheriff turned onto Rainey Road and picked up speed.

Dale rested his hand on the armrest between their seats. "Um, how're you doing? About, you know—"

"Fine." Taylor clipped the word off, then softened her voice. "I *really* don't want to talk about Michael."

Silence rode with them for a mile before Dale reached and patted her arm. "You were too good for him. You're young. Give it time."

She turned and stared though the window at the dimly lit houses whizzing by. Her biological clock ticked off another day every twenty-four hours. Of course, women bore children into their late thirties and early forties now. Which was fortunate, given her history with men. But that history made dreams of having children, the white picket fence, and the fairy-tale ending rather unlikely. The image of little Sarah Coleman in her dad's arms sent an ache through her chest.

The front tire centered a pothole, jarring her.

"Sorry, didn't see that." He cocked his head toward her without taking his eyes off the road.

"There's something I tell my girls. At the right time, God will bring the right man into your life, but you have to wait for his timing."

"Let it go, Dale." Like God even cared. "I'm not looking for anyone."

Nick Sinclair's face with his day-old beard surfaced in her mind. *No.* He would be the last person she would ever date. Too good looking, like Michael. Not that he'd be interested in her— she'd just accused his brother of stalking.

They neared her winding driveway, and the car slowed, then turned beside her mailbox. "If you'll let me out here, I'll pick up my mail." Taylor unbuckled her seat belt. She'd rather get her mail now, before he left. After getting out, she poked her head back in the car. "Go ahead, I'll walk."

Dale's brows knit together.

"Climbing back in just isn't worth the effort," she said.

"Make the effort. We've just been talking about someone stalking you. And, it's pitch black. Not even a moon."

"Come on, it's not like you're leaving me— you'll be at the end of the drive. Besides, you won't be here tomorrow night when I get in from the university." Taylor tried to laugh, but the sound stuck in her chest. She wished she'd never told him how she hated the dark. She straightened her shoulders. Time to face the monster under the bed. "I need to do this."

"Sorry." He shook his head. "You don't have to get back in the car, though. I'll just drive slowly ahead of you."

High winds moaned through the pines in her yard as she fished a penlight from her purse and pointed the beam toward the ground. Taylor retrieved several envelopes from her box, almost losing them in a gust of wind loaded with the threat of rain.

The tiny light flickered then came back to life, cutting a narrow swath through the darkness between her and Dale's cruiser ahead. Her feet crunched on the loose gravel, the only sound other than the wind. She focused on the bouncing light until she rounded the curve.

Dale parked and climbed out of the cruiser. He jerked his head toward her house. "Why didn't you leave your porch light on?"

Hadn't she? Taylor tried to think back to when she left. She remembered now, the bulb had burned out. "I meant to replace the bulb this morning, but I forgot."

They climbed the steps, and Taylor fumbled in her purse for her key. "You don't have to do this."

"Did you forget Nick Sinclair is dropping by?"

She slapped her head. "It's been a long day."

"It wouldn't matter if he wasn't coming." His face cracked into a grin. "I do it all the time for my girls. We get together for dinner, and afterward I go in and check out their apartment. Make sure it's secure—it's what dads do."

The words echoed in her empty heart. For a second, she envied Dale's daughters. She unlocked the door and let him go ahead of her.

"Where's the light switch?"

"I'll get it." Taylor followed him into the house. A strong odor of Old Spice filled her nose as she flipped on the living room light.

Nothing. Her flashlight cast an eerie circle on the far wall, then flickered and snuffed out. Taylor swallowed a cry and shook the light. Her heart hammered against her ribs. The light twitched on again, a faint shaft in the dark.

"Get out of here." Dale shoved her toward the door. He barked into his shoulder mic. "I need backup, 302 Rainey Road. Now!"

He unsnapped his holster and pulled his gun. Footsteps scuffed somewhere to her left. Before she pinpointed the direction, a bone crunched and Dale yelled. His gun spit flame, and a deafening roar boomed in the enclosed space. Gunpowder burned her nostrils.

"Dale! Where are you?" Taylor swept the dim light to her left. He lay crumpled on the floor. A man whirled toward her with a pipe in his hand, his face hidden by a hood, a Nike emblem on his jacket. The flashlight flickered off again. *No! Stay on!*

Darkness pressed in on Taylor. She couldn't

move. Old Spice threatened to smother her.

Air whooshed overhead. She jerked back, kicked, and slammed into soft tissue.

"Umph."

Taylor dropped to the floor and scrambled for Dale's gun, her fingers probing under his body. Blood pounded in her temples. The gun wasn't there. He groaned. Had to get him out. Her breath ragged, she stood and tugged at him.

The pipe sliced the air again. She ducked—not low enough. Pain slammed down the side of her skull then her shoulder. White light pierced her vision, splintering into a thousand points ringed with darkness. Taylor staggered, grabbing air. Strength flowed from her body. She fought the black fog filling her head.

2

Nick checked the GPS again. Another mile to Dr. Martin's house. She probably thought he was an idiot, but he'd known he'd never be able to sleep unless he told her the truth about the poem. It wasn't like him to hide something like that.

His headlights picked up a skinny figure in the middle of the road. Nick slammed on his brakes. He had a fleeting impression of a teenage boy, but a hoodie kept him from seeing a face as the kid disappeared into the wooded area on the other side of the road.

Nick shoved the car into park and jerked open his door and jumped out, his whole body shaking. No sign of anyone.

He returned to his car. At least he hadn't hit the kid, but he could have. His heart still racing, he eased down the road.

The GPS informed him he'd reached his destination at the same time his beams picked up a mailbox. Three-o-two. He turned onto the white slag and crept up the winding drive. His lights swept over a police car.

The house was dark, the front door opened. Nick jerked to a stop and got out of the car. "Dr. Martin? Sheriff Atkins?"

The faint sound of sirens reached his ears as he eased to the porch and climbed the steps.

Someone slammed into him, knocking him to the porch floor.

Nick grabbed at legs as he went down. This time it would be different. This one wasn't getting away. A fist slammed his ear. A blow to his diaphragm curled him into a ball, the spasm radiating through his chest as air whooshed from his lungs. The assailant wiggled from his grasp. The faint sirens grew louder as Nick hugged his stomach and gasped for air.

Groans from inside the house filtered through his wheezing. Nick struggled to his feet and stumbled through the doorway into the pitch dark room. He coughed, pain racking his chest. His foot kicked something, and it rolled across the wooden floor. A tiny light beam flickered on, illuminating a body crumpled on the floor. Too big to be Taylor.

"Ohh . . ."

Nick grabbed the light and flashed it in the direction of the moan.

Taylor was on her knees, struggling to stand. "Sheriff Atkins. Is he okay?"

Nick flashed the light back to the body and knelt beside it. The sheriff didn't look good. He yanked his cell from his pocket while he felt for a pulse. Weak. Using his thumb, Nick punched in 911.

"Nine-one-one. What is—"

"I need an ambulance. Sheriff Atkins is hurt."

"What's the address?"

His mind blanked out. "I don't—we're at Dr. Martin's house."

"I need the road and house number."

Nick flicked the light toward Taylor. She rocked back and forth, her head in her hands. "What's your address?"

No response. He spied an envelope on the floor and scooped it up. A bill from Macy's. "Three-o-two Rainey Road."

"I'm sending an ambulance. Could you give me your name, please?"

Nick breathed tension from his body. "Nicholas Sinclair."

"Can you tell me what happened, sir?"

"No. I just got here." Sirens blared up the drive. "Somebody's here. Cops, I think." Another spasm radiated from his stomach through his chest, and he pressed his hand below his rib cage. It'd been awhile since he'd been hit hard enough to get the wind knocked out of him, and he'd forgotten how much it hurt.

Car lights swept across the open doorway, and then footsteps pounded up the steps. Beams of light blinded him.

"Newton Sheriff's Department! Hands behind your head!" The order came from the doorway.

Oh, great. Now he was getting arrested. Nick gripped his phone. "I just called 911. I'm not the—"

"Do what I say! Now!" Metal clanked as the deputy relieved him of his cell and jerked Nick's hands behind his back.

Another deputy knelt beside Sheriff Atkins.

Nick winced as the cuffs cut into his wrists. "The guy you want is getting away."

"Yeah, right."

"Zeke, the sheriff looks bad."

The deputy prodded Nick. "If you've hurt Atkins, I'll—"

"Zeke, take the cuffs off." Taylor's soft voice carried authority. "You've got the wrong guy."

"You don't know that, Taylor."

"Is he wearing black?"

Zeke shined a light over Nick. "So, what if he isn't?"

"The guy who attacked us wore a black Nike jacket with a hood. Obviously, Nick isn't wearing black. That's who you've handcuffed. Nick Sinclair. You need to be looking for his brother."

"Taylor, let me take you home." Christine Nichols's voice penetrated the fog in Taylor's brain. Word of the attack had spread through the college town like wildfire, and her friend had come to the hospital immediately.

"I'm not leaving until I know Dale will make it." Every word pounded against Taylor's skull. A simple concussion, the doctor had said. It didn't feel simple, but at least *she'd* walked away with her life. The sheriff might not be as lucky. She turned her body toward the ER doors, pain shooting through her shoulder this time. Why didn't the doctors tell them something?

She glanced around the ICU waiting room, where small groups of people waited, their murmurs blending into the background of hospital noises. Deputy Zeke Thornton squatted in front of the sheriff's wife, patting her hand.

"If you won't go home, can I get you a cup of coffee or a Coke?" Christine asked.

"Coffee would be great." Taylor closed her eyes, trying to reconstruct the evening.

"You okay, Dr. Martin?"

Only four words, but no one had to tell her it was Nick Sinclair speaking in that Southern accent of his. Her heart kicked up a notch. She blinked open her eyes. "Call me Taylor. I'm Dr. Martin to my students. And, yeah, I'll live. Probably have a headache for a couple of days and my shoulder will probably give me trouble for a while, but at least it isn't broken. How about you?"

Nick touched his stomach. "Sore, but like you, I'll live. Mind if I sit down?"

"Please do. I need to thank you anyway—you probably saved both of our lives. It's a good thing you were stopping by."

The pupils of his hazel eyes narrowed. "Yeah. Has there been any word on the sheriff?"

She shook her head and immediately grabbed it. But head pain she could deal with. She'd frozen in the dark—she couldn't deal with that. If Dale didn't make it, Taylor would never forgive herself. She swallowed down the lump lodged in her throat. "They're still evaluating him. He hasn't regained consciousness. But thanks for checking on me." She rubbed her temple. "I'm repeating myself."

"Understandable. And thank you for not letting them arrest me." He smiled, exposing perfect white teeth. "If there's anything I can do . . ."

"Find your brother." The words popped out before she could catch them. Asking Nick to help put his brother in jail wasn't the best way to become friends . . . if she wanted the handsome writer as a friend.

He folded his arms across his chest. "My brother didn't do this, unless he's put on a lot of weight."

"I agree." Zeke Thornton's voice chimed in from behind her just as Christine returned with her coffee.

Taylor twisted around. The forty-something deputy adjusted the black cap that covered his receding hairline. "Have you learned something?" she asked. "Do you have a lead on Scott Sinclair?"

"I'm not worried about the Sinclair kid unless he's part of the burglary ring operating in the county. Your door was jimmied, and we found a pile of your stuff at the back door. Add that to your friend here seeing someone run across the road before he got to your house means two people were involved. I'm thinking we have a robbery gone wrong."

"How about the black hoodie?" She gripped the Styrofoam cup. "That's what Scott always wore to class. A black hoodie with a Nike emblem."

Thornton's heavy-lidded eyes blinked, reminding her of a skinny gecko. "Him and half the male students at the university. But I'll add your description to the file."

She gritted her teeth. By the tone of Zeke's voice, he'd made his mind up that she and Sheriff Atkins had interrupted a burglary.

He hitched up the belt that held his holster. "So, how are you feeling?"

She waved her hand back and forth. "So-so. I'll feel better when I know Dale is going to be okay."

"Me too," he said and nodded. "If I learn anything new, I'll give you a call."

As Zeke strode toward the exit, Nick gently took the cup from her. "What's going on between you two? I sense an undercurrent between you two."

She rubbed her arms. "Zeke sees everything in black and white. We don't agree about victim profiling, and he doesn't understand that it isn't an exact science, that instinct plays a big part. He gets impatient waiting for results." Actually, he'd never been totally on board with her being part of Dale Atkins's team, and even less since a hostage situation six months ago ended with Taylor losing the gunman and his hostage. But if she hadn't been brought into the situation so late, the outcome might've been different.

"He's just jealous you got the spotlight for saving that little girl today," Christine said.

She *had* saved Sarah Coleman and hopefully her mom. She chewed her lip. Zeke Thornton was dead wrong about this case being a burglary. She'd just have to prove it to him.

"I understand, Andy." Taylor held out her hand, palm down. God, please don't let this boy kill his stepfather. *"You feel like you don't have any other choice. But this hasn't gone too far. No one's hurt yet."*

The young man turned, and she stared into the eyes of death.

"You don't want to do this, Andy."

Taylor struggled against the paralysis trapping her in the nightmare.

God, please! Just this once.

"He hurt my mama. I won't let him hurt anyone else." Andy jerked the gun up, and a beam of light pinpointed his target—the dead center of his stepfather's chest.

"Andy, nooo . . ."

Taylor bolted straight up in bed, her breath coming in gasps. She hugged her knees to her chest, waiting for the hammering in her rib cage to slow. Even in her dreams, God didn't answer her prayers. Andy Reed still killed his stepdad.

Pain speared her head, clearing the remnants of the nightmare but not the lingering sense of failure that pervaded her life . . . the Reed case, the failed engagement to Michael, who'd left a "Dear Jane" note on the seat of her car, and now Dale Atkins. And the futile search for her dad overshadowed it all.

Taylor tested the lump on her head. Still tender.

And her shoulder still ached where the pipe had grazed it. If only Dale had gotten off as easy. After two days, he still lay unconscious in ICU. She picked up the phone by her bed and dialed the hospital.

No change, according to Dale's wife. But the doctors were hopeful. Taylor told her she'd visit later in the day. She slowly replaced the receiver. His wife sounded so tired. More guilt piled on her head.

She closed her eyes against the headache throbbing to the beat of her pulse. Burglary gone wrong. She still didn't buy it, and Zeke refused to listen to her, totally dismissing her theory about Scott and the note. Certainty burned in her gut that the two were related. Somewhere in the back of her mind, a memory tried to scratch its way to the surface.

Frozen . . . she'd frozen in the dark . . . Taylor leaned against the headboard, wanting to curl in a ball and hide from the world.

No. She was not a quitter. Not in this matter and not in the matter about her father. Heaving a sigh, Taylor threw off the coverlet and padded through the bedroom to the kitchen, avoiding the living room, where a bullet hole in the wall still waited to be repaired. She rummaged in the cabinet for her Earl Grey. The aroma of citrus blossoms mingled with black tea leaves would lift her better than any pill. After turning on the burner under the kettle, she took out Granna Martin's white porcelain teapot with its blue forget-me-not floral pattern.

Memories of her grandmother washed over her like a warm rain. Four o'clock tea on wintry Sunday afternoons. Granna dabbing a drop of Evening in Paris behind Taylor's earlobes; the sweet scent of roses and violets curling in her nose. She could not have been more than five or six when the two of them sat in Granna's small parlor at Oak Grove, the old home place, sipping Earl Grey from dainty porcelain cups that matched the teapot, both wearing white gloves and hats because her grandmother said ladies always dressed for tea.

Sometimes her father joined them, looking very handsome in his suit and smelling of Old Spice. Tears burned her eyes, and Taylor blinked them back. Her father. Didn't take a degree in psychology to figure out that the root of her failed relationships began and ended with him and the day he'd walked out of their lives.

The kettle whistled, piercing the air, and Taylor poured steaming water into the pot. After the tea steeped, she poured a cup and took it to the den, then retrieved her laptop from her bedroom. Some burglar . . . didn't even find her computer in plain sight.

Settling in the recliner, she sipped the tea and clicked on her email and waited. The university server had become so slow. Finally, her account came up, and she scanned the inbox. A reply from Livy.

She opened the email from her childhood friend, now a detective for the Memphis Police Department. She'd asked Livy to locate her father's old case files, since the MPD had investigated his disappearance—he'd last been seen boarding a Dallas flight at Memphis International Airport. Livy had finally gotten around to making inquiries last month, and Taylor had emailed her again Sunday, inquiring about any progress.

Sorry I haven't had time to look for your dad's files. When are you coming home? I can get authorization for you to look for them. Besides, I'd love to see you, kiddo.

Home. Logan Point, Mississippi. Twenty-three miles east of Memphis. Twenty-three *hundred* miles from Newton.

A wave of homesickness blindsided her. Livy had been her best friend until Taylor left home. Then she'd been too busy getting her doctorate and working with the Florida State Police, then the Georgia Bureau of Investigation to make a new best friend.

Taylor had opted not to teach the June session and had planned to visit Logan Point in July, mostly to get her mom off her back. She supposed she could move the date up.

It wasn't like she didn't have a relationship with her family—she talked to her mom every week. Taylor's fingers hovered over the keyboard. *I'm working on it, ma chère.*

She almost deleted the childhood term they'd used when one of them needed rescuing. Livy was the only person who understood why she hated coming home, and how much her father's desertion affected her.

Taylor hesitated, then typed once more.

In case I haven't said, don't mention to Jonathan I'm looking for Dad's files.

Her uncle had blown up when she'd called him at Thanksgiving and broached the subject of her dad. "Taylor, don't stir this up again. The gossip was bad enough the first time around. He's gone. It's in the past. Let it stay there. And why all of a sudden do you want to know?"

But it wasn't sudden. She'd always wanted to know, only no one in the family would ever talk about his leaving, and she put it behind her. Or so she thought. When Michael dumped her and the nightmares came back, the smoldering question of why her dad left flamed anew. What was so wrong with her family—with her—that he had taken ten thousand dollars from the farm safe and disappeared? But after her uncle had blown his stack, it'd taken four months and more nightmares before she started her search again.

Taylor couldn't understand Jonathan's problem —it was his brother who'd been missing for twenty years. She pressed her lips together. What her uncle didn't know wouldn't hurt him.

Taylor copied the contents of the email and added it to the other information she'd compiled in a file labeled James E. Martin. She added a few notes, then closed the file and checked her watch—still time to catch a little of the morning news.

Taylor clicked on the TV. The title of a book, *Dead Men Don't Lie*, filled the screen as the *A.M. News* co-host spoke in the background.

". . . debuted at number nine on the *New York Times* bestseller list and continues to climb."

As Taylor sipped tepid tea, the camera panned to host Laura West, tanned, blonde, and dressed in business black, and then to the guest. "Nicholas, welcome to the show."

Taylor caught her breath. Nick Sinclair? They never had gotten together after that awful night. "Thank you, Laura. Glad to be here."

Nick's laid-back Southern drawl countered West's clipped tone, and Taylor refreshed her memory of him. He still had that hint of a beard. On purpose, she decided. He'd gotten a haircut, though. She had kind of liked the dark curls on his neck. The camera backed off, revealing jeans and cowboy boots.

Unease pricked Taylor's heart. Nick had struck her as vulnerable, and Laura West was famous for ferreting out information her guest didn't always want to divulge. She almost felt sorry for this author she'd never heard of until two days ago.

Taylor's stomach rumbled, and she glanced toward the kitchen. Cranberry bagels a neighbor had brought yesterday or English muffins? She settled on the bagels. After refilling her cup, she popped a bagel in the toaster, half listening as Nick spent a few minutes talking about what it meant to grow up in the South.

She caught the words "RC Colas" and "Moon Pie" and "sweet tea." Nodding, she returned to her chair. It'd been years since she'd thought about the taste of banana-flavored marshmallow sandwiched between two graham crackers and the way it stuck to the roof of her mouth. Hard to believe she and Nick had grown up only twenty miles from each other. For a moment, she slipped into that time when she and her friends played hard, most nights lingering outside until well after dark.

The memory faded, replaced by another recollection, unbidden and unwanted. It'd happened the summer after her dad left, when her mom was on an out-of-town trip. Taylor and her friends were playing "Mother May I?" in the field beside her house, the light waning into that dusky time when day faded into night, and one by one, parents called their children home until she stood alone.

Taylor frowned. Why the memories all of a sudden? She threw off the haunting recollection and focused on the TV.

"So, I understand you're a fan of the blues. You even play a blues harmonica."

Nicholas laughed. "I try. It's hard to live in Memphis and not like blues. Or Elvis."

"True." Laura leaned forward. "Let's talk about your book. It's about college politics, intrigue, and murder. Was it difficult to write about murder after what happened to your wife?" The anchor had injected just the right note of sympathy in her voice.

Nick's wife had been murdered? Taylor frowned as the camera switched from the full-blown compassion in Laura's face and zoomed in on Nick, catching the quick smile that didn't quite reach those hazel eyes. Taylor applauded him as he held on to his smile.

"Death, even murder, is always difficult for me to write about. Life is precious, and I try to convey that in my books. It's very important when I write those scenes that I show the body being treated with dignity, no matter whose death it is." Nick leaned toward Laura. "Don't forget, *Dead Men Don't Lie* is also about love and relationships and good and evil."

Good job, Nick. Taylor wanted to clap.

"Still, I find it fascinating that you write about

murder. Do you think your wife would approve of your subject matter?"

"My wife did some of the research for the book, and a percentage of the sales will go toward building a camp for inner-city boys in Memphis, a project that was dear to her heart and now mine."

"Very commendable." Laura West glanced down at her notes. "I understand you have a new book coming out in November. Who did the research for it?"

He raised his hand. "I did all my own research this time. It's about the murder of a news anchor—"

"Really?" Laura's eyes widened. "Are you putting me on?"

Amusement stretched across Nick's face. "Why, Laura, I would never put you on."

She paused a minute, then tilted her head and gave him a genuine smile. "I want to thank Nick Sinclair for being our guest on *A.M. News* today. He'll be signing *Dead Men Don't Lie* at the Barnes and Noble on—"

Taylor raised the remote and pressed the off button. Nick appeared to be the real deal, a true Southern gentleman. Maybe even worth getting to know better. She bet he wouldn't leave a Dear Jane note on the seat of *his* fiancée's car.

3

I don't love you. Nick Sinclair stared at the words he'd typed and flexed his fingers. The mournful riffs of "Careless Love" from Big Walter Horton's harmonica filled his office even as the blinking cursor mocked him.

He tapped his foot to the slow rhythm of the blues tune. Maybe he should turn the music off. Instead, he hit the backspace key. At this rate he'd never finish the revisions his editor wanted by morning. It'd been this way ever since he'd returned from Seattle over a week ago. Taylor Martin kept getting in the way.

Nick bookmarked the page and went to the next section of revision, working for an hour before he hit a blank wall again.

"Come on, Nick, you can do this. You've done it before, remember?" Angie's voice crashed through his veiled memory like a tsunami, washing him in guilt and then in anger.

His leather chair creaked as he leaned back and folded his arms. There shouldn't be someone like Taylor to think about. *Angie* should be here. He focused on the music, letting it carry him to times before that dark night two and a half years ago.

His wife had been with him through the lean years, the days of beans and rice, always his cheerleader. She should be here now to see his success. Could she see from heaven that his last book made the *New York Times* bestseller list?

She'd always insisted success would happen before he turned thirty. She'd been right, and he ought to be floating around the room. He would be . . . if he had someone to float with. If he still had Angie. Somberly, Nick raised an imaginary toast to her photo on his desk. "Thanks for believing in me."

His cell rang, and he glanced at the ID, not recognizing the number. "Hello?"

"Nick Sinclair?"

The voice held a faint Southern undertone. Blue eyes and raven hair flashed in his mind. "Taylor?"

"I thought I had dialed the wrong number."

"Is everything okay?" His heart thumped in his chest. He should have already gotten back with her and explained about the poem instead of waiting until after he found Scott.

"Slowly getting back to normal, whatever that is. I saw your television interview last week. You held your own with Laura West. Came across as a true Southern gentleman."

"You think so?" At the time he hadn't cared how he sounded. West overstepped her bounds when she delved into his personal life. "At least she generated a buzz about the book. The signing at Barnes and Noble on Saturday was a huge success."

"Good. Um . . ."

He didn't like what he heard in her voice.

"Have you heard from your brother?"

Ah, the real reason for her call. Disappointment surprised him. "And here I thought you were calling just to hear the sound of my voice."

"I could fib, if you'd like."

"No, you've already wounded me," he said, faking a sigh. "Seriously though, I haven't heard anything. I've talked with the private investigator, but he hasn't found him. And just for you, I'll call him again later tonight, and if he knows anything worthwhile, I'll let you know. Are there any other suspects?"

"I don't know. Zeke Thornton doesn't exactly confide in me. He's still trying to say it was a burglary, but I don't buy it—they didn't even try to steal my laptop. I've been looking at some of the cases I've worked on with Sheriff Atkins . . . so far that's been a dead end. Your brother is still my number one suspect."

He hesitated, then plunged ahead. "Taylor, you have the wrong person. Scott would never hurt you."

"You haven't seen your brother in a while. He could've changed."

"Not that much."

"Nick, he wrote the poem. I'm almost certain of it."

That poem again. It was time to tell her he wrote

it. He doodled on his desk pad. *Not over the phone.* "How well did you know my brother?"

The line was silent for a moment. "Not well. I met him when he took my Introduction to Criminal Psychology last fall. He was quiet. Made a good grade, as I recall. I did find poems like the one I received doodled in the margin of his outlines."

Tell her.

No. He wanted to see her face when he told her, to judge her reaction. Yearning skittered through his heart, surprising him again, and he realized it was more than that. It wasn't just her reaction he wanted to see. He wanted to see Taylor.

He dropped his gaze, and Angie's photo pierced him. Her smiling face . . . laughing brown eyes . . . the mugger holding a gun to her head. He swallowed the lump threatening to choke him. "I'll . . . call you if I find Scott." After Nick hung up, he sat at his desk. Why did thoughts of Taylor lay a guilt trip on him? Angie was gone, and he didn't see himself being alone for the rest of his life. Or did he? Sighing, he scrolled through his contacts for the PI's phone number.

He'd contacted Carl Webster years ago while doing research on his first book. When Angie died, Scott had already taken off for who knew where. But Angie had been like a mother to Scott, and Nick wanted his brother to know. He hired Webster to find him.

With the help of Scott's lawyer, the investigator found his brother living in Alabama and brought him back in time for the funeral. What neither Nick nor the investigator had been able to do was keep him sober. Nick winced as he remembered how he'd gone off on Scott. Harsh words that couldn't be taken back.

The PI answered on the first ring. "What can I do for you, Nick?"

"Just checking to see if you had anything new on Scott."

"Actually, I do, but since it's late, I planned to wait until morning to call you."

Nick checked his watch. He didn't realize it was already ten-thirty. "What do you have?"

"A prepaid credit card with a $480 purchase three weeks ago at a jewelry store in that same town where he attended college. Newton, Washington."

"Three weeks ago? And you just now found it?"

"Like I told you when you hired me, I'm not law enforcement. I have to go through channels, and that takes time, especially with something like a prepaid card."

"But you found him so quickly before."

"Yeah, his lawyer helped last time because you were legally his guardian. That's not the case this time. He can't divulge information Scott wants kept private."

"I didn't mean to question your ability. It's just

that I'm frustrated." With himself as much as Scott. After his brother had shown up at the funeral drunk, Nick had washed his hands of him until a month ago when Scott called out of the blue, crying, wanting help, promising to do better.

He told Scott to come home, but he never showed up. Webster had traced the call to a cell tower in Newton.

"Do you want to handle it like last time, or would you like me to check it out?"

Nick glanced at the photo of Angie again and gripped the phone tighter. Return to Newton? His gaze shifted to his calendar. He could book a flight for Sunday, take a day to check out Webster's information, and return on Tuesday. "I'll go myself."

"Good deal."

"I need you to do one more thing. Eight years ago, I published a short story. I've googled it, but nothing came up. Would you check to see if you can find it floating around somewhere?"

Nick flew into SeaTac airport Sunday afternoon, rented a car, and drove the hour to Newton. He hoped there wouldn't be another disaster waiting for him. Scott was the only family he had left, and Nick needed to know his brother was all right and that he hadn't been the one to use Nick's poem for a death threat. Then he could clear Scott's name with Taylor.

A call to the sheriff's department netted him zero information on Scott. He did find out that while the sheriff remained in the hospital, he was recovering.

Three times he'd taken out his phone to call Taylor, and three times he'd returned it to his pocket, the call unmade. He'd only promised to call if he found Scott, and he hadn't. So what did he have to say? *Taylor, I'm really attracted to you, but there's this thing about my wife. She died and I don't know how to move on . . .*

Until he did, he better steer clear of the beautiful professor.

She had nothing to do with the fact that he flew twenty-five hundred miles to take care of something that could've been done over the phone. If he kept telling himself that, he might believe it. In a hundred years.

After a restless night, Nick drove downtown to Drexler Jewelry, the store listed on the credit card report, arriving a little before ten at the quaint little place in the older, artsy section of Newton. The door jingled shut behind Nick, drawing the attention of a stooped, balding clerk.

"May I help you?"

"I hope so." Nick pulled a note from his pocket with the information Webster had emailed him. "A purchase from your store showed it was paid for with a credit card belonging to my brother. I want to get a little more information about it."

50

"No can do." The clerk stared him down with watery blue eyes.

"Excuse me?"

"I can't give you information about someone's credit card."

"It's not his credit card I want to know about. It's the purchase."

The jeweler eyed him with tight-lipped suspicion.

"Let me start over. I'm Nick Sinclair, and I haven't seen my brother in almost three years. This purchase is the first lead I've had, and I hoped there might be an address on the receipt. I have the date of purchase and the card number."

The man hesitated, then his face softened, and he stuck his hand out to Nick. "Herman Drexler. My sister ran off whcn she was fifteen to get married. I looked for her for years . . . that was over sixty years ago. What's your brother's name, and when did he make the purchase?"

Nick grasped his hand. "Thank you. May 8, and it should be under the name Scott Sinclair."

Herman pulled a gray metal box from under the counter and flipped through the files. "Ah, here it is. I remember this. A phone order for a diamond tennis bracelet. It was mailed to a box number at a receiving service here in Newton that same day."

A diamond tennis bracelet? Nick's mind raced. He'd expected a man's watch maybe, but a woman's bracelet? He jotted down the number and the name of the service to give to Carl Webster.

Herman reached under the counter again and brought out a black satin box. "This is a bracelet like he bought."

He opened the box, revealing a simple yet elegant circle of round diamonds. At least his brother had good taste. "Thank you for your time."

"Sorry I couldn't be more help. I hope you find your brother."

Nick sat in his car, drumming his fingers against the steering wheel. He took out his cell and called the private investigator, only to be told he was out for the morning.

"Maybe I can help you."

"Just have him call me." Nick hung up. Moments passed before he pulled away from the curb and drove toward the university. He'd been kidding himself to think he wouldn't go see Taylor.

4

Taylor's footsteps echoed down the empty hallway to her office, a definite sign the semester had ended. Someone had stuck a newspaper in her box, one of her students probably. She retrieved it, then juggling the paper and her briefcase she unlocked her door and stepped inside.

The sweet aroma of Cavendish tobacco greeted her, courtesy of the former occupant, a crusty old professor with a penchant for pipes. Taylor left the curtains closed and flipped on a small lamp, enjoying the soft glow on the walnut paneling.

Perhaps today she could concentrate on wrapping up the semester and getting term papers read and grades posted instead of trying to figure out who assaulted her and Dale. Two weeks since the assault, and she was no closer to solving the case. At least Dale had improved and might even get to go home this week. Scott Sinclair had virtually disappeared from Newton, no more notes had arrived, and Zeke Thornton was still looking for burglars.

The opening notes of the Batman musical score jarred her. *Chase.* She'd assigned the theme song from his favorite movie as his ringtone, but the way the urgent notes pricked her senses, she might need to change it.

Furthermore, it was too early in the morning for this to be good news.

Taylor walked to the window and parted the curtain as she answered. "Morning."

"I didn't expect you to answer. Figured it'd go to your voice mail."

"Nope, you got me. How's my niece?"

"Abby's good. She's leaving for horse camp this afternoon."

"Is school out in Mississippi?"

"School ends the twentieth of May here. Something you'd know if you ever came home."

She flinched. But, blame was a two-way street. Chase only called when he wanted something. "So, what's up?"

Chase's answer was slow in coming. Taylor's stomach knotted as she stared out the window at Mt. Rainier. The mountain peak was visible, but not for long. Dark billows of gray lay to the west, waiting to descend and wrap around the summit.

"Can you come home before July? Like now?"

Oh no. She could tell things were not good with the family *again* from the urgency in his voice, reminding her of one of the reasons she shied away from Logan Point. "Chase, I'm really busy with a case."

"It's important, Taylor. Jonathan wants to sell our land."

Sell Martin land? Land that had been in the family since the early 1800s? "What are you talking about?"

"A developer offered a million dollars for the sixty-five acres behind the house."

Taylor almost dropped her phone. "Did you say—"

"Yeah. A million."

For once, words escaped her. Her mother always said that land was valuable, but—

"I can get Mom to side with me, and if you

agree, Jonathan can't sell. But he keeps pushing, says the offer won't be on the table long. You know Dad wouldn't want to sell."

Taylor focused on Mt. Rainier again. Clouds now obscured the very tip of the peak. Suddenly, she was nine years old . . .

"Your word is judgment."

"Judgment." Taylor's braids bobbed as she repeated the word. "J-u-d-g-e-m-e-n-t."

"I'm sorry, that is incorrect."

Sweat trickled down Taylor's back as Trudy Carter prissed to the microphone and shot a triumphant glance at Taylor. She repeated the word and began spelling. "J-u-d-g-m-e-n-t."

Applause sounded, and her classmate all but skipped to her seat. Taylor barely noticed. Her gaze focused on her dad's retreating back.

She never saw him again.

"Can you come this week?"

Chase's insistent question brought her back to the present. She couldn't just drop her search for Scott.

But why not? She'd hit a dead end.

Because she didn't want to go home yet. "This week? Impossible. It's the end of the semester. I've been out a few days and have a ton of work waiting. Besides, you said that Jonathan can't sell unless we all agree."

"Taylor, I don't ask a lot from you." Chase's voice cracked. "You're the only person who can do *anything* with him. Won't you do this one thing?"

The dark clouds completely obscured the mountain. Taylor's shoulders drooped, and air escaped from her lungs in a long sigh. "How about the end of next week?"

"The developer is pushing for an answer this week, and I'm afraid of what our uncle will do. Mom said to call you."

Why hadn't her mother called?

She knew why. Her mom hated confrontation, and she wouldn't want Jonathan to know she disagreed with him. Taylor didn't blame her. Getting into the middle of another conflict with her uncle was the last thing Taylor wanted. "Is Oak Grove included in the deal?"

"Yep. Can you believe he wants to sell the old home place?"

Who would buy land that contained a house on the National Register of Historic Places? Especially one that needed a lot of repairs, or had the last time she saw it. "What triggered this sudden urge for Jonathan to sell?"

"He claims he has financial problems that he's blaming on the new CPA office here in Logan Point. Says he has to have cash to keep it open, but I don't buy that. The office is making money. I manage it—I know. Look, Sis, you were coming home in July anyway. You can just come a month early."

Stubborn was Chase's middle name. Silence stretched between them. She could be just as stubborn. "Let me check my calendar and get back to you."

Taylor hung up and slid the phone in her pocket. Another problem to deal with. She walked to her desk, where term papers awaited her. She'd call him tomorrow and tell him she couldn't make it before the middle of the month. Maybe the problem with her uncle would be resolved by then. Only if Jonathan got his way.

Talk about a dysfunctional family. A weight settled in her chest as thoughts of her dad returned. The spelling bee wasn't the last time she saw her father—he left in the summer, and the competition had been in the dead of winter. Why would she recall it that way?

Taylor straightened her shoulders. Forget it. Move on. She splayed the weekly newspaper across her desk, immediately noticing that an article had been circled. "Small Child Rescued, Mother Recovering from Injuries."

The write-up on the Coleman case. Someone had penned "Criminal Minds: Newton" across the bottom of the two-week-old paper. Had to be one of her students. Each semester, at least half the students thought her classes would be one *Criminal Minds* episode after another. Most quickly learned otherwise. Her classes focused on the basics of victimology—figuring out how and why the victim was chosen and how to create a profile of the victim as well as the offender. That's what had led her to little Sarah's abductor.

A light rap at the door jerked her attention from the article.

"Come in."

Christine crossed the threshold, a satchel in her hands. "Good morning."

Her friend's voice held way too much enthusiasm, but then it always did. This morning Christine looked every bit the art professor in her tiger-striped dress that flowed loosely from the shoulders.

Christine placed her satchel on Taylor's desk. "I miss you at the track. How are you feeling?"

Taylor rubbed her left shoulder. "Head's better, but my shoulder still gives me trouble."

"At least you have a little color in your cheeks. Any special reason?"

"My brother wants me to come home, like yesterday."

"Oh." Christine gave her a knowing look. "But that might not be all bad. Doesn't Nicholas Sinclair live in Memphis? And isn't Logan Point close by?"

"I don't get the point." Taylor picked at a hangnail on her thumb.

"Taylor, the guy is smitten. At the hospital, I saw the way his gaze followed you. Have you heard from him?"

Taylor felt heat in her cheeks.

Her friend clapped her hands. "You have! He called you!"

"No. I called him to see if he'd heard from his brother."

"And you didn't tell me?"

"There was nothing to tell. He hasn't seen him, or so he said."

"Nicholas Sinclair wouldn't lie."

"Look, Miss Glass-half-full, you don't actually know the man. He could be a serial killer for all you know."

Her friend took a book from her satchel. "The man who wrote this could never lie. You need to read it. I'm going to leave it with you in case he ever comes—"

"He's not coming back." That door had slammed shut—Nick's voice had conveyed the message quite plainly. But what did she expect? She'd wanted to arrest his brother the last time she saw him. What she didn't expect was the way regret speared her heart.

"Just in case." Christine slipped the book on Taylor's desk, then turned to go. "Oh, wait!" She pulled a square white envelope from the satchel and handed it to Taylor. "Since you weren't here last Friday, the secretary asked me to give you this. It's your invitation to Dean Hart's annual fete this Wednesday night."

Taylor stared at the invitation like it was a

snake. Could the day get any worse? The summons, and it was a summons, meant she'd be stuck for at least thirty minutes in the same room with her ex-fiancé and his bride of three months. Rumor had it he'd been seeing the woman for quite a while before he broke their engagement. Too bad the friends who had been so quick to share that information after he dumped her hadn't been more forthcoming when it was going on.

She massaged her temples as a migraine threatened. Not attending wasn't a choice—unless she was dead or in the hospital . . . or in Mississippi like Chase wanted.

"I heard she's pregnant." Christine's soft voice didn't blunt the bomb she dropped.

Definitely a migraine coming on. Taylor pressed her lips together, blinking away the hot sting of tears forming in her eyes. It wasn't fair. She swallowed and forced words past her lips. "Thanks for telling me."

"I didn't want you to hear it from someone else." Christine's voice reflected concern. "Look, I have a student to see about a final grade, but if you need me . . ."

"I'll be okay. Really."

After Christine left, Taylor ripped the invitation in half and tossed it on her desk. She had two options, neither of which she liked. Stay here and pretend to be happy for Michael—no way would she fuel the university gossip mill again—or go home and deal with the life she'd fled. Going home looked better by the minute. Besides, how hard could it be?

Like scaling Mt. Rainier in a blizzard kind of hard.

She massaged her temples again. It was only Monday. She had four days before the party, so she didn't have to think about it this minute. Maybe she'd think about it . . . tomorrow.

Oh, great! Now she was quoting Scarlett O'Hara in her head. Wouldn't her ex-fiancé just love that? With a shake of her head, she reached for the stack of term papers.

Six term papers and two hours later, she stood and stretched. So far, she was pleased with the way her students had grasped the concept of victim profiling. The three-page essays reflected careful consideration and even examples of case studies. She actually wanted to pump her fist in the air.

Her gaze caught Nick's book on the corner of her desk, and Taylor picked it up. *Dead Men Don't Lie.* She turned the book over. Nick, with a brown sports coat thrown over his shoulder, grinned back at her, dimples creasing his cheeks. She just might contact him again when she went home. Another knock at her door shot a jolt of adrenaline through her body, and her fingers gripped the book tighter. Nick's lanky frame filled the doorway. "Nick? I didn't think—"

"Neither did I, but I was here in town and decided to stop by. May I come in? Maybe talk about Scott and convince you he isn't your stalker?"

"Maybe it'll work the other way around." She waved him in, trying to ignore the way her heart raced even as his cottony scent tickled her nose. Nick smelled like sunshine and a freshly ironed shirt. She glanced at his feet as he crossed the floor. Cowboy boots.

He followed her gaze. "Ever tried them? Cowboy boots?"

"Uh, no. Well, maybe when I was a little girl. I had a pair of ruby-red boots with pointy toes that curled up." Was she babbling or what?

"Are you over the concussion?"

She chuckled. "Is it that obvious?"

"No." He gave her a slow smile that started in his hazel eyes. "I like your laugh."

The way her heart ratcheted up, she didn't need to do the eye contact thing and dropped her gaze to the five o'clock shadow on his jaw. Warning bells rang in her head. *Say something.* "You and Scott don't look like brothers."

"He's my stepmom's son."

Her social skills really needed fine-tuning. But he made her feel like an awkward teenager. She took a calming breath while Nick took a seat in the wingback chair close to her desk.

"You're reading *Dead Men Don't Lie*?" Surprise laced his Southern drawl.

Taylor fumbled the book as she set it on her desk. "Actually, it belongs to a friend. She's hoping you'll autograph it."

"Be honored to." He reached for the book. "Her name?"

"Christine." She waited as he signed his name on the title page. "What was it like, being on *A.M. News* last week?"

A tinge of red started at his throat and worked up to the tips of his ears.

"I'd rather have a root canal." He slid the book back on her desk.

"I know . . . I've done a few interviews, and there's nothing quite like those studio lights and someone sticking a microphone in your face and having your mouth get so dry your tongue sticks to the roof."

"Sounds like the voice of experience." Nick shook his head. "I hope I don't have to do another one anytime soon."

"Don't blame you there."

A soft knock interrupted them again. Her office had turned into Grand Central Station. "Come in."

Her teaching assistant handed Taylor a small package and several envelopes. "This just came for you, and since I was coming to this building, I brought it."

"Thank you," Taylor said, dismissing him. She placed the mail to the side and picked up the small box. The postmark on the package caught her eye. Memphis, Tennessee. No return address. Maybe something from some of the family . . . except she wasn't expecting anything. She glanced from the box to Nick. "Do you mind?"

"Go ahead."

Taylor peeled off the brown wrapping paper, then used a letter opener to slice the tape on the shipping box. Inside she found a black satin case embossed with the Drexler Jewelry Store logo. She frowned, remembering a diamond bracelet she'd admired in Drexler's window a few weeks ago . . . actually drooled over it, but it'd been way beyond her budget.

She lifted the top, and her hand froze. Shrouded in black velvet, the same bracelet she'd admired glittered at her like a rattler coiled to strike.

A business card fell from the box, and she picked it up.

Death unfolds like a budding flower . . .

Cold chills raced over her body and wrapped around her chest, squeezing her lungs until she couldn't breathe.

A diamond bracelet like the one the jeweler had shown Nick only an hour ago gleamed hard and cold in the light. He was certain it was the same bracelet charged to Scott's credit card. Nick's stomach churned. There had to be a mistake. His brother could not be the one stalking Taylor. Not the little boy he raised after their parents were killed in a car wreck.

Lord, let it be a coincidence. Let the card have a name on it. "Taylor, are you all right? Does it say who it's from?"

"No! I'm not all right. And no, it doesn't say who it's from. I looked at this bracelet weeks ago. The same day I caught your brother following me."

"I don't know what to say." Maybe something like he had evidence his brother had purchased it?

She took out her cell phone.

"What are you doing?"

"Calling Zeke Thornton. Let's see what he does with this."

"Wait."

Her thumb hovered over the screen. "Why?"

"I need to tell you something first."

"Does it have anything to do with Scott?"

Nick sighed as he nodded. "It's one of the reasons I came to Newton. After I talked with you last week, I called the private investigator. A purchase at"—he glanced at the black case—"Drexler Jewelry showed up on a prepaid credit card belonging to my brother."

Taylor folded her arms across her chest. "So Scott *is* stalking me. That means he's the one who attacked me and Sheriff Atkins."

"I refuse to believe that. The bracelet was a

phone order. Anyone could've placed it." Nick leaned forward. "You don't know that Scott—"

"Stop!" Taylor held up her hands. "I'm telling you, he's stalking me. Even though Conway is now a satellite of a much larger institution, it's still a small university. I have, on average, eighteen students in each of my classes, most of them from the Newton and Seattle area. I'm not that well-known, yet Scott found his way here from Memphis, twenty-five hundred miles away. Which just happens to be close to where I grew up. Logan Point, Mississippi. Did you know that?"

"You grew up just outside of Memphis? No, I didn't know. How could I?"

"Same way your brother knew. Hello . . . internet."

"You're saying my brother found you on the internet and came here to stalk you?"

"Why else would he pick this university to attend? And this poem." She held up the card. "It sounds like your brother to me."

Taylor crossed her arms and gave him a look that dared Nick to contradict her. Nick stared at the bracelet again. It was the only piece of evidence linking Scott to Taylor—everything else was circumstantial. Unless he revealed he'd written the poem. Given Taylor's present state of mind, if she had that information, there would be no changing her opinion. She might even think Nick was in on it, and the last thing he needed

66

was for her to decide he was working with his brother on this. "Everything you say may be right, but you don't know my brother."

"Oh!" She raised her hands as if in surrender. "I give up."

He stood and paced in front of her and then stopped and leaned his hands on her desk. "I can't believe Scott is the only long distance student you have in this university. Have you checked?"

"Sheriff Atkins did." She tapped a pen on the desk. "We have less than a hundred from outside the northwest region."

"So he's not the only one."

"He fits the circumstances."

Nick chewed his bottom lip. "*If,* and I'm only saying if, Scott left the candy and flowers for you . . . you're a beautiful woman. Have you considered he might have a crush on his professor?"

"Right. I led him on." She glared at him. "Now I understand why you're a bestselling writer. You can fabricate a story out of thin air. But that doesn't explain the photographs."

She rolled her chair to a file cabinet behind her desk, plucked out a folder, and thrust it toward him. "Take a look at these pictures. They arrived in the mail in a large envelope, no return address but postmarked in Newton."

Nick opened the folder and flipped through photos of Taylor jogging, getting her mail, sitting in an auditorium. Someone had gone to a lot of trouble. "How do you know Scott took these?"

"Most of them"—she pointed at the photos—"are all the places I saw Scott, and when I confronted him, he turned white, almost fainted. He was guilty, all right. And he dropped my class right after that."

Nick's cell phone rang, and he unhooked it from his belt. The private investigator. "I need to take this."

He turned and kept his voice low. "Hello?"

"Nick, Carl Webster. My secretary said you called, but first, let me tell you what I've discovered. I finally received feedback from some of the other banking institutions. Scott had more than one card. He purchased a one-way ticket from Seattle to Memphis using a debit card."

"When?"

"Ten days after he bought the bracelet. The eighteenth."

The day after the attack. Nick gripped the phone. Doubt mushroomed, eating away at his belief in Scott's innocence. Could his brother be dangerous? If he was, Nick had to stop Scott before he hurt someone else.

There has to be another explanation. The small whisper echoed in his heart.

Either way, he had to find his brother. And Taylor had resources he didn't. If they could work together . . .

• • •

Taylor's hands shook as she used a tissue to slide the jewelry box and packaging into a large envelope. She couldn't live with these threats hanging over her. She had to find Scott and put an end to them.

Nick hooked his phone on his belt. "That was the investigator. Scott's in Memphis. Been there about two weeks."

Taylor caught her breath. If she'd had any doubt about Scott's guilt, that information erased it. "That's where the package came from. Memphis."

Nick stepped back. "What?"

She shoved the address where he could see it.

"No . . ."

His ragged voice touched a chord in Taylor. She hated this for him, but she didn't understand why the investigator hadn't found this information already. "If the PI can find out about the credit cards now, why not earlier?"

He stuck his jaw out. "He's not a cop, and this isn't a movie where the detective gets online and sends out a few queries or bribes someone for the information."

"Well . . . you could've gotten a court order."

Nick folded his arms across his chest. "What crime has Scott committed? Judges don't issue subpoenas without probable cause, and your own Deputy Thornton said my brother isn't even on his radar."

She cringed under the withering glance he shot at her. She hated to admit Nick was right, that PIs didn't have access to the same information law enforcement did. "Did your investigator say where in Memphis? It's a big city."

"No. Only that a plane ticket to Memphis showed up on a debit card." Nick shook his head. "I don't know what's going on, but I know my brother. Scott didn't do this. He was the kid who always took up against bullies and brought home stray cats. I'm going to find him and show you. Work with me. Help me to prove his innocence."

She steeled herself against the grief in his voice. Grief so palpable it breathed. But Nick Sinclair needed to face reality.

"Your brother is in Memphis. I get jewelry and another threat postmarked from there. You don't know what he's like now. Wake up, Nick. Scott is involved somehow."

"No," he said, determination settling into his voice. "There has to be someone else. Someone with a reason to threaten you. Scott doesn't have one."

Taylor gave Nick her best "I can't believe you" look. "Are you always this stubborn?"

He folded his arms across his chest. "That goes two ways."

"Just know this—I'll be looking for him too." She shot him a warning glance. "Don't get in my way."

Nick's eyes narrowed, then he gave her a curt

nod and without another word turned and walked out the door, his back ramrod straight.

Taylor bit her lip. She wished . . . what did she wish? She couldn't change the evidence, and the evidence pointed to Scott's involvement. But, her profiler instincts told her a good man just walked out the door.

And he was going to get hurt.

Her cell rang, and Taylor glanced at the ID. Livy. She punched the green button and answered the Memphis detective's call. "What's going on?"

"You tell me. You're the one who yelled 'ma chére.' "

"That was last week," Taylor said.

"I know. Your email got buried in an avalanche of spam, and I just read it. So what's going on?"

Taylor's glance slid to Dean Hart's dinner invitation on the corner of her desk, then back to the envelope containing the bracelet that she needed to get to Zeke. "If I come home this week, can you get me cleared to search for my dad's old case files?"

"You bet! When are you coming?"

"Tomorrow, if I can get a flight out." Her mouth curled in a wry grin. At least she wouldn't have to make small talk with her ex-fiancé.

Taylor opened her internet browser and typed in flights to Memphis, Tennessee. "But I would like you to do a couple of things before I get there. First, I'm trying to locate a Scott Sinclair . . ."

5

A sour odor fanned in Scott Sinclair's direction from the man who handed him a Movies 2 Go membership card. Scott managed to keep his lip from curling up. In the week and a half he'd worked at the video store, he'd come to know this one as a regular. A heroin junkie if he'd ever seen one—red-rimmed eyes, sallow skin, and wearing a dirty white long-sleeved shirt on a hot muggy night like tonight. And like always, he needed a bath.

Scott hated dealing with these people and would quit this job tonight if his trustee had come through with an advance on his monthly allowance. *"Work will do you good."* Ethan Trask's words rang in his ears.

One more day until the first and money would hit his bank account, but until then Scott only had the small amount of cash his boss paid him every night to live on. If his girlfriend hadn't let him crash at her apartment, he'd be on the streets.

As soon as he got his money, it'd be adios . . . to this job, maybe even to Memphis. In the meantime, he'd at least been able to walk to the video store from the apartment.

Scott handed the card back to the customer and glanced at the movie title. *Babes Gone Wild.*

Heroin wasn't the only thing this guy was addicted to.

The man's nicotine-stained fingers shook as he took the card, his gaze fixed on the video case. He pocketed the card, then rubbed the scraggly gray bristles covering his hollow cheeks.

Scott stepped back to take a quick breath and glanced toward the glass door, where a notice warned that customers had to be twenty-one to rent certain videos. *Yeah, right.* A purple Movies 2 Go sign flickered in the dark parking lot like a lightning bug on steroids.

Scott turned his attention back to the customer. "That'll be five dollars. It's a twenty-four-hour rental. Keep it longer and it'll be an extra five."

"I got a name. You been here awhile. You ought to know my name."

"Excuse me?" Was this joker for real?

"I said, I got a name. It's Ross. Albert Duncan Ross."

"All right, *Mr. Ross*. I need five dollars or I'm putting the movie back. Got it, Mr. Albert Duncan Ross?"

Ross handed him a crumpled five dollar bill. Scott stuffed it in the cash register and pushed the video across the counter. Then he turned away and wiped his hand on his cargo pants, his fingers brushing the pocket that held a pint of whiskey.

Ross grabbed Scott's arm, spinning him around. "Don't treat me like I'm trash."

Scott drew his fist back. "Don't *you* put your hands on me."

"I saw how you looked at me. Like I'm something you wipe your feet on."

Out of the corner of his eye, Scott spotted other customers watching, excitement lighting their dull eyes. He dropped his clenched fist and shoved past the man. "Next time you come, see the manager."

Leaving the cash register unattended, he hurried to the rear of the store, passing the store manager on his way. "I'm taking a break, Johnson."

Scott stumbled out the back door into the thick night air. Water dripped from the eave. Vaguely, he remembered thunder earlier in the night. He leaned against the brick wall, the damp odor of wet asphalt clearing the stench of Ross from his nostrils. If only his head would clear. Instead, his thoughts tumbled together, racing from one thing to another.

Dana. His girlfriend said not to come back to the apartment drunk. He fingered the bottle in his pocket. Maybe the friend he'd met in Newton would let him crash at his place. Nah, Scott hadn't seen him since he got the job at Movies 2 Go. His friend had never told him where he lived . . . or where he worked. He was always just *there* when Scott needed him.

He fumbled for the pint of whiskey in his front pocket and squinted at it. Half gone. He didn't remember drinking it. Just like he didn't remember overdrawing his checking account. Bank had cut him off. Maybe he did need to quit drinking, like Dana kept harping on.

He and Dana went way back, before he left for Newton. In fact, she'd encouraged him to go. Get your head screwed on straight, she'd said. And at first it'd been so good. Ethan had gotten him admitted to Conway, and he was staying sober and making good grades. He really liked Dr. Martin. Liked just being near her.

But then Newton went all wrong.

Flashing lights. Newton. Dr. Martin.

What happened that night?

He uncapped the bottle and drank straight from it, pushing the question from his mind. *Gotta think about something else.* Like getting a lawyer, breaking the trust. Bet old Ethan wouldn't like that. He acted like the money belonged to him. Scott wanted to see his face when he told him he was getting rid of him.

Tomorrow. Scott would tell him tomorrow.

He knit his brows together, trying to puzzle out the hazy memory that surfaced. Something about Ethan. Yeah, he'd tried to punch the trustee out when he wouldn't give him any money. Maybe he wouldn't go see him.

Scott took another swig from the bottle. Next month he'd be twenty. One more year and he wouldn't have to ask anybody for anything. The money would be his to spend any way he wanted. All five million.

"You don't need more money, Scott. Or alcohol. You need Jesus." He stuck his fingers in his ears. He didn't want to hear Angie's voice tonight.

"Jesus doesn't want me," he mumbled, draining the bottle. He wiped his mouth with the back of his hand and waited for the numbing relief. Maybe after tonight he wouldn't drink anymore. Angie had always wanted him to quit.

"I'm sorry, Angie." Scott's voice echoed down the alley. He should have been there. *He* would have protected her, not like Nick. Why hadn't Nick kept his wife safe?

Maybe he could crash at his brother's house. Scott ran his hand over the top of his head, the short stubble of his crew cut prickling his fingers. Nope. He'd only get a lecture there, and that he could get from Dana.

Nick wouldn't have time for him, anyway. Nobody had ever had time for him . . . except Angie and his mama. Scott squeezed his eyes shut. If they could see him now, it'd kill them.

He laughed. *But they're already dead . . . they can't die twice.* He laughed so hard his laughter turned into sobs. Great racking sobs.

"No!" The scream echoed down the alleyway. Scott hurled the empty whiskey bottle against a garbage bin, shattering it. A cat yowled and skittered from behind the green bin. The back door to the video store flew open and his boss stormed out.

"Sinclair!" he yelled. "You're fired."

Scott struggled to his feet, wiping his nose with his sleeve. "Fired? What do you mean?"

Johnson poked him in the chest. "Fired. F-i-r-e-d." He shoved him, and Scott staggered against the wall. "I'm tired of you showing up half drunk, arguing with the customers. Now clear out. I don't want to see your face around here ever again."

A slow burn started in Scott's chest. Ross. It was all *his* fault. He lunged for Johnson and spun him around. "Ross. Where is he?"

The manager shrugged his hands off. "Are you crazy?"

"I said, where is he?"

"I wouldn't tell you even if I knew. Now beat it." Johnson stepped through the doorway and slammed the door.

"Wait! You owe me money!" Scott grabbed the doorknob and shook it. Locked. Turning, he stumbled out of the alley and rounded the corner of the building. A wave of dizziness hit him, and he leaned against the wall. When he straightened, a lone figure walked in the distance.

Ross.

Nick reclined in seat 3-A and stretched his calves. Legroom alone made up for the extra cost in first class. And if he got the right seatmate, maybe he could nap through most of the flight to Memphis and have the energy to start looking for his brother when he deplaned. If Taylor found Scott first, she'd probably have him slapped in jail first and ask questions later. Not that she could, but she probably could make Scott's life miserable.

He'd spent half the night tossing and turning, rehashing his conversations with Taylor Martin and then with Deputy Thornton, who wasn't as convinced of Scott's guilt as the professor. Nick still didn't like the deputy, or the disdain he seemed to have about Taylor's work, but at least the guy didn't want to put his brother in jail.

The only real tie between Taylor and his brother was the bracelet charged to Scott's credit card, and even that could be questioned. No one could identify Scott as the buyer since it was a phone order. Besides, if he was stalking her, he wouldn't be stupid enough to put the gift on his credit card. More and more, Nick was certain someone had stolen Scott's credit card or even bought the card in his name and was using it to frame his brother.

Except . . . there was the Memphis zip code on the envelope . . . and the poem. He should have told Thornton it came from one of his short stories. No. If Nick told anyone, it'd be Taylor. Right after he found Scott and got some answers from his brother.

"Pardon me, but is this 3-B, young man?"

Nick turned toward the aisle. The soft voice matched its owner. Azure eyes peered from a face etched with years of living and were just a shade darker than her blue-rinsed hair. A faint memory of his grandmother stirred. He glanced at the boarding pass in her hand.

"Yes, ma'am, that's your seat," he said.

"Wonderful." She plopped in the seat beside him. "I've been worried silly about who I'd be seated next to, but I can tell by looking at you, I can quit worrying."

Nick saw his nap disappearing. Still, he smiled at her.

"Do you fly often?" he asked as she settled in.

"First time ever. Going to see my miracle grandson in Memphis. Laurie was thirty-nine when she learned she was expecting."

"Congratulations." Nick wasn't sure if the pride in her voice reflected the new grandson or courage in flying. Probably a little of both.

"I wasn't sure I'd make the gate on time." She clapped her hands together. "Just wait until I tell my daughter TSA wanded and patted me down because of my new hip. There I was, honey, passing through that metal detector gate and it starts beeping like crazy. Laurie will roll on the floor laughing."

He chuckled at the image of this petite granny

being searched. He bet it was one time TSA wished they'd accepted the hip explanation. "I'm glad you passed."

A commotion at the boarding door turned both their heads. Nick gaped as Taylor wrestled her luggage through the opening.

"Thank goodness, I made it," Taylor said to the flight attendant.

He tried to catch her eye as she came toward him, but she had her gaze glued to the row of seats on the right aisle.

He couldn't believe it. She hadn't mentioned flying to Memphis yesterday. Had she really hopped a plane just to track down his brother?

He had to talk to her, convince her to work with him instead of against him. *In your dreams, buddy, not after yesterday.* Nick winced at the voice of his conscience. He shouldn't have lost his temper. But Taylor Martin was so . . . inflexible. Maybe if he took a different approach —charming instead of rude. A wild idea sprouted and took root.

As soon as the "fasten seat belt" sign flashed off, Nick unbuckled and grabbed his computer. He walked toward the middle of the plane where Taylor sat in a window seat, rubbing her left shoulder. In the aisle seat, a twentyish mother nestled a baby against her chest, her eyes glued to a paperback. *Desire in the Wind.*

"Excuse me," he said.

The mother looked up from the book, and Nick's mind went blank. He scrambled for the right words. "Um, would you consider changing places with me for the flight? I'm in first class . . ." He ignored the astonished expression on Taylor's face. "But I'd like to sit with my friend."

"First class? Are you kidding?" Surprise crossed the young mother's face and quickly morphed into a yes.

Taylor gaped at him. She started to shake her head. The girl looked from Nick to Taylor and back to Nick. Her mouth dropped open. "Oh, I know what happened. I bet you two had an argument." She beamed at Nick. "And you want to apologize and make up."

Taylor's eyes widened. "No, I promise—"

"It's not like that at all," said Nick.

"It doesn't matter." The mother shifted the baby in her lap and unbuckled her seat belt. "This is too good to pass up. Besides, I'm not coming between lovers."

"Really, we're not." Nick grabbed the woman's diaper bag. Protesting only made it worse. "But there is a new grandmother in first class I think you'll love meeting."

As Nick settled in beside her, Taylor edged closer to the window but couldn't escape the clean, cottony scent of his aftershave. She couldn't believe he'd gone along with the story her seatmate had fabricated and had actually changed seats. She turned toward him.

"You let her believe we had a . . . a *relationship*."

At least he had the grace to blush.

"You heard me, I tried to tell her."

"Not hard enough."

"Well, you didn't mention *you* were flying to Memphis today."

Warmth spread through her chest as his gaze held hers. It'd be so easy to get lost in those eyes. She'd never noticed the green and blue flecks before. Against her will, her focus drew to his chiseled jaw and then to his full, sensuous lips. He seemed to be waiting for an answer, and she tried to recall the last thing he'd said. Something about flying. Oh. "I decided to fly home after you left."

"To find Scott?"

"Uh, no." She shot him the look she reserved for arrogant freshmen. Once more a blush crept up his neck.

"I did it again." He dropped his gaze. "That's why I wanted to change seats—so I could apologize for yesterday. I thought this way would be a little more private."

She snorted. "Sure. Now everyone within five rows thinks we're in love."

"Okay, so now I have three things to apologize

for—embarrassing you and being nosey today and my rudeness yesterday. I'm sorry." He tilted his head. "Accepted?"

Somehow Taylor didn't think he was sorry about today. To her surprise, she didn't care. She hadn't looked forward to the long flight to Memphis, and especially so after finding out the baby was teething. At least she wouldn't feel bad telling Nick she didn't want to talk, might even get satisfaction out of it. "Apology accepted, on one condition—no arguing about Scott."

"Deal." He hesitated. "Can we talk civilly about him?"

"Yes." She sighed. "And for the record, Scott isn't the reason for my trip home—not to say I won't try and find him." Nick didn't have to know that Livy was looking for his brother even as they flew. She turned her attention to the refreshment cart as it rattled past their seat.

"Coffee? Or a soda?" The attendant waited for their order.

"Coffee," she replied.

"Sprite for me and a bag of pretzels."

Taylor accepted the cup and a napkin and sipped the black brew. Strong. She blotted her lips and shifted in her seat toward Nick. Questions hovered in his green-flecked eyes. Questions she didn't want to answer, she was sure. Maybe she could get him to talk about himself. Men liked to do that. "So, you grew up in Memphis."

"Yep." He popped open the tiny package of pretzels and offered her one.

"Never thought about leaving for somewhere like New York City?" Taylor asked.

"Nope." He wrapped his napkin around his soda. "My turn with a question. How did a Southern girl end up teaching college so far from her roots?"

So much for directing conversation away from herself. "Hmm." She munched on the pretzel. "I couldn't wait to get away from Logan Point. Left for New York University the summer I finished high school. After getting my bachelor's degree, I enrolled at Florida State University in a dual master's and doctorate program in forensic psychology. That led to working with law enforcement, and that's how Conway learned about me. They offered me a position teaching criminal psychology."

"But Conway is so small," he said. "How did you transition into teaching something as specialized as victim profiling?"

"Conway was bought out by Seattle University the first year I taught. They expanded Conway's programs and offered me the opportunity to create a pilot program on victimology, one based on the methods I used while working with the Georgia Bureau of Investigation."

"I remember Sheriff Atkins mentioning your fame as a victim profiler. In Georgia?"

She tilted her head toward him. "Are you sure you want to hear all of this?"

He nodded. Taylor Martin intrigued him, and he couldn't quite figure her out. Maybe if he knew more of her background . . .

She took a deep breath. "Three years ago, there was a series of murders in Atlanta. Prostitutes. I was working for the Florida Department of Law Enforcement, actually FDLE is where I did my research project for my doctorate, and afterwards they gave me a job. Anyway, because of a couple of cases I worked on, the GBI requested, and I was loaned out to them. To make a long story short, my victim profiles led to the serial killer."

"I remember that case." He sipped the Sprite. "Your family—what did they think about you working on a serial murder?"

"They don't have a clue I worked on that case. It would worry my mother to death if she knew. She thinks I only teach psychology."

"You weren't in the news on that case?"

She held up her hands. "No. I stayed in the background. But my work caught Seattle University's eye, and that's how I came to teach victimology at Conway."

"Very interesting. One more question."

She waited expectantly.

"How did you lose your Southern accent?"

"I worked *really* hard to get rid of it, so I'll take that as a compliment."

"You know, there's no shame in being from the South."

Heat blazed across her cheeks as her ex-fiancé's words rang in her ears. *With that accent, people will think you're stupid.* "Never said I was ashamed, but I've found in educational circles a certain bias against a Southern accent."

"Then you missed a good chance to prove them wrong." He popped the last pretzel in his mouth. "Why couldn't you wait to get away from home?"

Fire started in Scott's stomach and washed upward to his throat, pushing him out of a drugged sleep. He rolled over and threw up on the wet grass. Where was he? And who was pounding that jackhammer against his head?

Scott swallowed back another wave of nausea as sweat ran down his face. He needed water . . . or something stronger. He cracked open an eye and immediately closed it against the light.

"When you dance, you have to pay the piper."
Shut up, Nick.

Don't let me be in a public place. Scott struggled to a sitting position against a huge tree and used his hands to shade his eyes. A silver pole shimmered straight up to a ball. A flag pole. Slowly his vision adjusted to the light, and he looked around. A huge pencil on the ground. An orange lion. He rubbed his eyes. Was he still drunk? He cracked his eyelids and saw a white iron sign. Peabody School. A groan escaped Scott's cracked lips. He'd sunk to a new low, passing out on a school playground. He rubbed his eyes and tried to remember how he got here.

Thinking hurt, but slowly memories surfaced. He'd followed Ross. Shadows . . . fighting . . . The jackhammer pounded against his temple. With the morning heat wrapping around him, Scott crawled to the flagpole, used it to pull himself up, then stumbled to a covered walk-way. His mouth tasted like he'd been eating with hogs. Pretty sure he smelled like it too. Had to be a water fountain around here somewhere. He staggered around a corner and froze. "Ohh."

A body lay sprawled across the walkway, face up.

Scott crept closer.

The blank expression. Unseeing eyes fixed on the sky.

Ross.

Dead.

6

Taylor's eyes darkened to almost violet and flashed a back-off warning. Were they destined to cross swords on every topic? Although Nick would have to admit this time was his fault. He'd crossed a line—her life was none of his business.

Except for a brief second, he'd seen a pain so deep it pierced him like an arrow and made him want to help her. Another thought worked its way through his mind, numbing his brain. Taylor reminded him of Angie. Not her looks, although she was ever-so-easy on the eyes in that red sweater. No, her raven-black hair and porcelain skin were totally unlike Angie's coppery curls and freckles.

It was more in the way she listened to him. Like Angie, she focused in on what he was saying. And Taylor stuck to her guns just like Angie when she believed she was in the right. Made for some unwinnable arguments . . . but Angie always challenged him to reach deeper. How he missed that.

Right now he owed Taylor an apology. Again. He unwrapped the white napkin from his drink and waved it. "I surrender. I should not be prying. How about a do-over?"

"You want a do-over? I haven't heard that expression since I was a kid."

Nick laughed. "But it always worked, and that last question bordered on being nosey. Again."

"You've got that right."

"How can I make it up to you?"

"Let me see . . ." A gleam lit her eyes. "Tell me about Nick Sinclair. What makes you tick?"

She drove a hard bargain. He thought a minute. "My writing, a camp for troubled boys, the blues.

88

There's something about the beat that just gets in your blood."

Taylor's lips tightened. "My dad liked the blues, played the saxophone." She picked at a spot on her jeans. "You mentioned the boys' camp on *A.M. News*. Tell me about it."

Evidently her dad fell into the off-limit category as well. He shifted his thoughts to the camp. "Originally it was my wife's dream way before we had the money to accomplish it. I caught it after Scott's trouble with drugs and alcohol started. He'd moved out, and it almost killed my wife. He'd lived with us since my dad and Scott's mom were killed in an accident."

"I didn't know Scott had lost his mom," Taylor said. "What about his dad?"

"Never met him. When my dad married Cecelia, he gave Scott his last name."

"How old was Scott when he moved out?"

"Sixteen."

"And you were okay with that?"

"I didn't have a lot of choice. Scott threatened to take us to court to become an emancipated minor, and I didn't want to go through a nasty court battle." It'd been hard enough dealing with Angie's depression over miscarrying their baby.

"So, your dad brought home a new wife and baby. That couldn't have been easy for you. You were what, a teenager, and suddenly you have a little brother?"

"Yeah, almost thirteen." He smiled, remembering. "Actually, I wanted a mom so bad I gladly put up with a three-year-old. And I know you don't want to hear this, but Scott was always a good kid . . . until he started drinking. Four years ago, all I knew about addictions came from a book. Scott's dependency educated me pretty quick."

"Four years ago? He was so young. Where'd he get the money?"

"Trust fund his grandfather left him. After that, trouble found Scott, not the other way around. With trust money jingling in his pocket, he attracted bad friends like a sunken ship attracts barnacles."

"Wow." She took a sip of her coffee. "I didn't know."

"I wish we could work together to find him. You know, combine your talents with my investigator."

"We'll see," Taylor said. "You were saying about the camp . . ."

When Nick was a kid, "we'll see" meant no. He'd have to change that, if he could figure out how. "Since we couldn't help Scott, we decided we'd try to help someone else—inner-city boys who might not realize there were options besides gangs and drugs. Angie did the research and planning. Came up with a name—the Walls of Jericho."

"Where'd you build the camp?"

"We didn't. She died before we found any land."

A wince flitted across Taylor's face. "That . . . must have been hard."

"It's taken a year to get back on track with the camp." And everything else in his life except writing.

"You must have loved your wife very much."

"I did." Her blue eyes pierced the layers of his heart, and Nick looked away. A man two rows up tucked a blanket around the woman beside him, a gesture too intimate for anyone other than a girlfriend or wife. It was something Nick would have done for Angie. But never again.

"It's okay, Nick, you don't have to talk about it. It must have been terrible, losing her like you did."

The warmth in her voice wrapped around him like a comforter. He wanted to tell her. "We . . . were mugged coming out of a restaurant in Memphis. The Midtown area. It happened so fast. We were walking to the car, and next thing I know, a guy shoves a gun in Angie's face and demands our money. I tried to keep him calm, handed over my billfold and told Angie to do the same thing with her purse. I don't know if she was confused, or just frozen, but she wouldn't give it to him. Then she shoved him, and the gun went off."

He swallowed, not wanting to remember what came next. "Angie bled out in my arms in that dark parking lot. The ambulance came, and they took her to surgery, but it was too late."

"Nick, I'm so sorry."

"I keep replaying that night, thinking if she'd just given him her purse." His voice cracked.

"You don't know if it would have changed anything."

"If only she'd listened to me . . ."

Taylor had never met a man like him before. The kind of man who stood by those he loved. She didn't think she'd ever experienced that kind of love. Certainly not from Michael, who'd only wanted a clone of himself, and most certainly not from her father. Not even her uncle, who'd tried to take his place.

She struggled with something to say, but in spite of all her training, she came up empty. Probably why she hadn't gone into counseling.

"Beating yourself up won't help." It was the best she could offer, and his subdued smile almost broke her heart.

"It's hard not to, but thanks for listening."

Taylor reached into her bag and pulled out his book. "I got this in the airport."

Nick's eyes widened, and she almost laughed, glad she'd distracted him from his grief.

"You bought my book?"

"Actually two." She pulled out another one. "One's for my mom, the other for a friend—they like murder mysteries. Although since I've gotten to know you, I might read it."

"Wow, you know how to keep a guy humble."

She handed him the books. "Would you autograph them?"

"Sure."

"My mom's name is Allison and my friend is Olivia, but you better make it Livy."

Nick inscribed the title pages and handed the books to her.

"Thanks." She tucked them back into her bag.

A question crossed his face, and she waited for him to put it into words. But the query didn't come.

"What?" she finally asked.

"I wondered something, just not sure how to ask."

"How about straight out?"

"How did you crack the Coleman case?"

Taylor hesitated. The case was closed and the kidnapper was dead. "Off the record?"

He nodded.

"Let me give you a little background first. With most crimes, victims have a link to their killer, so I start looking at the victim's past, trying to find where they've crossed paths with the perpetrator."

"Something like *Criminal Minds*?" Nick asked.

She laughed. "Not at all like the TV show. First of all, I don't usually work on murders in Newton. There just aren't that many, and I don't work on serial killings anymore."

"Why not?"

Her hands closed in tight fists, and she glanced out the plane window. They were above the clouds, and the white cotton-candy floor reminded her of a time before she learned just how sick the mind could get. The things that man did to those women . . . She turned back to Nick. "After Atlanta, I don't have the stomach for it."

He covered her fist with his hand, his touch warm, reassuring. "I can see how that could happen."

She shook her head to clear it of the memories and reclaimed her hand. "What I do is look for links between the criminal and the victim."

"So what was the link in the Coleman case?"

She steepled her fingers. "Off the record again, Jim Coleman had been involved in an accident when he was a teenager. And while he wasn't hurt, and it wasn't his fault, all four passengers in the other vehicle died—Ralph Jenkins's family. Evidently Jenkins brooded for years until one day he kidnapped the now-grown teenager's wife and child. And then kills himself at the scene . . ." Everything fit together perfectly. Maybe a little too perfectly.

"So you'll never know exactly why he did what he did?"

She nodded. That was one of the things that bothered her about this case. It was like the solution had been wrapped in a pretty box and bow and handed to her, but the box was empty. Sometimes she wished profiling *was* like television and she could see the script.

Nick whistled. "Wow. How did you find out about the wreck?"

"By asking the right questions . . . of the right people. Sometimes you get lucky—and the only person you can ask is where the link happens to be."

"Are there any other cases you can tell me about? Off the record, of course."

She cocked her head. "Are you picking my brain for one of your books?"

He gave her a thumbs-up. "Nailed me. I can see writing about a heroine much like you."

Taylor didn't know how to respond.

His gaze held hers, then his chiseled lips spread into a heart-stopping smile. For five heartbeats, Taylor forgot to breathe as she imagined his lips on hers. Like that would ever happen. Men like Nick didn't fall in love with women like her. She was a loser. With a capital *L*.

7

Two in the afternoon and downtown traffic in Memphis worked like ants on the trail of bread crumbs. Taylor braked the rented Rav4 for a construction worker as he directed traffic. The pungent scent of asphalt seeped through the floorboard, burning her eyes.

At a stoplight she flipped on the radio, seeking one of the hard-rock stations she'd listened to as a teenager. Elevator music streamed through the speakers. Just her luck. She massaged the back of her neck. It'd taken half an hour to claim her bags. Then Nick, ever the Southern gentleman, had driven her to the rental agency and waited with her until she was in the car. She wasn't used to being looked after. It was kind of nice, and made her feel bad, considering she had Livy out beating the bushes for his brother.

Remembering the intensity of his gaze even now sent a shiver through her chest.

It was fruitless to go there. But he'd changed seats just to sit with her. No, only so he could change her mind about his brother. The argument raged in her head. No matter. He'd been a nice diversion on the plane. Nick Sinclair was a complex man, and it surprised her how they'd clicked.

Writer, humanitarian, man of his word, blues player. The last one she could do without, although she'd loved going with her dad when he played his sax with his friends. They played slow blues, and the pull of that lonesome sound had drawn her in, made her one with the music. As a teenager, she'd even learned to play the piano, trying to recapture those days. Then she decided he was never coming back and quit the lessons.

Now, the first ragged notes of a blues tune brought her dad fresh to her mind. So she didn't listen anymore.

Nick was a nice guy—too bad she'd sworn off relationships. But then, it wouldn't matter anyway. Even if she weren't trying to put his brother in jail, his heart belonged to his dead wife. Taylor wasn't about to compete with a ghost.

Maybe that's what attracted her—she couldn't win his heart, so she didn't have to risk her own.

Taylor turned onto Washington Avenue and whipped the SUV into an empty space, the hour left on the meter enough for her meeting with Livy. She entered the doors of the Shelby County Criminal Justice Center and crossed the slate floor to the elevators. Taylor had called Livy from the airport and left her friend a voice message that she was on her way. When the doors opened, she crowded into the elevator with a dozen others. "Eleven, please."

A uniformed officer obliged, and Taylor took a breath for the upward ascent. She hated being closed in, but ten floors were a bit too much to climb. And who knew what she'd encounter in the stairwell of the Shelby County CJC.

She couldn't hold her breath all the way up either, although it would have been preferable to the body odor permeating the elevator. Taylor caught a whiff of another scent, heavy and sickly sweet. Marijuana.

More than likely it belonged to the barefoot kid in handcuffs with the silly grin pasted on his face. The doors opened to the second floor, and the kid and arresting officer got off. Most of the scent left with them.

Nine stops later, Taylor escaped the elevator. A sign pointed left for the homicide division, and she followed the hall to the double doors.

The receptionist looked up from her computer. "May I help you?"

"I'm here to see Detective Olivia Reynolds. I was supposed to be here half an hour ago."

"Are you Taylor Martin? Everybody's in a meeting, but Livy left a message for you to wait at her desk. Said you'd know which one is hers."

Taylor surveyed the room. All six desks were empty, but she easily picked out Livy's. Only the desk in the corner had no papers or folders littering the work space or pencils strewn about . . . and no Styrofoam cup. She walked toward the desk, and a brass nameplate engraved with "Dt. Olivia Reynolds" verified her deduction.

A door opened to her right. Livy lingered behind the stream of colleagues exiting it. When she spied Taylor, her face lit up with a welcoming grin, and she hurried across the room. "You made it!" She gave her a quick hug.

Taylor returned Livy's hug. "Sorry I'm late, but my bags were the very last ones off, and then it took forever at the car rental agency."

Only the Glock at her waist gave a clue the petite, tanned blonde was a cop. "You look great as a blonde," Taylor said. "I like the pixie cut."

Livy ran her hand through the wispy haircut that flattered her heart-shaped face. She grinned, and dimples popped in her cheeks. "Still trying to get used to the shorter layers."

She gave Taylor the once-over. "You look tired. What's going on?"

Like a Gatling gun, a flashback of the assault shot through her mind. Darkness. Metal crunching on bone, gunpowder stinging her nose, Dale Atkins on the floor. She struggled to breathe and shuddered, blinking back unexpected tears.

"Hey, are you okay?"

What was wrong with her? Taylor's emotions had never nosedived like that. And why the sense of doom circling like a vulture?

Livy pulled up a chair. "Sit. Tell me what's going on."

Taylor took a shaky breath and sank in the straight-back chair. *Get a grip.* "I didn't tell you everything about Scott Sinclair."

In fact, she'd told her friend little, only that she needed her help in locating him. She filled Livy in on the details.

"You're sure Scott purchased the bracelet?"

"It was on a prepaid credit card that has been traced back . . ." The words died on her lips. If

Scott was stalking her, why would he purchase the bracelet with a credit card that could be traced to him? A chill shivered down her spine. The bigger question was why it had taken her this long to figure it out. She glanced at Livy and realized her friend hadn't been as slow as she. "A stalker wouldn't do that, would he?"

Livy tapped her fingers together. "My thoughts exactly."

Taylor stretched her neck and massaged the knotted muscles. "I've got to rethink this, but I'm not ruling Scott out. Not yet, anyway. The bracelet came in a package postmarked in Memphis, and Scott's debit card has a trip to Memphis on it. That's too many coincidences, and I don't like coincidences. Scott's involved somehow."

"I have a few more coincidences for you."

"What do you mean?"

"I just got a new murder case, and guess who's a person of interest."

"Not Scott?"

Livy nodded. "One and the same."

Taylor caught her breath. Even though she'd warned Nick his brother's violence could escalate, she'd hoped it wouldn't happen. Nick would be devastated when he found out. "Is Scott your only suspect?"

"Oh no." Livy grimaced. "The victim was a heroin junky, ex-con—we have a big pond to fish from. Sinclair floated to the top because he had words with the victim last night. That and your history with him."

"Do you have Scott in custody?" Taylor asked.

"Don't have enough for that," Livy said. "Besides, we haven't been able to find him. Hoping you might help with that part."

Taylor was familiar with that scenario.

"At this point, we only want to question him." Livy opened a thin folder on her desk. "What information I have is sketchy—no autopsy report yet, no crime scene photos either, except these on my phone." She took out her iPhone, tapped the screen, and handed the phone to Taylor. "Here. Shots of the crime scene."

"Should I be seeing these?"

Livy pressed her lips together, and the dimples popped up again. "I haven't gone through the formalities yet, but I asked Mac—that's my partner—if I could add you as a consultant on this case. He okayed it, providing you'd work cheap, so I kind of volunteered your services."

"What?"

Livy lifted a shoulder and palmed her hands up. "Come on, you won't have to do much. Just a profile. From what I read in the newspapers, you can do that in your sleep."

"Livy Reynolds! I didn't come home to work on one of your murder cases. I came home to look for Dad's records, and maybe find Scott."

Livy leaned across her desk. "And maybe to

help Chase convince Jonathan not to sell the sixty-five acres behind the house?" Her friend snorted. "Like that's going to happen. Your uncle isn't about to let a million dollars get away."

"You've heard?" Taylor stared at a crack in the institutional-gray walls. If Livy had heard about the land deal, then probably everyone in Logan Point had heard.

"Kate told me Sunday."

Maybe not everyone. Kate was Chase's mother-in-law and Livy's aunt. "What are you not telling me?"

"I heard not only is someone offering a lot of money for the land, but that your uncle needs cash. It's no secret he and Chase can't get along. If Jonathan hadn't moved Chase from the Memphis office to the one in Logan Point, they would have already parted company."

Neither her uncle nor her brother was easy to get along with. Chase especially since his wife left. Her shoulders sagged. Could she simply stay in Memphis and avoid going home altogether? Her nerves were too shot to deal with her family and their problems, particularly the land deal. "It is a lot of money. How often do you see my family?"

"Whenever I make it to church in Logan Point. I really hurt for Chase and Abby. Abby especially. I mean, your brother is doing a good job of raising her, but he's a man, and let's face it, he doesn't have a clue about the finer points of raising a daughter."

"At least he has a few years before she reaches her teen years."

"Thank goodness," Livy said. "I get so mad at Robyn sometimes I could throttle her, even if she is my cousin. Abby asked me about her mom last weekend."

Oh, Robyn, why did you leave? Taylor's excitement over her best friend marrying her brother had always been shadowed by the fear they were too young, but Abby was already on the way . . .

"What did you tell her?"

"That we were the three musketeers."

"Yeah, that was us." Taylor said the words very softly as unspoken thoughts of Robyn hung in the air.

Livy blew out a breath that wavered between a sigh and a groan. "We were tight. *Ma chère.*"

"Which one of us came up with that code?"

"I think it was Robyn. And it wasn't always about some boring guy one of us needed rescuing from, either. How about the time that nasty Susan Palmer was going off on you because you beat her out as class president in the seventh grade?"

Heat flushed Taylor's cheeks as Susie's words echoed in her head. *"You may have won this time, but it was a fluke. You're a loser, Taylor Martin. Everyone knows it. Even your own daddy couldn't stand you. Else he wouldn't have run off."*

"Robyn and I locked her in the bathroom."

And pretended not to see Taylor's tears. "We were so close back then. What happened?"

"Life." Livy's lips quirked down. "You went off to college, I came to Memphis, and Robyn ran away. No warning, either. Thing is, I know she loves Chase and Abby. I think about it sometimes, trying to figure it out until my head wants to explode. She's left virtually no trail except for a phone call to Chase a few days after she left, saying she was okay, that she wanted to *find* herself. Said the same thing a few months later in a letter to Kate. If she's working, it's not under her Social Security number. No hits on her credit history. I check."

Taylor didn't like the look in her friend's eyes. "Do you think she's dead?"

"If I didn't see so many similar cases here in Memphis of a mother or father just walking away, I would." Livy's lips formed a tight line. "I just never thought Robyn would do something so selfish."

Taylor's background kicked in. "Did anything traumatic happen before she left?"

"Not that I know of, but then, I might not know if it had. After Abby's birth, she withdrew, and even after she went to work at the Roadhouse, she didn't seem like her old self."

"Was she depressed?"

"She kept insisting she wasn't, but I don't know. That's more your field than mine."

"And I wasn't around."

"I didn't mean it that way."

A throat cleared behind her, and she turned, but not before noticing her friend's eyes brighten.

"Taylor," Livy said. "My partner, Evan McCord —better known as Mac."

She stood and accepted the hand he held out. Mac stood a head taller than Taylor, and his meaty palm engulfed hers, the handshake firm but not squeezing. She studied Livy's partner and in turn felt his frank gray eyes appraising her.

Mid-thirties, she guessed, so the gray sprinkling his hair had to be premature. His broad shoulders strained against the white dress shirt. Worked out too. As he went to get another chair, his movements reminded her of a cat. No, a panther. Mac would be a good man to cover your back if a situation went bad.

"Livy has spoken highly of you, Lieutenant McCord."

"Be the first time," he said with a snort. "And just call me Mac. Has Olivia told you she volunteered your services?"

"Just now. I'm a little surprised. You don't really know me or my qualifications."

"That's where you're wrong. Talked with a Sheriff Atkins in Newton just this morning after Olivia mentioned you." He cocked his head. "You come highly recommended."

"Um, thanks, I guess. Sheriff Atkins is back at

work?" Thank goodness Mac hadn't talked with Zeke Thornton.

"No, but when the dispatcher learned what I wanted, she gave me his home number. We'd appreciate any help you can give us—right now it's only Olivia and me on the case."

Taylor didn't know how this meeting had gone so far astray. She'd only wanted to get started looking for her dad's files, and now Livy had involved her in a murder investigation. "I'll do what I can," she finally said. "I'll need access to everything you have."

"No problem. Just glad to have you on board." He turned to Livy. "Get her what she needs."

After Mac left them, Taylor glared at Livy. "Nice ambush."

"No apologies, and I'll have you a file put together by morning—I want to wrap this case up ASAP. Budget cuts are coming down the pike, and I don't want the powers-that-be to have any reason to include me in those cuts."

Livy's job was in jeopardy? That put a different slant on things. Taylor picked up a small yellow pad from Livy's desk. "Okay, fill me in, *O-livia*."

Livy crossed her arms. "Don't call me that. Mac's the senior partner, and I can't stop him, but you, I can."

Taylor palmed her hands up in mock defense. "Like you did Susie?"

Livy ignored her and picked up her pad. "Let me

give you an overview of the case, then I'll call Archives and get you set up for searching their records for those files." She looked at her notes. "Victim is Albert Duncan Ross, a heroin junkie. He had a Movies 2 Go receipt but no movie. It's a sleazy video store. Probably one of those where you watch the video in a tiny cubicle." Livy looked up. "The manager wasn't too helpful but did admit that Ross and an employee of his, Scott Sinclair, had words last night. Sinclair threatened Ross after the manager fired—"

"Wait, are you saying Scott Sinclair worked there?"

Livy nodded. "Manager said he'd been there a little over a week."

Taylor rubbed her forehead. "Scott Sinclair lives on a trust fund. Why would he be working at a place like that? Or working at all?"

"You're kidding. How do you know that?"

"His brother, Nick Sinclair. You need to talk to him." Taylor pulled her cell from her purse and scrolled down to Nick's name and jotted his number on a sticky note. "Although I doubt he'll be very helpful. He's also looking for Scott and thinks his brother is being framed for stalking me."

Livy stuck the note on the folder. "When did you last talk to the brother?"

"Today, on the flight from Seattle. We sat together. You may have heard of him—he's from here and a writer. In fact . . ." Taylor reached into her bag and pulled out *Dead Men Don't Lie.* She checked to make sure she had Livy's copy. "I have this for you."

Her friend's eyes widened. "Nicholas Sinclair? I love his books."

Taylor did everything she could to keep from groaning. Had everyone but her read his novels? "I figured as much. He autographed it."

Livy grabbed the book. "And you have his cell number? Wow, I'm impressed."

"Well, don't be. He's not too happy that I want to see his brother arrested, or at the very least, questioned closely. Any leads on where Scott might be?"

Livy shook her head. "He didn't have any friends at the store, and employment records are nonexistent. Evidently Movies 2 Go paid him daily, in cash. Manager still owes him for yesterday, and I told him to call me if Scott showed up for his money."

"How did he get the job?"

"Good question. I'll check with the manager on that."

Taylor nodded. "What happened between Scott and the victim?"

Livy glanced at her notepad again. "According to the manager, they got into an argument, a little shoving went on, then he fired Scott." She closed the pad. "Scott blew up and left the video store muttering about it being Ross's fault. That was around eleven-thirty. The body was found about a mile from the store, and the medical examiner put the time of death around midnight, which fits the time frame for Scott."

"How was he killed?"

"Garroted."

"Eww." Taylor's lip curled. "Find any prints?"

"Nope. Not even smudges."

Taylor's cell phone rang the special ringtone she'd programmed for her mom.

" 'It's your mother calling and you better pick up'?" Livy shook her head. "Where did you get that ringtone?"

"Somewhere on the internet." Taylor punched the accept button. "Hello, Mom."

"Where are you?"

Taylor held the phone away from her ear. Her mom's voice carried loud enough for Livy to hear. She found the button to turn the volume down. "I'm in Memphis."

Livy made a *tsking* sound and leaned forward, whispering, "Aren't you going to tell her you stopped to see me first?"

Taylor made a face and waved her off.

"Good." Her mom's voice was even louder.

She fumbled with the button again and moved a few feet away.

"Um, did Chase call today and tell you that Jonathan sent him out of town overnight?"

"No." That meant she would have to beard the lion in his den alone tonight. "When will he be home?"

"Tomorrow. Will you be here in the next hour?"

"I'm not sure. I'll call you when I get out of Memphis traffic."

"Be careful."

Taylor stared at the phone. Her mom ended almost every call that way. "I guess you heard?"

Livy laughed. "You better hit the road."

"Not before looking for my father's records."

Livy's eyes widened as she gaped at her. "Today?"

"Why not?"

Her friend closed her mouth. "First of all, records that old aren't digitalized. You'll have to find where they're warehoused, then comb through miles of records. You're looking at spending at least a day or two in the archives."

Her shoulder slumped. No wonder Livy hadn't looked for them. She sighed, calculating exactly when she could get a whole day away from her family. "I'll have to do my searching piecemeal starting tomorrow when you get the file on your murder victim compiled—I'll find an excuse to come to Memphis." She stood. "Who knows, maybe I'll get lucky and find them right away."

They walked to the elevator together, and Taylor punched the down button.

"Thanks again for doing a profile on Ross,"

Livy said and jabbed the elevator button in quick succession.

"You know that won't make it come any faster."

Livy's grin punched dimples in her cheeks. "I've missed you! Visiting you out in Washington just isn't the same as having you here."

"Don't start on me—Mom's going to be bad enough."

Livy flipped her a wicked grin. "Good luck with that."

8

Nick read the email from his editor on his phone, then with a sigh clicked out of the account. More revisions. He'd do them tonight.

He retracted the top on the Mustang and hit the interstate. A few miles later, the wind had whipped the early June heat out of the car. He merged into the right lane on I-240, and at the Poplar exit, Nick took the 72 West exit. Even after helping Taylor rent a car, he'd beaten the afternoon traffic.

Taylor. She'd wanted a red convertible like his, something else they had in common. But she'd settled for the Rav4, saying if she couldn't have flash, she could at least have dash.

He'd never forget the expression on her face when he offered to exchange his seat in first class with her seatmate, but again she'd recovered nicely.

The move had surprised even him. If he'd had time to think it through . . . would he do it again? His heart rate quickened. *Admit it.* Taylor Martin was the first woman who'd sparked his interest since Angie.

He'd met interesting women since his wife's death, beautiful women, but none like Taylor. Was it because she didn't seem aware of her looks? Or was it the way she listened to him? Or was it because she seemed so vulnerable? Sometimes her blue eyes filled with an emotion he couldn't identify, one that reminded him of the injured animals Scott had brought Nick to "fix." Some-one had inflicted a deep wound in Taylor's heart.

Stop. She wants to put Scott in jail.

Maybe he needed to write that on the palm of his hand where he could see it.

The problem of the poem burned in his gut. He'd tell Taylor as soon as he found Scott and got answers from him. For now he put the issue on hold. His cell rang as he turned the red Mustang into his drive. He didn't recognize the number. "Sinclair."

"Mr. Sinclair, this is Olivia Reynolds. I'm a detective with the MPD homicide division. Taylor Martin gave me your number, and I would like to ask you a few questions about your brother, Scott. Do you have a minute to talk?"

"A minute is about all I have." So that's where Taylor had been in such a hurry to get to—the Memphis Police Department. And to think he'd helped her rent the car to get there. Now he was glad he hadn't mentioned where the poem came from. The detective would probably have an all-points-bulletin out for Scott if he had. Maybe him too. "If you think I know where Scott is, you're wrong."

"Would you tell me if you knew?"

"Why are you looking for him? Because of Taylor?"

"No. Scott is a person of interest in a homicide that occurred late last night."

The detective's words sucker punched him. "You . . . you think Scott *killed* someone?"

"I didn't say that. Just want to ask him a few questions. Maybe it'd be better if you came downtown and we talked at my office."

"About what? I've already told you I don't know where he is." He tried to keep his tone neutral while his fingers itched to throttle Taylor. No telling what she'd told the detective.

"I need a little more information on your brother, and since I can't find him, you're the next best thing."

Nick rubbed the bridge of his nose as he considered the request. At least it wasn't a demand.

Plus, he might learn something about Scott from this detective.

"All right, Detective Reynolds, but I can't today." The revisions had to be finished and emailed to his editor by morning. And he wanted to look for his brother.

"Tomorrow, before noon, then?"

"Ten o'clock?"

"Great. And Mr. Sinclair, if you hear from Scott, would you please let me know?"

"I'll see you in the morning." Nick ended the call and sat in his driveway, making no move to get out of the car. A murder investigation? He squeezed his eyes shut. *What next, Scott?*

Maybe he needed to talk to a criminal lawyer as well before he met with this detective. But which one? Memphis had a plethora of attorneys. Scott's trustee practiced corporate law, but perhaps he could recommend a good criminal defense attorney, if it came to that. If Ethan Trask would talk to him.

He'd contacted Trask about Scott's whereabouts before calling the private investigator, only for Trask to inform him that since Nick was no longer Scott's guardian, he couldn't help him. Maybe he'd get a different outcome in a face-to-face conversation.

Nick glanced at his watch. A little after four. Perhaps he could reach Trask before he left for the day. He grabbed his bags and entered the house

114

through the back door. In his office the light on his answering machine blinked with two messages. He pressed play.

When no one spoke, Nick reached to press delete, but a low moan stopped him. Scott?

"Nick, I know you're mad at me . . . but I need your help. I had this argument with some dude, and now he's dead. I'm afraid the cops are lookin' for me."

The message ended abruptly.

"Tuesday, two-o-five," intoned the robotic voice.

Another message. "Nick, where are you? Please come get me."

Scott didn't say where he was. Nick scanned the caller ID. The calls came from pay phones. He jotted the numbers down and turned on his computer. While it booted up, he found Trask's number in the phone directory and dialed. When the secretary answered, he identified himself and asked to speak with Trask.

"I'm sorry, but he's out of the office this afternoon. Can you call back in the morning?"

"Can I make an appointment for tomorrow?"

"Tomorrow?" Her tone indicated she assumed Nick was joking.

"Unless he'll be back this afternoon."

After a brief wait on hold, she informed him that because of a cancellation, the lawyer could see him at nine. Nick thanked her and hung up as icons appeared on his computer screen. He clicked on the internet and found the site he'd bookmarked for pay phone locations. He'd discovered the website while doing research for his book . . . the one the editor wanted revisions on by morning. Maybe he could get a little grace there.

Nick jotted down the addresses for the pay phones and logged them into MapQuest. One was on Cooper, the other on Young. He logged off and grabbed his keys. Maybe someone around there would know where he could find Scott.

Taylor. Should he call her? He had promised to tell her if he heard from Scott. But that was before she'd gone straight to the Memphis police.

Taylor swung from I-240 onto the Bill Morris Parkway. Traffic moved efficiently, and in another twenty minutes she left the Parkway behind for a four-lane highway and rolling green hills dotted with horses and cattle. Every mile brought her closer to home . . . and dealing with her family.

Before she knew it, Taylor was on the bypass around Logan Point with her exit coming up. She checked her watch. It had taken thirty minutes from downtown Memphis to the bypass. The big city crouched at their door. She made the turn, glancing at a black SUV in her rearview mirror. It had been behind her since she left Memphis. When she turned onto Coley Road, she slowed to see if it turned. Unease crept into her mind when it came into view. Was someone following her? She deliberately slowed the Rav4. When she looked into her rearview mirror again, the SUV was gone. Taylor released a pent-up breath, and heat flushed her face. She hated the residual effects of the assault.

Taylor topped a hill and stepped back in time. On the left was the pasture where she rode her mare . . . and the pond where she and Livy and Robyn swam. The places where she'd ridden her bike . . . the old oak she used to climb. The memories soothed like good chocolate. She lowered her window, inhaling air laced with fresh-cut grass.

The Duncan house came into view, then the open meadow where her dad had talked old Mr. Duncan into letting him build a baseball field for the neighborhood kids. She slowed her car, looking for signs where they'd run the bases, and remembered how her dad had coached the ragtag seven- and eight-year-olds, molding them into a team. A shadow raced across the field, and unexpectedly she ached for what had been one of the best summers of her life—the summer before her father left. She raised the window and gunned the SUV, leaving the memories behind.

Taylor pulled into the circle, and her heart caught when she spied her mom waiting on the porch. Allison Martin embodied the steel magnolias of the past. Her quiet strength had been tempered in the trial of her husband's abandonment, and she had chosen the path of graciousness rather than bitterness.

Dressed in white cropped pants and a blue silk blouse that fluttered as she descended the porch steps, Mom was a picture of genteel beauty and charm. So opposite of herself. Much to her mom's chagrin, Taylor had never been a girly-girl, preferring instead to climb trees and tag after her brother. She smoothed her wrinkled shirt and climbed out of the Rav4. The smell of fresh-cut clover tickled her nose.

Her mother wrapped her arms around her in a long hug. "It's about time." Then she stepped back and cocked her head. "You're too skinny."

Taylor pressed her lips together. "Nice to see you too, Mom."

"Oh, don't be so prickly. At least I didn't say anything about how tired you look," Mom said, the corners of her lips curving upward slightly.

Taylor followed her mom up the steps, catching the screen door before it banged shut. The sweet scent of honeysuckle pervaded the foyer. *"Mom, look what I picked for you."* The memory of her mom laughing and accepting the tangle of vines from her small hands pricked Taylor's heart. Her steps slowed, and she looked around at all the changes.

"I didn't know you'd replaced the carpet."

"We put new hardwood down five years ago when we painted."

Which you would know if you'd been home. That's what Mom would like to say, Taylor was certain. "I like it. And I'm glad the green fleur-de-lis wallpaper is gone too. Everything looks so much bigger."

"Thank you, dear. I wish you'd been here to help remove it."

She shot a quick glance at her mom. No accusation on her face, only wistfulness . . . Taylor jerked herself up short. She didn't know what was wrong with her. Yes, she did. Guilt. She could've come home before, but it had been so much easier to stay in Newton rather than come back to the place where she wasn't good enough. Not good enough to keep her father from leaving, not even good enough to be valedictorian of her graduating high school class, coming in as salutatorian instead.

Honeysuckle tickled her nose again, and she followed the fragrant aroma to a vase in the dining room, noting the ecru walls extended there as well. She trailed her fingers across the smooth cherry table and breathed in her favorite fragrance.

"It's good to finally have you home," her mother said softly from behind. "Jonathan wanted to be here when you arrived, but you know how it is when the hay's ready, but he'll be around. He's taking a few days off from the office. He should be in for supper, and Chase will be home from his conference tomorrow in time for lunch."

Taylor nodded and inhaled the honeysuckle again. A shadow crossed her heart, and she shivered. *Someone's walking over your grave.* She tried to shake off Granna Martin's old wives' tale, but the feeling settled in her bones and spread.

"The land Jonathan wants to sell," Taylor said as she turned around. "Chase said you want to keep it. Is that right?"

Her mom hesitated. "I don't know yet. I'm still praying about it."

That figured. Her mom prayed about everything.

Upstairs, Taylor absorbed the changes in her bedroom, which was no longer her bedroom but a guest room. Walls were now a soft robin's egg blue and accented by a white ruffled coverlet and strategically placed Delft vases—a reflection of her mom's tastes and definitely not Taylor's at eighteen, or even now. She kind of missed the ruby-red walls and Mick Jagger posters, though. She might even take the posters back to Newton if they were still around.

She paused at her dresser and picked up a clunky bowl filled with potpourri that seemed out of place with the Delft. The first decent piece of pottery she'd made, a Mother's Day present. Taylor set it back on the white dresser, and the shadow crossed her heart again, only this time it filled her with longing. She almost wished . . . She stiffened her spine. Staying had not been an option. Not with a full scholarship to New York University in her hands. After that it was easier to let Mom, and everyone else, visit her.

Taylor brushed her regrets away and quickly unpacked, then descended the stairs in search of her mother. When she wasn't in the kitchen or her office, Taylor backtracked to the library. Empty as well. As she turned to leave, the Baldwin piano in the corner caught her eye. The torturous hours she'd spent on that bench, but she had learned to play. She flipped the lid up and ran her fingers over the keys. Someone kept it tuned.

Automatically, her fingers picked out the notes to "Chopsticks," probably the first song she had learned. She pulled the bench out and sat behind the piano.

"Play 'Summertime' for me," her mom said from the doorway.

"I don't know. I'm rusty." As her mom entered the room and sat on the arm of a chair by the piano, Taylor started the slow melody, wincing when pain shot down her left arm, and she hit the wrong note. "I'm better at this." With a laugh she plunked out "Chopsticks" again using only her right hand.

Her mom laughed with her. "You should practice more. What's wrong with your arm?"

Mom missed nothing. Taylor massaged her arm, rolling it around in the socket. "I ran into something, bruised my shoulder."

It wasn't a lie. She had run into a pipe, but she wasn't about to tell her mom an intruder had been attached to the other end. The grandfather clock in the foyer chimed, and Taylor checked her watch. Seven o'clock, but only five in Newton.

"How about a sandwich?" her mom asked. "I thought we'd have a light supper tonight and wait until tomorrow night for your welcome home dinner when everyone will be here . . . except Abby, of course. She'll be home Saturday."

"Sounds good." Taylor followed her mom toward the kitchen.

That night Taylor stood at her bedroom window. The sandwich had turned into more than a light meal with fruit and cheese, chips, and finally, white chocolate brownies. Mom had only brought up moving back home once, but Taylor knew it had been only the first volley in her campaign to get Taylor home for good. Like that was going to happen. She was happy in Newton.

In the distance, a giant moon rose over Oak Grove, casting an eerie light on the old homestead and the ancient oaks. Not exactly the best image to imprint on her mind just before going to sleep.

Was her tree house still nestled in the big limbs of the sprawling oak beside the house? Maybe tomorrow she'd go see. That'd be a nice respite from what she expected to be a tumultuous day with Chase and her uncle. At least she'd been spared that today with Chase gone and her uncle tied up with mowing. In fact, she'd only seen Jonathan long enough to give him a quick hug.

A light appeared below the tree. It moved, bouncing against the dark, and Taylor followed it until it disappeared around the back of the house. Maybe it was Jonathan. She grabbed her cell phone and called her uncle. After seven rings, she hung up.

Taylor stared out the window again. No light. No movement.

Just an old house standing in the moonlight like a sleeping dragon.

9

A new day, new possibilities. Or another brick wall. The revisions had been the only thing Nick had accomplished yesterday. Heat waves shimmered up from the concrete as he exited the parking garage near Trask's downtown office and walked the block to the attorney's building. Automatically, he avoided the cracks in the sidewalk, which was about as useless as his search yesterday.

He'd found the pay phones, but they weren't

located in an area where people readily answered questions. Especially if the questioner was looking for someone. His options were running out. If Trask couldn't, or wouldn't, help him, he didn't know where he'd turn next.

Nick entered the building through the glass door and paused to orient himself, trying to remember the location of Trask's office. He spied a directory on the lobby wall beside the elevator. Trask was on the second floor next to Martin Accounting. Suite 208.

Trask's secretary informed him the attorney had stepped out for a minute and asked him to take a seat. Nick opted to stand. Trask probably had him cooling his heels for payback—their history hadn't always been cordial, and this meeting could go south fast.

While Trask had helped locate Scott when Angie died, Nick and Trask had exchanged sharp words a year earlier over the amount of Scott's allowance, and Nick's opinion hadn't changed— a sixteen-year-old shouldn't have a thousand dollars a month for an allowance. Not a teen involved in alcohol and drugs.

Nick walked around the room, pausing in front of a framed newspaper clipping about the Battle of Antietam. More clippings were grouped on the same wall—Shiloh, Corinth, Vicksburg. The other three walls sported black-and-white portraits of Southern generals.

Eventually, the secretary ushered Nick into another office, where the motif continued. Nick gravitated toward a table where Trask had set up a battlefield, complete with soldiers, roads, fortifications, even a river. Nick read the markers. Buckland, Hornets' Nest, Peach Orchard, Bloody Pond. *Shiloh*.

Trask entered from a side door. "Nick, sorry to keep you waiting."

He had the kind of voice that could easily sway a jury. Compelling.

Nick shook the offered hand, noting the cut of Trask's designer suit. It fit him perfectly, down to the sleeves that left enough cuff to show off expensive links. The lawyer took a seat behind the massive desk and motioned Nick to a wing-back chair.

"How can I help you?"

Nick sat in the chair and leaned forward. "I need two things. I'm still trying to locate Scott, and—"

Trask held up his hand. "I'm sorry, I can't help you there. When your brother turned eighteen, he made it plain I am not to share any information concerning him with you."

"Would it make any difference if I told you he called me yesterday and wanted me to come get him? He just didn't leave an address or phone number."

"Personally, I would love to tell you, but he's

my client, and until he tells me differently, my hands are tied."

Nick leaned back in the chair. Yep. Another brick wall.

"I tell you what I can do," Trask said. "I'll get a message to him and ask permission to give you his current address and phone number."

It looked like that was the best he was going to get. "I'd appreciate it." He hesitated. "Have you seen my brother lately?"

Trask rubbed his jaw. "Unfortunately, we had a disagreement over an advance on his allowance. And after he'd been doing so well."

"Are you saying Scott hit you?" Nick gripped the chair arms. What had happened to his little brother?

Trask leaned forward, bracing his elbows on the desk. "Let's just say I'm staying on as his trustee right now because I had so much respect for his grandfather, and the fact that the trust ends next year. Although, if I get the appointment to the Tennessee Court of Criminal Appeals, that may change. I won't be able to do that job and handle the case load I have now."

"That's right, I remember reading that you're on the governor's short list for that nomination. Congratulations."

"Thank you. And while you're here, I'd like to clarify something. I know you opposed the amount of money I initially sought for Scott."

"My wife and I didn't think he was old enough to handle that much money."

"Your wife. I'm sorry about what happened."

Nick acknowledged the condolences, and the attorney continued.

"Scott insisted that I ask for that much, and I went along with him because I knew the judge scheduled to hear the case would approve the amount and perhaps more. I feared, too, that Scott might hire another attorney, one who could have been disposed to break the trust. If that had happened, he could've received the entire trust."

"Something he clearly doesn't need," Nick replied.

"I just wanted you to know," Trask said. "And if you find your brother, get him back in rehab."

"Get him back in rehab? What are you talking about?"

"He completed a ninety-day program last year. I thought he'd turned a corner, and I helped him get into a little university out in Washington State."

"You're the one who helped him get into Conway?"

Trask's eyes narrowed. "You know about that?"

"That he attended, yes."

"I don't know what happened, but I know he's drinking again." Trask shuffled papers on his desk. "You mentioned two things you wanted to discuss with me."

"Yes. I received a call yesterday from a Detective Olivia Reynolds. She indicated Scott was a person of interest in a murder case. He might need an attorney."

"I see." Ethan tapped his pen on his desk. "George Anthony is probably your best bet."

"Thanks." Nick checked his watch. "I'll probably know more shortly—I'm on my way to the Criminal Justice Center to meet with her." He stood and held out his hand.

"Before you go, come over and look at my toys." Ethan walked toward the battle table. "Ever been to Shiloh?"

The attorney must be kidding. Every school kid within a hundred miles of the battlefield had been bussed there at least once. "A couple of times."

"Every month or so I create a different battle from the Civil War, and I just finished this layout. It's the Battle of Shiloh." Ethan positioned two soldiers opposite each other, one in gray and the other in blue.

Why? Nick caught the question before it spilled out of his mouth. But it must have shown in his face.

"You don't approve of war games per se, or is it just the Civil War?" Ethan's gray eyes seemed to be measuring him.

"The Civil War was not our finest hour," Nick said. "As for war games, they're just not my cup of tea."

"I find playing them to be very stimulating. I've actually used battles like those at Shiloh, Gettysburg . . . Antietam to work out courtroom tactics."

"You're kidding." He wasn't. "How?"

Ethan moved a Confederate soldier from a Union direct line of fire. "Both Grant and Lee were brilliant strategists. And in war games, you get into the mind of the opposing generals. Right now, I'm playing 'what if' at the Battle of Shiloh. What if General Johnson hadn't been killed? What if Beauregard had not ordered his Confederate soldiers to cease firing with an hour of daylight remaining?" He cocked his head. "Sort of like what you do on paper."

"You've read my books?"

The attorney nodded. "You have a knack for sucking me in on the first page, and I enjoy trying to guess who did it. Not that I have much luck. Especially with your last one."

"Thank you." His readership was broader than he'd imagined.

The steel-gray eyes measured him again. "So, when you get stuck, what do you do to spark your imagination?"

Nick considered his question. "I play Solitaire . . . and sometimes I play an online game of chess."

"I suppose chess could be comparable to the war games." Ethan smiled suddenly and held out his hand. "Let me know if you find Scott. I really did try to help your brother."

Nick shook his hand. "I will, and thank you again for your time."

It had been a long morning of working through the tasks she'd brought with her to complete. Seated at her bedroom writing table with her laptop, Taylor entered another grade into the system, pausing only as her cell phone rang. Livy. She really needed to assign her friend a special ringtone. The theme from *Dragnet* maybe.

"I don't think I'll make it to Memphis this morning to help you look for Dad's file," she said instead of the customary hello.

Livy chuckled. "Since it's ten o'clock, I don't think you will either. What happened?"

"The university's website crashed last night and wiped out all the grades I had posted. I'm reentering them."

It didn't surprise her that the site had crashed. Lately her internet connection at the university had been slower than dial-up. "My new plan is to be in your office by two. That's if another disaster doesn't hit."

"Good. Autopsy report came in on Ross, and I've pulled a report together—crime scene photos, statements, known associates, his rap sheet. If you don't make it, I'm coming to Logan Point this afternoon. Aunt Kate called and wants me to come for supper tonight. I'll drop it by then."

"I'd still like to get started on my search." Taylor stood and stretched, then walked to the window, where a light breeze billowed the curtains into the room, bringing in the sweet scent of wisteria growing on the trellis beside the house. She caught sight of her uncle near the barn, doing something in the bed of his truck.

"Wear something cool. The air-conditioning is out on this floor, and they may not get it fixed right away," Livy said. "How was the home-coming yesterday?"

Taylor slid the gauzy curtain material through her hand. "Quiet. Abby is away at camp until Saturday, I saw Jonathan briefly, but he'll be around since he's taking off a few days, and Chase hasn't made it back from his meeting. And Mom is . . . Mom, still plotting ways to get me back to Logan Point. How about you? Have you talked to Nick?"

"I did, and your friend has agreed to come by my office and answer a few questions about Scott. He should be here any minute."

"He's not my friend. Just someone I met recently. And I doubt he's very happy about me giving you his cell number."

Livy laughed. "You're probably right about that. He just walked in the door, and he doesn't look pleased. Call me before you come—just in case I get called out."

Taylor agreed and slid her cell into her pocket. She'd like to be a fly on the wall about now at the Criminal Justice Center. Or maybe not. Nick just might splat her against that wall.

An hour later, Taylor closed her laptop and stretched her shoulders. Finished entering grades, at least. She hoped the website didn't crash again. The rich aroma of cinnamon wafted through her open door, making her mouth water. She followed her nose to the kitchen and peeked in the oven. Apple pie, her mom's specialty. She wandered outside and found her mother in her herb garden.

"There you are," said Taylor.

"I figured you'd find me. I needed rosemary for the potatoes tonight." Her mother tucked the herb in her apron, but not before Taylor caught a whiff of its pungent aroma.

"Roasted potatoes?" Her mouth watered.

"And braised tenderloin and sautéed green beans."

All her favorites. A soft nicker drew her attention, and she looked toward the corral. A sorrel mare stood at the white fence, and behind her a colt pranced in the paddock. "Scarlet?"

"Yep, with her newest addition. Why don't you go see them while I finish making lunch?"

"I'll help."

"Not today. After you visit Scarlet, get reacquainted with the farm. You might even find Jonathan at the tractor shed."

The horse nickered again as she approached. Was it possible the mare remembered being bottle-fed by Taylor as a foal after her mother died? More likely she was expecting a treat.

"Hello, girl. I see you've done well for yourself." She rubbed the mare's forehead, and Scarlet nuzzled her arm. Taylor laughed. "Sorry, no sugar cubes."

The colt trotted toward them, but when Taylor reached out her hand, he snorted and cavorted off. She stroked Scarlet's head again. "Someone needs to teach your boy some manners."

"Want the job? You were good at it once."

Taylor turned, and Chase caught her up in a bear hug. "Welcome home."

She held him tight. "You're back early!"

"Just for you."

She hugged him again. "Let me look at you."

He'd lost weight since she saw him a year ago in Newton. Dark circles under his eyes emphasized the gauntness. Chase, the one who'd always held it together for Taylor, wore brittleness like a cloak.

An ache the size of Texas weighted her heart. She should have known, should have been able to tell in his voice when she talked to him. She managed a shaky smile. "You're too thin. Everything okay?"

He eyed her and shrugged. "Finding a way to keep Jonathan from selling the land will help."

"Yes, the land." Her shoulders sagged.

"Taylor, don't tell me you're taking Jonathan's side."

"Goodness no! I just dread opposing him."

Chase's jaw shot forward. "That's why I wanted you to come home. With all three of us standing firm, he'll have to listen."

"You might want to bring Mom on board. She didn't seem too sure last night. Are we calling a family meeting?"

Chase looked away. "I hoped if you talked to him first, like this afternoon, we might not have to do that."

He was throwing her to the wolves, or rather wolf. Her stomach knotted. As a child, she'd been able to twist her uncle around her little finger. Not so much after she became a teenager. "Okay, I'll do it this afternoon."

The thin line of his lips twitched, finally forming a sheepish grin. "Sorry. Didn't mean to put pressure on you, but it's our heritage he's trying to sell."

Out of the corner of her eye she spotted a white minivan and pointed toward it. "Is that yours?"

Chase turned. "Yep." He caught the sidelong glance she shot him. "Hey, I have an eight-soon-to-be-nine-year-old. I need something to haul kids and soccer balls in."

She laughed. "I never thought I would see Chase Martin in a mommy mobile."

"Yeah, well, now you have." Scarlet nosed

134

against Chase's back. "All right." He rubbed her nose, and she snuffed his hand, nibbling his fingers.

"You've spoiled her rotten."

He grinned at Taylor. "I know. Let me get a treat, or she won't leave us alone."

He went to the barn and came back with a flake of clover and pitched it in the corner of the lot. The mare tossed her head and trotted over to the hay.

"Does Abby ride Scarlet?"

"A little, but Scarlet is more horse than she can handle. She's been bugging me for an Indian pony for her birthday. Mom thinks I ought to wait a couple of years."

"Mom would." Taylor inhaled, taking in the sweet scent of the hay. The colt bounded away from Scarlet and kicked out his back feet. The last time she saw her niece a year ago in Newton, Abby was going through a growth spurt and had been all gangly and awkward, just like the foal. "How is Abby? You know . . . about Robyn."

Tight-lipped, he braced his foot against the bottom fence rail and leaned with his arms over the top. "Abby's okay."

Taylor stiffened at his terse reply.

Chase fiddled with something around his little finger. Finally, he cleared his throat. "We need an understanding."

"What do you mean?"

"You may be a psychologist, but nothing's broke here, so don't come home and try to fix us. Let Abby work through this problem with her mother in her own way—just like we did with Dad."

Maybe you did but not me, Taylor wanted to shout. If the subject of her father hadn't been taboo, maybe some of her questions would have been answered. And maybe she wouldn't be having nightmares about him now.

The nightmares. There hadn't been one last night. Maybe they'd ended. They had before. She glanced at Chase. What did he keep twisting on his finger? Taylor's breath stilled in her chest. The ring.

Chase still wore the small gold ring engraved with his initials. Seeing it reminded Taylor of her necklace, and she touched her neck. A ring for Chase and a necklace for her—gifts from their father the day he'd walked out of their lives—like a ring or necklace would make up for his presence. But the memory of the golden heart with her name on it was all she had. She'd lost the necklace that same day.

Taylor's hands curled into tight fists. She didn't know if she could do it—stay here where her father's absence and betrayal slapped her in the face at every turn.

10

Nick shifted in the straight-back chair. Barely cool air filtered into the small room Lieutenant Reynolds left him in. Where *was* the detective? She'd brought him here and immediately left.

He glanced around. Drab gray walls. No windows, only a mirror. A two-way? Was she watching him even now? He almost laughed at his writer's imagination running amok. The door opened, and Olivia Reynolds stepped inside.

"Sorry about the air-conditioning. They've just gotten it repaired."

That explained the heat, but not being put in an interrogation room. Nick sized up the detective. In person Lieutenant Reynolds had been very different from his mental image. He'd pictured someone taller, more muscular, not a petite blonde with disarming dimples in her cheeks. She placed a folder on the table, then combed her fingers through her short hair.

"I don't understand why you wanted me to come downtown," he said. "I've already told you, I don't know where my brother is."

The detective pulled out a chair and sat across from him. "I know. But I wanted to meet you face-to-face."

"You could've come to see *me,* Detective Reynolds."

She acknowledged his point with a nod. "But then we would have been on your territory."

Her point-blank honesty surprised him.

"You can call me Livy." She opened the folder. "And thanks for autographing *Dead Men Don't Lie*. I feel like I already know you through your writing, anyway."

Interview Technique 101. Create a sense of familiarity with the suspect's brother. *Wait.* "You're that Livy?"

She nodded.

Taylor's *good* friend, and if he were a betting man, he'd bet she had shared more than just basic information. Probably all her biases. He leaned forward. "I really don't know where Scott is. I do know he's in trouble, but I'm not sure it's of his own making. I think he's being framed."

"Taylor thought you might say that. Who would frame him?"

"Someone who has a grudge against her."

The detective seemed to consider his point. "You could be right. From Taylor's assessment of him, your brother is too smart to charge a bracelet to his account then send it to her with a death threat. Except, there's Scott's presence in Newton and the Memphis postmark on the envelope. And then there's *my* victim. He has words with your brother, they almost come to blows, and an hour later, the guy is dead."

"That could be a coincidence. But someone is

138

framing him for the attack on Taylor." The detective raised her eyebrows, and Nick shifted in his chair. The scenario the detective described sounded like the plot of one of his books. "What's Scott's motive?"

"I don't know. Maybe he's a psychopath—"

"No!" Nick's hands curled into fists on the table. "My brother is a sweet, gentle kid."

"How do you know?" Detective Reynolds folded her arms across her chest. "I understand you haven't seen him in several years."

"Only two and a half years." Nick reined in his emotions. "Look, I'm sorry for my outburst. But I raised Scott for six years. He has a tender heart. He couldn't do what you're accusing him of."

"Does your brother know how lucky he is to have an advocate like you?" She sighed. "We're going in circles, so I won't keep you any longer. If Scott contacts you, would you give me a call?"

Unsure of whether he would or not, Nick remained silent.

"Don't try to handle this yourself. You're not a cop." Then Livy smiled. "But, if you're anything like the characters you write about, I know you'll do the right thing. Thank you for coming by."

Detective Reynolds was good, but he wasn't quite ready to be dismissed. Nick held up his hand. "Wait. The victim. How did Scott know him?"

"Albert Duncan Ross frequented the place where Scott had worked for the past two weeks. Movies 2 Go." Livy's eyes questioned him. "I understand your brother receives a substantial allowance from a trust fund. Do you know why he'd be working?"

Nick flared his nostrils. "Because he blows his money on drugs and booze before the month is over?"

Taylor stacked the dirty lunch plates on the counter. The restlessness inside her was like an itch that needed scratching. Jonathan hadn't come to lunch, and that talk still loomed before her. Maybe meeting with Livy and searching for her dad's records would help soothe the itch. "I'll be going in to Memphis later to see Livy."

"Tell her I said hello."

Taylor nodded and put the mustard jar in the refrigerator, marveling at how easily she'd slipped into the routine of mundane Martin family life. But mundane was better any day than constantly looking over her shoulder. At least she wasn't alone.

She leaned against the marble countertop. "I forgot to tell you last night, but I like your haircut."

"Thanks. It's easier." Her mom filled the sink with sudsy water.

Was that a blush creeping over her mom's

cheeks? Puzzled, she grabbed a drying cloth, and they fell into a quiet rhythm of Mom washing and Taylor drying, just like old times. The kitchen had always been her favorite room. Something about the way the windows let in the light, bouncing against the warm maple cabinets and the light sage-green walls.

Her mom broke the silence. "You've been awfully quiet since you got home. Anything wrong?"

"It's been a tough year." She had to be careful what she discussed with Mom. She definitely couldn't mention Dad. Taylor never knew how she would react. The last time she asked something about him, her mom ended up in tears. And any hint of danger and there'd be no let up of pressure to come home—where it was safe. Sometimes, Mom created her own reality and didn't hear anything to the contrary.

Her mother dunked the last plate into the suds. "I'm sorry about Michael. He seemed like a nice young man. Want to talk about it?"

Taylor reached for the plate as her mom rinsed it. "There's not much to say. Michael said I didn't need him, and he found someone who did."

"I'm sorry, honey."

"Me too." Taylor rubbed the middle of the plate with a vengeance. "I don't get it. I didn't know I was supposed to *need* him. I thought marriage was about love."

"Oh, Taylor." Her mom dried her hands. "Marriage is about love, but a man's definition is often different from a woman's. I imagine Michael wanted to be your knight in shining armor."

Taylor snorted. "No wonder our relationship was doomed. I don't need someone to take care of me or rescue me. I can take care of myself."

"Yes, you can. I just wish your father had been here and you could've seen what—"

"Don't! I needed him, and he left, and it hurt. No one will ever do that to me again."

Her mother took her hand. "Your father didn't reject you. For whatever reason he left, I promise, it wasn't about you."

Taylor stared at her mom. "Do you know what happened to him? Where he is?"

Her mother paled. "No, of course not . . . Just don't let his absence keep you from finding love."

"I'm not looking for love." After Michael, she wouldn't trust her judgment if she found someone. Nick Sinclair and his chiseled jaw and broad shoulders materialized in her thoughts. She shook away his image.

"Honey," Mom said, "the right person is out there, and God will bring him into your life at the right time."

Her mother sounded like Sheriff Atkins. Taylor squeezed out the drying cloth and spread it across the drainer to dry. "Ever read Nicholas Sinclair's books?"

Her mom gave her the "we're not done with this discussion" look. Taylor ignored it and waited.

"He's one of my favorite authors. I caught his interview on *A.M. News* recently."

"Really? Would you like to have an auto-graphed book?"

"Of course I'd like one."

"Wait right here." Taylor hurried to her bed-room and retrieved Nick's book. Her mom beamed when she put it into her hands.

"How did you get this?"

"Oh, I—"

The back door scraped open, and she glanced toward it, expecting her uncle. The man entering the kitchen bore no resemblance to Jonathan.

"Mail, Ms. Martin." The lanky farmhand wasn't looking at her mother as he waved a large envelope and several business-sized letters. His scrutiny sent a shiver down Taylor's back.

"Thanks, Pete. Would you mind putting it in the office? I'll have you a glass of iced tea waiting." Her mother nodded toward Taylor. "You remember Pete Connelly?"

Pete? From high school? What happened to the skinny little runt the older boys always picked on? This Pete stood a menacing six-one with biceps that strained against his white T-shirt and a buzz haircut. Suppressing a shiver, she folded her arms across her chest as his black eyes traveled the length of her body and then back to her face.

"Good to see you again, Taylor." He tipped his head.

Her eyes narrowed as he sauntered toward her mother's office. She didn't like the way he stared at her any better now than in the past. "What's he doing here?"

"He's staying in that little camper of Jonathan's. Works off and on for your uncle. The rest of the time he works for Ethan." Ice cracked as her mom poured tea into a tall glass.

"Ethan?"

"Your uncle's longtime friend and business associate. Ethan Trask. He's an attorney. Do you remember him?"

"Mmm, somewhat. Tall? Good looking? Something about magic?"

"That's Ethan. They were college roommates." Her mom shot Taylor a curious glance. "But it was such a long time ago that he and Jonathan did magic tricks. I'm surprised you remember that."

Taylor had a vague recollection of being a flower girl at his wedding, and a marriage she didn't remember lasting too long. "Did he ever remarry?"

"Uh, no."

An inflection in her mother's voice caught Taylor's ear. "Tell me more about Ethan."

Her mom's cheeks reddened. "Well, he and Jonathan have adjoining offices in downtown Memphis, and Jonathan keeps the books for several of Ethan's trust accounts—"

"I meant personally."

The redness deepened, but before she could answer, Pete returned. "Here's your tea." She handed him the glass, avoiding Taylor's eyes.

"Thank you, Ms. Allison. It's hot out there."

"Did Jonathan finish the tractor repairs?"

"Yes, ma'am. He wants to make a few rounds, and then I'll finish baling." Ice clinked against the glass as he drained it and set it on the counter before turning to Taylor. "Are you home for good?"

"Just for the summer. I heard you left town after high school."

He rocked back on his feet, an amused gleam in his eye. "I come and go." Then he nodded at her mom. "I better check on Jonathan."

The door banged shut, and she wanted to bolt it behind him. "Does he always just barge in?"

Her mom shrugged off her question. "Sure. Pete's worked here off and on for quite a while. You don't like him?"

"He's—" She caught the word *pervert* before it shot from her mouth. He'd never actually done anything in high school except leer at her. But she'd always felt him undressing her with his eyes. "He creeps me out." She'd make it her business to stay out of his way.

"Taylor, it's not like you to be judgmental. Especially with someone who's had it hard all his life."

Her mom didn't know the same Pete Connelly that Taylor knew.

The tractor clattered by, and Taylor peered out the window as her uncle made a round on the field. Every few yards the baler dropped a rectangle of hay. Soon, hundreds of hay bales would dot the field, a scene she'd seen time and again. "You haven't said much about Jonathan and the land deal. Have you decided how you'll vote about selling it?"

Her mother didn't answer right away. Misgiving grew in Taylor's mind. "You aren't thinking about selling, are you?"

Mom sighed. "I don't know . . . I would hate to see the old home place go." She smoothed her hands on her pants. "We need to talk."

Uh-oh. Taylor knew that drill. Anytime her mother wanted a serious discussion, it began with those words, moved to the kitchen table, and usually ended with Taylor doing something she didn't want to do. She took her usual chair. "I know you didn't want to talk about it last night."

"No need to go to bed stewing about something that can wait until morning."

Taylor recognized one of Granna Martin's old sayings. "Why would you sell? The land's been in the family forever."

"It's only land, Taylor, and a million dollars is a million dollars." She took the chair opposite Taylor.

Taylor pressed her fingertips together. "Is it worth dividing the family over? You know Chase doesn't want to sell. Even Dad would never agree to it."

"I know, but your dad's not here. If we do accept the offer, I plan to sell this house and move into town."

"What?" Her mother couldn't sell this house. No wonder she hadn't wanted to talk about it last night.

"This place is a constant reminder of what I don't have."

Taylor rocked back in her chair. She didn't always consider how her father's desertion had affected her mother's life. Her heart sank. And she'd certainly been no help. So anxious to get away from home, then staying away for nine years. Even though getting her education consumed her for so many years, she should have taken the time to come home. *But Mom had Chase and Abby.* The guilt didn't ease. She'd have to come home more often.

The telephone rang, and her mother rose to answer it. After a few words, she pointed toward the phone and mouthed, "Farm business. I'll be in the office."

Taylor set the glasses in the sink and turned to

go upstairs for her keys to drive into Memphis. The back door scraped open again.

"Well, girl, it's time for a better hug than I got last night." Jonathan's smile stretched from ear to ear on his jowly face. He bent over and wrapped his arms around her. "How's my favorite niece this fine day?"

A small chuckle escaped her lips. "I'm your only niece."

"Darlin', if I had fifty nieces, you'd still be my favorite."

He hugged her again, and she rested her head on his chest and breathed in horses and hay and the pipe he smoked when her mom wasn't watching. He oozed safety . . . security. For the moment, she forgot the land issue.

Her uncle released her. "Let me look at you."

She hadn't seen Jonathan in years, not since he'd come to her college graduation in New York. He'd lost a little more hair on top, making his long face seem even longer, and he'd put a little weight on his lanky frame. But the skin around his blue eyes still crinkled when he laughed.

Jonathan squeezed her hand. Taylor patted his small potbelly. "I see you haven't missed any meals."

"Your mama sees to it I don't go hungry." He hitched up his khaki pants. "Where's Allison?"

"In the office."

He nodded. "So, how long are you staying?"

"I don't know. Classes begin again in August."

"Good. That'll give us the rest of the summer to work on getting you back home for good. You could teach at the University of Memphis."

"Are you still doing community theater?"

His sidelong glance told Taylor she hadn't fooled him, but thankfully he played along.

"Occasionally," he said, "but mostly I take Abby to practice. She's really into this acting thing, and if there's a good part for an old, balding, character actor, I'm their man."

"You're not old. What are you, forty-four?"

"Twenty-nine!" he retorted, then grinned. "And I have been for the past fourteen years."

Taylor remembered the mysterious light. "Were you up at the old home place last night? I was looking out my bedroom window and saw a light go around behind the house."

"It wasn't me. I turned my phones off and went to bed at nine. Could've been Pete, though. Teenagers around here have discovered the legend about the tunnels beneath the house, so I asked him to keep an eye out. Wouldn't want one of them to get lost down there."

"I didn't realize the tunnels at Oak Grove were still open." Dug long before the Civil War to aid slaves escaping to the North, they connected the old house to caves in the nearby river bluff.

"Only a couple of them go all the way to the river bluff."

Taylor's skin prickled, and she rubbed her arms. "You won't get me near there. Close me in, no light—I would die on the spot."

"That's one way you're not like your mama. Before you and Chase were born, Allison spent hours exploring those tunnels with your dad."

Taylor's heart hammered in her chest. "Jonathan . . . why did my daddy leave?"

Disbelief darted across his face and then a flash of something else. Something so fleeting, Taylor wasn't sure it had been there at all.

"Taylor, you aren't still pursuing that, are you?"

"I don't understand why you don't want to look for him."

"I did look. When he first went missing." He planted his feet wide and gestured with his hand. "Don't you know if someone wants to disappear, they can do it? Please. That's all behind us. Don't stir it up fresh again."

What happened to the uncle she always went to as a ten-year-old? The uncle who always said the right things, told her one day they'd go find her dad. She was thirteen before she realized he was placating her. That's when she quit asking. Until now. "My nightmares are back. I . . . thought if I could find him and ask why he left, they'd go away. You used to tell—"

"If your father is alive, it's plain he doesn't want anyone to find him."

Hard and cold, his words stung. Taylor blinked

back tears. "This time you have to do better than that. I have to know."

"Some things are better left alone. You can't change the past. Let it go."

She lifted her chin. "I can't."

"Even if it means destroying your mother? This family?"

"Truth won't destroy us." She touched her chest. "And how about me? I need to know."

His face softened. "Is that why you came home?"

"Not entirely. A case I was working on in Newton has a Memphis connection, and Chase wanted me to weigh in on the land deal."

"Oh." He rubbed his balding head. "Well, I want you to hear my side before you come to a decision. This is a really good deal, actually more than the land's worth. We'll call a family meeting after dinner tonight and fully discuss it."

"Why not now?" Chase demanded from the doorway. "We're all here."

Startled, Taylor jumped and turned as Jonathan jerked his head toward the doorway.

Her uncle's eyes narrowed. "I thought you'd already left for the office." Then he curtly nodded his head. "But now is fine. Get your mother."

While Chase went to find their mom, Jonathan folded his arms across his chest, and the "my mind is made up, and I'm not changing it" scowl settled on his face. It was a look she'd come to know well growing up. Her stomach tightened. She did not want to be here.

Silence thickened in the wake of Chase's exit.

"I need you to hang with me, darlin'."

"But Jonathan—"

"Taylor, I need the money this sale will bring." Desperation edged his voice.

"I have a little saved up. Let me loan—"

"I'm not borrowing money from my niece."

Chase returned to the kitchen with Mom. She carried a large white envelope in her hands. "Do we have to do this now?" she asked.

"Mom, let's get it out of the way. It's been hanging over us too long as it is." Chase pulled out a chair for her.

From the look on her face, Mom didn't want to be here any more than she did. Taylor returned to the seat she'd vacated only a short while ago and waited for the meeting to begin, but first her mom handed her the envelope. "This came for you today. Who knows you're here?"

Taylor stared at the white envelope her mom handed her. A dull ache started in her temple. No. It had to be something from Christine or the college, and she laid the envelope on the table. "It's probably from the university. I'll look at it later."

Mom took her seat. "Who wants to go first?"

"I do." Jonathan leaned forward and put his arms on the table. The scowl had disappeared.

"First of all, as usual, we'll abide by majority rule, and we'll vote after everyone has spoken."

Chase's jaw shot forward. "I say we vote now and save time."

"No." One word, but it carried weight. "I know how you're going to vote, but Taylor doesn't know all the particulars, and your mom still has a few questions. I'll go first with why selling is a good idea, and you can end with why we shouldn't."

Her brother pressed his lips together in a grim line and sat back in his chair, arms folded.

"So Taylor will know, the offer is from someone working with the contractors who built the subdivision across the road. It's a million dollars for the sixty-five acres of farmland behind our three houses and does include Oak Grove. That breaks down to roughly two hundred and fifty thousand for each of us. The buyer will pay the realtor, but there are a few other fees." He looked around the table. "Any questions so far?"

Mom leaned forward. "I thought you were going to negotiate with the buyer to keep the old home place."

Jonathan rubbed his jaw. "We need to let it go, Allison. Do you know what it would cost to fix it up? With Oak Grove being part of the Underground Railroad and on the National Register of Historic Places, do you want the hassle of dealing with the restrictions to renovate? I don't.

The agent wants an answer by the first of next week. If we accept the offer as it stands, we'd have our money within a month."

Taylor lifted her finger, hoping Jonathan wouldn't snap it off.

"Question or comment?" he asked.

"Why do we have to decide now? Why can't we take a few more days?"

"Because I'd like to tell the realtor our answer today."

"No way!" Chase gripped the table. "Unless it's a no vote."

Her uncle closed his eyes briefly, then shook his head as if to clear it. "Before you say any more, Chase, let me explain why I think we should sell. Fifteen thousand an acre is top dollar for that land. You think those two-hundred-thousand-dollar houses across the road are expensive? The houses built on our land will *start* at three hundred and fifty thousand dollars—we're not talking about cheap tract houses. Now, say your piece."

"First," Chase said, "I want to know why. Why now, why ever?"

Jonathan snorted. "It takes a small fortune to keep this place up. Taxes, mowing—which you never help out with—repairs . . . do I need to go on?"

"You won't let me help. I've offered."

"Maybe that's because I want it done right."

"You won't—"

Mom banged her hand on the table. "That's enough, you two."

Both startled but closed their mouths.

Her mother massaged her hand. "Chase, go on."

He swallowed. "I just want to remind us all that this land has been in the Martin family since before the Civil War. The land and Oak Grove are our heritage. Think about Granna and Papa." He glared at Jonathan. "I can't believe you'd sell your own parents' place. Oh, but I forgot. You don't have a sentimental bone in your body."

"Chase . . ." Mom touched his arm.

The dull ache in Taylor's head had morphed into full throbbing. "Can we wait until later to do this? My head is killing me."

Three pairs of eyes turned toward her.

"I think that's a good idea," her mom said.

"Could we at least have a prelim—"

A hard look from her mom silenced Jonathan.

"I'm going up to my room to try to ward off a full-blown migraine." Taylor stood and started for the stairs.

"Wait," Jonathan called after her. "You forgot your envelope."

He handed it to her, and she hurried up the stairs.

In her bedroom, Taylor examined the envelope. The postmark was blurry. How did she miss that downstairs? She looked closer. Memphis. She covered her mouth with her hand as the room spun. Scott? But how did he find her? She ticked off the people who knew where she was and came up with only five. Livy, the secretary at the university, Christine, Sheriff Atkins, Nick.

Nick? He didn't have her address, but how hard would it be to find the Martin address on Google? She tried to remember if she'd mentioned either her mom's name or Jonathan's.

Maybe she was worrying for nothing. Tight-lipped, Taylor grabbed a tissue and opened the flap. When she pulled the contents out, a wave of weakness swept over her. The poem. Three photos. The first two were the same as others she'd received—her sitting on a rock, her standing in her kitchen. She flipped to the last one and choked out a gasp.

The Coleman crime scene.

How had Scott taken this? She stared at the photograph that showed her watching the para-medics load Beth Coleman into the helicopter bay, the husband and daughter hovering beside her . . .

I KNOW WHERE YOU ARE. The words were neatly printed with a black Sharpie across the bottom. The same Sharpie had circled her image . . .

She snatched her cell phone from her pocket and called Sheriff Atkins at home. "Dale, are you up to talking to me a minute?" she asked when he answered.

"I was actually going to call you shortly. I just found out the Coleman kidnapper didn't commit suicide."

"What?" Blood pounded against the top of her head.

"The doctors finally allowed one of my deputies in to take Beth Coleman's statement. Appears there were two kidnappers. She believed at first that only Ralph Jenkins was involved and tried to escape from him with little Sarah. They struggled, and that's when his partner shot her."

"Could Beth describe the second man?"

"No. She never saw him." Dale inhaled a shaky breath. "But he whispered something in her ear before she lost consciousness."

She steeled herself.

He continued. "Something about death unfolding like a flower. When Zeke showed her the poem, she recognized the rest of it. Taylor, you need to be very careful."

The photos slipped from Taylor's hands. A numbing chill gripped her stomach and spread to her lungs, choking off her breath.

A man dead, a woman shot.

And now, by coming home, Taylor had drawn her family into a murderer's direct line of fire.

▌▌

"Taylor, are you there?"

"I'm here, Dale." *Breathe. Think this through.* What kind of person kidnaps two people and kills their partner to send a message?

A very sick person. The same one who wanted to kill her. Who knew where to find her.

If she didn't stop him, someone else would die, and it would be her fault.

Taylor sat on the side of her bed and concentrated on breathing. "Whoever it is, he knows where I am. I just received another package with photos that included the Coleman crime scene."

That up to this moment she truly believed Scott had sent. But his profile didn't support the type of planning it would take to pull off such an elaborate scheme. And it didn't support such cold-bloodedness.

"I want a copy of everything in the package."

"Yes, sir." Now she knew why the Coleman case had nagged at her. That was why it had been so easy. "It was a setup . . ."

Taylor closed her eyes and tried to snag the elusive hunch that wouldn't stay put. *Talk it out.* "Beth Coleman and her daughter were taken in Newton County . . . they were chosen because the kidnapper knew you would call me in on the case. If I'm the primary target—"

Beth, little Sarah . . . *My fault. All my fault.*

She balled her hands into fists. "The kidnapper had to find someone in our county he could manipulate."

"Right. This probably eliminates Scott Sinclair. Nineteen-year-olds don't typically have the ability to plan a complex situation like this."

"I know," Taylor said.

Dale broke into a coughing fit. "I'm sorry," he finally wheezed. "Lost my breath there."

Guilt flushed her cheeks. She hadn't even asked how he felt. "Are you okay? You haven't gone back to work, have you?"

"Not full-time. Working a little bit from home since Zeke left for a conference in your area."

"Zeke Thornton is here, in Mississippi?"

"He's attending a conference on cyber crimes at the National Forensics Training Center in Southaven. I think it ends Saturday." His voice cracked. "I'm getting tired here. You need help on this. I'll have Zeke call you."

"I'd rather call my friend at the Memphis Police Department." She shouldn't have kept him on the phone so long.

"Don't fight me on this, Taylor. Zeke has your cell number, and he'll be calling you."

She didn't look forward to butting heads with Zeke. "You take care of yourself."

Taylor paced her room. She had to tell her family—they had a right to know she'd brought danger to their doorstep. They needed to watch themselves, be careful. But first she'd call Livy. Taylor punched in her number.

"Reynolds." Livy's voice sounded hurried.

"I have a major problem."

"What's going on?"

"I received another package . . . photos. Here, at

Mom's. And it includes a picture of me taken at the last crime scene I worked in Newton."

"You're kidding." Livy paused. "Hold on a second, Mac."

"You're busy."

"Have a meeting with the captain in two minutes. Why don't you call Ben Logan?"

Logical. Taylor should have already thought to call the Bradford County sheriff. It would be Mississippi jurisdiction, anyway. "Do you have his cell number?"

Livy gave her the number. "Call me after you talk to him."

"I will. Doesn't look like I'll make it to Memphis today." She'd really wanted to start looking for her dad's files.

"I'll take care of it. And you might want to think about moving in with me until whoever is doing this is found."

"That's a thought. Then I would only have to worry about you getting hurt. I was thinking along the lines of a motel."

"Do what you have to, but you're welcome anytime."

She broke the connection and dialed the sheriff's number. Ben answered on the second ring.

"Taylor? I heard you were coming home, but I didn't expect to see your name on my ID," he said with a chuckle.

"I didn't expect to call you, either."

"What's going on?"

"I have a problem, and I don't want to discuss it over the phone. Or here, at Mom's." Taylor wanted a plan ready before she told her family.

"How about at Kate's? I had planned to stop by there later today, anyway. Mom's birthday is next week, and she's been hinting for one of Kate's porcelain pieces."

Kate Adams's pottery studio would be perfect. Nothing ruffled Livy's aunt, and anything said there would stay there. "How soon can you meet me?"

"I stepped out of a meeting with the mayor to take your call. Shouldn't take over half an hour to finish up."

"Great . . . and Ben, don't mention this to anyone."

"Come on, Taylor. It's me you're talking to."

"Right. Sorry."

Taylor ended the call. Half an hour seemed like an eternity. Using a tissue, she stacked the photos with the envelope and put them in her briefcase. Maybe she needed to invest in latex gloves.

Downstairs she found a note from her mother on the table. *Gone to town. Be back by three.* Good. Maybe by then, she and Ben would have a plan in place. Taylor left her own note telling her mom where she'd be and grabbed her car keys.

As Taylor slid into her rental, she glanced

toward the barn and noticed Pete getting into a black pickup. He drove toward the house and gave her a half salute as he passed, then continued on to Coley Road and turned toward town.

In high school, Pete had floated on the periphery, always hanging around. She had to admit to more than a little curiosity about what he'd been doing since graduation. He'd gone away to college, or so she'd heard, so why was he working as a flunky for her uncle and his partner? Maybe Livy or Chase would know. She fastened her seat belt and followed the same path as Pete, only at the end of the drive, she turned the opposite way.

A wooden sign caught her eye as she approached the Adams's drive. The Potter's House Bed and Breakfast. A bed and breakfast? Kate had been a potter for as long as Taylor could remember, and now she ran a B and B? Questions buzzed her mind. When did this happen? As she drove the winding, tree-lined drive to the hundred-year-old house, she had to admit the two-story Victorian looked like a bed and breakfast with its three-gabled roof and wraparound porch.

Taylor followed the drive to the rear of the house and the pottery studio. Kate's husband had transformed an old carriage house into a place for Kate to work. Taylor pulled into the parking area that had been added since she left.

She stopped to admire the array of vases and bowls in the display window. An impossibly thin bowl caught her eye. Porcelain. She bet that was the piece Ben's mom wanted. The soft whirring from a potter's wheel caught her ear, and Taylor walked toward the sound.

Kate leaned over her potter's wheel and coaxed a cylinder higher and higher. She was so focused on pulling up the sides of a vase she didn't see her, giving Taylor time to study the woman who'd been like a second mother. Only the silver streaking her French-braided hair indicated she was in her early sixties.

Kate looked up and broke into a smile that stretched to her dark eyes. Eyes that missed nothing when Taylor was a teen and could stare the truth out of anyone in their path.

"Taylor! I thought I heard the buzzer." She waved a muddy hand. "Come on in. I'll have this vase off the wheel in a jiffy."

Her own hands itched to touch the clay as Kate made one last pull from the bottom of the pot and then compressed the rim with her fingers. The cylinder had to be at least twenty inches high. "Is that porcelain?"

Kate grunted an affirmative as she pushed from the inside, stroking out the belly of the cylinder in slow, even pulls. Then, she trimmed the base and lifted the bat off the wheel, balancing it on the tips of her fingers.

"Very good!" Porcelain was probably the most difficult medium for a potter to work in. Taylor knew—she'd tried it. And failed.

"You ought to come and work in the clay while you're here."

It'd been years since she fooled around with the wheel, not since she was a freshman in college. Taylor could almost feel the cool clay in her hands. "I will, if you have some stoneware."

"You know I do." Kate washed up before wrapping Taylor in a hug. "Allison told me about the broken engagement. I'm sorry."

With Kate's arms around her, Taylor was sixteen again and crying over the quarterback who broke her heart. She blinked away the tears that stung her eyelids. "Thanks," she squeaked out. Then she straightened and shook her head. "He was a rat. Didn't even care enough to tell me in person. Just left a note on the seat of my car. And then he up and married that . . ." She pressed her hand against her mouth. "That woman." Taylor spit the word out.

"Do you know how blessed you are, child? God was protecting you from the wrong man." Kate folded her into another embrace. "You just rant and rave all you want."

"She's pregnant, Kate."

"Ohhh." The older woman rubbed her hand up and down Taylor's back, then held her at arm's length. "Your time will come, Taylor. God will bring the right man to you. Then you'll have those babies you want."

Kate and her mom must subscribe to the same advice columnist. Taylor swallowed the lump in her throat. "Enough about me. You look good. Your pottery"—she swept her arm around—"is so beautiful."

"Thank you." Kate acknowledged the compliment with a nod. "Now, why don't you tell me what you're doing here your first day home."

Kate always did know how to cut to the chase.

"I have a little problem. Actually, a big problem. And I've asked Ben to meet me here since I don't want Mom to know about it yet."

"Then you and our sheriff need a cool place to talk. Why don't we go to the house?"

Taylor stopped at her car to retrieve her briefcase and caught sight of the sign again. "What's with the bed and breakfast?"

A blush crept up Kate's neck. "It's something I always wanted to do, and with the girls gone, this old house is too quiet with just me and Charlie, so I decided to give it a whirl. Don't have that many guests, usually only when Memphis has an overflow, but word's getting around."

Taylor had never known Kate wanted a B and B. "If you still cook like you used to, the food alone will bring them."

They entered through the kitchen door, and it was like stepping back in time. Sun-yellow walls, white cabinets, blue gingham on the windows. Taylor pulled out a ladder-back chair and sat at the oak table Kate's husband had made. "How are Charlie . . . and Bailey?" She didn't ask about Robyn.

"Charlie is as contrary as ever." Kate's voice held affection for her husband. "He and your uncle were supposed to go over to the casinos today, but I think the tractor repair took care of that little excursion."

"Casinos? Jonathan?" It didn't surprise Taylor that Charlie went, but her uncle? A memory of an argument with her dad and uncle scratched at her mind. If Jonathan was gambling and losing . . . Suddenly pieces of the land deal puzzle clicked into place. "Does Mom know?"

Kate nodded. "And probably everyone else in Logan Point. I think they go several times a month. It bothers me, just like it bothers me that none of you girls wanted to stay in Logan Point. But you and Livy have done well, and Bailey is thriving as a teacher in Mexico."

It was plain she was proud of her oldest daughter.

Kate cleared her throat. "And let's get rid of the elephant in the room. I don't know why Robyn left or where she is, but every day since she left— for two years—I've asked God to return our daughter to us. I believe he will."

Taylor hoped Kate had better results with God

166

than she'd had. She had sense enough not to voice her opinion, though. And evidently Livy hadn't shared with her aunt her suspicion that Robyn was dead. "I know Chase and Abby would be happy if she came home."

"Chase can take care of himself. It's my grand-daughter that concerns me," Kate said.

"Chase says she's doing okay."

"Hmph. She's hurting for her mama. That's something else that bothers me, because there's nothing I can do about it." Kate set a plate of biscotti on the table. "How about a glass of iced tea?"

Taylor laughed. "I had forgotten how everything a person does in the South revolves around food and iced tea. I've had at least three glasses already today."

"Then one more won't hurt you."

As Kate rattled ice into glasses, Taylor's gaze travelled around the familiar walls and rested on one of Kate's cross-stitched pieces. *I can do all things through him who gives me strength.* One of Kate's favorite verses to quote. Another one . . . *"For I know the plans I have for you," declares the Lord, "plans to prosper you and not to harm you, plans to give you hope and a future."*

Taylor had decided long ago she was the only person who determined her future. She alone was the master of her fate, the captain of her soul.

Could that be why she felt so empty?

The screen door swung open. "Anybody home?"

Ben.

"Come on in. I have a glass of tea waiting." Kate pointed toward the table.

Ben Logan set a bag on the floor and enveloped Taylor in a hug. He released her, and she stepped back.

"You've grown a beard!"

He rubbed his hand over the trim beard covering his jaw. "It'll probably come off with the hot weather," he said with a chuckle.

When she'd left Logan Point, the great-grandson of the town's founder was a skinny college sophomore bent on becoming a lawyer. Skinny had turned into lean, and he'd changed his degree from law to criminal justice and become a deputy. After his dad's shooting, he'd been appointed acting sheriff.

She glanced at the third finger on Ben's left hand. Still no ring. It surprised Taylor that some ambitious mother hadn't snapped up this rugged lawman for her daughter. She gave him another quick hug. Her childhood friend didn't always play by the rules, but his quiet strength reassured her. "Thanks for coming."

He picked up the glass of tea, then turned to Taylor. "What's going on?"

"Drink your tea first." Now that Ben was here,

Taylor needed a minute. "I'm sorry about your dad. How is he?"

He ran a hand through unruly black hair. "Not much progress. Still can't communicate."

Mom had told her that Tom Logan had been shot on a back road in Southeast Bradford County, then suffered a stroke while the doctors operated to remove bullet fragments from his head.

"I hope he recovers soon. Are you going to run for the office?"

"Haven't decided yet." Ben turned a chair around and straddled it. "Congrats to you. You're the only person I've ever known who got published in the *American Journal of Criminal Psychology*."

"You read my paper?"

"Yep, and you're absolutely right about the importance of profiling the victim. But you didn't call me over to talk shop. Fill me in."

Kate rose from the table. "I think I'll check on my pots and leave you two alone. Be outside if you need anything."

After the door closed behind Kate, Taylor used a napkin to pull the envelope and photos from her briefcase. "I have a stalker back in Washington, and this came in the mail today. It wasn't forwarded from Newton—it's from Memphis. I'm afraid he's followed me here. And is taunting me about knowing where I live."

"Any suspects?"

"Until today, I believed it was a former student. Scott Sinclair. I haven't completely ruled him out."

Her circled image jumped out at her. Maybe she *wasn't* such a great profiler. If she was wrong about Scott, what else had she been wrong about?

Ben pulled a pair of latex gloves from his back pocket and slipped them on before taking the packet from her. His mouth tightened as he perused the photo and poem.

"I take it you've received something similar in the past."

"A diamond bracelet, the poem, several photos, and a few inexpensive gifts. The crime scene photograph is new, as is the wording 'I know where you are.'"

There was no longer any question of when that note had been put in her pocket. Her skin crawled, thinking how close her stalker had been in those woods. "I don't know what this has to do with anything, but I smelled Old Spice on the first note, and another time at my house."

"Tell me everything." Ben took out a notepad.

She explained what had happened in Newton, ending with the message Dale had relayed earlier. "So, what seemed fairly straightforward is now quite tangled. We had assumed the kidnapper—his name was Ralph Jenkins—killed himself at the scene."

Different possibilities whirled through her

mind, one thought chasing another. "It always bothered me that Jenkins waited twenty-two years to exact revenge and then committed suicide. Now it appears someone manipulated Jenkins into kidnapping Coleman's wife and daughter, then killed him. My gut tells me it's because he knew I would be profiling the case, and he could photograph me at the crime scene."

Who would go to that much trouble, and why toy with her? The answer to *why* came quickly. Power.

"Scott Sinclair was a former student? How old is he?"

"Nineteen."

"Any priors?"

"None."

He shook his head. "It sounds awfully sophisticated for a nineteen-year-old with no history of this type of crime."

"I know, but he seemed very knowledgeable when he took my class on criminal psychology last year. On the other hand, anyone as smart as Scott wouldn't charge the bracelet to his credit card, except . . . he has a drug and alcohol problem, which can mess with a person's decision-making process."

"Tell me a little more about this student."

"He started attending the university where I teach last September, took my introduction to criminal psychology and was an excellent student.

No evidence of alcohol or drug addiction at that time. In January, he took my victim profiling class." Taylor massaged her temples. How did Scott creep back onto her list of suspects? She'd thought she'd put that to rest. This seesawing back and forth was driving her crazy.

"What kind of student was he?"

"Like I said before. An excellent student, although he seemed to deteriorate early this spring. His papers became disorganized and messy."

"It doesn't sound like he's your man."

"I know. Except . . . he is a person of interest in one of Livy's cases." She explained the connection between Scott and the murder victim. "I'm profiling that case for her, so I'll let you know if I think he's involved."

"My brother is not capable of violence." Nick's words rang in her head. Taylor looked up at Ben. "He probably isn't involved, but don't mark him off your list. He could be a pawn in this, feeding someone else information. That's why I'm not dismissing him completely."

Ben looked over the poem again. "This sounds familiar. Have you googled it?"

"Yeah. Nothing turned up."

He stared at the note. "Maybe it was in a movie or something recently." Then he tapped the envelope. "Can I get a copy of the earlier photos and note? Maybe a copy of the sheriff's report?"

She took out her cell. "On it."

Taylor gave the dispatcher in Newton a brief explanation, then thanked her and hung up. "The photos and the note will be in your in-box this afternoon."

"Good. I'll send your sheriff a copy of what you received today." He tapped the photos. "How many people have handled this envelope? I'll need their prints."

"Me, Mom . . . Jonathan. And Pete Connelly. But do you have to fingerprint them? You know how fast that'll spread through Logan Point."

Ben rubbed his chin. "Let's see . . . Jonathan's are on record already. He volunteers at the juvenile jail, but I'll need your mom's and Pete's."

Taylor wrinkled her nose. "Oh, wait a minute," she said. "Pete drank a glass of tea earlier at the house. The glass should still be in the sink. Mom's too."

Ben shrugged. "It's worth a shot, but if I don't get clear prints, I'll have to involve them. Let me get yours now."

He took a small ink pad from the bag he'd brought in.

"Wow, you came prepared."

"Did you forget I was an Eagle Scout?" He pressed her left thumb to the pad and transferred the print to an index card. "We have an electronic fingerprinting machine, but I figured you didn't want to do this down at the jail."

"You have that right. If someone saw me being fingerprinted, it'd be all over town in an hour."

Ben chuckled. "Don't know how it is out in Washington, but it'll probably take five to ten days to get the results once I send them in. Depends on the backlog in Jackson."

"I know. Too bad it's not like TV," she joked, then sobered. "So, what's the plan? How do I protect my family? Do I need to move out?"

"I doubt they'll let that happen. Knowing Chase and Jonathan, they'll want you where they can see you."

"I can take care of myself." She scrubbed the ink from her fingers. "I've been doing it for over ten years now."

Ben stood. "Let's see if those glasses are still in the sink, and then we'll bring your family up-to-date."

Taylor shifted in her chair as her family stared at her. Too much information. Ben had told her family way too much about the attack, and about Scott. Now she had to downplay it. But at least they'd found the tea glasses, and Ben had gotten good prints from both.

Mom spoke first. "A stalker, an attack, concussion . . . why didn't you tell me?"

"I didn't want to worry you." Taylor folded her arms across her chest. She quickly dropped her arms to her side. They were not going to put her on the defensive. "You always said I had a hard head. I think it'd be a good idea if I move to a motel—"

"You'll do nothing of the sort." Jonathan halted his pacing long enough to give her his what-have-you-gotten-yourself-into look. He hooked his thumbs in his belt loops. "Talk about worrying."

"It'll be safer for you to stay here." Chase rubbed his hand over his face. "Think about it. It's open space from here to the road."

"And I'll have my deputies increase their patrols by the house," Ben said.

Taylor had actually been thinking of Memphis. "All right. But what about Abby? I don't want to put her in danger."

"She won't be home until Saturday," Chase said. "We'll look at the situation then and decide if she needs to stay with a friend. But it's not like Abby will be staying here—she'll be at my house."

"Scott Sinclair." Jonathan said the name slowly. "Why is that name so familiar to me?"

"I don't know. He's Nicholas Sinclair's brother. You know, the mystery writer. According to Nick, he lives on income from a substantial trust."

Jonathan snapped his fingers. "Of course. Ethan is his trustee, and I've audited his account. Troubled young man."

"That would be the one," Taylor said as the doorbell rang.

"I'll get it," Chase said.

When he returned with Livy in tow, Taylor's heart sank. Livy couldn't have picked a worse time to show up. "I wasn't expecting you, *chère*."

"I was on my way to have dinner with Kate and Charlie and thought I'd drop these files off."

Mom cleared her throat. "I remember the code phrase, so can the play acting." She turned to Taylor. "Did you call Livy first?"

Taylor shrugged. "Seemed logical. She told me to call Ben."

Mom nodded. "Is that why she's here?"

Taylor sighed. "No . . ."

Her mother waited. Why did Taylor feel like a ten-year-old caught in the cookie jar? Instead of a grown woman who solved crimes. It was time her mother knew.

"I'm profiling a murder case for the Memphis Police Department, and Livy brought the file to me."

Her mother's mouth formed an *O*.

"It's what I do."

12

Twelve rings and no answer. Nick's thumb hovered over the end button. Finally, he pressed it. After he'd returned home from meeting with Livy Reynolds, he'd checked his caller ID. Maybe yesterday wasn't the first time Scott had called. He'd found three numbers he didn't recognize. Two turned out to be businesses, and now, the third one didn't answer. He might as well get back to writing.

That almost made him laugh. He'd risen at five with writing in mind and had some success putting words on the screen. But now it was four o'clock in the afternoon, and all he could think about was Taylor, picturing her raven hair loose from the French braid, the stubborn tilt of her chin. And that brought on the guilt. Which had made for a blank page for the last hour.

Not interested in her? Yeah, right.

Maybe she'd meet him tomorrow for lunch. They could compare notes on Scott. Nick scrolled to her name and pressed call before he changed his mind.

She nearly took his head off when she answered. "Did you tell Scott where I am?"

"Of course not. Why?"

"I received another one of those packages. Here. At my mother's house. Same poetry, same photos, plus a new one with 'I know where you are' written across it."

He flinched. She thought Scott sent it, but if he was drinking, would he have enough presence of mind to track her to Logan Point? "I don't think my brother sent that to you, but if he did, I'm sorry."

"If you didn't tell him . . ." Her voice trailed off.

"Taylor, I didn't tell him. I haven't found him yet." Nick stared at the number he'd found on his caller ID. "Was there anything new in the package?"

Taylor hesitated. "Now is not a good time to discuss it. I'm in the middle of something. Can I call you back?"

"Meet me for lunch tomorrow, and we can discuss it then."

"Are you kidding? I'm still not sure you didn't tell him where I am."

"I may have a lead on his whereabouts." Nick paced his office floor.

Quiet ensued. "I'm listening."

"Tomorrow. Noon. A place called Blues Espresso. It's quiet, plenty of privacy. I'll text you the address."

"That lead better be good."

He disconnected and texted Taylor the address. Taylor had the wrong person in her sights. And finding Scott was the only way to prove it—an easier task to plan than to accomplish. Nick's shoulders dropped. If he didn't find his brother before tomorrow, he would tell her about the poem.

"What do you mean, it's what you do?"

Taylor tapped her cell phone. She wished she'd told Nick her doubts about Scott being her stalker instead of barking at him. She'd also hoped his call would give Mom time to move on to something else. In her dreams. Slipping the phone into her pocket, she turned to face her mother.

"I help catch criminals, Mom. I go to crime scenes, and I create profiles on both the victim and the criminal. And right now I'm the victim, and I need to figure out who tracked me to Logan Point. And how." She schooled her voice, using her best teacher tone.

Her mother lifted her chin and squared her shoulders. "No, Taylor, what you do is teach psychology, not run around masquerading as some kind of policeman."

Taylor ground her back molars and counted to ten. "Mother . . ."

"Actually, Allison," Livy said, "Taylor is one of the best victim profilers in the country. That's why I asked for her help in this case."

"Is Livy right?" Awe tinged Chase's voice.

"You bet she is," Ben chimed in.

"They're laying it on a little thick, but . . . yeah, I've written a few papers on victim profiling and helped solve some cases. You can google me."

Her mother's lips pinched together. "And so your extracurricular activities have come home to roost. None of this would have happened if you'd just come home and gotten a job teaching at the University of Memphis."

Leave it to Mom to state the obvious.

The rest of the afternoon passed in a blur. After Ben and Livy left, Taylor took the case file Livy had compiled on Albert Duncan Ross to her bedroom and started work on it. At the same time she tried to process the threat to her life. With Scott basically out of the picture, she'd returned to square one. Which should make Nick happy.

Except she couldn't quite shake the feeling that Scott knew something.

That evening she took her usual spot at the dinner table and glanced around, studying each family member. What little civility Chase and Jonathan had shown each other earlier in the day had evaporated. Chase hadn't said five words, instead focused on picking at his food. She wanted to tell him to eat, that he needed more meat on his skinny bones. Her gaze shifted to Jonathan, who was lost in his own world. Nothing wrong with his appetite. Only her mom kept the conversation going, her voice a little too loud, a little too bright. Creating her own reality again.

And then, there was the empty seat at the end of the table for Ethan Trask. She'd been surprised when her mom had indicated he might join them for dinner. He was already late, if he was.

She startled when her mother tapped the side of her goblet.

"Attention, please." When everyone looked up, her mom continued, "Taylor, I want to apologize."

She swallowed her surprise. "For what?"

"For the way I reacted this afternoon. You're a grown woman, perfectly capable of deciding what you do with your life."

She stared blankly at her mother. Who was this person and what had she done with her mom? Allison Martin changed her mind about as often as it snowed in July.

"And from what I read on the internet this afternoon, you do what you do really well. I'm proud of you. And I promise I'll try not to worry."

Her mom was proud of her. Taylor worked her mouth, but nothing came out. She cleared away the lump that threatened to overcome her. "I . . . will hold you to that. And thanks. I never expected you to approve."

"Didn't say *that,* but I'll try to get there."

"Well, I've always been proud of you, Sis."

Taylor beamed at Chase as the doorbell rang.

"I'll get it," Jonathan said. "It's probably Ethan."

Energy filled the dining room when Ethan entered. Her mom even seemed to bloom with a smile that radiated from within. Her suspicion that something was going on between the two deepened.

Since he and Jonathan had been college roommates, Ethan would be in his mid-forties, younger than Mom. A golden tan set off Ethan's salt and pepper hair, and she bet he spent a fair amount of time working out as well—definitely no little potbelly like her uncle's.

Jonathan nodded her way. "You remember Taylor."

"How could I forget anyone as lovely as this young woman?"

Like honey, Ethan's voice flowed warm and smooth. He reached his hand toward her ear, and a quarter materialized in his hand. "Especially one who has money coming from her ear." He handed her the coin.

Taylor pasted a smile on her lips as she took the money. Even when she was a child, his magic trick had made her skin prickle. Probably because he invaded her space.

Ethan took the vacant seat. "Jonathan told me about the problem with Scott, and I'm truly sorry. I feel like it's my fault."

"Your fault?" Taylor and her mother spoke simultaneously.

He nodded. "I'm the one who suggested he attend Conway University. He'd straightened up and showed an interest in criminal psychology, and since your mom has given you rave reviews, I recommended Conway. Thought in a new place, he might straighten up. I assumed he would tell you of our connection. Never occurred to me he might become obsessed with you, but I probably should have anticipated the possibility, since he's done it in the past."

"What? Scott's done this before?" She wondered if Nick knew about this and had neglected to tell her.

Ethan's face turned crimson. "I shouldn't have said that. Scott's my client." He fiddled with his knife. "But you're like family, and I would be negligent if I didn't tell you to be careful around him."

At least that solved the mystery of why Scott travelled across the country to attend Conway. She started to tell Ethan she no longer believed Scott was her stalker when Mom cleared her throat with a loud *ahem*.

"Have you read the Nicholas Sinclair book you brought me?"

Taylor had almost forgotten her mother's ban on unpleasant conversation at the dinner table. "Not yet."

"I have." Ethan took the hint. "And it's the best one he's written."

Mom turned to her. "So, when am I going to meet this new friend of yours?"

Taylor almost dropped the bowl. She didn't want to encourage her mom into thinking she and Nick had some sort of relationship. "We're not exactly friends. More like two people on the same mission. Could someone pass me the banana pudding?"

"When will you find out about the judge nomination?" Chase asked Ethan as he gave Taylor a wink.

She'd have to do something nice for her brother for directing conversation away from her.

Ethan forked a slice of roast. "Probably within the month. The waiting is about to kill me. Never dreamed I would be on the short list for a seat on the Tennessee Court of Criminal Appeals."

"That's only the beginning. I believe we are sitting in the presence of a future Supreme Court judge." Jonathan raised his tea glass. "I think a toast is in order."

"That's a little premature, my friend." A broad grin belied Ethan's words as everyone raised their glasses. "And before I forget, I need your signature on a form first thing in the morning."

Jonathan's mouth twitched. "I've taken a few days off and hadn't planned on coming to the office tomorrow. Just sign my name—you can write it as well as I can." He turned to Taylor. "It's a good thing he's on the right side of the law. With Ethan's talent for forgery, there's no telling where he could be."

"Certainly not on a governor's judgeship list." Ethan's dry response brought a laugh. "I'll wait for your signature."

Taylor raised her eyebrows. "That's an unusual talent. How did you develop it?"

"Your uncle exaggerates. It was something I had fun with in college but long since left behind." Ethan tilted his head toward her. "Has your uncle ever told you how we came to be such good friends?"

"No." Taylor leaned forward.

"I'm sure you remember that we were roommates at Memphis State, and one night your uncle crashed a frat party. He got suckered into playing Texas Hold 'Em, and by the time he called me, he'd already lost his shoes and was down to his pants."

"What did you do?"

"I went and got him, of course. I wish you could have seen that tenderfoot running to get in the car."

"They were using marked cards," Jonathan growled as laugher erupted around the table.

"Maybe so, but you never got much better at poker." Ethan directed his attention to Taylor's mother. "I understand you're having a picnic Saturday. Can anybody come?"

"Picnic?" Taylor paused with her fork in mid-air. She'd heard nothing about a picnic.

"It's to celebrate Abby's birthday, and now your homecoming too," Jonathan said. "We're having it down at the lake."

At least it wasn't at Oak Grove. The Martins hadn't held a picnic since her dad left, but before that there'd been at least one every year under the oaks at Granna's house with the whole town invited. In fact, the day he left . . .

Her mother broke into her thoughts. "Abby

found some old photographs, and one thing led to another. She's really excited."

"I suppose everyone will be there." Taylor could see it now. The prodigal returns. Might as well display her like a pinned beetle.

"I only posted information about the picnic at church." Taylor groaned, and her mom raised her eyebrows and then turned to Ethan. "You know you're welcome."

After dinner, Taylor helped her mom with the dishes and then excused herself to take another look at the material Livy had dropped off and to write a preliminary report. If she could keep her mind off her own case.

Questions about it kept popping in her thoughts as she climbed the stairs to her bedroom. Like who was investigating the leads in the Coleman case back in Newton? Zeke was at a conference here in Mississippi, and Dale was still recuperating. She wished she'd asked. But she didn't want to bother him tonight, and she wasn't calling Zeke just to be blown off like always.

Although Zeke might have been right about Scott. She picked up Livy's report. Just like Scott probably wasn't involved in the Ross murder. Not unless he'd gotten mixed up in a drug ring in the two weeks he'd been back in Memphis. Livy had pulled several cases where the victim had been garroted, and they all had one thing in common— all were known druggies. Evidently someone wasn't paying their drug bill. Ross had a history of not only using but selling as well. If they could find his supplier, they'd probably have his killer.

She reread the autopsy report. A horrible death that even clinical language couldn't soften. Petechial hemorrhaging and not just at the ligature site. The small pinpoint dots of blood were also in the eye and eyelid area. Whoever killed him tightened and loosened the cord . . . played with Ross's mind, indicating the murder was not only personal but sadistic. A cold-blooded, premeditated crime with a highly organized perpetrator. She opened a new document on her computer and started typing.

An hour later, a car door slammed. Taylor padded to the window, and as Ethan's black Navigator pulled away, she caught a glimpse of Mom coming back to the house. Taylor wasn't sure how she felt about her mother's interest in Ethan.

Jonathan appeared from the shadows and got into his pickup, going in the opposite direction, toward Oak Grove. Tomorrow, or whenever Jonathan called another meeting, she would have to vote against him on the land. Not something she looked forward to.

Taylor moved to the other window and followed the pickup taillights until they disappeared around the rear of the house. Like the night before, the full moon illuminated the old two story. Chill bumps raised on her neck, and Taylor hugged her arms to her body as half-forgotten dreams surfaced of walking the halls, her shoes clattering on the hardwood floors, opening doors to empty rooms, inching down the dark basement steps . . .

She shuddered.

Maybe tomorrow she'd visit the place from her dreams and confront the hold it had on her.

13

Dusk settled over the tree-lined boulevard as Nick searched for 1210 New York Street, the address reverse directory had given for the number on his caller ID.

Twelve-six, Twelve-eight. He slowed in front of an older, two-story house and found the street number on the doorpost. Twelve-ten. This was it. If he didn't find Scott here, he might as well quit looking.

A 1940s porch, complete with wicker chairs and a swing, stretched across the front. Made for a time when people sat outside and visited with their neighbors, the furniture now boasted flaking paint and dry rot. A rattling window unit drew his gaze to the second floor, where it labored against the hot evening. The building appeared to be an older home converted into apartments. Unfortunately, Google hadn't told him which apartment.

Nick tried the glass security door, found it unlocked, and stepped into the foyer. There appeared to be two apartments downstairs and a stairway that led to the second level. He could see one door at the top of the stairs and assumed it was another apartment. The muffled sound of a television came from the apartment on the left along with the odor of cigarette smoke. His rap on the door brought a flurry of barking and footsteps.

"Hush up, Daisy. Can't hear nothin' for your infernal barking. Who is it?" The woman's voice, at least he thought it was a woman, rasped from the other side of the door. Nick formed a mental image of dyed hair, baggy eyes, and tobacco-stained fingers.

"Nick Sinclair. I'm looking for Scott Sinclair."

"No Scott Sinclair living here."

"Do you know if he lives in the building?"

There was a pause, and then a bolt rattled back. The door opened as far as the chain allowed. Nick stepped back, as much from the cigarette odor as the small Chihuahua that growled through the crack at the bottom of the door.

"Hush up, Daisy!" Watery blue eyes peered at him from a mass of wrinkles. "You the cops or a bill collector?"

"Neither." He gave her his best you-can-trust-me smile.

"Like I said, there ain't no Scott Sinclair living here."

He needed to work on that smile. "Well, thank—"

A loud crash from the second floor apartment interrupted him. He glanced toward the sound as Daisy erupted into another barking frenzy. Seconds later the door on the second floor opened, and a bundle of clothes flew out onto the top of the stairs. A pint-sized woman in her twenties emerged next. She stood just outside the door, her hands planted on her hips.

"That's it, Scott. Get your things and get out of here!"

Nick's brother stumbled against the door frame. "C'mon, Dana, let me sleep here tonight."

"Do you want me to call the police? I told you not to come back here drunk. Go call your high-and-mighty lawyer and get some money to stay somewhere else."

"But—"

"Out!"

"I gotta sit down." Scott slid down the wall and propped his head in his hands.

The old woman had stepped out in the hallway with the wiggly dog in her arm, and Nick shot her a quizzical look.

Smoothing back copper-red hair that had an inch of white roots, she winked at him. "Didn't say he wasn't *staying* here. You the lawyer?"

Nick grinned. "Nope." He started for the stairs. "You!"

He raised his head. Dana had her fiery gaze fixed on him. Carrot-colored hair curled in every direction on her head.

"Who are you and what're you doing here?"

"I'm his brother. Nick Sinclair." He nodded toward Scott, who stared at him, then closed his eyes and slid a little farther down the wall. "I've been looking for him."

Recognition came into her eyes. "The one he called the other night?"

Nick nodded. "I found a number on my caller ID, but no one answers. I googled it and got this address."

"Phone's been out two days." Dana jerked her head toward Scott. "Are you taking him with you? 'Cause he's not staying here."

Nick climbed to the top of the stairs. "I'll take him. Could you get his clothes together for me?"

She wiped her hands on her blue scrubs. "Might be better to just call the police. He's a lot of trouble when he's like this."

For the first time, he noticed a hospital ID badge identifying Dana Rogers as a nurse's assistant. "You sound like you've had experience."

Dana's expression softened. "Yeah, well, he was different when I first met him. Wasn't drinking like this. He's really sweet when he's sober, a different person, really. Somebody needs to get him help, get him dried out . . . or something."

"Yeah, I know." Nick bent over his brother. Soured bourbon almost knocked him down. "Hey, wake up, Scott. We have to go."

"Hey, you came and got me." Scott looked up at Dana. "Didn't I tell you he'd help me?"

"Come on, buddy, help me out here." Nick slid his hand under Scott's arm. "Come on, push yourself up."

Scott tried to shake him off. "Don't wanna move right now."

Nick persisted, and finally Scott heaved himself up. "Put your arm around my shoulders so I can get you down the stairs."

Between dragging and carrying, he got Scott down the steps and to his car. Dana followed with Scott's clothes. After Nick got his brother in the front seat, he took them. "Thanks."

"Maybe he'll sleep it off—he usually does." She hesitated, then jotted a number on a scrap of paper and handed it to him. "Gets too bad, call me on my cell phone. I'll come help you out, and if you get him sober, keep him away from that Digger guy."

"Who?" Nick wasn't sure he heard her correctly.

"Digger. I don't know his real name. He's some guy Scott met out in Washington. He keeps him supplied."

Nick thanked her and slid under the wheel. As

he pulled away from the curb, Scott sagged against the door with a moan. *Lord, please don't let him be sick.* Just before he turned the corner, Nick glanced in the rearview mirror. Dana hadn't moved from the sidewalk.

Wrinkling his nose, he fanned away the stench of alcohol and vomit that filled the small car. Evidently, Scott hadn't had a bath in days, either. Nick ought to let the police haul his drunken carcass to jail. He lowered the top on the Mustang and glanced at his brother. Oh, great, he was turning green. It'd be a miracle if they made it home before Scott threw up again.

14

Eight-thirty and the temperature already approached ninety. Taylor's feet dragged as she approached Oak Grove. Someone wanted to kill her, and she should be finding him instead of wasting her time digging into old memories. In spite of the heat, a cold shiver stabbed her stomach. Last night had brought more dreams about this place and her dad and clowns chasing her.

In the dream, she'd been in the basement, and the clown was chasing her, his red lips leering and his fingers reaching to grab her. Taylor wiped sweat from her brow. Something deep inside shied away from climbing the steps and opening the door to those memories.

Maybe the nightmares would go away on their own. They had once. After her dad left, Taylor had experienced these same nightmares off and on for almost two years, and then they'd stopped . . . until six months ago—about the time Michael dumped her.

Tires crunched on the gravel lane behind her, and she turned. Jonathan. A reprieve.

He lowered his window. "Be careful if you're going inside. I was making a few repairs before we received the offer on the land and haven't cleaned my mess up."

"Thought I would look around."

"I'd go in with you, but Ethan called a few minutes ago. That signature won't wait."

"While I'm here, I think I'll at least look around the first floor."

"Just be careful of the scrap lumber and nails scattered everywhere."

The truck jerked forward as an incoming text beeped on Taylor's cell phone. She glanced at the screen and groaned. It was too early in the morning to hear from Zeke Thornton. He wanted to meet with her.

At least she had his attention now.

What time? she tapped back.

Seconds later her cell rang, and Thornton showed up on her ID.

"Good morning, Zeke."

"I'd like to meet within the hour," he said. "The conference starts at noon. I can come to the farm, or would you rather meet in Logan Point at the sheriff's department?"

"You know where I live?"

"You're in Logan Point. How hard could it be to find the Martin farm?"

She ignored his joke. "I'll meet you at the sheriff's office."

"How soon? I don't want to be late for the introductory session."

The memories would have to wait. Taylor glanced down at her shorts and running shoes. Not quite appropriate for a meeting with Zeke and Ben. She might as well go ahead and dress for her lunch with Nick. "I'll be there in forty-five minutes."

In exactly forty-five minutes, Taylor parked the Rav4 beside the rambling white-bricked jail. Inside the building, the dispatcher caught her before she could orient herself.

"Taylor! About time you came home."

"So I've heard." Maggie had been a fixture at the county jail for as long as Taylor could remember, and she flashed her a smile. "Is the sheriff's office still in the back?"

"Hasn't moved. Ben and some banty rooster are waiting on you."

That would be Zeke. Taylor took a deep breath at Ben's door and pushed it open. Last time she was in this office, the whole gang was here, Ben included, withering under Sheriff Tom Logan's wrath for toilet papering the mayor's yard. Seemed like a big deal at the time. Now she knew what a big deal was.

Ben nodded a welcome and handed her a manila envelope. "Copies of yesterday's photos. And the fingerprints are in Jackson."

"Thanks." She tucked them in her briefcase and glanced at Zeke. Not for the first time, she wondered where he purchased clothes to fit his scarecrow frame. "Morning, Zeke."

"Morning." He hitched his starched khakis. "You're late."

She glanced at the digital clock on the gray wall. "One minute, Zeke. And who made you boss around here, anyway?"

His mouth twitched, then he palmed his hands up. "You're right. I'm sorry, but I really need to leave here by eleven-thirty to make the opening session of the conference."

"Then let's get to work. Where do you want to start?"

"This is as good a place as any." Zeke pointed to the Coleman crime scene photo as he took a pad from his shirt pocket and flipped it open. "Whoever took this had a clear view of you. Did you notice anyone snapping photos at the crime scene?"

She searched her memory. "No one other than you. Have you checked the people in the background of your crime scene photographs?"

He shook his head. "Until yesterday, I didn't know I needed to. The case was closed. Dale put Billy Carson back on it last night, and he's processing the people in the photos. If this conference hadn't been paid for, I would be on the first flight back to Seattle."

She could imagine the battle in Zeke's mind over wasting taxpayer dollars versus working on the case. She turned to Ben. "Yesterday you said the poem seemed familiar. Have you remembered why?"

"I wish. It's one of those things just below the surface . . ."

"Maybe if you let it go, it'll come to you." She rubbed her hands on her capris, wishing Zeke hadn't put a deadline on their time. It made her want to rush. She took a calming breath and cleared her mind. "Okay, let's look at what we know."

"We know the killer planned this thing to a T."

"I agree. Whoever masterminded the kidnapping chose Jenkins and the Coleman family. I'm thinking he cruised bars looking for someone he could use and encountered Jenkins. According to the people who knew him, Jenkins was loud and vocal about hating Jim Coleman. And if it hadn't been Jenkins, it would have been someone else."

"Okay, I'm following you. I'll call Carson and have him check out all the bars in Newton, show Jenkins's picture."

Ben examined the photo of her jogging. "This looks like it was taken with a long lens."

Taylor picked up another photo, the one of her sitting on a flat rock. "It was. Just like this one. The camera is probably an SLR digital and expensive, or we'd have some grainy photos. But the one taken at the crime scene looks like a point-and-shoot was used, and it could've been taken by anyone at the crime scene. It was also taken before I found the note in my pocket. Are we all on board that the actual kidnapper is my stalker?"

When they both nodded, she continued. "We thought the kidnapper was dead, and everyone's attention was on Beth Coleman and little Sarah. Whoever he is, he could've easily gone unnoticed. It's possible our killer didn't leave the crime scene until after I did. Then I think he showed up at my house and attacked Dale and me."

"And he beat you to your house?" Zeke lifted his eyebrows. "Come on, Taylor, you're better than that."

"Okay, so maybe he left earlier."

"Why didn't he kill you when he had the opportunity?" Ben asked.

She'd asked herself that question more than

once. "I don't know. Maybe Nick scared him off, or maybe it's a game to him, like a cat toying with a mouse. He seems to know everything about me, where I am, my tastes . . ." She looked around Ben's office. "Do you have a white-board? I'd like to compile a list."

Ben rolled in a whiteboard and handed Taylor a dry-erase marker.

"Let's start with the crime scene and work backward." She wrote "stalker" at the top, and under that, she wrote "photos," then glanced at Zeke. "Off the top of your head, what do you think when you see that?"

"Two things. The photographer values quality and has access to money. The camera is expensive, and even though the last photo is shot with a cheaper camera, he used quality paper to print it."

Taylor blinked. She'd already concluded those points, but for Zeke to recognize them . . . "You'd make a pretty good profiler, Zeke."

He snorted. "I know quality when I see it."

That he did. She'd noticed that he bought the best in everything, even things like his business cards and the pen he guarded like it was made of gold. "You said two things?"

"He was following you, or he knew you'd be there."

"Good."

"He hung around even though it was risky."

199

"Bingo." She wrote "risk taker" on the board. "How did he know I was in Logan Point?"

"Maybe he hacked your email account."

Taylor stood stock-still. "The university website crashed a couple nights ago, and if someone is hacking into their system, it could explain why my email has been slow lately." She hadn't thought of that and nodded toward him. "That's good, Zeke."

She wrote "computer whiz" on the board. "I booked my flight online. And I've been emailing a friend about coming home." She winced. "And I have Mom's phone number and address in my contacts."

"If someone can hack a university system, they'd have no trouble finding where your family lives." Ben stroked his beard. "What I want to know is, why? Why are you being targeted?"

"I've hunted that dog to death."

Ben chuckled. "I can't believe you remembered that old saying."

She couldn't either and turned to Zeke. "Do you have any theories?"

"You're a threat to someone."

Taylor stared at Zeke, surprised once again. She'd been operating out of her original assessment that she was being stalked because someone was obsessed with her, not because she was a threat.

Chill bumps prickled the back of her neck. She

wouldn't be a threat to a stranger. No, like 75 percent of all victims, she had a link to him, had crossed paths with him somewhere. And people who felt threatened, killed.

Someone she knew wanted to kill her.

15

Nick rubbed his hand over his day-old beard and stared at the blinking cursor. Spending most of the night listening to Scott's drunken ramblings did not make for fresh writing. It didn't help that he kept seeing Taylor's face and remembering they had a lunch date.

He'd debated cancelling the date. What if Scott woke up and took off again? Nick didn't think he would, given the way his brother kept thanking Nick for coming after him and for letting him come home. If he woke, which Nick doubted since Scott didn't go to sleep until four, more than likely he would go back to sleep—it would take more than a few hours for the alcohol to wear off . . . long enough to meet Taylor.

And that made for a whole new set of problems. Like having to tell her about the poem today—before someone else did. If only he could've gotten information from Scott last night. But his brother had been too drunk. Once Taylor found out Scott was here, she'd want to talk to him. That would be fine, except Nick had counted on talking to his brother first.

He padded down the hallway to Scott's old room and looked in. He hadn't moved since Nick got him to bed. In sleep, Scott looked so much younger than nineteen. Innocent too.

How did they get to this point? Scott accused of stalking, maybe involved in a murder? Wrong choices, for sure, and not all of them Scott's. Nick should have listened to Angie when Scott first rebelled. She'd told him to fight the important battles and let the others slide instead of nit-picking his brother to death. No, he'd chosen battles like Scott's long hair and not attending church with them. By the time Nick had realized his mistake, his brother was gone.

Nick flexed his shoulders, trying to loosen tight muscles caused from too little sleep and too much time at the computer. He rummaged through Scott's sack of clothes, trying to find something other than black, then gathered the grungy jeans and shirt he'd peeled off his brother when they'd arrived home. Holding them at arm's length, Nick took them to the washer, turned the water on, and dropped them in.

He checked his watch. An hour and a half before he met Taylor for lunch. He wanted to check out the sound system at the restaurant for the Friday night crowd, but there was time enough for one last cup of coffee before he left.

In the kitchen, he eyed the nearly empty coffeepot. He didn't remember drinking a whole pot of coffee. Nick poured the last dregs into his cup and set the pot in the sink. His gaze traveled to Angie's cookbooks, settling on her favorite, and he took it to the table, where he reverently turned the pages. His heart caught at the sight of "Nick's favorite rolls" scribbled in the margin.

He closed his eyes and imagined her writing the note. What they'd shared had been exceptional. So why couldn't he remember her face some-times? He closed his eyes and focused on her memory, recalling the curve of her cheek, the freckles splayed across her nose. No dagger to his heart today. Some days he couldn't bring up a clear image of her features.

He'd loved his wife, still felt married. So how could he be so drawn to Taylor?

Maybe because it was time to move on, step out of the lonely half-life he'd created, and embrace life again. But how could he do that when part of his heart died with Angie? Grieving had become familiar, almost comfortable.

Nick couldn't deny his growing attraction to Taylor. Could he open himself up again to the kind of love he'd shared with Angie? What if some-thing happened and Taylor died? After all, she was involved in a dangerous situation. Why couldn't she simply be an uncomplicated college professor instead of living life on the edge?

He finished the bitter coffee and returned the cookbook to its place, then went to shave and get dressed. Before he left the house, he checked on Scott one last time. Judging from the sound of his snoring, his brother would probably sleep until Nick returned.

Traffic was always busy in Memphis, and today was no different. Nick pulled into the parking lot of the Blues Espresso at half past eleven, parked, and went inside.

"Hey, Nick!" Big Joe Tyson's voice boomed across the café.

He turned and waved to the owner of the restaurant. The former linebacker for the Detroit Lions jerked his ebony head toward the pit area.

"You got your harp? Maybe jam a little?"

Nick patted his shirt pocket. "I don't come to this place without it. Help me check out the sound system. Don't want it messing up tomorrow night."

Friday nights some of the regulars had started getting together and jamming. Big Joe on the guitar, a couple of ex-cops on the saxophone and drums, and Nick playing a mean harmonica, mostly as backup but occasionally solo. He flipped on the microphones and slipped into his regular spot beside Big Joe's guitar. After a few riffs to warm up, he slid into "Walking by Myself."

• • •

Someone wanted to kill her. Probably someone she knew. Taylor couldn't get the thought out of her mind as she drove west on Highway 72, crossing from Mississippi into Tennessee. The old pickup in front of her belched a plume of exhaust, and she slowed, changing lanes. She hoped Nick's lead took her to Scott—even if he wasn't the actual stalker, Scott might hold the key to his identity.

Her phone rang, and she glanced at the ID. Livy.

"Get my profile done?" Livy sounded hopeful.

"A preliminary one. Thought I would drop by your office after I have lunch with Nick Sinclair."

"Ooh. Where are you meeting him?"

"Blues Espresso."

"I love that place. Very romantic."

Taylor could imagine Livy's eyebrows doing a Groucho Marx. "We're meeting to discuss his brother. How about we try for two o'clock again today?"

"Call me if you lose track of time." Livy chuckled. "I know I would."

"Not going to happen. See you then."

Ten minutes later she swung off of I-240 onto Poplar. She found the café in a small shopping mall and spied Nick's red convertible. After parking beside him, she stepped out of the Rav4, smoothing the wrinkles from her white capris, and glanced down at her strapless sandals. Taylor wiggled her hot-pink toes. Hot pink? What had possessed her? She always painted her toenails with a simple white coat.

"God has someone for you." Her mother's words popped into Taylor's mind, and she dismissed them. She wasn't looking for anyone. Been there, done that. Had the broken heart to prove it. She squared her shoulders and hurried to the door but stopped long enough to check her makeup before she pushed it open.

Toe-tapping music stopped her. She scanned the eatery and found the source at the back of the café—Nick, blowing a harmonica, and a giant of a black man on guitar. She walked closer, drawn by the magic and the man with the mouth harp cupped in his hands.

If she had any sense, she'd fly back through that door and leave the music and memories behind, but it was as though her feet had grown roots, anchoring her to the floor. She closed her eyes as the notes wrapped around her and filled her soul. Soothed a dry ache . . .

When the music stopped, she opened her eyes and stared straight into Nick's. His pleasure showed itself in the slow grin that started at his mouth and spread to his hazel eyes.

"I didn't know you were here," he said, his voice husky.

"I'm early." The music played on in her head. "I didn't realize you were so good."

"You don't know how good I can be."

The wicked grin he shot her sent heat rising in her cheeks.

He tapped his harmonica in his hand and turned to the guitar player. "Good set, man. I think the microphones are fine. I want you to meet my friend, Taylor Martin. Taylor, Big Joe Tyson."

Joe's hand engulfed Taylor's. "This is a good man," he said, nodding toward Nick. "Don't let anybody tell you any different."

Taylor laughed. "That's good to know."

Nick took her by the arm and escorted her to a table by the window. "Is this okay?"

She nodded and took the seat he pulled out. "I love this atmosphere, but I thought all the blues places were on Beale Street."

Nick waved his hand toward the pit. "This just sort of evolved. Do you know what you're hungry for? The menu is on the wall, but I always recommend the shrimp po'boy."

She was glad he suggested something because her mind hadn't kicked in yet. "That sounds good. And sweet tea."

Oh my word. Had she actually said sweet tea? How easy it was to slip into old habits.

Nick gave the college-age waiter their order, then turned to Taylor. "So, how do you like being home?"

"I liked it fine until that package arrived. I really need to talk to your brother. When are you going to tell me about this lead you have?"

A look she couldn't decipher crossed his face.

"Let's save business for after we eat."

"But—"

He held up his finger. "How about for one hour we don't talk about where Scott is, or that poem, or anything bad."

Nick was good at slipping in and taking control. Which was fine—she could use an hour without thinking about the threats that hung over her like a guillotine poised to drop. She propped her elbows on the table and crossed her arms. "Okay. One hour."

"Good. That'll give you enough time to tell me about your family. Do you have any brothers or sisters?"

Her family? Was he just curious, or was it more? "There's not that much to tell. You know about my mother—she was very pleased with the book, by the way. I do have a brother, and a niece, and an uncle. And that's about it."

"Your dad. Did he die?"

"No. Or at least, I don't think he did."

The waiter brought their tea, and she focused on the lemon wedge adorning the tall glass, avoiding the question in Nick's eyes. She squeezed the lemon and dropped it into the tea before turning her attention back to Nick. The question remained.

"Okay. He left for a business trip and didn't come home."

Nick sat back. "What happened to him?"

Taylor pressed her lips together and swallowed down the knot that jumped into her throat. "He just walked out of our lives. Your music brought back one of the good memories." She worried a hangnail on her thumb. "Mostly I only have nightmares about him."

"Are you certain something didn't happen?"

"Memphis police investigated and concluded he abandoned the family." Blood seeped from the hangnail, and Taylor dabbed a napkin against it. "I thought he loved us."

"I know how you feel."

"You couldn't."

"My mother left when I was five. Said she wanted to *find* herself."

The grim set of his mouth . . . Yeah, maybe he did know how she felt.

"Can cause attachment issues," he added.

"Don't I know it." Taylor spied Big Joe approaching their table. "Here's our food."

Joe set their plates in front of them with a flourish, then set a basket of fries in the middle of the table. "I hope you folks enjoy this."

"Thank you, man," Nick said. "You outdid yourself."

The sandwich, framed by two dill pickle spears, looked delicious but messy. White capris may

209

not have been the best choice. Using her knife, she cut the po'boy into bite-sized pieces, while Nick dug into his.

"This is good," he said between bites.

Nodding her agreement, she picked up one of the pickles and bit into it, relishing the tangy-sour taste.

"Those attachment issues . . ." He tilted his head toward her. "Is that why you're not married?"

Taylor almost bit her tongue. "I knew I shouldn't have agreed with you. And it's really none of your business."

His hazel eyes twinkled. "Maybe not, but a beautiful woman like you . . . I just wondered why some guy hadn't snatched you up. Have you ever considered it? Getting married?"

"Again, none of your business." He thought she was beautiful?

"I'm sorry, you're right. I seem to have a knack for asking the wrong questions."

He did that. She speared a shrimp that had escaped the bun as Michael's image invaded her thoughts. She sighed. "I was engaged once. He married someone else. Can we drop it now?"

Nick dredged a fry through the ketchup and bit into it. Then he wiped his mouth with his napkin. "Attachment issues, fiancé abandons you, nightmares about your dad . . . ever considered all this is related?"

"Never crossed my mind."

He had the grace to blush. "Sorry. The mind protects itself, but it doesn't heal whatever it's shielding us from. Maybe the nightmares are a sign you need to deal with what your dad did."

"And you know this, how?"

"Common sense."

She folded her arms across her chest and waited.

"Okay . . . I had a character that blocked certain memories from her past, and I did a lot of research on the subject."

"That's what I thought. You might want to try six years of psychology courses." She tented her fingers. "Of course I know it's all related, and after the nightmares started again, I decided to try and find my dad. Made my uncle furious."

"Why wouldn't your uncle want to find his brother?"

"He said it would cause another scandal if I rehashed all that ancient history."

"But you don't believe that."

"Jonathan wants to sell some of the farm, something I'm sure my dad would never allow. Besides, my uncle is somewhat of a control freak. I don't think he'd relish giving up the top-dog spot."

"Can he sell without your dad's signature?"

That hadn't occurred to her. "I'm sure Jonathan can figure out a way."

"So you dropped your search?"

"No. Just going about it a little differently. I

have a friend in the Memphis Police Department helping me."

"Olivia Reynolds."

Heat crawled up her neck. "About that . . ."

He held up his hand. "After we finish eating. Remember—nothing unpleasant until then."

Taylor ducked her head and concentrated on her sandwich.

"This fiancé, was he nuts?"

"I thought no talking about bad stuff."

"Come on," Nick said. "That's just getting to know more about you."

Taylor crossed her eyes at him, but he only laughed. She picked up the glass of tea and leaned back. "Okay. Michael would tell you he was being practical. Said I didn't love him. That I never had." Then she took a long draw of tea, savoring the nectar of the South. She'd forgotten how good it was.

"Was he right?"

Boy, Nick wasn't letting this go. "Michael knew I wasn't madly in love with him when he proposed."

Nick's eyebrows came together in a frown. "So, why did you say yes when you knew something was missing?"

She wanted to look away, but his gaze held hers. "He said his love was enough for both of us, that he could wait for me to love him the way he loved me. Evidently, he got tired of waiting." She lifted her chin. "Passion's not everything."

"You have to be kidding." Nick paused with his fork in midair. "It's one of the three components of love. You know . . ." He held his thumb, then first two fingers up. "Intimacy, commitment, and passion."

"You're quoting Sternberg to me now?" She'd studied the famed psychologist's triangular theory of love her first year in college. Taylor squirmed a little under Nick's intense scrutiny. "Okay, looking back, I probably just wanted to check another item off my to-do list . . . finish school, get the MRS degree, then start a family. I could have done worse than Michael."

Nick groaned. "You don't really believe that. Life's too short to settle for a marriage that's not everything it can be."

Heat infused her cheeks. She didn't want him to be right. Knew he was.

"I think marriage is important to you, and not just as an item to check off a list. What was the real reason you were willing to marry this Michael?"

"That was the real—" His lifted eyebrows stopped her. "Okay, maybe the part about starting a family was more important than that MRS degree. I happen to believe marriage comes before sleeping together, and a baby should have both a mother and a father."

"Good for you. But shouldn't love be even more important?"

"Like my daddy's love?" She lifted her chin. "I don't believe the kind of love you're talking about exists. Marriage is nothing more than a union between two people who have a common need and are attracted to each other, and I *was* attracted to Michael."

From his look she must have sprouted horns.

"I can't believe an intelligent woman could buy into that baloney. If you don't have love, what's going to sustain you when you hit a rough patch?" He shook his head. "You should be glad Michael realized it wasn't there."

A snappy retort came to her lips. And died. She drummed the table with her fingers and willed herself not to cry.

"Taylor, all men aren't like your father." Nick placed his hand over hers, stilling it. His touch was warm and rough at the same time. "You're an incredible woman, confident, smart, beautiful . . ."

Her heart fluttered against her ribs as Nick's hazel eyes held hers. She could almost believe his words. Even more, she could almost believe Nick cared.

"In fact," Nick said, "I would—"

"Sir, can I get you anything else?" The waiter plopped the bill beside Nick's plate.

"We're fine." Nick waved the young man away.

Taylor pulled away and leaned back against

her chair. She knew he was about to ask her out again, and not just to talk about Scott. But once he got to know the real Taylor, he'd be gone, just like all the others.

"Taylor—"

"Let's talk about that lead you promised me."

Nick steadied himself, and that look crossed his face again. Fleeting, but something was definitely going on. Taylor tensed. "Okay, what are you not telling me?"

"I, ah . . ." Nick gripped the table edge. "I found Scott last night."

"What? Why haven't you already told me? Have you called Livy?"

"He's not going anywhere. When I found him, he was so drunk he couldn't stand. I wanted him sober before anyone talked to him."

"Okay," she said, stretching the word out. "Where is he?"

"My house."

"Your house? And you're here? Aren't you afraid he'll take off again?"

"No. He was so drunk last night, believe me, all he wants is to sleep for at least twelve hours without being disturbed."

"Are you speaking from the voice of experience?"

"I might know something about it from my younger days. Come on, we'll go wake him, and you'll see he's not this monster you think he is."

She held up her hand. "First of all, I don't think he's a monster. I'm not even sure he's my stalker. And I'm taking a report to Livy with my professional opinion that Scott isn't involved in the Ross murder."

"I never believed he was involved in either one. What changed *your* mind?"

"He didn't fit the profile. I didn't say I've completely ruled him out as my stalker, or at least being involved in some way. Just rethinking it a little . . . well, a lot. The thing is, about the time I come up with a reason it's not Scott—like a stalker wouldn't use his own credit card to purchase a gift for the person he was stalking— something else pops up. But did you know Scott was involved in another stalking case? One that his attorney, Ethan Trask, resolved?"

"How do you know Ethan? And how did you know he's Scott's lawyer?"

"Ethan is a longtime friend of my uncle's. He said last night Scott is one of his clients, that he administered a trust for him."

"I can't believe he discussed one of Scott's cases with you. He wouldn't even give me his phone number."

Even though that had bothered Taylor, she'd excused it because Ethan was close with her family and he'd seemed concerned. She felt the need to defend Ethan's actions. "He only mentioned it to me because of the photos that came yesterday and what Sheriff Atkins told me when I called him."

She explained about the message the killer had whispered in Beth Coleman's ear before he shot her. "The photo I received yesterday was taken at the crime scene."

"Why didn't you tell me?"

"I wanted to when I first got here, but you were so insistent on eating first. I'm telling you now. I've been thinking about it, and the whole thing is too sophisticated for a typical nineteen-year-old, and just like the Ross murder, it doesn't fit Scott's profile. That's the upside."

"What's the downside?"

"Scott's not your typical nineteen-year-old. And every time I reach the point of completely scratching him off my lists of suspects, something holds me back." She leaned forward. "Maybe you can help me. Tell me who would frame Scott. And since victims almost always have a link with their perpetrator, we probably share that link. Who could it be?"

"I don't know." Nick scooted his chair back. "But why don't we go talk to Scott and see if we can find out?"

16

Nick kept Taylor in his rearview mirror as she followed him. The more he got to know her, the more he wanted to know, even though part of him wanted to run the other way. Especially since his heart did crazy things when he was around her, like beat so hard sometimes he almost couldn't hear what she said.

Her tough exterior hid a vulnerable core. He'd seen it when he played his harmonica. The music touched her. He saw it again when she talked about the children she wanted. But she was most vulnerable when she talked about her father. He ached to help her find him.

Nick turned onto his street, and a light flashing in the middle of the block caught his eye. He looked closer. Two fire trucks and an ambulance sat like harbingers of doom in front of his house.

He parked on the other side of the ambulance and raced toward his house as firemen emerged from the backyard. Taylor pulled in behind him. A fireman stopped him in the driveway. "Sorry, can't go any farther."

He tried to push past him. "This is my house. What's going on? Where's my brother?"

"You the owner? Been trying to find you." The

fireman turned and shouted over his shoulder. "Inspector, the owner's here."

Nick didn't wait. He sprinted for the door. The acrid scent of smoke and burnt electrical wire stung his nostrils.

"Hey, wait! You can't go in there!"

He reached the door as paramedics shoved Scott through on a stretcher. Nick's heart plummeted. His brother lay corpse-like on the gurney as oxygen hissed through the mask covering his nose and mouth. Tinges of soot stood out against the grayness of his face. "Scott!"

No response. Nick grabbed a paramedic by the arm. "What happened? Is he going to be okay?"

The paramedics pushed the stretcher past him. "We need to get him to the hospital."

"Which hospital?"

"Baptist. It's the closest."

Had he found Scott only to lose him? The thought constricted his chest. He had to go with him. Nick turned to follow the gurney, but a Memphis fire investigator blocked his way. "Hold up."

"I need to be with my brother."

"You'll just be in their way in the ambulance, and you won't see him at the hospital until he's stabilized. Give me a minute."

"Now?" Nick scrubbed his face.

The investigator flipped open a badge: Mike

Hurley. "Give me two minutes so I can finish my report." His face softened. "Your brother's in good hands."

Nick glanced toward the ambulance. Hurley might be right, but that didn't make staying behind any easier.

"I promise this won't take long."

Nick clenched and unclenched his hands. "Okay, two minutes, then I'm out of here."

He followed the investigator to the spreading elm tree in his yard.

"First of all, you can't go into your house."

Nick glanced toward the house. He didn't see any damage. "Why not?"

"Damage is on the back side," Hurley explained. "Fire got your breaker box. No power. Should be able to get in later this afternoon to get personal effects, but you'll have to rewire before you can stay here again."

Nick glanced back at the ambulance. Taylor said something to one of the paramedics, then turned and walked toward them. Before she reached him, the ambulance pulled away from the curb, siren blaring.

"What'd he say?" Nick asked.

"His vitals are better." She turned to the investigator. "How did the fire start?"

"Let me ask my questions first." He took out a notebook. "Your name is Nicholas Sinclair, and you live alone. That right?"

Nick nodded. "My brother spent the night with me."

"Do you have insurance?"

"Of course." Nick took a deep breath. "Call my insurance agent." He scrolled through his phone for the number. "Anything else?"

Hurley glanced up from his writing. "I need you to sign a consent-to-search form for the fire marshal."

"Fire marshal? Why?"

"To make a determination that the fire wasn't deliberately set."

"You think—"

"I don't know. That's why I want an expert to look at it." He asked a few more questions, then looked over his report. "That'll do for now. When the investigation is finished, you'll be contacted, and a report will go to your insurance company."

"Can't you tell me something now?"

The investigator tapped his pen against the pad several times. "Appears the fire started in the kitchen. Found your brother near the stove, a pint whiskey bottle beside him."

Nick rubbed his hand across his eyes. He didn't keep alcohol in the house, but there was a liquor store at the end of the street.

"When the fire marshal finishes, we'll know for sure." He held his notebook out for Nick to sign the form.

Nick hesitated briefly, then signed.

Hurley closed his notebook. "That about does it for me. There'll be someone posted here until a determination is made. Don't go into the house before you get the okay." He touched his cap brim. "Hope your brother makes it."

"Thanks." He turned to Taylor. The care in her blue eyes made his heart skip a beat.

"He'll make it, Nick."

"I hope so." He stared in the direction the ambulance had gone.

"Would you like me to follow you to the hospital?"

"You don't have to."

"Someone should be with you."

The last time he'd sat in a hospital waiting room was the night Angie died. The paramedics had gotten her heart beating long enough to get her to the ER. "Thanks."

Changes had been made to the ER waiting room since Angie's death. New, softer chairs and earth-toned stained floors, but nothing could change the anxiety permeating the air. After Nick took care of the admission papers, he paced the floor, waiting for an update.

Taylor disappeared briefly. When she returned, she handed him a Coke. "Thought you might need a pick-me-up." She nodded toward two empty chairs in a corner of the room. "Let's sit over there —the doctor will find you when he comes out."

222

Nick followed her to the chairs. "I've never liked hospitals. They make me feel so . . ."

"Inadequate?"

That was the perfect word. He popped the top on the soda. "Especially since Angie."

"Tell me about Scott when he was growing up, before the alcohol and drugs."

Nick was quiet a minute. Memories flowed through his mind—the first time his dad brought Cecelia and Scott to the house, years later, Scott with his two front teeth missing, the home run he'd hit when he was twelve . . . Sometimes, he felt more like Scott's father than his brother. "Once when he was in the second grade, Mom—that's what I called Cecelia—tried to teach him the value of money. She expected him to save half of his allowance. He went along with her, amassed a nice savings, then one day he wanted fifty dollars from his account."

"Fifty dollars? Whatever for?"

"He wanted to buy his girlfriend a present."

"In the second grade?"

"Mom responded the same way. Boy, did she preach to him, but he wouldn't give up. Finally, she asked what he wanted to buy for this girl." Nick paused. "Guess what it was."

"A bicycle, maybe?"

"Nope. A pair of New Balance tennis shoes. This girl had three sisters, and her divorced mother struggled to keep food on the table. Her only pair of shoes came from a yard sale, and they weren't name brand. The other kids made fun of her, and he wanted to do something about it. New Balance was the 'in' shoe that year."

"What did your mother do?"

"They bought the shoes, wrapped them, and left them on the girl's doorstep with her name on the package." He caught her gaze and held it. "Drunk, sober, or anything in between, I don't think that tenderhearted little boy could grow up and be involved in something that could hurt someone else."

A voice blared Nick's name from the intercom, and he jerked his head toward the front as the intercom repeated it. A man too young to be a doctor stood at the front desk, scanning the room. Nick rose and waved, and the man hurried to their corner.

"I'm Dr. Anderson. Your brother is going to make it."

"Oh, thank goodness." He eyed the young doctor in his white lab coat with stethoscope draped around his neck. He looked more like a fuzzy-faced teenager playing grown-up than a physician.

"We'll admit him to ICU and wean him from the oxygen later tonight, but he'll stay in the unit until I'm certain there's no pneumonia." In spite of his youthful looks, the doctor's voice was strong, confident.

"Has he said what happened?"

"No, but from the size of that knot on the side of his head, it appears as though he fell and hit his head." Dr. Anderson scanned the chart. "When they brought him in, he had a blood alcohol level of point-three-seven."

Point-zero-eight was the legal limit for driving. Nick whistled.

"Yeah." The doctor nodded his agreement. "Your brother is extremely fortunate. That level very often is fatal. The next few days will be difficult as he goes through detox. Has he ever been in rehab?"

"Earlier this year, I think. I don't know where, though." Nick liked this doctor and his straight-forward manner. "Is there anything I can do?"

"Get him back into rehab."

After the doctor left, Nick let out a deep sigh of relief. At least Scott would survive this time.

Taylor glanced at her watch. "Wow. It's after five."

"You need to go home."

"Will you be okay?"

"I will now." He stretched his arms back and flexed his shoulders.

"You're going to need a place to stay."

He gave her a blank stare, then tapped his forehead. "I haven't even thought about that. I'll stay here tonight. After that . . ." He slumped in the chair. Fatigue swept over his body. "I'll cross that bridge tomorrow."

Taylor hesitated. "There's a bed and breakfast next door to me in Logan Point, and the owner, Kate Adams, didn't have any guests yesterday. It's twenty miles away . . . but if it were me, I'd rather stay there than in a motel."

Stay in Logan Point? He'd only been there once before, and the memory of a lake and trees came to mind. Peaceful. The idea sounded good. "Do you have the number?"

"It's in my phone. Let me check and see if she's booked." Taylor found the number and called, but there was no answer. She frowned. "I'll call her later tonight or first thing in the morning and let you know if she has a room."

"Thanks for staying with me." He took her hand, noticing how long and tapered her fingers were. He lifted his gaze and connected with her luminous blue eyes. Nick's heart thudded against his chest. He wished she wouldn't look at him like that.

Their footsteps echoed in the dimly lit hospital parking garage. She was glad Nick had insisted on escorting her to her car. After unlocking the Rav4, she turned to him, her hand still tingling from his touch when he'd held her hand. Exhaustion lined his face. "Sure you'll be okay on your own? I can stay longer."

His gaze held hers, and the tingling spread to her heart.

"I'll be fine," he said. "You need to get back to your family."

It was time to leave, but she hesitated, wishing she could tell him everything would be all right. "Nick, I'm truly sorry about what happened to Scott. I never wished him any harm."

"I know." He kicked at a pebble on the garage floor.

Silence charged the air between them as their gazes locked. Her whole body pounded with each heartbeat. Imperceptibly, he drew toward her. Taylor waited, her lips parted.

Abruptly, Nick jerked a half step back. A slow flush crept over his face. "I . . . thanks again for being here."

In her wildest imagination, she hadn't dreamed Nick might want to kiss her. So why did she feel so let down? Even if she had been waiting for someone like Nick her whole life.

"Just glad to be of help," she said, forcing a stiff smile to her lips. Nick opened the car door, and she slid behind the steering wheel.

He tapped on the window. "Taylor—"

She tensed. He had that look on his face, the one that said he was going to apologize for almost kissing her. Taylor lowered the window halfway. She wasn't giving him a chance. "No need to thank me again."

He started to speak, then simply nodded. "Be careful."

She worked to keep the smile in place. "Sure."

Taylor raised the window and backed out of the parking slot. The void in her soul widened as she blinked against the stinging in her eyes.

Frustrated, she flicked away a tear. What was the big deal, anyway? So what if Nick was probably the most honorable man she'd ever met. His heart belonged to his dead wife.

She didn't need him.

She didn't need anyone.

17

Her father swung Taylor up in the air. She squealed as his hands let go, and then he caught her as she came down. He was so strong. He held her close. He smelled so good, all spicy and woodsy.

The dream shifted and Taylor was older, not yet eight as her dad fastened a necklace around her neck, then hugged her.

"Daddy, you're squeezing me!"

"Come on. Let's go see if we can find Uncle Jonathan. I have a plane to catch." He set her down. *Hand in hand they walked toward Oak Grove.*

"Can I go to the airport with you?"

"Of course you can. You're a princess, and a princess gets to do whatever she wants."

"Oh! Daddy! I forgot my princess purse."

"Well, we can't have the princess without her purse, can we? Run get it, and I'll find Uncle Jonathan."

Taylor looked up at her father. But the man holding her hand wasn't her father. And they weren't outside. They were someplace dark. The basement. Her necklace dangled from her hand as she scrunched her eyes, trying to see who it was. Black eyes with fierce black brows peered from a white face, the mouth an angry red slash. A clown. But the clown stared beyond her.

She turned and saw her father. Taylor started to run to him, but he wasn't alone. He was dancing with someone, holding her close.

The clown rushed toward her father.

"No!"

He stopped and turned toward Taylor. She caught her breath. Then the clown was gone, and Andy Reed stood with a gun pointed at his stepfather.

"No! Don't do it, Andy! Noooooo!"

Taylor jerked up, gasping for air. Newton, the Reed boy, the hostage situation that went bad . . . She tried to shake the nightmare off as her heart hammered against her ribs and the room slowly came into focus. Sunlight spilled through open curtains against pale blue walls and familiar white dresser. Her bedroom in Logan Point. She jerked her head toward the pounding on her door.

"Taylor, are you all right?"

"Mom?"

Her mother burst into the room. "You were screaming. What's wrong?"

"Do you smell it?" Taylor pressed her hand to her forehead.

"Smell what?" Her mom sniffed the air.

"Old Spice." She sucked a deep breath through her nose. A faint scent lingered . . . didn't it? "Dad's aftershave."

"Oh, Taylor. No, honey, I don't. Is that why you screamed? Were you having a nightmare?"

She nodded and hugged her knees to her chest.

Her mother sat on the edge of the bed, stroking Taylor's baby doll quilt. "You're having the dreams again?"

Taylor leaned against the headboard and nodded. "I smelled Old Spice. It was so real."

"How long have the dreams been back?"

"Since before Christmas. I . . ." Taylor swallowed. "About the time Michael broke our engagement. And there was a case . . . a young man, not even twenty years old . . . he had a gun. Had his mind set, determined to kill his stepfather, who had just beaten his mother almost to death. I tried to talk him down." She turned and stared out the window. "The stepfather was drunk and called the boy's mother a name. The boy lost it, started shooting. When it was over, both were dead." Taylor squeezed her eyes shut against the memory. *Failure.*

Mom brushed a strand of hair from Taylor's face. "Honey, it wasn't your fault."

"I know. Or at least in my head, I know. Just not in my heart yet."

"Did you get counseling?"

"Yes, the psychologist went for counseling." She glanced up at her mother. "I need to find Dad."

Her mother stiffened, and she put her hand at the base of her throat. "Is that what the counselor recommended?"

"I never talked about Dad with her. I didn't have to. I already know he's at the root of the nightmares, my failed relationships." She moistened her lips. "Mom, it's something I have to do. I have to know why he left."

Unshed tears rimmed her mother's eyes. "Why he left doesn't matter. It had nothing to do with you."

"Then tell me what happened. Why did he leave?"

"I don't know. I've asked myself that question every day since he got on a plane and didn't come home." A slight tremor crossed her mom's face. "In the letter I received a week later, he just asked me to forgive him. That's all. No reason, not even a hint."

"He wrote you a letter?" She had never heard anything about a letter. "Did you keep it?"

"The Memphis detective took it as evidence. They never gave it back."

Taylor had to find those files. But this was more than she'd ever learned. "Dad didn't give any clue the day he left that he wasn't coming back?"

"No." Her mother twisted the corner of the sheet. "It was the Fourth of July. Such a happy day. Half the town was here. Picnic tables and chairs were set up under the oak trees near the old house. Your granna had already moved in with us. Oak Grove was empty except for the farm office in the basement. Your father had to be at a conference in Dallas the next morning, and he planned to leave mid afternoon for the airport in Memphis. I was so busy that afternoon I barely remember him kissing me good-bye and going to find Jonathan to drive him to the airport."

Her mother dabbed the corner of her eye and took a tremulous breath. "My last memory of your father is seeing the two of you walk toward Oak Grove."

"What?" Taylor sat straighter in bed. "What's wrong?"

"Before it became a nightmare, I was dreaming about Daddy. We were walking together to Granna's old house. He called me his princess, then he tossed me in the air and caught me."

Her mother's chin quivered. "When you were a

baby, he was always doing that. He loved you so much. You were his princess."

Taylor touched the hollow of her neck. "In the dream, he fastened a necklace around my neck, and then I'd forgotten my purse and went to find it."

"Your necklace." Her mom struggled, blinking back the tears in her eyes. "The heart-shaped pendant he'd given you that morning. You were brokenhearted when you lost it that day."

Her mother was quiet for a moment. "You were supposed to go to the airport with him, but when it was time to leave, no one could find you. I think we finally found you in your tree house, hours after Jonathan returned from the airport. You were crying about the necklace."

The tree house her dad had built. It'd been her sanctuary in the months after he left.

"When he didn't come home, you withdrew, just closed yourself off. Oh, you functioned— went to school, that sort of thing—but it was a long time before you laughed again. And the nightmares. They were horrible."

Her mom stood and walked to the window with her back to Taylor.

"I'm sorry, Taylor. I didn't handle that time in our lives very well. I thought if I didn't talk about it, it would be all right."

"I know that now, Mom. I kept thinking he'd come home."

"Well, he didn't." Her mother turned around, the lacy curtains billowing around her. "There's something I should have told you and Chase long ago." She shut her eyes and stood very still. Then she sighed. "We had your father declared legally dead."

Taylor's breath caught in her chest. "You had Daddy declared legally dead, and you didn't tell me? When?"

Her mother stared down at her fingers.

"Mother, please. I know this is hard, but tell me . . ."

"Seven years after he left. Jonathan said we had to, that none of the insurance would pay unless we did. It was evident your father wasn't coming back, no one had heard from him, and the private investigator your uncle hired couldn't find any trace of him. We needed the money to run the farm, for your college education. Then we decided it would be better to wait until you were older before we told you."

The words, spoken in monotone, hung flat and dismal between them.

"How much older?" Taylor's voice cracked. "I'm twenty-eight. Chase is thirty. When were you going to tell us?"

"I know we should have, but there was never a right time." Mom returned to the bed and sat on the edge. "Besides, I just knew your father would come back someday."

Taylor's anger dissolved in the face of her mom's heartbreak. Now she knew why Mom created her own reality sometimes. It was a coping mechanism. Her mother had handled the situation the only way she knew how. "Do you think he could be dead?"

"No!" Her mom touched her chest. "I would know in here."

Silence settled in the room as Taylor processed what she'd learned. "Is there anything else?"

Her mom traced her finger around the stitching on the quilt. "Until the day he left, your father was a good man. You must believe that."

"How can you say that? A good man wouldn't have left us."

"I'm talking about before that." Her mother paused. "I have something I want you to see."

She hurried from the room and returned in less than a minute with a packet of letters in her hand. "Read these, and you'll know his true heart."

"He wrote you more than one letter after he left?"

"No. These are from earlier trips. Notes encouraging us, love letters, really. I know he never changed the way he felt. He loved us."

Was her mom trying to convince Taylor or herself? She took the packet. A thin blue ribbon held them together.

"Read them, and if you want to talk again, I'll

be downstairs with coffee and cinnamon rolls waiting."

After the door closed, Taylor stared at the packet. Letters from her daddy. Mom had saved them all these years. With a deep breath, she untied the ribbon and took out the first letter. It had been unfolded and refolded many times. Strong, bold handwriting flowed across the page. She checked the date. Six months before he disappeared.

My darling Allison, it began. *I've been gone only a day and it seems like a month.* Taylor read slowly, absorbing each word. It was impossible to stay detached and uninvolved. The man who had written this letter obviously loved his wife and two children.

Or was a very accomplished liar.

Each letter was several pages long with numerous references to Taylor and Chase. In one, he mentioned the outcome of Chase's basketball games and talked about Taylor's upcoming dance recital. In another, he encouraged them to get good grades. One by one she read them. When she finished, she stacked the letters together, retied the ribbon, and placed the packet in the nightstand beside her bed.

Taylor wanted to believe what was in the letters, that her father loved them, but his words didn't jibe with his actions or the letter he'd sent from who-knows-where. She'd like to see *that* letter. She shut her door and went downstairs to the kitchen.

"Well?" her mother asked.

"He seemed to love us."

"He definitely loved us. When he went on his trips, he wrote at least one letter."

"Why didn't he just call?"

"He did," she said, a wistful smile curving her lips. "But he said a letter was something to hold on to, to read over and over. Your father was a romantic."

The image from her dream of her father dancing with another woman materialized. She wished she could erase that from her mind like her mother erased the last letter he'd sent. If she could, she might believe the letters. "May I keep them a few days? I'd like to read them again."

"As long as you return them." Mom took down a plate. "Cinnamon roll?"

"Sounds good." Taylor poured a cup of coffee and took the roll to the breakfast nook.

"What are your plans for today?" Mom asked as she sat opposite her.

"Thought I'd visit Kate." She'd decided to talk to Kate in person about a room for Nick. "Maybe make something on the wheel. Livy is dropping by the shop around ten."

Taylor had called Livy from the hospital to let her know she wouldn't be coming by her office and that Scott was in the ER. She had the preliminary report on Ross finished, and perhaps they'd actually get together today. And maybe she could learn a little more about her dad from Kate. She caught her mom staring at her with a slight frown on her face. "What? Do I have sugar on my chin?"

"Should you be going out alone?"

Taylor's spine stiffened, and she folded her arms across her chest. "I will not become a prisoner in this house."

"You will be careful?"

"Of course I will, but I don't think he'll attack me in plain daylight."

"Just don't let your guard down." She stood up from the table. "I have an appointment in town today. There's plenty of food in the fridge for lunch, but I should be home in time to throw something together for supper."

"Will Ethan be coming by again?" Taylor tried to sound casual.

Her mother blushed. "I'm not sure."

"Is anything going on I should know about?"

"I told you, he's just a friend."

"Is he now? I saw him watching you, and I don't think friendship is all he's thinking."

She looked at her mother with new eyes. It was hard to believe she'd be fifty her next birthday. Maybe because she didn't look it. Her trim figure testified that working out paid dividends. Taylor hoped she'd inherited her mom's youthful genes.

Mom rubbed her left hand, and Taylor noticed her mother no longer wore her wedding ring. When had that happened?

"Nothing will ever come of it. I don't have the energy or inclination for a relationship." Resignation tinged her mom's voice. "Besides, he's too young for me."

"Ethan's what, a couple of years younger? That's nothing."

"More like five. In ten years when I'm sixty, he'll be fifty-five."

Taylor laughed. "Haven't you heard? Sixty is the new forty."

"I'm serious. You've seen him. Ethan is very good-looking. I'm surprised he isn't dating one of those pretty young lawyers in Memphis. I don't even know how this . . . attraction started. He's always been around, but it's like now we're seeing each other for the first time."

"Well, I think he knows a good thing when he sees it."

"You're talking foolishness. Don't you have something better to do? I thought you were going to Kate's."

Taylor stood and lifted another cinnamon roll onto a napkin. "I am."

"Then go and stop tormenting me."

The lingering scent of smoke and charred wood pinched Nick's nose as he viewed the destroyed kitchen. Angie's kitchen. He scowled at the burn pattern etched up the wall behind the stove, blistered paint, blackened curtains, and soot everywhere. A charred iron skillet sat on the stove top, the once chrome-plated knob still turned on high.

He stepped through the rubble. Spied the broken whiskey bottle. Booze . . . a wasted life. Nick shook his head. That was not going to be Scott's future. It was time to shake some sense into his brother's head, and he would as soon as Scott could put two sentences together.

Nick had come out to his house to pick up a change of clothes. Scratch that idea unless he wanted to smell like a chimney. Unwillingly, his gaze traveled to where Angie's cookbooks had lined the wall. Now the shelf and cookbooks lay in a charred clump on the blackened floor. His anger burned hot against Scott. Probably a good thing he couldn't get his hands on his little brother right now.

Nick knelt and dug through the heap, seeking the cookbook he'd looked through yesterday. Was it just yesterday? He pulled the waterlogged book from the bottom of the pile and placed it on the kitchen table. At least it hadn't been completely destroyed.

Unbidden, Taylor's image popped into his mind . . . Blue eyes that deepened to violet as she'd listened to his story about Scott. Nick's hand went to his wedding band. He'd done nothing wrong yesterday. He slid the band back and forth on his finger.

Other than want to kiss Taylor.

18

Taylor made one last pull on the wet clay and admired the height of her pot. It was good to lose herself in the clay before Livy arrived. Then would be soon enough to return to her problems, but for the moment, all she wanted to do was put aside thoughts of someone trying to kill her.

Kate stopped by her wheel. "I miss you three girls in the pottery room, but I see you still have the touch."

"I wish." She'd never had Livy and Robyn's skill, but she'd had determination. Taylor wiped her forehead with the back of her hand. An oscillating floor fan swayed from side to side, stirring the air.

She stood a ruler beside the cylinder. Tall enough for a nice vase. Not bad for someone who hadn't sat behind a wheel in a while. "Don't know why I quit this."

Feeling the clay as it became smooth under her hands and then transforming it into something beautiful touched deep inside her. She cocked her head to the side and studied the cylinder. "If I turn

241

this into a pitcher, would you attach the handle?"

"Sure, honey. I'll do yours when I do mine."

Taylor spun the wheel, carefully bellying the cylinder. After she formed the pouring lip and trimmed the bottom, she admired her work, pleased that she hadn't collapsed the whole thing.

"Good job." Kate placed a freshly glazed vase in the kiln and then set Taylor's pitcher on the drying rack beside the ones she'd made earlier. "I'll roll these outside. In this heat, they should be leather hard by afternoon and ready for the handles. Want to make something else?"

Taylor glanced at the clock. Almost ten-thirty. It'd taken her four attempts and an hour to make the pitcher. "I'd like to, but Livy should be here soon. I think I'll come back another day."

She slipped off the mud-splattered apron she'd worn to protect her clothes and hung it on a peg. As she washed the clay from her hands, her cell rang. She grabbed a towel, then fished the phone out of her pocket. Her heart kicked an extra beat. Nick. She had not mentioned him to Kate yet. "Hello?"

"Good morning."

His brother must be a lot better. She tried to match his upbeat tone. "Good morning to you too. How's Scott?"

"They took the oxygen off early this morning and are moving him out of ICU today. I wanted to share the good news with you."

Taylor caught a guarded note in his voice. She picked at a tiny lump of clay on the wheel. "I'm glad."

"Um, did you ask Kate about a room?"

"Not yet."

"If you'd rather I not stay there, I can find a place around here."

"No, don't do that," she replied. "Kate's right here. I'll ask and call you back."

"Are you sure?"

"Positive."

Kate's eyes questioned as Taylor pressed end. "I have a friend who needs a place to stay until repairs are completed to his house. Nick Sinclair." Taylor went on to explain about Scott and how the fire occurred. "I told him about your bed and breakfast, and he was interested."

"Would the brother be coming?"

Taylor hadn't thought about that. "I assume Scott will go into rehab."

Kate lifted another vase and ran a damp sponge over it. "I've taken in a few teens with problems, so it wouldn't be a big deal with me. As long as it wouldn't be a big deal with you."

"I'm sure Nick will insist on rehab. He's very busy working on edits for his next book."

Kate's brow pinched together. Her eyes widened and her mouth dropped open. "Wait a minute—are you talking about *the* Nick Sinclair? The writer from Memphis?"

Taylor nodded, and Kate's voice rose with excitement. "I've read every one of his books. Call and tell him he's more than welcome."

She dialed Nick's number. "Kate will be pleased for you to stay here."

"Good." He sounded relieved. "I'll try to be there by three. I'm meeting with a restoration company around one to get an estimate on the repairs. Hopefully, I'll only need a place for a week or so."

"I'll tell her."

Nick hesitated, and Taylor heard him take a deep breath.

"I'd hoped to stop by your house, but I doubt now I'll have time. Will you be home tomorrow? I'd really like to see you."

Her breath caught. He wanted to see her? "Tomorrow we're having a picnic at the lake behind the house. Why don't you come?"

"What time?"

"Fivish."

"Uh, sure—I ought to be able to work a picnic in around hospital visits. I'll call you if something comes up."

"Good." She ended the call and relayed what Nick had said.

"I appreciate that you recommended the B and B to him." Kate set the now-glazed vase on the rack. "In case Nick Sinclair asks, how would you feel about the brother coming here?"

Good question. While she didn't believe Scott was her stalker, her gut said he knew something. Maybe with him next door, she'd at least get to question him. "I'd be okay with it."

"From what you've said, though, the boy needs to be in rehab."

"I agree." Taylor rubbed a smudge from the white case on her phone. All morning she'd been waiting for the perfect opportunity to ask Kate about her dad, and it hadn't materialized. And probably wouldn't. *Just ask.* "Do you know why my dad left?"

Kate paused with a mug halfway to the glaze bucket. "What?"

"I'm having those nightmares again, and I thought if I knew more about why he left . . ." Taylor sighed and looked off. "Kate, I really have to find him."

Kate set the mug on a table and peeled her latex gloves off. "I don't think anyone really knows why, Taylor. I personally believe—" She pressed her lips together. "Never mind what I believe. The important thing for you to remember is your father loved you very much. All of you."

"Then why did he leave?"

"I don't know."

"You know Mom and Jonathan had Dad declared legally dead?"

Silently Kate nodded. "They didn't have any choice, honey. Your mom asked my advice about it before they actually started the process, and I told her I thought it was the only thing she could do. She needed to get on with her life—not that she did."

"They could've told us. Mom insists that he's not dead."

"I know," Kate said. "Sometimes your mom . . ."

"You think he's dead."

"The way he loved you kids and Allison . . . I just don't see it being anything else." She closed her eyes. "But I understand where she's coming from."

"Robyn?"

Kate nodded. "It's a little different with your dad, though. I've heard from Robyn, and except for that letter right after he left, Allison never heard from James."

"What about the rumors that he ran away to start another family?" She remembered the taunts from some of the kids in school. "I mean, the ten thousand dollars he took with him pretty well indicates that."

"There were lots of rumors flying then, and if you stir this up, you'll hear a lot more than you want to."

A memory blasted through her mind. *"I love you, Taylor. Don't ever forget it."* He'd been planning to leave even as he told her he loved her. Just like her ex-fiancé. "Kate, what's wrong with me? Why couldn't I keep my dad from leaving or hold on to my fiancé?"

Kate took her hands. "Now, you listen to me. For whatever reason your father left, it had nothing to do with you. Don't look to men for your worth, Taylor. You have a heavenly Father who thinks you're pretty incredible. He created you because he loves you."

She wanted to believe that, but if it was true, why didn't God answer her prayers and bring her father home?

Tires crunched in the gravel parking lot, saving Taylor from saying something she might regret. A minute later Livy appeared in the doorway.

"It's about time," Kate said. "I thought you were going to change your hair."

Livy ran her hand over the short blonde spikes. "Nah, think I like it this way." She glanced over the rack of pitchers. "Which one's yours?"

Taylor laughed. "The smallest one."

"Not bad. One of these days, I'm going to work on the wheel."

Kate hooted. "I'll believe that when I see it."

Livy turned to Taylor. "I did the impossible and located your dad's records, but they hadn't reached my office when I left."

"You found his files? Why didn't you wait for them?"

"Because I wanted to talk to Ben about another case before he got out of pocket. It'll probably be late this afternoon before I get them. I'll call you as soon as I do."

"Well, I have something for you." Taylor reached into the bag she'd brought and pulled out Ross's profile. "Here's a preliminary on the Ross murder investigation. I don't think Scott's involved in it. With everything that's happened, I haven't had time to finish it up."

"That's okay. This case is going nowhere. Anything you can give me will help." Livy placed the folder in her bag. "We are—"

"Excuse me," Kate said. "When you two finish talking police business, I'll be in the house with lunch ready."

"Sounds good," Livy said as her cell phone rang. She glanced at the screen and made a face. "Mac." She pushed the answer button. "This better be important."

Livy's expression changed from teasing to sober, then disgust. "I'll be there as soon as I can," she said, then hung up.

"Something wrong?" Taylor asked.

"A kid discovered a woman's body. It's not our case yet, but Mac wants me to cover it just in case it gets dumped in our lap."

"I'm sorry."

"Me too. Even sorrier for that poor woman."

Like floating in a blanket of cobwebs, Scott drifted in and out of consciousness, never quite rousing. He barely sensed being moved, rolling through the hallway. People came in and out of his room. Occasionally, someone applied pressure to his right arm. He smelled soap and aftershave and briefly wondered if they'd bathed him. No, *that* he would have remembered.

He liked this place in between waking and sleeping. A wave of nausea hit, and he retched. Strong hands turned him. A nurse pressed a wet cloth against his mouth, and later a voice, deep and soothing, spoke words of comfort. Nick? The swish of soft soles and the light fragrance of jasmine curled inside his nose before he slipped back into his surreal world.

"Fired. F-i-r-e-d." Johnson shoved him, and Scott staggered against the wall. "I'm tired of you showing up half drunk, arguing with the customers. Now clear out. I don't want to see your face around here ever again."

Find Ross. Make him pay for getting him fired. Follow Ross . . . struggling . . .

"Drink this. You'll feel better."

"Digger?" Relief. His friend was here.

Fire! Flames shot up the wall. Where did Digger go? Gotta put out the fire. Pain exploded in his head . . .

"Mr. Sinclair! Wake up!"

His heart jerked in his throat. Sweat drenched his body. A nurse hovered over him, her voice a din in his ears.

"Mr. Sinclair, are you all right?"

"Fire," he mumbled. "Gotta get the fire out."

"There's no fire. You're in the hospital."

Hospital? He shuddered a breath and stared at the nurse as she concentrated on something over his head. He twisted to see. A monitor. Then she inserted a hypodermic needle into his IV. "What are you giving me?"

"Valium. It should help."

A slightly sweet metallic taste filled his mouth, then his muscles relaxed. The next time he roused, Nick was standing at the foot of his bed. Scott pretended sleep, hoping his brother would go away. He didn't want a sermon. He'd had enough of those to last a lifetime.

"I know you're awake."

Scott cracked an eyelid. "No preaching," he croaked.

"Okay. Can I get you anything?"

"How about a pint of Jack Daniels for starters."

"They're trying to dry you out."

Nick didn't sound mad. Another wave of nausea hit, and Scott curled into a fetal position. Spasms racked his body. He hugged his arms to his stomach. The dry heaves had started.

His brother was in full-blown withdrawal. Nick glanced at the monitor and groaned at the 163 pulse rate. Where was the nurse? He pressed the call button. The usual "can I help you" did not come.

Nick's heart broke as he laid a wet cloth on Scott's forehead and waited for the spasms to end. It killed him to see how Scott was wasting his life. The anger he'd harbored at the house dissolved as his brother writhed on the bed. Finally, the jerking subsided, and Scott lay limp and pale, panting for breath.

"Can I do anything to help?"

Scott drew a shaky breath. "Get the nurse," he whispered.

Nick pressed the buzzer again. This time someone answered, and he explained what had happened.

"I'll be right there."

Seconds later, a ponytailed RN burst into the room. "I'm so sorry, Mr. Sinclair. The technician watching your monitor was distracted by an emergency."

She bent over him with a stethoscope, listening to his heart, then took his blood pressure. "You're calming down."

"Explains why I feel so good," Scott rasped out.

"Scott, she's trying to help you. You're lucky to be alive."

"Just give me the Valium."

The nurse glanced at Nick and winked as she wiped the cap on the IV catheter with an alcohol swab and inserted the needle. "If this doesn't help, let me know."

"Don't worry, I will," Scott said.

The nurse patted Scott's leg. "Buzz me if you need anything else, sugar."

Scott closed his eyes, and Nick sat in the chair beside the bed while his brother feigned sleep. "You might as well look at me—I'm not leaving until I get some answers."

With a groan, Scott opened his eyes. "No law against hoping, is there?"

Nick counted to five before he answered. "I'm waiting for an explanation."

Their gazes locked. Scott looked away first. "What do you want me to say? You wouldn't believe me if I told you I was sorry."

"Try me."

Scott closed his eyes. He swallowed, and the corner of his mouth twitched. "It was Angie's kitchen. That's what bothers me the most." His voice cracked. "How bad is it?"

"Bad enough. But fixable. You could've died in that fire."

"So? Everybody would be better off."

Nick sat on the side of the bed. "You know better than that."

"I . . . I didn't mean for it to happen. But I had to have a drink." Scott had opened his eyes but avoided looking at Nick.

"How'd you get the whiskey?"

"Walked to the corner. Threw up the first drink, took another. Then another. By the time the bottle was gone, I was hungry, and French fries sounded good. I remember pouring the oil in a pan and turning up the burner. I don't remember anything else until I woke up here."

Nick pressed his lips together. Did Scott think he was stupid? His brother had no more walked to the corner and bought a bottle of whiskey than Nick had. He'd already checked out the liquor store. They'd never seen Scott. Nick rewet the washcloth in the bathroom sink and wiped his brother's face. "The clerk at the liquor store said she never saw you."

Scott cracked an eye. "You think she'd admit she sold Jack Daniels to a minor?"

Nick flushed. "I talked to Dana. She said I ought to ask you about Digger. Who is he? And did he buy your whiskey?"

Scott rubbed his hand across his mouth. His chest heaved with short, shallow breaths.

"Scott, who is he?"

"A friend, that's all."

"I assume he has a name besides Digger."

"It's the only name I know," Scott said, shrugging Nick off.

"How do you know him? Where'd you meet him?"

"At . . . the university, in the library."

"Is he a student there?"

Scott shook his head. "He's too old to go to college. He's just a good friend. Helps me out sometimes."

"And now he's here, in Memphis?"

His brother licked his lips. "I . . . I don't feel good."

This was going nowhere fast. Nick tossed the cloth on the rolling table. "Can you handle some water? Or maybe ice chips?"

"Chips."

Nick spooned slivers of ice into his brother's mouth.

"I found your cell phone near the stove. Destroyed, by the way. So, who'd you call? Who brought it to you?"

"Nobody. I have a fake ID. It's like I said. I found twenty dollars on your dresser." Scott scowled at Nick. "You're never going to believe me, and I don't want to talk about this anymore."

"Okay, let's talk about Dr. Martin."

Scott's head jerked up. "How do you know about her?"

"It's a long story, but I know about the stalking."

He tried to pull up and collapsed on the bed. "I wasn't stalking her! Not really."

"What do you mean, not really? Either you were or you weren't. How about the gifts and those photos? And I understand this isn't the first time you've been accused of stalking."

"I . . . don't know what you're talking about. Can't this wait until I can think?"

"No, Scott, it can't. You're in serious trouble. Did you break into her house and attack her and that sheriff?"

His Adam's apple bobbed as he swallowed.

"Well, did you?"

"I didn't hurt her. I really liked Dr. Martin. She was always so nice to me. Sometimes, I just liked to be where she was."

"Don't you know that can be construed as stalking?"

"I promise, I didn't stalk her. You have to believe me."

The same eyes that so many years ago begged Nick to make the wounded bird live begged now. "Why, Scott? Why do I have to believe you?"

"Because . . . you're my brother."

Nick released a slow breath. A knot clogged his throat. Not blood brothers, but maybe something more. "Okay, Scott, I believe you. Now, let's see if we can get Dr. Martin to do the same."

Scott's body started shaking.

"C-can we w-wait?" Scott's teeth chattered. He hugged his ribs. "Until I f-feel b-better?"

"Sure, Scott." His brother's thin body shook beneath the sheet. "Are you going to be okay?"

"You c-can't help me. S-ee about more V-valium."

"It's too early for that, but I'll see if I can get you something for nausea." Nick pressed the call button, and a nurse arrived shortly. Slowly the tremors subsided and Scott dropped off to sleep. Nick checked his watch. Barely enough time to get home and meet the cleaners.

He stopped at the nurses' station. "Could you put up a 'no visitors' sign?"

Until his brother's condition improved, he didn't need to answer questions from anyone, not even Taylor.

19

Taylor wasted no time getting to the Criminal Justice Center after Livy's call that her dad's records were sitting on her friend's desk. Finally, she would get answers, maybe even a lead on where her dad was.

Livy looked at her watch. "What'd you do, fly? It hasn't been forty-five minutes since I called."

"No in-coming traffic." Taylor grinned. "It's all going the other way. Besides, it's almost five—I didn't want to hold you up."

"Don't call me when a black-and-white pulls you over. I don't fix tickets."

"No, honestly, I didn't speed."

"Yeah, right. The small conference room down the hall is empty. Would you like company?"

Taylor wasn't sure she wanted anyone with her as she examined the contents of the box. "Maybe later."

She started toward the room and paused. "That woman who was murdered, were you assigned that case too?"

Livy shook her head. "Not this time. Looks like it might be a serial killing, and the feds want it. A couple of other detectives get to work with them on it." Her grim look said "better them than me."

Taylor walked down the hall to the conference room and put the box on the table and stared at the faded white card on the end. *James William Martin*. Her body tensed. What secrets did the box hold? Or had she been chasing a dead end? Taylor squared her shoulders and lifted the lid.

A few sheets of paper clipped together and what looked like pages torn from a small notebook lay in the bottom. One report, a few notes. And a letter-sized envelope—probably the letter her father mailed after he left.

She began with it, taking out an expensive-looking sheet of stationery. Bold handwriting that she remembered from the letters Mom let her read. *Dear Allison, I don't know where to start, only that I have to leave. The pressure is too great. I'm sorry. Please forgive me.*

He'd signed it "James." Taylor could not imagine how Mom felt when she received this bombshell that left the lingering question of why. She checked the envelope to see where it'd been mailed from. She blew out a breath. Dallas.

She set the letter aside and lifted the smaller sheets and counted eight. Then she took out the larger pages. Her father's name appeared in the upper left corner and below that the name of the lead detective, Lt. Robert Wilson. Taylor removed the paper clip and began reading the two typewritten sheets.

She learned nothing new from the first paragraph. The second paragraph listed people Wilson interviewed. Her mother, Jonathan, Ethan Trask. Taylor hadn't realized Ethan was there that day. The other names she recognized as her father's friends and acquaintances. The next paragraph gave a brief summary of the day he left. Jonathan and Ethan took him to the airport. *Interview with airline: manifest shows Martin boarded the plane. Flight attendant indicated she didn't remember him per se, but the crew had been short staffed that day.* A comment at the bottom of the page noted he never arrived at the Palace Hotel in Dallas.

The second page mentioned the missing ten thousand dollars from the safe, along with the name of a private investigator Jonathan had hired. Wayne Russo. She needed to check that out. Wilson had ended the second page with the conclusion James Martin deserted the family and made off with ten thousand dollars. Case closed.

Nothing new, but seeing the detective's words along with her father's in black and white made it so final. When her dad had gotten on that plane, he had never intended to return. He deserted them. Jonathan was right—her dad didn't want to be found. The heaviness in her heart spread through her body. She'd pinned so much hope on this case file.

Taylor pulled her thoughts together and picked up the handwritten notes. That was odd. Unlike the report, the note pages were in random order. Reading the report, she'd imagined a meticulous lawman and not someone who'd just toss the notes in the box.

When she finally put them in order, she noticed that the last page ended in midsentence. Why would any part of these notes be missing? She examined the papers. Most cases had two detectives working them, and they worked on the report together. This looked like the work of one person. Maybe there was another report somewhere.

She looked over Wilson's working notes again that showed the lieutenant's penchant for concise statements. He would have made sure all his notes were in the file. If one thing was missing, could other items be missing as well? Was it possible Wilson was still around?

"Livy," Taylor called as she came out of the

conference room. "Do you know—" She halted. Livy was engaged in conversation with her partner, Mac. They both looked toward her.

"Sorry, I didn't mean to interrupt." Taylor turned to go back into the conference room.

"You're not interrupting anything important," Livy said. "I'm sending the boy here to get coffee. Hazelnut, to be exact. Want some?"

"You bet." Taylor glanced down at the report in her hands. "You guys know a Lieutenant Robert Wilson?"

Livy shook her head while Mac repeated the name. "Robert Wilson . . . Rob . . . yeah, I remember him. He retired at least ten years ago. Why?"

"He was the investigator on my father's case," Taylor replied. "I wonder if he's still around."

"I can check and see." Livy picked up the phone. A few minutes later she jotted a number on a sticky note and broke the connection. "Jody in personnel says he's still kicking." She handed Taylor the note. "This is his address and phone number."

"Can I use your phone?" Livy nodded and Taylor dialed the number. Rob Wilson answered on the seventh ring.

"Hello?" his voice wheezed over the line.

"Lieutenant Wilson?"

"That's me."

Taylor identified herself and explained she was

investigating her father's disappearance. "Mac McCord and Livy Reynolds will be sitting in on our conversation," she added as she put the call on speaker.

"That you, Mac?" Wilson's breathy voice rasped into the room.

"How're you doing, Rob?"

"Gettin' by."

"I know that feeling," Mac replied. "Appreciate it if you'd help us."

"The James Martin case," Wilson said slowly. "It's odd. Y'all are the second ones to ask about that case lately. Hasn't been a week since a reporter came out and interviewed me for a story on it. Said he was doing a series on unsolved crimes in Memphis. I haven't seen the article yet."

"What did you tell him?" Taylor asked.

"You say you're the daughter?"

"Yes. What did you tell the reporter?"

"Didn't remember anything at first. Then, it came back to me. Told him Martin lived over in Logan Point. I got the case because the Memphis airport was the last place he was reported seen. The way I recollect, the Martin fellow just up and left. Took some money with him." The old man paused, and Taylor heard him suck in air. "There was always something about that case that bothered me, though. Some things just never added up—that's what I told that reporter that came around. Got my personal notes out—the ones I kept so I could write a book someday."

"Did you figure it out?" Taylor's hopes rose.

"I think so." Wilson's wheezing filled the room as he stopped once again to get his breath.

"Can you tell me?"

"Don't have time right now. My daughter is sitting in the driveway, waiting to take me to her house."

"Could I visit you and talk about the case?" Taylor asked. "Maybe I could take a look at your personal notes."

Wilson hesitated. "Have to be the first part of the week. I'd have to find the notes again, and my daughter won't bring me home until she goes to work Monday morning, but I ought to find those notes real quick. Come Monday morning around ten."

"I'll see you then." As she thanked him for his time, a thought struck her. "Lieutenant Wilson," she said before he could disconnect. "Do you remember your partner on that case?"

This time there was no hesitation. "Sorriest partner I ever had. Allen Yates. He committed suicide a few years later, or so the story goes. Got my doubts about that too. Look, my daughter's honking, so I need to go." He broke the connection.

Taylor handed the phone back to Livy. "Well, guess that's that until Monday. Except for checking out the detective Jonathan hired."

Mac tapped his lips. "I remember the Yates story. It happened right after I got out of academy. There were rumors Yates was a dirty cop, extorting some of the drug dealers downtown, but nothing concrete ever developed—drug dealers aren't known for cooperating."

"*Was* it a suicide?" Taylor asked.

"I think there was a note." He shook his head. "Happened at least fifteen years ago, and the details are a little murky."

Strange that one of the detectives involved in her dad's case was dead under questionable circumstances. Or was she making too much of his death? After all, people died every day. "Thanks for the help," Taylor said. "As soon as I copy my dad's files, I'm out of here."

"I'll help you," Livy said and walked with Taylor to the conference room.

"Let that be your last official act of the week," Mac called to Livy's back. "You're working way too many overtime hours for this month. Take the weekend off."

"I might just do that," Livy called over her shoulder.

Taylor grinned. "Good. You can run interference for me tomorrow at the picnic."

"Sorry I'm late, Mrs. Adams." The appointment with the restorers had taken longer than Nick had expected, and then he'd stopped to purchase clothes for him and Scott, along with a pair of sneakers. Not one article of clothing for Scott was black.

"Call me Kate—none of that Mrs. Adams stuff. And I'll call you Nick."

He set his overnight bag in the foyer and followed her as she showed him around the old Victorian. Upstairs, Kate gave him his choice of two bedrooms. Both were large and airy and furnished with antiques. The one he chose had a private shower and separate dressing room. He liked the solid lines of the oak bedstead and dresser.

"Once you get settled, come downstairs. I'll be in the kitchen. Most days I make supper, and you're welcome to eat here, no extra charge."

Nick's stomach growled, reminding him he hadn't eaten lunch. "Thanks. I may take you up on that."

"Supper will be in one hour."

When he returned to the main floor, the rich aroma of corn bread baking in the oven drew him to the kitchen. The sunny room with its country curtains and cross-stitched verses on the wall reminded him of his childhood home. Kate even made him think of his stepmother as she stood at the stove, stirring three different pots of vegetables.

"You go ahead and fix your plate," she said.

Nick hadn't had a home-cooked meal in days.

He helped himself to the vegetables while Kate took the corn bread from the oven and flipped it onto a plate.

She frowned at his small portions. "That chicken is my specialty."

He obliged her by forking another piece onto his plate. Kate joined him at the table. "How is your brother?"

"Getting better. I'll be going back to the hospital after I finish eating. I should be back in a couple of hours." But he wasn't leaving the hospital until he got the information he wanted.

"I always stay up for the ten o'clock news." Kate gave Nick a gentle smile. "Taylor told me about Scott. Is he going to rehab?"

"I hope so, but I'm not sure he'll agree to it." Nick looked around the kitchen, recognizing the Bible verse from Jeremiah. This was a happy place, much like the home he grew up in. "You know, this would be a good place to bring Scott. Maybe fatten—" He stopped, his face burning. "I'm sorry. This is your home, not a hospital. I shouldn't assume that it would be okay for Scott to stay here. And Taylor lives close by, doesn't she?"

"Taylor is like family. My daughter married her brother." Kate tilted her head. "Taylor has already mentioned you might want to bring him here. Do you think the police will release Scott to your custody?"

"He hasn't been charged with anything."

"Oh." She seemed puzzled. "I just thought this thing with Taylor . . ."

"My brother is not the one stalking her."

"How do you know? And are you willing to risk her life to prove it?"

Was he?

"Let me tell you a story," Nick said. "I came home from school one day. Scott was under the old elm tree in our backyard, and he held a small wren with a broken wing in his hands. He held that bird up to me with tears in his eyes and said, 'Fix it, Nick. It's hurting.' I don't think that little boy could grow up and intentionally hurt anyone. I know he has an alcohol problem, but violence is so foreign to his nature. Taylor doesn't have anything to worry about from him."

Kate's eyes softened. "I believe you're right. And he won't be the first person staying here who has problems."

"Oh?" Nick forked a piece of chicken into his mouth, savoring the spicy chipotle flavor.

"My daughter took off a couple of years ago. Can't figure out how we went wrong."

Taylor hadn't mentioned that. "Maybe it wasn't anything you did."

"Wasn't all us." Kate smoothed her apron. "But we failed her in some way. Ever since, I've tried to open my home to anybody God brought here. There were a couple of runaways that Sheriff

Tom Logan, the current sheriff's dad, asked me to take in. They went home to their families, so maybe I'm doing some good."

"Did Taylor tell you I'm looking for land to build a camp for troubled kids? It'll be only boys at first, but . . ." Nick's heart quickened. Kate was a potter, a skill she could pass on. "Have you ever thought about giving pottery lessons?"

A broad smile stretched across her face. "I can't take on anything full time or even part time, what with the pottery studio and all the orders, but I could spare a couple of hours a week."

"Is there any land around here for sale? I'd like to get at least twenty acres, with access to a lake, if possible." Nick wasn't rich, but with his savings and Angie's insurance money, he should be able to swing twenty acres.

"You'd need plenty of money to do that. Developers are grabbing up all the good land, offering outlandish prices."

Reality check. Memphis was knocking on Logan Point's door. Land would sell by the foot here rather than by the acre. "You're right. I doubt I could afford it."

She patted his hand. "I wouldn't worry too much about it. If God wants it here, it'll go here."

Nick had experienced open doors too many times not to recognize another one. He squeezed Kate's hand. "I don't believe it's a coincidence that we've met."

• • •

Nick stared out the fifth floor window of Scott's hospital room at the parking lot below. A monitor beeped a steady rhythm from above his brother's bed. "So tell me a little more about this Digger person your girlfriend mentioned."

When he didn't get an answer, he turned around. Scott was dozing again. The hamburger Nick had brought was still on the tray, untouched. Nick crossed to the bed and shook him. "Scott, tell me about Digger."

"Somebody . . . I met in Newton." Scott slurred his words.

Nick sat on the edge of the bed and waited. Overhead, the faint beeping from the monitor indicated an increase in Scott's heart rate. "Did he take Dr. Martin's class?"

"What? No, I told you he was too old . . ."

"What do you mean by too old? Scott!" He shook him again. "We need to talk."

"Not now . . ."

"Did you give her the bracelet?"

Scott's eyes blinked open, and he squinted at Nick. "What bracelet?"

"She received a diamond bracelet in the mail Monday. It was postmarked from Memphis and charged to your credit card. A five hundred dollar purchase, Scott."

His eyes widened, and he struggled to get up as

he shook the sleep off. Nick raised the head of his bed.

"I didn't send her a bracelet. Yeah, I went to her house. But because she texted me to come. Look on my phone. You'll see it."

"Your phone was destroyed in the fire." Taylor had never mentioned a text to Scott, probably because there never was one. Nick expelled an impatient breath. "How did you get to her house? You didn't have a car."

"I got a ride part of the way and walked the rest."

"Were you drunk?"

"Not then. I'd maybe had a couple of drinks." He rubbed the side of his head. "Do we have to do this tonight?"

Nick crossed his arms. "Tell me what happened when you got there."

Scott pressed his hands against his head. "The front door was open, and I rang the doorbell and knocked, and when Dr. Martin didn't come to the door I went in to make sure she was okay. I don't remember anything after that until I heard a loud bang. Knew I had to get away, so I started running."

"How did you get back to town?"

Scott laid his head on the pillow and closed his eyes. "When I heard the sirens, I called Digger. I walked about a mile before he came." He took a shuddering breath. "Please." He closed his eyes. "I don't want to talk about this any longer."

Cold chills ran over Nick as he sat silently as Scott drifted off. Before he went to bed tonight, he needed to write down what his brother had just told him and email it to Taylor. He sighed.

Scott was in deeper trouble than he had ever guessed.

20

The sun topped the trees in the Martin backyard, promising a hot Saturday as Taylor stretched first one leg then the other. After a fitful sleep, she hoped running would revitalize her, but even now her father's case gnawed in her gut. Missing evidence and one of the investigators dead. Maybe a suicide, maybe not. The wait until Monday morning seemed interminable.

She pulled her hair up in a ponytail, then jogged the quarter mile to Coley Road and turned toward the bed and breakfast. Years ago she and Livy routinely ran a two-mile stretch of the road and back. Sometimes they even added the mile to the lake. She would forgo that leg of it today.

A horn honked, and she almost stumbled as a pickup eased beside her. She recognized one of Ben's deputies even though he was out of uniform.

"Wade Hatcher, you scared me to death," she said.

"Ben know what you're doing?"

She winced. At the least, she should have called the sheriff and advised him that she planned to jog a little. "No, but it's good to see he's sending patrols by."

"I'm not exactly part of the patrol, just on my way to check on my mom. I'll radio dispatch and let them know to send a deputy by."

"I don't think I'll need it, but thanks."

By the time she reached Kate's drive, she'd slipped into a groove again as she focused on the feel of the road under her feet. Lost in a world of her own, she didn't hear or see Nick until he spoke.

"Good morning."

Taylor jerked her head up. She lost focus as he fell in beside her. Her traitorous heart thudded against her ribs as she took in his lean body. "You scared me half to death," she panted.

Nick grinned wickedly. "Sorry. Want me to run the other way?"

She shot him a sharp glance. "Think you can keep up?"

"Try me."

Taylor's jaw shot out. She'd do just that—as soon as she got her pace back, a difficult task with him running beside her, his body lean and taut. He hadn't shaved, and his five o'clock

271

shadow had grown into a day-old beard. An eye patch and he'd look like a pirate.

Breathe. In. Out.

Muscles. Rippling. Body. Glistening.

Her mind backslid as he matched her stride for stride. They rounded a curve in the road. Killer Hill lay ahead, so named by Livy because of the sharp incline. She'd leave him in the dust. Taylor upped her pace, stretching out her legs. Halfway up the hill she drew from reserves. Again, he matched her stride for stride. She glared at his back in disbelief as he pulled ahead before they reached the top.

Nick jogged several yards beyond while she slowed to a walk, her chest heaving. He turned around and jogged back. "You're good," he panted.

"I would have beaten you if we'd started even." At least he was winded. "You didn't tell me you were a runner."

"There's a lot you don't know about me." He reached and brushed back a strand of hair that had escaped her ponytail. "Thirsty?"

Her heart erupted into a flurry of rapid-fire beats that had nothing to do with running. Taylor pinched her T-shirt and fanned it. "I'm dying here."

His gaze lingered, and then he smiled. "Be right back."

While she stretched her calves, Nick disappeared

into the woods beside the road. When he reappeared, he held two water bottles in his hands.

"You knew about Killer Hill?"

He laughed. "I scoped it out last night and stashed a couple of bottles of frozen water Kate gave me." He handed her a bottle. "One will be enough for me."

"Thanks." Taylor unscrewed the cap and took a long draw. "I gather you stayed at the bed and breakfast last night."

Nick nodded, then turned his bottle up and drank, the water trickling out the side of his mouth. He wiped his chin with his hand. "Kate's an interesting woman."

"She's special."

He took a breath. "The hospital will probably release Scott tomorrow, and he's refusing to go to rehab, says he can do it himself this time. If you don't have any objections, I'd like to bring him to Kate's for a few days, until I can find a drug and alcohol facility he'll agree to go to."

"Bring him to Kate's?" Even though she'd mentioned to Kate that Nick might want to bring Scott to the bed and breakfast, it still unsettled her.

"Before you decide, there's more."

From the look on his face, she wasn't going to like the "more" part. "What?"

"I talked to him last night about what

happened the night you and the sheriff were attacked, then I went home and wrote down what he said. I'd like to email it to you."

She gave him her email address. "Give me the highlights."

He looked into the distance, then turned back to her. "He admitted he was at your house that night. But he said you texted him to come. I—"

"I what?" She gaped at him. "I don't even know his cell phone number."

"That's what I thought. But he was adamant." Nick licked his lips. "I'm not saying *you* texted, but that someone could have from your house. Maybe on your computer?"

Her computer hadn't been moved from her desk, one of the reasons she didn't believe robbery was part of the attack. Even so, she'd checked the computer out, and everything seemed normal. "My computer is at the house. I'll check and see if a text was sent from it as soon as I get there."

"I've been saying all along someone is framing my brother."

He might just be right. But even if Scott wasn't the attacker, he almost burned Nick's house down. "You're sure Kate is okay with Scott coming there?"

"We talked about it, and she indicated it was mostly up to you. Of course, I'd have to make sure he didn't get any alcohol, but that shouldn't be so hard to do at Kate's house. I don't think there's any place he can buy it closer than five miles."

She chuckled. "That's true. If he comes, can I talk to him?"

"I want you to. I want him to tell you everything that happened that night . . . but let me get him settled first."

"Hopefully sooner than later? After all, I might be able to help him."

"We'll see."

She slugged down the last of the water and looked at the empty bottle. She didn't want to throw it away, and she didn't want to carry it to the house.

Her gaze flitted to his chiseled lips. How could anyone look as good as Nick this early in the morning? Nearby, a mockingbird let loose with a melody, and his mate answered. Her breath shortened, and she tried to ignore her thumping heart.

Nick's hand brushed hers as he reached for the empty bottle, and a charge raced up her arm. She raised her head and met his gaze, drowning in his liquid hazel eyes. The air between them surged with an undercurrent. Desire to feel his lips on hers raced through her body.

Nick dropped the water bottles and leaned toward her, cupping her face in his hands. His lips, tentative at first, tasted salty and sweet at the same time. Then he claimed her mouth with such intensity that it took her breath away. Desire she'd never known ignited in her heart, and she melted into his arms as the pleasure of being held by him blew everything else away.

"Oh, Taylor," he said, his voice husky as his finger trailed down her cheek. "I didn't mean for that to happen."

She stiffened and tried to pull away.

"Wait . . . That didn't come out right. I don't regret it. I just didn't see it coming."

Taylor took in a shaky breath. She could live with that. "That makes two of us. So, what's next?"

She could kick herself. Did she always have to be so direct? Did it even matter? His low chuckle was like butterfly kisscs to her self-doubt.

He released her and stepped back, amusement glinting in his eyes. "That remains to be discovered."

With a new awareness of Nick charging her senses, Taylor struggled for rhythm as they jogged toward home. Just before Kate's drive, they slowed to a walk, and Nick took her hand. A car blew past them, creating a cooling breath of air. Another vehicle followed and a horn tooted as one of Ben's deputies drove by. Taylor waved a thank-you.

Nick squeezed her hand. "See you at the picnic?"

"Five o'clock," she reminded him.

Taylor's feet barely touched the ground as she jogged to her drive. The lyrics from a song about being loved every waking moment played in her head. The day stretched before her and with it the promise of seeing Nick again.

Jonathan's dark maroon pickup inched slowly toward her in the distance. Her gaze slid past the truck to Oak Grove, and the weathered old house cast a pall on her mood. He stopped and lowered the window as she came even with him.

"Have a good run?"

"I did." She pulled the damp T-shirt away from her body as she glanced in the back of his truck. Several worn boards lay in the bed. "Been working up at the old house this morning?"

He nodded. "Cleaning up some of the boards lying around."

"Wish you'd told me. I would've helped." It would have been the perfect time to put her ghosts to rest.

His bushy eyebrows came together in a frown. "Last time you helped me, you ended up in the emergency room with five stitches."

She'd forgotten that. "Why do you keep working on Oak Grove if you're going to sell it?"

"At first I was only cleaning it out, but one thing led to another, and I decided to replace a few boards, patch a few places in the walls." He chewed his bottom lip. "I'm calling a meeting after the picnic. The contractor wants an answer."

"Come on, Jonathan. Let it rest this weekend. I need a little more time."

"So you're not a definite no?"

She couldn't deny the two hundred and fifty thousand dollars tempted her, so she could honestly say yes. "Not definite."

A broad grin broke across his face. "Good enough for me. I'll wait until Monday evening."

"Kate said you and Charlie go to the casinos. Is that why you want to sell? You're in trouble?"

The grin disappeared. "Kate needs to keep her mouth shut. I win more than I lose."

Taylor had read that line before in her research for graduate school. Compulsive gamblers, like all addicts, lived in denial. "Is Wayne Russo still doing investigative work?"

His head jerked back. "Russo's dead. You're not still fooling around with James's case, are you?" His mouth tightened. "You are. Taylor, don't open this can of worms."

She looked away from his piercing eyes, toward Oak Grove. How could her uncle not want to find his brother? She straightened her shoulders and turned back to Jonathan. "I don't understand why you're so dead set against looking for him."

"I'm trying to spare you some pain. Your father doesn't want to be found." He slowly enunciated each word. "If he did, he would contact you."

"Have you heard from him?"

"Don't be silly. And I don't have time to fool with this now. Need to dump these boards and get some chairs your mama wanted." Jonathan put his arm across the back of the truck seat and turned to look behind him as he shifted the truck into reverse.

She fanned her T-shirt again. Her uncle was hiding something. Maybe he had helped her dad disappear. That would explain a lot. Slowly, she walked to the back door and embraced the cool air inside the kitchen. Her mom turned as she closed the door. "It's getting hot out there," Taylor said.

"Have you lost your mind?"

She blinked at her mom. "What?"

"Someone sent you a threatening note. Shot another woman to send you a message, and you're out running the roads?" Her mom jerked a towel from the rack and scrubbed the already spotless table. "What were you thinking? I was almost ready to call Ben Logan."

Taylor swallowed the defense that sprang to her mind. "Ben had it covered and nothing happened." Except Nick kissed her. "Might not have been my wisest decision, though. It won't happen again."

"It better not." Her mother popped open the oven and took out a pan of cinnamon rolls.

Taylor's mouth watered. "Those look so good."

"They're not for you." She set the pan on a trivet. "They're for Abby. Chase has gone after her."

Abby. She wished her niece had another week

at the camp. "Then I better get showered and dressed."

At the door, she remembered the reporter and turned back to her mother. "Did anyone contact you about a story on Dad?"

Her mother gave her a blank stare. "What do you mean?"

"I was talking with the lieutenant who investigated Dad's disappearance. He indicated someone was writing a story about it."

"Why?" her mother demanded. "It's been twenty years."

"People are fascinated with unsolved mysteries —it's those television programs about cold cases."

A gasp caught in her mom's throat as her hand flew to her chest.

"Cold case, that's what he called it," she said slowly. "A reporter did phone about a month ago. I refused to answer his questions, other than to tell him we had gotten on with our lives. The newspaper can't write about that without my permission, can they?"

Taylor winced. "I'm afraid so, Mom. It's a matter of public record."

For a second, her mom stared transfixed at Taylor, then like a fragile flower, she wilted. Taylor wrapped her arms around her. "I'm sorry. I didn't mean to upset you."

Her mom pulled away, her face splotchy. "You

were talking to the detective who investigated your father's disappearance?"

Taylor pinched the bridge of her nose. Talk about opening a can of worms. "Briefly. I should have waited until after the picnic to bring it up. Right now, I better go take a shower." And check to see if someone used her computer to send Scott a text.

An uncertain smile touched Mom's lips. "Sure, but let's do talk about this later, after the picnic is over."

"Sounds good." Taylor hurried upstairs and flipped on the shower. She hadn't meant to hurt her mom. Sometimes her single-minded focus made her insensitive to the feelings of others . . . something she obviously needed to work on. But she needed answers to the question of her father's whereabouts, and they were locked away somewhere.

Maybe Monday Lieutenant Wilson would know where to find the key.

When Taylor opened her computer, Nick's email was there. She opened the document and quickly scanned it. When she read the part about the text, she stopped and checked her sent folder, then the trash. Just as she expected, there was no text sent from her computer to Scott. But anyone smart enough to set him up would not leave evidence. She called Ben Logan and filled him in.

"Can you get me the cell phone number this text was supposedly sent to?" the sheriff asked.

"Why don't I have his brother call you? His name is Nick Sinclair. And I'll forward the email he sent me."

After she showered and dressed, Taylor descended the stairs, and a child's voice filtered through the kitchen door. Her heart lifted. Abby was home. "Where's my favorite niece?" she called from the bottom of the stairs.

"Aunt Tay!" Abby burst from the kitchen and jumped into Taylor's outstretched arms.

As a toddler Abby couldn't say Taylor, and the Aunt Tay stuck. "I've missed you, pumpkin."

Abby's answer was to wrap her arms around Taylor's neck.

Taylor nuzzled her hair, inhaling strawberry shampoo. "Did you have a good time?"

"It was the best. I rode horses, and swam, and canoed, and my horse's name was Buttermilk, and I'm going to ask Daddy for a pony."

Taylor laughed. Chase had been right about the horse. "Whew! Sounds like you did have fun. Hop down, and let's see how much you've grown."

"I've grown two inches since we came to see you." Abby slid to the floor, her curly blonde ponytail bobbing. Smaller than most eight-year-olds, she stood straight, trying to appear taller. The curls, the blue eyes, the freckles peppering her nose. Except for the color of her hair, Abby was the spitting image of Robyn at that age. The realization caught Taylor unaware, and she blinked back tears. How could Robyn bear not seeing her child? She didn't like the answer that came to mind. She didn't want to believe what Livy did—that her sister-in-law was probably dead.

Abby cocked her head to the side. "Is something wrong, Aunt Tay?"

Taylor touched the tip of Abby's nose. "No, nothing's wrong. I'm just glad to see you." She held her arm out, measuring her niece's height. "I believe you have grown two inches."

Chase appeared in the doorway. "Y'all standing out here in the hall all day?"

Taylor grabbed her niece's hand. "We're coming."

As she passed Chase, he stopped her. "Can we talk later? About the land? Jonathan says he's going to call a meeting after the picnic."

"I talked to him earlier this morning, and he's going to wait until after the weekend."

Chase hugged her. "I knew you could still wrap him around your little finger."

In the kitchen, Abby climbed on a stool by the breakfast bar and patted the one beside it. "Sit here."

Her mom was her old self as she placed a cinnamon roll in front of her granddaughter.

"Who wants to help me load the van and take the food down to the lake?"

"Me!" Abby cried.

"I'll help," Taylor replied in answer to a "look" from her mother. Anytime she received a pointed look and raised eyebrows it was best to agree with whatever her mother suggested.

"Good. I'll start loading around three." She took a ham from the refrigerator and arranged pineapple slices around it, securing them with toothpicks, and then opened a bottle of maraschino cherries.

"I want one!" Abby cried.

Laughing, Mom plopped a cherry in her granddaughter's open mouth. She turned to Chase. "Would you load the ice chest?"

Chase nodded and pulled Abby's ponytail. "Come on, pumpkin. You need to unpack, and after lunch you need to rest."

"Aw, Dad, I'm not tired."

"Abby . . ."

She turned to Taylor. "Would you help me unpack?"

"Sure, honey." As they climbed the stairs, Taylor smiled. Chase was a great dad. Her thoughts wandered to Nick, and immediately she forced them away. No need to go there.

21

By five o'clock, if Taylor had explained where she'd been the last ten years to one person, she'd told a hundred. She'd endured matchmaking attempts and smiled until her cheeks hurt. Once or twice she even caught herself watching for Nick. Tired of mingling, she sought out a cool place under a huge oak where a light breeze touched her cheek. Abby and her friends caught her attention as they jumped off a wooden pier. Her heart hitched as she saw herself twenty years ago. Jumping off the pier. Swimming to the raft anchored a hundred yards off shore, then swimming back to the shore. Her dad watching.

Taylor brushed away the memories, but she couldn't brush away the ache of not knowing why he left. She wanted answers, and somehow, she had to find a way to get them.

"So this is where you got off to."

Taylor looked around. Jonathan was pulling up a chair beside her. "I'm hiding out," she replied. "If one more person says they can fix me up with a date, I'll scream."

"That bad, huh?" Jonathan stretched out his long legs and crossed his hands over his belly.

"Yes." Taylor was half-tempted to ask Jonathan more questions about her dad. No. She didn't want a repeat of this morning. She studied her uncle. Would her dad be balding now? Overweight? In her dreams, his features were indistinct, blurry.

"What are you working on with Livy? That new murder case with the woman found by the interstate?"

Jonathan's question brought her back to the present. "Nope, another murder case." Taylor glanced across to the dirt road where the cars were parked. Livy had arrived in her white Chevy SUV. She nodded toward her friend. "But Livy might know something about that case. Not that she'd tell you anything."

Jonathan turned and looked. "Bet I can get something out of her."

Taylor threw down the challenge. "Bet you can't."

He shot her a sly glance. "You're on."

When Livy plopped into a chair beside them with a sigh, Taylor laughed. "You sound tired. Thought you were taking the weekend off."

"I did. I called Kate and discovered she had a to-do list a mile long, so I offered to help. Just delivered the last order of mugs."

"How about a glass of lemonade?" Jonathan asked.

"Wouldn't want to put you to any trouble." Livy's tone said otherwise.

"No trouble." Jonathan stood and ambled to the drink table.

"It's a bribe," Taylor said. "He wants to know what's going on in that woman's murder investigation."

"He's wasting his energy. The feds aren't leaking anything. Do you want me to go with you to interview Lieutenant Wilson?"

"That'd be great," Taylor said, then nodded toward a grassy area where Abby and two of her friends had moved to practice their gymnastic moves. Abby arched her back and bent backward until her hands touched the ground. "She's good."

Livy laughed. "Glad she took after you instead of me. By the way, I had a long conversation with Nick while I was at Kate's. He's such a nice guy." She lifted her eyebrows suggestively.

"Don't go there." Taylor wagged her finger. The memory of his kiss sent a warm flush to her face.

"Mmm-hmm."

Taylor's gaze slid past her friend. "Oh, look, there's Rachel."

Livy turned. Their former schoolmate had stopped to swing a toddler into her husband's arms. At their side, a smaller, towhead version of the husband pulled at a German shepherd puppy.

Livy shook her head. "The little one there, he's all boy. And there's another one running around somewhere. Never figured Rachel for the three kids routine. Figured she'd be a lawyer or something."

If she and Nick . . . what would their child look

like? *Don't go there. He's too good to be true.* Taylor traced her finger around the cup holder on the chair arm. "Would you trade places with her?"

"No!" Livy shot a sharp glance toward Taylor. "Would you?"

Taylor hesitated. "No, I guess not. She got a good man, though . . . and speaking of men, I almost called you earlier yelling '*ma chère.*' "

"Who'd you need rescuing from?" Livy glanced across the picnic area. "Old Mr. Peabody?"

"Mr. Peabody I could deal with. Mrs. Lizzie and her cronies I can't. 'Taylor, honey, you simply must meet my nephew Bert.' " She mimicked the older woman's high-pitched nasal tone.

Livy burst out laughing. "They got you, did they?"

"Now I know why you avoid Logan Point as much as possible."

Accompanied by her mom and Ethan, Jonathan rejoined them and handed Livy a tall glass of lemonade. "Here you go, Ms. Reynolds."

Livy accepted the drink with a twinkle in her eye. "Thank you, Mr. Martin. And before you ask, I'll tell you, I know nothing."

Jonathan shot Taylor a frown. "Did you—"

"Not one word." Taylor palmed her hands. Then she grinned. "Well, maybe two . . ."

"The feds are keeping a tight lid on this case," Livy said.

"I'm glad you could make it, Livy." Her mom

reached down and gave Livy a hug while Ethan hovered in the background. "Are Kate and Charlie coming?"

"Not sure about Charlie, but Kate was packing her basket when I left."

Mom glanced toward Ethan. "Livy, do you know Ethan?"

"I've seen him around the CJC a few times." Livy extended her hand. "Congratulations on making it to the governor's judgeship list."

"Thank you."

Taylor flicked a glance toward the couple. Ethan stood with his hand resting on the small of her mom's back, as it had been off and on all afternoon. A question wormed its way into her mind. How would she feel if something really did develop between the two? Unease settled in her stomach. Somehow, she couldn't see her mother with anyone other than her father. Which was ludicrous.

Taylor's attention was drawn to her niece as she raced toward them.

"Aunt Tay! Come watch me dive off the pier!"

Abby stopped short and squealed when she saw Livy. "Aunt Livy!" Bounding toward them, she grabbed Livy's hand, and then Taylor's. "Both of you, come."

Laughing, they rose and followed Abby to the water's edge.

"Watch me!" Abby shouted. She raced down the

pier and jumped, flipping in midair before diving into the water.

"Good dive!" Kate yelled behind them when Abby surfaced.

Taylor turned and grinned at Kate. She hadn't seen her arrive. "I'm glad you made it."

Kate's answer was lost as Taylor caught sight of Nick. Instantly, the sky deepened a little bluer, and a golden glow settled on the picnic. A warning sounded in her head, but Taylor ignored it as she remembered his lips on hers and felt an idiotic smile stretch across her face. She probably looked like a Cheshire cat.

"You look good." His eyes reflected his words.

Taylor barely noticed as Livy took her aunt's basket and the two walked toward the picnic tables. She touched the French braid, glad she'd taken the time. "Thanks. Do you want to sit in the shade?"

"I can't stay."

The three words sank her good mood. "Why not?"

"The hospital called. They're discharging Scott."

"Now? Today?"

He nodded. "He's waiting. Oh, and I talked with Sheriff Logan and gave him Scott's phone number. He's going to check for the message. Did you get my email?"

"Yes. I forwarded it to Ben," Taylor said. "Not

sure what I think about Scott's story, but I do have a few questions to ask him."

He nodded. "I wish I could stay longer. How long will the picnic go on? If it's not too late, maybe you could come over to the B and B later?"

"I don't have to talk to Scott today. After church tomorrow will be good with me."

His eyebrows rose. "You're going to church?"

Taylor grimaced. "Short of dying, there's not much way of getting past Mom on this one."

"Good for her." Nick leaned closer to her. "And I wasn't asking you over to see Scott."

She lowered her gaze as her heart turned somersaults.

Nick lifted her chin. "I want to see you."

"You do?" Were those the only words she could get out of her mouth? Any other time she'd have something witty to say. That's why she hated the dating thing—she was no better at banter now than she'd been as a teenager.

"Of course I do." He glanced around the picnic area. "I guess I better go . . ."

He made no move to leave, and instead swept his arm toward the lake. "This would make a great boys' camp."

Taylor turned and tried to look at the area from that perspective. "It would, wouldn't it?"

"Any chance your family would sell twenty acres?"

"I don't know. My uncle seems to be in a selling mood. I can ask him."

"That would be great. Well, I better go." He stepped back, almost colliding with Pete Connelly.

Taylor jerked her hand toward him. "Watch out!"

Too late. Nick tried to catch the plate that sailed through the air and landed food side down. "Sorry, man!"

"No problem." Pete scooped the plate off the ground.

Taylor couldn't keep from laughing. She thought she was the only one who did things like that. "I'll take that," she said and reached for the plate. "Nick Sinclair, meet Pete Connelly. He works for my uncle here on the farm."

Nick's face matched his red shirt. "I hope that wasn't the last piece of ham."

"Nah. I saw plenty more."

"Good." Nick took a deep breath. "Okay, this time I'm leaving. Nice to meet you, Pete."

As Nick walked to his truck, Taylor looked for a place to dump the plate.

"I want to apologize for the other day."

She glanced sharply at Pete. "For . . . ?"

"I was kind of rude, staring at you like I did. But it's been a while since I've seen you and you looked great. But I could tell I made you uncomfortable."

Taylor wrinkled her brows in a frown. "You didn't—"

"It's okay." He lifted his hand as if to reassure her. "Just sort of hoped things had changed since high school."

Maybe she'd misjudged Pete. "It's not that I don't like you. We just never had a lot in common. And I don't like the way you stare at me."

"It won't happen again." His lips curved upward. "I'd like to be friends . . . seeing as we'll probably be running into each other a lot while you're here."

Friends? Taylor didn't know if she could go that far. Besides, she wouldn't be here that long. But she held out her free hand. "Okay, I'm willing to give it a shot."

He flashed a quick grin and shook her hand. "Anytime you need help with anything, let me know. Your mom always lets me work on things for her. Computer, printer, get the mail, most any-thing."

"I'll keep that in mind. But right now, what I need is a garbage bin." She liked this new version of Pete Connelly, now that he wasn't staring at her like a lizard contemplating lunch. The "William Tell Overture" played from her shorts pocket.

"See you," Taylor said and fished her phone out. She looked at the caller ID. Christine, her friend and colleague from Newton.

"Hey, Taylor. What's going on in Logan Point?" Christine asked.

"Nothing much, just a picnic." Taylor had meant to call Christine earlier.

"Sounds nice. Did you find Scott?"

Taylor trashed the plate, then fanned herself with her hand. "Sort of, but he's been in the hospital, so I haven't questioned him yet."

"Hospital? What happened?"

Taylor filled her in about the fire. "He's not my stalker, but I do think he knows something. Just don't know what."

"His brother wouldn't have anything to do with your change of mind, would he?"

"You do have a vivid imagination," Taylor replied. "Did you ask at the administrative office if anyone called looking for me?"

"I did, and no one remembers any calls, but if someone gave out your information, they might not admit it. Oh, I almost forgot. There was a breach in security—someone hacked into the university email system."

So, Zeke nailed that one when he suggested someone had gotten into her email.

"That explains why the site crashed the other day." She smoothed back a strand of hair that had escaped the braid. She'd bought her plane tickets online. Maybe that's how her stalker knew where she was. "Do they know who did it?"

"Not a clue. And even though the administration

claims they straightened it out and no harm was done, you might want to make sure no one is using your credit card."

They talked a few minutes more, and Taylor promised to call Christine the first of the week before she hung up and walked to the picnic tables.

Livy joined her in the food line and gave her a nudge. "So what's going on with you and Nick?"

"We're just friends." What was it with everyone wanting to know about her love life?

"The looks you two exchanged tell a different story. Just be careful you don't get your heart broken." Livy's soft words had an edge to them.

Taylor narrowed her eyes. "What are you talking about?"

"Just sayin'. I understand his wife died not too long ago."

"It's been two and a half years."

"Sometimes grief takes longer than that. He may not be ready to commit to a serious relationship."

"I'm not sure *I'm* ready for anything serious. And what makes you an expert on relationships, anyway? I'm the psychologist."

Livy's green eyes darkened. "Yes, but I read more romance novels."

Did she detect sadness in Livy's voice? Then her friend laughed, and Taylor laughed with her. "Well, we're just talking, that's all," Taylor added.

Livy lifted her brows.

"That's all." Taylor grabbed two paper plates and shoved one into Livy's hands. "Isn't that Kate's potato salad?"

"Just be careful with your heart," Livy said and started filling her plate.

It might be too late for that. Taylor turned to the food on the table. After she filled her plate, she spied Ethan sitting by himself. "I'll join you in a bit. I've been meaning to talk to Ethan since seeing his name in Wilson's report."

Taylor balanced her plate and a drink as she strolled toward Ethan. "I see you've been deserted. Mind if I sit with you?"

"Love to have you." He grinned at her before he speared a piece of ham.

She took the chair beside him. She'd noticed all afternoon that energy seemed to radiate from him, but maybe that was his normal persona.

"So, are you glad to be home?"

Taylor thought before she answered. "Yeah, I am."

"You sound surprised. Your mom has really wanted you to come for a visit."

"I know." Just how close were they? Evidently close enough to discuss her travel plans. Taylor picked at her food. She caught sight of Pete talking to her mom in her peripheral vision. She nodded in his direction. "Pete's worked for you a long time. What kind of work does he do?"

"Oh, a little of this, a little of that. I wish he would finish his last year of college and go to law school. I'd help him get started in a heartbeat."

"Pete?" A lawyer. Wonders would never cease.

"Pete would make a great lawyer. He has a phenomenal memory—beats your uncle all the time at blackjack . . . and chess, and he has a grasp of the law that amazes me. Unfortunately, he'd rather drift from one place to another. When he shows up in Logan Point for a few months, Jonathan and I nab him before anyone else can."

"Do you know where all he's traveled?"

Ethan took a sip of tea. "Let's see. New York . . . Florida . . . I think he was in Atlanta for a while . . . Louisiana too, I think. He really should write a book about his travels."

Pete had lived in some of the same states she had. "Do you know if he's been to Washington State?"

"Hadn't heard him say. You ought to ask him sometime."

Her mother waved, and they both waved back. "Have you received word about the judgeship nomination yet?"

Now he really seemed about to burst, and she stared at him. "You've heard!"

"It'll be officially announced Monday morning, but yes, I am the new judge on the Tennessee Court of Appeals."

"Congratulations! Does Mom know?"

"I told her earlier."

Her mother could certainly keep a secret. "So will you be moving to Nashville?"

"Oh no. I'll be on the panel that meets in Jackson, so I'll be staying in Memphis most of the time. Although I have bought a condo to stay in so I don't have to drive back and forth when we're in session. Actually, Pete is driving over in the morning to start work on it."

She glanced toward her mother again. "I can't believe Mom didn't say something."

"She is very discreet," Ethan said. He put his plate down and turned to face Taylor. "I'm fond of your mother. I hope that's acceptable."

His eyes challenged her. She gulped a breath of air. "I'm not sure how I feel. It's hard to see my mother in that light. Even though my father's been gone a long time, I just—"

"Your mother deserves to be happy." His tone indicated he could provide that. "I don't think you should keep reminding her of the past."

"What are you saying?"

He shrugged. "Your questions about your father are upsetting. Not only to her but your uncle as well."

"They told you that?"

"They didn't have to. I see it."

"I'm sorry, but I don't think hiding from the truth is a solution. We'd all be better off if we found him and got some answers." She worried her food around the plate. "You went with Jonathan to take him to the airport. What do you remember?"

"That was a long time ago." He turned and stared toward the lake, then shifted back to face her. "I came to the picnic, and afterward Jonathan and I dropped your father at the airport. We probably didn't even park." He gave her an apologetic smile. "I was in my twenties, didn't pay much attention to things like taking people to the airport."

"You don't remember anything else?"

"I'm sorry. I wouldn't even remember that if he hadn't disappeared. And for your mom's sake, let this go."

Taylor sighed. "I wish I could."

22

The wicker swing faced the west, giving Nick a perfect view of the sun edging toward the horizon. His soles scuffed against the boards on Kate's front porch as he glided back and forth in a slow rhythm. The hospital had discharged Scott, and he was sleeping peacefully upstairs. Nick had talked with Taylor. She was coming over. He traced his finger around the links in the chain holding the swing.

For the first time since his wife's death, the

jagged edges of his heart had begun to heal. Not that he'd forgotten Angie, but he'd moved past the pain. In some ways, Taylor was like Angie. Gutsy and bulldog determined.

Her car swung into the drive. Seconds later, his heart kicked up a notch as she got out of her SUV, and he took in the length of her tanned legs, the trimness of her body, the curve of her lips as she smiled at him.

"Beautiful evening," Taylor said as she climbed the porch steps and sat beside him on the small swing, bringing with her the light fragrance of honeysuckle.

"Yeah, it's my favorite time of day," he said. Conversation waned as the swing creaked back and forth and the sun dipped below the horizon, leaving behind streaks of pale apricot, burnished reds, and smoky blues.

"Mine too. Everything is all soft and beautiful," she said.

Like her. She had taken her hair out of the French braid, and it curled delicately around her face and neck. *Focus.* "Thanks for coming."

She ducked her head, a blush creeping into her face as she turned, facing him with one leg tucked beneath the other. "How's Scott?"

"So-so. Still shaky. Sleeping a lot." He rested his arm on the back of the swing, very much aware of her nearness. "He talked a little on the way home from the hospital, repeated what he said last night—still swears he never stalked you. Before you came tonight, I remember something he said once before about liking to be where you were because you were nice to him. I think that's why he kept popping up wherever you were."

"That's a stretch."

"If I remember correctly, Newton is pretty small. Wouldn't be hard to keep running into the same person."

Taylor gave him a gentle smile. "You just don't give up on your brother, do you?"

"I'm all he has." He wanted to quit talking about his brother and just take her in his arms. But he couldn't, not until he laid his case out. "I still believe someone set him up to take the fall the night of the assault. Deputy Thornton said your door was jimmied. I believe Scott was lured there by your assailant to take the fall."

Taylor leaned back in the swing, a frown creasing her brow. "Any ideas on who this assailant is?"

"He met a guy in Newton who befriended him."

"This guy, does he have a name?"

"Digger."

"You're kidding, right?"

"I wish." Nick took a deep breath. He hadn't mentioned Digger's name in the email, only that Scott had called someone. "Scott claims he doesn't know his real name. But he's the one Scott called to come and get him from your house."

"I'll call Sheriff Atkins. Maybe one of his deputies can ask around at the university and see if anyone remembers seeing Scott with someone."

He could see Taylor processing the information. He didn't blame her for being skeptical. Even knowing his brother and how he always got himself into messes, it still sounded crazy. "I think Scott is telling the truth."

She dropped her hands in her lap and held his gaze, her blue eyes the same color as the smoky blue streaking the sky. A wayward strand of hair curled across her cheek, and he wanted to touch it, brush it behind her ear.

"I admire your loyalty," she said, her voice husky.

Taylor's voice lured him, and he touched her cheek, trailing his finger to her jaw. Her luminous eyes held his, and his heart caught at the hope and fear in them. The intoxicating scent of her perfume drew him closer until his lips touched hers, soft and warm, igniting a bonfire in his heart. When she responded, everything faded. Nothing else mattered. He pulled her closer, kissing her long and hard.

"Wow," he murmured when they broke apart.

"Double wow."

Nick flicked off the lamp beside his bed. He'd spent the last hour trying to figure out this growing relationship with Taylor. He flipped on his side, but his thoughts followed him. Taylor made him excited about living again . . . but was he ready to unlock the door to his heart?

Fine time to wonder that, after he'd kissed her twice. He was pretty sure she didn't give her kisses to just anyone.

What was the worst that could happen?

Taylor could get hurt. She already felt that her father, then Michael, and even God had rejected her. If their relationship didn't work out, she would see it as another rejection, and he didn't want that. But—

"No! Stop!"

Scott.

Nick bounded from bed and ran into his brother's room. Scott kicked at the sheet twisted around his ankles.

"Scott! Wake up!"

"Stop him!"

"Stop who?" Nick asked.

Scott's eyes flew open. He stared at Nick, his eyes wild. Gradually he relaxed. "Nobody," he mumbled. "I was dreaming."

"More like a nightmare. Here, drink this."

His brother's hand shook as he reached for the glass of water Nick handed him. He gulped the water and wiped his mouth with the back of his hand. "Where am I?"

"Logan Point."

"Oh . . . yeah. The old lady's house. What time is it?"

"Midnight," Nick replied. "Have the shakes started again? Do you need to go to the hospital?"

"No." Scott's voice cracked. "Don't take me back."

"Scott, I really think you need more help than I can give you."

"I'll be okay. Done this before on my own. Couple of days is all I need." He held his ribs and rocked forward. "Give me two of the Valium they sent home with me."

Nick went to his bedroom and shook two pills into his hand. He returned and handed them to Scott. There should be something else he could do.

"Thanks." Scott popped the pills in his mouth and swallowed them with a swig of water. He sank into the bed and closed his eyes.

"Want me to tell you a bedtime story?"

Scott cracked one eye open. "Are you serious?"

Nick grinned. "I can sit here and talk until you get sleepy." He moved a chair to the side of the bed. "Remember that home run you hit in the playoffs when you were twelve?"

A spark of interest flicked in Scott's eyes. "Yeah, I had a pretty good game that day."

Fifteen minutes later, Scott's eyelids drooped. Nick stood. "I'm going to bed."

"I'll try not to wake you again."

"Okay, but remember I'm across the hall if you need me."

He was almost out the door when Scott called his name. Nick turned around.

"I didn't hurt Dr. Martin or that sheriff."

Nick studied the guileless face of his brother. "I believe you, Scott. We'll find a way out of this mess."

23

Tenth pew, middle of the row—Taylor took her seat beside her mom just as she had every Sunday morning of her childhood. She noted that when sunshine filtered through the stained-glass windows, it still splashed a rainbow of color on the pew in front of her. Just like when she was a child and believed God answered prayer.

Seeing Nick's faith made her question if she might be wrong about God. But if God cared about her, wouldn't he have answered her prayer about her dad? What would Nick say about that? She smoothed a wrinkle that creased her white linen skirt, then tucked a stray curl behind her ear, remembering how Nick had done the same thing. Right before he kissed her. She closed her eyes, savoring the memory of his kiss. She wanted to believe he was ready for a relationship, but maybe it was too soon, like Livy said.

The organ struck the first chord of the call to worship, and everyone stood. Chase and Abby sat two rows up with Kate. Taylor craned her neck around to find her uncle. "Where's Jonathan?" she whispered to her mother.

"He came to the early service," her mother whispered back.

Early service? There'd been no early service when she was a teenager. She opened the songbook her mother handed her. "Praise God from whom all blessings flow." In spite of her resolve to do nothing more than sit, Taylor joined in on the familiar song. "Praise him all creatures here below."

Taylor sensed someone to her right, and then a warm baritone joined in the song, and her heart fluttered in her throat. Nick.

"Praise him above ye heavenly hosts; praise Father, Son, and Holy Ghost."

She cut her eyes to the right and gave him a shy smile. He winked, and Taylor reminded herself to breathe. The song ended, and as they sat, Taylor leaned over and whispered, "Who's with Scott?"

"Kate's husband, Charlie."

Taylor tried not to react. Letting Charlie look after Scott was like putting the fox in charge of the henhouse, but she didn't tell Nick. No need to worry him.

After several songs, some she remembered and some she didn't, the pastor came to the pulpit.

Taylor glanced at the bulletin. *Reverend Carl Thompson, senior pastor*. Not the same one who'd been here when she left.

The reverend directed the congregation to a passage in Luke. When Nick turned to the Scripture, she flushed. She hadn't brought a Bible. Nick's eyes flicked to her empty lap, and he placed his where she could read along with him.

The book was worn, and Nick had underlined some of the verses. She half attempted to focus on the sermon, but her thoughts kept wandering to Nick and how his leg was almost touching hers. He reached for a pen from the holder attached to the pew in front of them, and Taylor jerked her mind back to the pastor.

As Reverend Thompson spoke about lost sheep, her mind wandered again. *Don't think about Nick. Think about the meeting tomorrow.* She needed to leave the house by nine to meet Livy at Rob Wilson's house. She tried to imagine why some of the notes in the case file were missing. Hopefully, Wilson could find his personal notes on the case.

Her mother nudged her and looked pointedly toward Taylor's left foot, which was swinging furiously. She stilled her foot, and finally it was time to sing the closing hymn.

Nick's baritone and her mother's alto blended, creating a sound so beautiful that chills ran down Taylor's spine. "Come home. Ye who are weary, come home . . ."

As the last note ended, Taylor turned to leave, and her mother intercepted her. "Taylor, do you want to introduce me to your friend?"

Not really. Knowing her mom, she would read more into their relationship than what it was, even seeing it as a way to get Taylor back to Logan Point. But as she was trapped between the two, and Nick seemed to expect an introduction, she pasted a smile on her lips. "Uh, Nick, I'd like you to meet my mom, Allison Martin."

He grasped her mom's hand. "It's my pleasure, Mrs. Martin."

"Call me Allison. I've read all your books so I feel like I already know you." She linked her arm in Nick's. "And thank you so much for autographing my copy of your last one."

"My pleasure."

"Would you like to join us for Sunday dinner?" her mom asked. Taylor held her breath. As much as she'd like to spend time with him, Nick and her family and Sunday dinner wasn't what she had in mind.

Nick hesitated. "I'd like to, but I better get back to the B and B and check on my brother. Maybe another time."

She breathed again.

"We'll see after your brother," Kate said as she and Chase and Abby joined them.

Taylor introduced her brother to Nick.

"You visit with the Martins," Kate said. "It'll

give you an opportunity to tell them about that camp."

There was going to be no escaping it, she could feel it in her bones.

"I've made chicken and dressing," Mom added.

"In that case, I accept."

Oh, boy. Taylor's emotions swung from one end of the spectrum to the other. She wasn't ready to share Nick with her family. Now every time she talked to Mom, her mom would want to know what was going on with them. It was too early for that kind of pressure. Yet part of her wanted him there—the part that enjoyed torture.

Exactly as she expected, Nick was a big hit with the family. He and Chase connected right away. Jonathan joined the conversation when it turned to sports, and Nick even wowed little Abby. Taylor couldn't deny feeling a little left out. She could understand him wanting to make a good impression, but to practically ignore her? Evidently, she had totally misread the kiss last night. Nothing new there.

Sometime during the meal, her mother left the table and returned with Nick's other two books. She placed them on the buffet. "Would you mind autographing those before you leave?"

"Sure."

Taylor noted a redness creep up his neck. It

amused her that he was uncomfortable with his fame.

"When will your next book be out?" Mom asked as she sliced a chocolate cake.

"Publication date is set for November. I'll see to it that you get an advance copy."

Mom beamed. "Thank you. I'll treasure it."

"What did Kate mean about a camp?" Chase asked.

Nick turned to her brother. "It's my dream to start a boys' camp, and Kate thought I might find land around here."

"How much land are you talking about?" Jonathan asked.

"At least twenty acres." As Nick shared his dreams with her family, his words drew Taylor into his vision.

After the meal, when the men adjourned to the library, she wanted to join them but instead helped clear the table.

"It's good to hear Chase laugh," her mother commented. "And maybe Nick looking for a piece of land is an answer to my prayers."

"What are you talking about?"

"Over the years, we've bought up several tracts of land at the lake. One of them has twenty acres. Doesn't have much lake frontage, but it has a boathouse. Maybe if we all signed our part over to Jonathan . . ."

Taylor saw where her mom's thoughts were

going. That would be one answer. "Did Nick autograph your books?"

"Not yet, and if he forgets, something tells me Nick Sinclair will be returning."

"What do you mean?"

"The way he looks at you—he'll be back."

"Really, Mom, he's barely even spoken to me this afternoon." And she wasn't going to give him another opportunity to ignore her. Pleading a headache, Taylor escaped upstairs as soon as she could. She unbraided her hair and brushed it, letting it fall softly around her shoulders, then changed into shorts and a shirt and considered her running shoes. As tempting as running away was, it would be rude, and Southern hospitality was one thing Michael *hadn't* drummed out of her. Beside the fact she'd promised her mother she wouldn't go out running alone.

She picked up her father's file instead and sat on her bed, searching for the detective's notes. Taylor frowned. Okay, where were they? She was certain she'd copied them. She flipped through the case file she'd profiled for Livy and found Wilson's notes and the copy of the letter her father had mailed near the back. She didn't remember putting them in the victim's folder. As she perused the notes, a knock interrupted her. "Who is it?" she barked.

"It's me, Abby." Her niece's voice sounded small.

"I'm sorry, honey, come on in."

The door opened, and Abby peeked around the door frame, her blue eyes huge. "Are you mad, Aunt Tay?"

"No, not mad, just kind of busy. But never too busy for you. Climb up here with me." Taylor set the files on the table beside her bed. "What's that in your hands?"

"I colored a picture for you during church. Daddy says coloring keeps me still. It's David and Goliath."

"Let me see." Taylor held the picture up. "Good job. I'll take this back to Newton with me."

"Why don't you stay here?"

"Oh, I have a job there and things I have to do. How are things going with you?" she asked, wrapping her arms around the girl's thin shoulders.

"Okay."

"Really?"

"Most of the time." Abby picked at a loose thread in the bedspread, and Taylor stroked her niece's hair. After a few minutes, Abby took a deep breath. "Did you and Mommy play together when you were my age?"

"We sure did."

"Did she look like me?"

Taylor grinned and poked Abby in the belly as she tickled her. "She looked a lot like you. She was *skinny* like you, and she had *freckles* like you."

Abby giggled and tried to wriggle away. Taylor held her fast, and she giggled again. "No, really, Aunt Tay. Do I look like my mommy?"

Taylor hugged her. "Except for your hair, you do. Her hair was almost the color of carrots."

Abby heaved a child-size sigh. "Why did she go away? Did I do something wrong?"

The questions echoed in Taylor's heart. The same questions she'd asked about her dad for twenty years. And no matter how many times Taylor told herself that it wasn't her fault her dad left, she never believed it, not down deep where it mattered. She had to do a better job convincing Abby.

"No, honey, you didn't do anything wrong. Sometimes adults do really dumb things. I want you to always remember that it wasn't your fault your mommy left."

"Promise?"

"I promise." Why couldn't she claim that same promise? Why did she feel responsible for her father's disappearance?

"Then why did she leave?"

"I'm not sure." Taylor chose her words carefully. "Sometimes a person's thinking gets messed up. They think that everything they do is wrong, and if they go away, everyone will be better off. That's what might have happened to your mommy."

"So, if her thinking gets better, she'll come home?"

Taylor didn't want to give Abby false hope. "I don't know. I hope so. But you have your dad, and your two grannas, and me and Livy, Grandpa Charlie . . . and Uncle Jonathan. So don't be sad."

"I'm not, but I miss my mommy." Abby turned so her face was even with Taylor's. She cocked her head to the side. "Aunt Tay, are *you* sad?"

"Sometimes."

"You shouldn't be, not if you have Jesus in your heart. Did Daddy tell you I'm going to be baptized before school starts?" Abby placed her small hands on either side of Taylor's face. Her blue eyes locked into Taylor's. "Do you have Jesus in your heart? He doesn't want you to be sad. He cares about you."

She'd believed that once. Enough to walk down the aisle one Sunday morning with Livy. "I—"

Jonathan's voice boomed through the closed door. "Abby, you in there? Time to go to play practice."

She squeezed Abby's hands. "We'll have to finish talking about this later. Come on in, Jonathan."

Jonathan cracked the door. "Y'all having a hen party?"

Abby giggled. "That's funny, Uncle Jonathan." She turned to Taylor. "Do you want to go with us? We're doing *The Wizard of Oz*, and I'm Dorothy."

"*The Wizard of Oz*?" She looked at Jonathan. "That's an undertaking. What part do you play?"

"I am Professor Marvel, aka the Wizard," Jonathan replied with a deep bow.

"Wow."

"Will you come with us?" Abby pleaded.

Taylor glanced toward the papers on the bedside table.

"I think she has other plans," her uncle said.

Taylor shot him a quizzical glance, but her uncle simply smiled.

"Another time," she promised.

Jonathan turned to leave. "Oh, by the way, Nick's looking for you. He's waiting downstairs. That's a nice young man you have there."

"He's not *my* nice young man." Why did her heart have to betray her, fluttering like a canary on steroids? "Did he say what he wanted?"

Jonathan's shoulders lifted in an exaggerated shrug. "Now why would he be telling me what he wanted?"

Taylor followed Jonathan and Abby down the stairs. Nick leaned by the door, sport coat slung over his shoulder and tie dangling from his hand. He straightened when he saw her. From the look in his eye, she knew he was remembering their kiss.

Abby stopped in front of Nick and cocked her head up at him. "Are you going to be Aunt Tay's boyfriend?"

"Abby!" Mortified, Taylor tried to avoid Nick's gaze.

"And on that note, we'll take our leave," Jonathan said with a chuckle. "Out the door, young lady, before your aunt skins you."

"Sorry about that," Taylor said. She almost wished she could follow Jonathan and Abby. "You were looking for me?"

"Would you like to drive down to the lake with me?" A smile teased at Nick's mouth. "That's if your headache is gone, or you don't have something else you need to do."

Her heart skipped a beat. "The lake?"

"Yep." The smile spread to his eyes, and the green flecks deepened. "The rest of your family said they would consider selling me twenty acres on the other side of the picnic area. Of course, you'd have to agree."

"You're kidding. That's great! Which piece of property?"

"Jonathan said something about it being part of the Roberts's place. Starts at an old oak tree?"

"I know where it is. We'll take the farm truck, but let me get my sneakers. Be right back."

Humming, she hurried upstairs to change shoes and put her hair into a ponytail.

Nick wanted her to go with him . . .

Scott forced another spoon of potato salad down his throat. If he didn't eat at least some of the food Kate Adams had brought, she'd stand over him until he did. A ceiling fan whirred softly, stirring the air on the porch. On the wall, an oversized weather gauge hovered at the ninety degree mark. Even so, he shivered as he sipped sweet tea and wished for whiskey.

"Scott, can I get you anything else?" Kate asked, swinging open the screen door. Her nose wrinkled when she noticed the tiny amount he'd eaten.

"No, ma'am. I think this is enough. Thank you," he added politely. His mama would be proud. He slouched in the swing, wishing Kate would leave. Where was the old man? Charlie. That was his name. He was a drinker. Scott could tell. "Where'd your husband go?"

Kate sat in the chair by the swing, her black eyes boring into his. Now he knew how a grasshopper felt pinned to a board.

"Won't do you any good to find him," she said. "He's not drinking now."

A slow flush burned up his neck. "It's not easy, stopping like this."

"I know, but do you want to be like my Charlie? Struggling to stay sober at his age?"

He shifted his gaze beyond Kate Adams to a nearby field.

"Do you want to get clean and stay that way?"

"Sure." He turned back to her, the word slipping easily from his mouth. Immediately, her eyes pinned him again. Sweat beaded his upper lip. "Everybody expects me to."

"No," Kate corrected him. "Everyone *wants*

you sober. There's a difference. The question is what do *you* want?"

Scott's mind scrambled for an answer. Instinctively, he knew his glib replies wouldn't work with this woman. He swallowed hard. Did he want to be sober, or did he want to keep living like this? He searched his heart. He couldn't remember the last time he'd stayed sober for a whole week. "I . . . don't know if I can."

"I won't tell you it'll be easy, but you can do it. God will help you."

"God? After everything I've done? No way." He wanted to look away again, but her gaze held him fast.

"We've all done terrible things, Scott. You don't get cleaned up to come to him. He cleans you up afterward."

Her words sparked a glimmering from the past. He'd learned all about God in Sunday school when he was a kid, but . . . "Would he really forgive me?"

The phone rang, and Scott jumped.

"Yes." Kate squeezed his hand. "We'll talk about this later. I better get that before it wakes Charlie."

Scott leaned back in the swing as Kate went to answer the phone.

"Yes, he's awake and doing fine." There was a pause. Her voice changed. "I'll tell him."

24

"About last night . . ." Nick's voice trailed off as the farm truck hit a rut in the road.

She knew that tone of voice. Had heard it before with Michael, and the boyfriend before him . . . she'd expected it all along. She rocked forward as the truck hit another rut. "Look, it was just a kiss or two. Don't put too much spin on it. I understand—we live in different worlds."

He shot her a startled look.

She pointed to herself then to him as she tried to hold her heart together. "You didn't think *I* thought you . . ."

"No, of course not," he said a little too quickly. "I—"

"It's okay, forget it." She turned and stared out the window as Pete waved at them from Jonathan's travel trailer. Circles ringed his sleeveless shirt and his tanned biceps glistened in the afternoon heat. She returned the wave. Ethan must have changed his mind about sending him to Jackson today.

"Pete Connelly, right?"

"Yeah. We went to high school together." Oak Grove loomed to her right. "I see Jonathan pulled off those old boards."

"He's repairing that old house?"

"He was before we received an offer on the sixty-five acres the house sits on. He and my dad grew up there." An unexpected shiver slid down her back. "A lot of the time, Oak Grove is where I am in my nightmares."

"You mentioned nightmares at the restaurant."

"Yeah. Well, this is where they take place. They get pretty wild sometimes with a clown chasing me."

"Clown? What's the significance of that?"

She took a shuddering breath. "I don't know. Except clowns have always terrorized me. But it doesn't end with the clown."

"It gets worse?"

She nodded. "About six months ago I was working a case. Wasn't called in until the last minute, and someone died. Sometimes the clown in my dreams is the shooter."

"Taylor, I'm so sorry. After I met you, I read about that case online. From what the article said, there was nothing you could do. That kid meant to kill his stepfather."

She closed her eyes. She'd tried to tell herself that over and over. Didn't stop the feeling that she'd failed.

"Have you been inside the house since you've come back home?"

"No. Things keep coming up. Not sure I want to explore by myself. Jonathan had said he'd come with me."

Nick slowed the truck. "Why don't we stop now? You wouldn't be by yourself, and exploring the place of your nightmares could—"

"No, thanks." He didn't want to date her but yet he wanted to be the white knight that chased away her inner demons? Not likely.

"On the way back, maybe?"

She bit her lip. "I'd rather ask Scott a few questions."

"Let me call Kate and see how he's doing." Nick took out his phone and called the bed and breakfast. After a brief conversation, he hung up. "Kate seems to think he's up to it. She said she'd tell him to expect us."

"Thanks."

"How about your dad's file? Did you get it yet?"

"Got it Friday afternoon. Tomorrow I'm going with Livy to interview the detective who investigated the case."

"That sounds promising. Learn anything you didn't know?"

She wrinkled her nose. "One of the cops who investigated his disappearance died suspiciously."

"Coincidence?"

"No such thing as coincidence when it comes to crime. Next on my list is to check the Logan Point newspapers printed around the time he disappeared. They're archived at the library."

"I'm a pretty good researcher. Why don't I do that for you?"

"I hate for you to bother." The lane forked. "Take the right lane. The old oak I used to climb should be just ahead."

"Wouldn't be any bother at all. And when you're out and about, you really need to be careful. Your mom reminded me of that after lunch."

She grunted. "She wasn't happy I went out running yesterday."

"I know. But she's right. Just because nothing's happened in the past few days doesn't mean the threat is gone."

"I'd like to think he's lost interest," Taylor said as they climbed out of the truck. At least that's what she hoped. She was more than a little frustrated with her inability to get into her stalker's mind and his on-again-off-again pursuit.

Unless her stalker *was* Scott. She tried to dismiss the thought—she'd settled in her mind that Scott didn't meet the profile. But with him incapacitated, it could explain why she hadn't received any more threats. She pushed the thoughts away and concentrated on showing Nick the land.

An hour and a half later, Taylor sat beneath the spreading limbs of the oak, listening to the soulful riffs of "Summertime" coming from Nick's harmonica. They'd walked the land, and he'd infused her with his enthusiasm. The plan he carried in his heart was perfect for the twenty acres. As he'd talked, she'd pictured the cabins, the repairs to the existing boathouse, even the kids. It'd be great to see kids romping these woods and swimming in the lake like she had.

Her head nodded to the slow rhythm of the song as Nick wound the music down and then sat quietly beside her. "I can play that on the piano," she said.

"You play the piano?"

"Learned how after my dad left." She looked at him. "Do you always carry your harmonica with you?"

"Usually." He sighed and tapped the harp against his knee. "Playing calms me, helps when I'm trying to make a hard decision."

"Buying this land?"

He nodded. "I'm pretty sure it'll be more than I've budgeted, but I keep thinking about how many lives could be changed. Without intervention, the boys I want to bring here don't have much of a chance. If they could just live a different kind of life for a few months, they could see they don't have to continue down the wrong road."

"It's a worthy goal."

"Can you imagine what it would be like for a boy who's known nothing but concrete and asphalt to come here?"

Nick's wistfulness captured her heart as a light breeze from the lake stirred the air. "You're going to do this, aren't you?"

"Depends on whether I can afford it."

"Did Jonathan quote you a price?"

"No. He said to look at it first, but Kate has already warned me that land around here will be high."

"Jonathan says we've been offered a million dollars for that sixty-five acres."

Air whooshed from Nick's lips. "That's more than fifteen thousand an acre." He glanced toward the water. "This will probably bring more, being on the lake." His shoulders slumped.

"Can you afford it?"

"It's a lot more than I've budgeted. Nonprofits don't usually buy prime real estate." He slid the harmonica in his shirt pocket. "There's enough from Angie's insurance policy to pay for it, but I'll need donations to build the cabins and run it. Potential donors might view the land purchase as extravagant."

"You don't have to advertise what you paid for it."

He gave her an odd look. "No, but they'll want to know, and I'll tell them."

Taylor thought about the boys he'd described and tried to imagine growing up in a big city, never knowing what it was like to roam the woods or swim in a lake. As a child, she'd never known anything else. Two swans glided from beneath the weathered boathouse, occasionally plunging their heads into the water, searching for food. Were they descendents of the ones who were here when she was a child?

Nick stirred beside her. "Kate says God will provide."

She bit her lip to keep from laughing. "Not even God can get my uncle to reduce his price."

"You never know . . ." He turned to her. "I try not to limit God."

"And I do. That's what you're really saying." She clasped her hands together and softly asked, "How can you trust God? He took your wife. Your brother almost killed himself . . ."

"So you think God doesn't care about me." Nick plucked a blade of grass and folded it in half. "I won't lie to you. I struggled with my faith when Angie died." He broke the end of the blade off. "But in the end, my faith is what sustained me."

Taylor absorbed his words. Then unfolding her legs, she stood and walked out on the pier past the boathouse, stopping to scoop up a couple of small stones. The lake stretched before her like a sheet of glass.

Abruptly, she sailed one of the stones out across the lake, and it rippled the water in their little cove with each skip. She turned and sailed another one and caught her breath as the rock startled one of the swans and it lifted off the lake. Years vanished, and she saw another swan in another time . . .

It'd been in autumn the year she turned seven, and she and her daddy had come to the lake to gaze at the night sky. She tried to count the stars. "Oh, Daddy, there must be a billion stars up there."

He threw back his head and laughed. "I'm sure there are, honey. Did you know God set each and every one in place and named them?"

Her father's laughter had startled a swan. She would never forget the sight of it lifting off the lake in the moonlight, her hand in her daddy's. They'd been a family.

She clenched her jaw. No, she'd only thought they were a family. It had all been a lie.

Still, she'd give anything to feel her daddy's hand wrapped around hers one more time.

She walked back to Nick. "Want to know why I don't agree with you?"

"If you'd like to tell me."

Taylor sat beneath the tree again, wrapping her arms around her knees. "Mom and Daddy took me to church every time the doors opened. He was a deacon, Sunday school teacher, you name it, he did it. When I was eight, I asked Jesus into my life. I believed God loved me. My daddy was so proud—so proud that the next week he walked out of my life. Didn't even stay around for my baptism."

She rested her chin on her knees. "When he first left, I believed with all my heart that if I prayed hard enough, God would bring him home. My Bible even told me he would. 'Ask and you will receive.' It didn't happen. I asked and I did not receive."

Overhead the haunting *kee-ee-ar* from a red-tailed hawk filled the air as it soared against the cobalt sky.

"That's when I decided if there *was* a God, either he wasn't powerful enough to bring my father home, or he wasn't listening to my prayers." She lifted her face toward Nick and narrowed her eyes. "So, don't tell me he has a plan for my life or cares about me."

Nick remained silent, and she got to her feet and walked to the end of the pier.

"Taylor."

Strong hands turned her around. When she wouldn't look at him, he lifted her face. His green-flecked eyes caught her gaze and held it.

"I wish I could take your pain away."

She allowed Nick to draw her into his arms and rested her head on his chest, feeling his strength wrap around her. "It's my fault he left. I did something wrong."

"You know that's not true." He stroked her back.

She relaxed into his embrace and wished she never had to move. Finally, she sighed. "I know. I even told my niece the exact same thing this afternoon about her mom . . . It just hurts so much."

"Oh, Taylor." He cupped her face in his hands.

Desire smoldered in his hazel eyes, and Nick lowered his head, capturing her lips. There was nothing tentative about this kiss. She slipped her hands around his neck and lost herself in his arms, giving back as much as he gave.

Holding Taylor, kissing her, came as naturally to Nick as breathing. In spite of his determination otherwise, he was falling in love with this beautiful woman.

He lifted his eyes, and his gaze caught the weathered boathouse. It'd stood the test of time. He turned his head from the lake to the land they had walked together. He wanted this land, and he wanted Taylor beside him, helping him build the camp. He simply didn't know how he'd get either one.

In the bedroom closet, Scott found a pair of jeans and a T-shirt Nick must have bought. With a shaky hand, Scott wiped sweat from his eyes. How could he sweat and freeze at the same time? He stripped off his pajamas and almost stumbled pulling on the jeans. Dr. Martin. She was coming to talk to him. Probably have him arrested.

Black dots swam before his eyes as he took a shaky step toward the door. He glanced back at his bed. One look and they'd know he was gone. He stuffed pillows on the mattress, then covered them with the blanket. Ought to buy him a little time. The door creaked open, and he held his breath as he looked down the hall. Empty.

His wallet, with his ID. He hadn't seen it in his room. He tiptoed across to where Nick slept and searched, finding it in the drawer with his brother's socks. Now to make it down the stairs without running into anyone, especially Kate. *"God loves you. He will forgive you."* Her words rang in his ears. Scott wished he could believe that.

At the bottom of the steps, he paused. Snoring came from the room across from the stairs. Scott peeked inside. The old man who'd babysat him this morning laid stretched out in a recliner, his mouth half-opened, dead to the world. Scott zeroed in on a half pint of whiskey on the desk in the corner. Scott licked his lips. He hesitated. The old man—Charlie—had been kind to him. His glance slid to a shelf above the desk, and he caught his breath. A Ford key ring with two keys dangled from a peg. *Yes!*

Charlie shifted in the recliner, and Scott froze, waiting for the snoring to resume. Finally, it did and he lifted the keys, then turned toward the door. He took two steps before the whiskey won, and he turned around, grabbing the bottle. The old man had never even opened it. Three twenties caught his eye in the open drawer below the bottle, and he stuffed them in his pocket.

A dart from his conscience pricked his heart.

He'd liked the old man and his stories about being a merchant seaman. And Charlie hadn't tried to make him eat. Scott fished one of the twenties from his pocket. He hated to take it all. But what if he needed it? *Wait.* It had to be after the first of the month, and he had money in the bank. The twenty went back in his pocket. He'd stop at an ATM in Memphis and withdraw some money— enough to pay the old man back. He eased the drawer a little wider. His hand froze as a .22 caliber pistol came into sight. A gun might come in handy. He stuck it in the waistband of his jeans and slipped out of the room.

Heat blasted his face as he stepped out the kitchen door, stealing his breath. Scott scanned the drive then the parking area in front of what looked like some sort of shop. Where was the old man's truck? No way could he get away from here without wheels. Then he spied a seventies model Ford pickup pulled beside the house. He was in business.

25

Nick slowed in front of Oak Grove, and Taylor tensed. "Why are we stopping? I told you I didn't want to stop here."

Her anxiety grew as he turned into the lane beside the old home place.

"I know, but let's talk about it." He parked the truck under a tree. "This place causes you nightmares. It's connected in some way with your dad. And it frightens you."

"But—"

Nick held up his hand. "You know that's true or you wouldn't have a problem exploring the place. So what about it scares you?"

Taylor licked her lips. "I . . . don't know."

She turned and stared at the empty house. What *was* she afraid of? That she had seen something she shouldn't have . . . perhaps the woman her father had danced with?

"You won't be by yourself." Nick's voice broke into her thoughts. "Whatever is in there, we can face together."

Taylor swallowed. "Okay."

The musty scent of old wood greeted them as they stepped into the foyer.

"Hey, this is just like your mom's house," Nick said.

"Only bigger. The living room and dining room were here." She pointed to the rooms to their left. "And over here"—Taylor's shoes made hollow echoing sounds as she walked across the hall—"was the library. Granna's bedroom was down the hall."

"How long has the house been empty?"

She tried to remember. Granna moved in with them a few months before her dad left. Jonathan moved out afterwards. "Almost twenty years."

"It's still in pretty good shape. And it's cool in here," Nick said. "Must be the high ceilings and trees."

They wandered down the hallway that divided the house, and Taylor halted at the basement door. A shiver ran down her spine. The door in her dreams. With her stomach churning, she touched the glass doorknob. *Don't go down there.* The voice from her dreams.

An invisible band squeezed her chest, cutting off her air. Nick said something, but the beat of her heart drowned out his words. Tremors shook her body. With the walls closing in, she slid to the floor and wrapped her arms around her stomach.

"Taylor, it's all right." Nick's body warmed her as he knelt and drew her into his arms. "You're safe. Everything will be okay. Look into my eyes. It's Nick."

His voice penetrated the fog in her head, soothing her jagged nerves. Slowly, she raised her eyes. "Nick?"

"Breathe. Slow and easy."

"What happened? What am I doing on the floor?"

"I don't know. You freaked out."

The basement . . . the nightmares. She couldn't live this way. "Help me up. I . . . I have to face this."

"I don't think so. We'll come back another time."

"No!" She pulled away from Nick and climbed to her feet. "Help me do this."

"Are you sure?"

No, she wasn't sure. Taylor swallowed, trying to wet her parched throat. With a deep breath, she twisted the doorknob.

Silently, it swung open, and Taylor peered down the pitch-black steps, her heart still hammering against her ribs. A silver Maglite hung on the wall. Another breath, then she slipped the flashlight from its hook and flicked it on. Light arced into the darkness.

"Let me hold it, and you grab that rail there," Nick said, pointing to the narrow banister along the wall.

Halfway down, the skin on the back of her neck prickled. Her fingers curled tighter around the rail as stale, dank air filled her nostrils, and she tried not to hyperventilate. Nick shined the light ahead of her, and briefly it reflected something shiny at the bottom of the steps. "What's that?"

"Where?"

"There." They stepped onto the basement floor, and she guided the light to where she'd seen the sparkle. Something was caught between the bracing and the step.

Taylor bent and cautiously ran her finger along the dried-out crack between the step and brace. A metal ring? Yes. And it was attached to a smooth metal object. She tugged on the loop, but it wouldn't budge. Taylor traced her index finger around a barely visible double curve. Her heart caught in her throat.

Could it be her necklace? Taylor broke her nail as she dug furiously in the wood around the metal. She pulled on the object again, and it shifted.

"Let me help you." Nick put his weight against the bracing.

"Wait," she said as the pendant slipped deeper in the crack, leaving only the loop visible. She grasped the loop. "Now."

Nick pushed, and slowly she inched the pendant upward until it was free.

Transfixed, Taylor stared at the small object in her hand. "Taylor" was inscribed on one side. She turned it over. "Love always, Daddy."

The relentless drumbeat of her pulse pounded in her temples. Taylor's fingers closed over the gold heart, and she clasped it to her chest, remembering when her dad had fastened it around her neck, his fingers clumsy on the tiny clasp.

She recalled looking for him so they could go to the airport. Where did he go? She remembered. To the basement to find Jonathan. And she came down here to tell him she was ready . . .

The stairs were dark. She clutched the heart so tightly the chain broke in her fingers. Then she saw him. Her daddy stood in front of the pool table, his back to her. Daddy! His name froze in her throat. Someone was with him, and they were dancing. Impressions of red hair and flowing clothes flashed through her mind. Who was she?

Taylor slipped behind the stairs, crouching in the shadows. Where was her necklace? It'd been wrapped in her fingers, and now it was gone. Shouting distracted her.

"You can't—"

"You're not stopping me!" Her dad's voice.

She cringed and slapped her hands over her ears.

"Taylor! Are you okay?"

Nick's voice snapped her to the present. Slowly he came into focus, and her gaze dropped to the pendant in her hand.

"I . . . I was here that day. My dad argued with someone. Whoever it was tried to keep him from leaving."

"Do you remember who it was?"

She shook her head. "I . . . think it was the woman I see in my dreams sometimes." She stared at Nick. "I don't want to think it, but he must have been having an affair. Maybe he saw me hiding behind the stairs and knew he'd been caught."

"What else do you remember?" Nick asked.

Taylor tried to pull the memory out. "There was a pool table here, and Dad stood beside it with his back to me. There was a woman with him. They were dancing . . . no, arguing . . . no . . ." She shook her head. "I don't know what they were doing or who she was."

She turned toward the steps. "I hid here, behind the steps," she said, pointing to the open stairway. "Even with a light on, this corner is dark."

"Did anyone see you?" Nick asked.

"I don't think so."

"What did the other person look like?"

Taylor stared where the pool table had been that day. She could almost see the other person. Red hair, loose clothes, then the image disappeared, replaced by someone sitting at the desk that had been beyond the pool table. Was it the same person? Then the memory was gone, leaving only the empty basement. She flicked the light around the room. Nothing but concrete walls, the old fireplace that had been sealed for no telling how long, cobwebs, dust, and the door to the tunnels. Nothing that would unlock her memory.

Nick walked to the door near the back of the basement. "Where does this lead to?"

"The tunnels."

"As in passageways?"

She nodded. "Oak Grove was a station on the Underground Railroad, and the tunnels were built to smuggle slaves to the caves near the bluffs, where they could rest for the next leg of their journey. Then they would make their way to the boathouse down at the lake under cover of darkness and be loaded into small boats that carried them to the river and on up North."

"Same boathouse we were just at?" He slapped his forehead. "Sorry, stupid question."

"Yeah. There are a lot of boathouses on the lake," she said with a grin as her cell phone chirped, startling her. She dug it from her pocket and checked the ID. "It's Livy," she said and answered. "What's up?"

"Remember the woman who was murdered the other day? The feds have called everyone in on the case, and I mentioned you to the agent in charge. He'd like you to sit in on the meeting. How about it?"

"What time?" Taylor was both honored and amazed at the invitation.

"In forty-five minutes."

"Just a sec, Livy." Could she make it to Memphis that quickly? She covered the phone and looked over at Nick.

"Do you need to get going?" he asked.

Taylor explained to him about the FBI meeting, and he said he would hurry her home.

She nodded and spoke to Livy again. "I'll try to be there by the time the meeting starts."

After she hung up, they climbed the stairs and hurried to the farm truck. "Will it be too late to talk with Scott when I get back?"

"Call me. I'll see how he feels."

They pulled onto the lane leading back to the house, and Nick turned to her. "So the FBI wants your input. Ever think about going to work for them?"

She shook her head. "I worked with them in Atlanta on the prostitute murders. I don't think I can handle the violence an agent encounters day in and day out."

"That would be hard." As they neared the house he said, "Those tunnels. Do you think I could explore them? They'd make a great backdrop for a book."

"Sure. Just don't ask me to go with you." She shivered. "I wouldn't be able to breathe down there, but my mom might guide you. Jonathan said she explored every square inch."

"I'll talk to her about it one day next week. And tell Jonathan I'll call him tomorrow about the land."

They parked the farm truck beside Nick's convertible and got out. Taylor smiled at him. "I hate to run, but . . ."

He brushed his knuckles across her cheek. "I understand. Just be careful."

Her heart fluttered. "I'm sure I'll be back before dark."

Taylor turned and hurried toward the back door, pausing to watch as Nick drove away. She'd been right. He was a good man. One she could see herself trusting . . . maybe even loving. With a sigh, she stepped inside. Her mother and uncle sat at the kitchen table.

"I'm going to run into Memphis—" Her mom's red, puffy eyes stopped her. "What's wrong?"

Her mom pushed a Memphis newspaper toward Taylor. "This."

Taylor's heart sank as she read the headline. *"Cold Case Files—Man Still Missing after 20 Years."* A computer-generated image of her father showed how he would look today.

"Are you responsible for this?" Jonathan demanded.

"Of course not." She scanned the article.

"We've gotten on with our lives." The same thing Mom said yesterday.

She skipped down to a quote from Lieutenant Rob Wilson.

"At the time, Martin's disappearance mystified me. Man just vanished. The case always nagged at me, and I think I know why now. One of these days I'm going to write a book, and this case will be in it."

The reporter asked Wilson to share his solution, but the lieutenant declined. As she read on, she noted several references to her father's charitable work, probably gleaned from the *Logan Point Tribune* archives at the library. That was one stop she could put at the bottom of her list. Had there been anything important in the archives, the reporter would have discovered it. She stared at the computer-generated photo. There was a strong resemblance to Jonathan.

"We weathered it before, we will again." Steel rang in her mom's voice.

"If someone else doesn't keep it stirred up." He crumpled the newspaper into a ball. "Enough of this. Did you and Nick look at the land?"

"That's where I've been. He loved it, said he'd call you tomorrow. And on the way back, we stopped at the old house. Look what I found." She fished the pendant from her pocket and held it out.

"The necklace your father gave you!" Her mom reached her hand out and grasped the gold heart.

Jonathan leaned forward. "Where did you find it?"

"Wedged into the bottom step in the basement. The flashlight beam caught it." Taylor slipped the pendant in her pocket, and a memory surfaced. A birthday party, Jonathan dressed as a clown juggling balls, wild yellow hair. "You . . ." She swallowed. "You were a clown."

He frowned. "For a while."

Was her uncle the clown in her dreams? "I remember now. My ninth birthday party. You scared me."

"You scared *me*. I was juggling and you started screaming and shaking. I didn't know what was wrong, but after I changed out of the costume, you calmed down. And I never put it on around you again."

"I remember that," her mom said.

"I still don't like clowns." Taylor checked her watch. "I need to get going, but I hope to be home before dark."

"Be sure you do that," her mom said. "Storms are predicted for later this evening."

Nick parked under the oak tree beside the bed and breakfast, his heart aching to help Taylor. Someone out there wanted to hurt her, and she took unnecessary risks, trusted in herself a little too much. Just like Angie. He pushed away the thought, but it would not stay away.

With a troubled heart, he entered the house through the back door and checked on Scott. He found him burrowed under a quilt, asleep. Taylor still thought his brother was involved in her stalking case, that even if he wasn't the stalker, he knew something about it. He hoped she was wrong.

A commotion stirred downstairs, and Nick closed the door before the noise woke Scott and walked to the landing.

"Kate, where'd you hide my keys?" Charlie Adams's voice bellowed from below.

"What are you talking about?" Kate answered.

"My keys. They're gone. That pint of whiskey too."

Whiskey? Maybe leaving Scott with Charlie this morning hadn't been such a good idea.

"Anything wrong?" he asked.

Kate and her husband looked up at him.

"She hid my truck keys," Charlie huffed. Wiry white hair protruded from beneath his Cardinals baseball cap. "Ain't right."

"Charlie, I haven't had your keys. Or the liquor." Kate sniffed the air. "Have you been drinking again?"

"I ain't ever opened that bottle. Just had the pint settin' on the dresser. Easier to stay quit when I know I can get it if I want to. You had no call to mess with my things."

"For the last time, I didn't touch your keys. They're probably wherever that whiskey is. Did you look to see if you left them in the truck?"

Nick came down the stairs. "I'll check for him," he said, glancing at Charlie's bare feet under his bib overalls. "Where's it parked?"

"Right side of the house in the shade," Charlie said. "Appreciate it."

"Next to the oak tree? I parked there five minutes ago. There's no truck."

"It's gotta be there. I ain't moved it."

A bad feeling started in the pit of Nick's stomach and spread. "Let me see if Scott knows anything."

He took the steps two at a time and didn't bother to knock at Scott's door. "Do you know where

Charlie's truck is?" he asked as he burst into the room.

Scott didn't move. Nick jerked the blanket away.

Pillows.

26

Blue lights on the side of the road sent ice rushing through Scott's veins. Surely the old man hadn't discovered his truck was gone yet. No, the Memphis cop was ticketing a speeder. His relief was short-lived. They'd be looking for him. Soon. He slapped his forehead. "Idiot."

Borrowing Charlie's truck had been dumb. But he couldn't wait around for them to come and arrest him. He regretted telling Nick he'd been at Dr. Martin's house that night. If he couldn't convince his own brother he hadn't attacked her and that sheriff, Dr. Martin sure wouldn't believe him. Or the cops. He had to get away.

Scott glanced down at the pint of whiskey in the seat, still unopened. His fingers shook as he wrapped them around the bottle, desire blind-siding him. *No.* The last thing he needed was to get pulled over for drunk driving and for somebody to find the gun he'd stashed in the glove compartment. Not to mention he was driving a stolen truck.

His insides quivered like a strummed guitar. He needed to rest. And his mouth tasted like he'd been drinking with pigs. Should've brought a bottle of water instead of the whiskey. An exit sign on I-240 loomed ahead. Perkins Road exit. Wasn't there a city park somewhere close by? He whipped off the Interstate. Audubon Park. Nick and Angie used to take him there for picnics. A few minutes later, Scott pulled into the entrance to the park and found an empty spot beneath a huge oak. Not many people around. Maybe no one would notice him. He scanned the area and couldn't find a water fountain.

Scott slid the whiskey under the seat and rolled down the window, wishing he'd never left Kate's house. He shouldn't have run. Nick would be so angry, he'd never help him . . . Dr. Martin wanted to put him in jail . . . but what if she'd only wanted to talk to him? His thoughts chased through his head like a mouse caught in a maze.

A light breeze wafted through the cab of the truck. His head nodded . . . so tired . . . maybe he'd just sleep, then figure out what to do. Scott nestled his head against the door and slipped into a troubled sleep as Kate's words whispered in his heart. *God loves you.*

"Agent Keller, Taylor Martin," Livy said.

Taylor tucked the interview notes she and Livy had discussed for tomorrow's meeting with

Lieutenant Wilson in her purse and held out her hand to the silver-haired FBI agent. Unlike his subordinates, he'd shed his coat and tie. Even so, she sensed a no-nonsense manner.

"I'm glad you could join us, Dr. Martin. I read the paper you published on the need for a stronger focus on victim profiling. Excellent work." He checked his watch. "Time to get started. I'll be interested in hearing your take on the victims."

Livy gave her a discreet thumbs-up as they walked toward the door. When Taylor turned the corner, she almost ran over Zeke Thornton. She didn't know which of them was more surprised. Taylor recovered first. "I thought your conference ended yesterday."

"It did, but I got to talking with a couple of the Memphis detectives and found out the FBI was taking over this case. Billy's handling the investigation back in Newton as well as I could, and I thought I might learn something that would help in other investigations. How about you— you're not FBI."

"Agent Keller invited me."

His eyes widened. "I'm impressed." Zeke licked his bottom lip. "There's something else . . . I want to apologize for the way I've acted in the past. I've never thought victim profiling accomplished anything, but after the Coleman case, I figured out I was wrong. Should have already told you." He offered his hand. "Okay?"

"Thanks," she said, accepting his hand. She'd waited a year to hear him admit that. "You want to sit with Livy and me?"

He nodded toward a couple of detectives. "Think I'll sit with them."

Taylor took the seat next to Livy, then turned off her cell as Agent Keller handed out packets.

"We have four victims prior to this case. Raped, beaten, and strangled, each murdered in a different state, seemingly random. The only common denominator is they were all prostitutes, and their mouths were glued shut."

Ladies of the street were the easiest target. Taylor sorted through the photos and tried to block out memories of the Atlanta case as she focused on the pictures of the women when they were alive—before this monster did his work. She wrote each of their names on her notepad along with a brief physical description. Straight black hair, blue eyes, with ages from early to late twenties. "When and where was the first murder?" she asked.

"The first murder was ten years ago in New York City." Keller pinned a photo of the youngest victim.

Someone else asked about the other locations.

"Florida, Georgia, Louisiana, and now Tennessee."

Her hand stilled as Keller wrote the states on a whiteboard and put a date by each name. She'd lived in four of the five states at the time of the murder.

"Dr. Martin, do you have any comments?" Keller asked.

She looked over her notes. "At first glance, the only thing these five women have in common is their looks and occupation. A good percentage of violent crime victims have come in contact with their perpetrator in the past, but I don't think that's the case here. I think with these murders you'll find the connection in *his* past. He has a mental illness that may or may not be obvious, but at some point in his life someone wronged him, and it triggered emotions he couldn't deal with. Perhaps a woman he fixated on scorned him, but he wouldn't kill her because he believes one day she will be his. So, he finds a substitute. These five women had the bad luck of having characteristics similar to the woman he's fixated on, and they were readily available."

"Thank you. Good observations. Questions anyone?"

Several questions were asked, then Agent Keller moved on to other details of the murders. When they finally took a break, Taylor had five front and back pages of notes, and Keller had asked her opinion twice more. "Whew," she said to Livy as they stood. "Keller can talk faster than anyone I've ever known."

"He's good, all right, but so are you." Livy

glanced toward the photos of the women. "Does the first victim remind you of anyone?"

Taylor walked to the board where Keller had pinned the photos. There was something vaguely familiar about the victim. All the victims, actually. "Not really."

"The way she wore her hair reminds me of you ten years ago."

"You're kidding." Livy wasn't and Taylor looked at the photo closer. The woman's black hair was pulled up in a ponytail, Taylor's regular hairstyle in high school. She supposed she could see a slight resemblance.

"Are you sure you don't mind interviewing Detective Wilson by yourself tomorrow?"

"Be better if you were there, but I understand." Taylor glanced at her watch. Almost eight. Less than an hour before dark. "I'm going to scoot out of here and see if Nick will let me talk to Scott."

Livy nodded. "I'll take good notes, and if a miracle happens and I can get away tomorrow morning, I'll meet you at Wilson's. Ten o'clock?"

"That'd be great." Taylor gathered her purse and notebook and looked around for Agent Keller. He stood near the doorway.

"You're not leaving us, are you?" Keller asked.

"I need to work on another case." Out of the corner of her eye, she saw Zeke get on the elevator and waved. "But thanks for letting me sit in."

"I appreciate your insight on the victims. If

you're ever interested in a career with the FBI, give me a call."

"Thanks, but no thanks," she said with a smile. The high praise lifted her spirits, and she hummed as she rode the elevator down to the first floor.

Heavy clouds had hastened nightfall. Goose bumps raised on her arms as she crossed Washington Street to the parking garage. She would not panic. Lightning arced across the black sky, revealing heavy clouds to the west. A gust of wind pushed against her, carrying the coolness of hail in it. The storm hadn't crossed the Mississippi River yet—hopefully she'd make it home before it started.

As she started her car, Taylor slid her cell phone from her pocket and turned it on. Immediately, a beep warned of a low battery. She groaned. She'd left her car charger in Washington. Taylor glanced at the cell screen. Five missed calls. Three from Nick, one from her mom, the last one from Livy.

She hit the call-back button and Livy's number dialed. No answer. She glanced at the fuel gauge. Less than an eighth of a tank. Why hadn't she noticed that earlier? She had no idea if there was a gas station in downtown Memphis. Surely she had enough gas to make it to the Walmart in Logan Point. She dialed her mom's number.

"Taylor where . . . you? Nick's . . . reach . . ."

"I'm in a car garage, and you're breaking up.

I'm on my way, but I have to stop at Walmart."

"Don't—"

The phone died.

Scott stared at the families in the park, walking, spread out on blankets enjoying a picnic; in a far field, a few people played baseball. He and Nick and Angie had done that. His thoughts drifted . . .

"Why did we have to leave Seattle?"

"You know why." Digger poured more of the amber liquid into Scott's glass. *"You did those bad things . . ."*

"No! I didn't do it!"

A fly buzzed near Scott's ear. He jerked upright, slapping the air. Sweat dribbled down his face. He must have dozed off. Day had slipped into night, yet the air remained still and hot. Lightning flashed to the west followed by a low rumble. Maybe not for long.

The conversation with Digger returned. Did he really do what Digger said he did? No! He didn't hurt that sheriff. Or Dr. Martin. Did he? Digger was his friend—he wouldn't lie to him. He pressed his hand to his sweaty head. He needed to talk to him. But first he had to get a phone.

Thirty minutes later Scott exited a Target store with a throwaway phone, a soda, two candy bars, and thirteen dollars and fifty-three cents of Charlie's money he'd borrowed. He'd decided not to use his debit card, fearing the cops might trace him. It hadn't rained, but the threat still held. He dug through his billfold, looking for his friend's number, and found the photo of the two of them—Digger with his arm draped over Scott's shoulders. He put it back in the billfold and kept looking for Digger's cell phone number, finally finding it. Digger answered on the second ring.

"What's going on, Scotty boy? Where are you?"

"At a Target store." Scott climbed into the truck cab.

"Doesn't tell me much."

"It's near Audubon Park." He couldn't remember the name of the street. "Dr. Martin wants to talk to me. You gotta help me. Tell her I didn't do it."

"You been smoking too much dope, boy?"

"No! I'm sober. You—"

Sirens wailed into the opposite end of the parking lot. Scott snapped the phone shut. Maybe the cops made Charlie's truck, and they were coming after him. Or maybe Digger told them where he was. He shook his head. He wasn't thinking straight. Digger didn't have time. But he had to get out of Memphis.

Immediately, his phone chirped. He ignored it as he eased the truck out of the parking lot into the night. Maybe he didn't need to trust anyone.

Or, maybe he just needed to do what was right. Take the truck home and face the music.

27

Meeting or no meeting, he wished Taylor would answer her phone or text he'd sent. The call went to voice mail again, and Nick left another message for her to call him. Reluctantly, he scrolled to his recent calls for the Martin number. He'd already talked to Allison once, explaining that Scott had disappeared.

He never dreamed Scott would steal Charlie's truck. He'd asked himself over and over why his brother had run. And came up with only one answer—he was afraid to talk to Taylor. According to Kate, after Scott learned Taylor wanted to talk with him, he'd been nervous and then disappeared upstairs. Evidently, when Charlie was taking a nap, his brother had snuck into Charlie's room and stolen the truck keys. And the whiskey along with sixty dollars. And Charlie's .22 caliber pistol was missing, presumably taken by Scott. Nausea burned up Nick's esophagus. Evidently, he didn't know his brother at all. He touched the Martin number, and it redialed.

"Hello?" Allison answered.

"Have you heard from Taylor?" he asked.

"She just called, but the phone went dead and now she won't answer. I didn't get a chance to tell her that Scott's missing. Ethan just left to intercept her at the exit off the bypass. She said something about stopping at Walmart, so Jonathan is going to wait there in case Ethan misses her."

"Call me if you hear from her." He hung up and paced the floor as thunder rumbled overhead. Finally, he grabbed his keys. Driving to Walmart was infinitely easier than waiting.

Lightning exploded from an ominous wall cloud that dipped almost to the ground. Taylor pressed the trigger on the pump at Walmart and willed the gas to flow faster. She did not want to get caught in the approaching storm. She stopped at ten gallons and didn't wait for the receipt.

Wind rocked the Rav4 as Taylor drove the SUV faster than she should on the dark highway from town to Coley Road. Headlights flashed in her rear mirror and were lost as she rounded a curve. Another bolt arced across the sky, then darkness swallowed the night once more.

A vehicle approached from behind.

Fast.

Someone else wanted to get home before the storm hit. She hugged the right side of the road, giving a wide berth for the car to come around. High beams reflected in her rearview mirror, blinding her as the vehicle rode her bumper. Had to be a truck—lights were too high to be a car. She tapped the brake pedal, but the warning went unheeded.

Taylor slowed for the driver to pass, but the truck stayed on her bumper. Her chest tightened, cutting her breath. This wasn't someone wanting to get home. She gripped the steering wheel and stomped the accelerator. The truck matched her speed. She scanned the road ahead and glimpsed pin dots of light. Another vehicle.

Too far away.

The dots disappeared, leaving her alone with the truck once more.

Another two miles before she turned onto Coley Road. She envisioned the winding, lonely road. No, not going there. Her headlights picked up a road sign. The old Memphis–Logan Point Highway that looped back into town. Perfect. She slowed to make the turn. Her body jerked against her seat belt as the truck rammed the Rav4.

Taylor slammed the accelerator to the floor and shot forward, missing the road. The lights swung out and the vehicle pulled even. She cut her eyes toward it.

A flash of light.

Her window exploded.

Another flash.

The jerk was shooting at her!

She yanked the steering wheel to the right and braked hard. The SUV fishtailed. Taylor fought for control as the front tire skidded into loose gravel.

"No!" The scream hung in the air as the Rav4

flipped over. Time slowed to a standstill as glass flew everywhere. The SUV landed hard, jarring her grip loose from the steering wheel. It flipped again, landing on its wheels.

Like a shroud, deathly silence enveloped her.

Her head was braced against the steering wheel. Blood trickled between her eyes and down her nose, dripping on her pants. She raised her head up, but dizziness forced it back down as the odor of gasoline permeated the air. *Got to get out.* Taylor fumbled to unfasten the seat belt.

Footsteps crunched toward her.

She stilled her hand, her whole body. The footsteps stopped. Taylor held her breath and barely cracked her eyelids. Legs stood close enough to touch through the shattered window. Faded jeans. A man's legs. Her mind snapped a picture to recall later.

If later came.

The deathly quiet was broken only by his raspy breathing.

Rrrack.

No! She'd heard that sound too many times not to know a bullet had just been chambered. She didn't want to die.

Dear God, please, no! She waited for the bullet. *If you're real, God, help me.*

Click.

The empty sound echoed in her brain.

She struggled not to move.

The distant sound of tires broke the tomblike silence. The man spun around, and once again gravel crunched, fast, like he was running. Seconds later, a motor revved to life and tires squealed. Taylor released her pent-up breath and gulped another one, inhaling the musty scent of rain mingled with gas fumes.

Gas. Hot motor. Her fingers fumbled with the seat belt again. Nausea came in waves, and her chest heaved against the seat belt.

Got to get out . . .

Nick's unease grew as he turned off Coley Road onto the narrow highway to Logan Point. The impending storm did little to calm him. He hadn't felt such a strong need to pray for someone since Angie lay dying in his arms.

Minutes later, he glimpsed headlights from the opposite direction. Maybe it was Taylor. He slowed. The approaching lights blazed in his eyes, and Nick flashed his high beams. "Come on, bud, dim them."

The vehicle roared past. Half-blinded by the lights, he couldn't identify the type of vehicle, much less the driver. He was certain it wasn't Taylor, though. She had too much sense to drive that fast on this crooked road. He drove on. If he didn't meet her by the time he reached Walmart, he'd wait at the exit.

Half-dollar-sized raindrops splattered his windshield. He rounded a curve and spied a car on the side of the road. Wasn't Taylor's Rav4, but he slowed. Twin beams of light blazed from the tree line. Someone was in trouble.

He pulled onto the shoulder of the road and jumped out just as the thunderstorm broke. Driving rain whipped him across the highway. A man raced toward him.

"There's a car in the ditch, and a woman trapped in it."

Nick could barely hear the man over the din of the rain.

"I can't get the door open. You got something we can use for a lever?"

Nick wiped rain from his eyes. "Have you called 911?"

"My wife did."

Nick ran back to his Mustang and threw open his trunk. There was a tire iron somewhere. There. He grabbed it and sprinted toward the wrecked car.

Lightning revealed a gold Rav4. Nick's heart almost stopped. In the driver's seat, Taylor struggled with the seat belt. Blood flowed from a gash on her head.

No! He clambered down the ditch and jerked on the door jammed into the frame. Taylor turned toward him, her eyes frantic. The odor of gasoline filled his nostrils.

"Nick, help me!"

• • •

Hopelessly lost, Scott slowed the old truck as flashing lights revealed an ambulance on the side of the road. He was a goner. He searched for somewhere to turn around so he could return to Memphis, but a flashlight already motioned him forward. Blood thumped in his head, drowning out everything else. He eased forward and caught sight of Nick's convertible, then a woman being loaded into the ambulance. Dr. Martin. For a second, he didn't breathe.

Whatever happened to her, the cops would say he did it. He thought his chest would burst as he came alongside the state trooper, but evidently the trooper wasn't looking at license plates, only directing traffic. He signaled Scott to keep moving.

Once past the wreck, Scott pulled his thoughts together. He wanted to do the right thing, but he didn't want to go to jail. Maybe if he called Nick, talked to him, his brother would help him out of this mess. He pulled over on the side of the road and punched in Nick's number, then waited, his thumb hovering over the end button.

"Hello." Nick's voice sounded strained.

"I shouldn't have run away."

"Scott? Where are you? Did you force Taylor off the road?"

"No!" Why would Nick think that? "Is she going to be okay?"

"How did you know she was hurt?" The hollow sound of Nick's voice filled his ear. "So help me, Scott, if you're the one who hurt her . . ."

"You gotta believe me, Nick. I'd never hurt her."

"Then how did you know?"

"I was bringing Charlie's truck back when I saw the wreck."

"Then why didn't you stop? Turn yourself in?"

"I got scared."

"I'm not buying your story. Scott, where are—"

Scott pressed the red button, cutting Nick off. It was no use. Nobody believed him, not even his brother. He rested his head against the steering wheel. He had to get out of Logan Point before someone recognized Charlie's truck. But where could he hide?

His cell rang and he answered it. "Nick, I promise, I didn't hurt Dr. Martin."

"Taylor's been hurt?" Digger's voice crackled through the receiver.

"Somebody ran her off the road, and Nick thinks I did it. She's hurt. Bad. But I didn't do it, I promise."

"I believe you, Scotty boy."

Silence filled the airwaves.

"You still there, Digger? Where are you?"

"I'm out of town, but I'm on my way home. Call your attorney. He won't turn you in."

"Why can't you help me?"

"You don't need me, you need a lawyer."

"I don't know—"

"Do it, Scott."

Nick's gut wrenched as the ambulance doors closed. Just like the surgery doors that swallowed Angie's gurney. He couldn't do it again. Wouldn't.

His phone vibrated in his pocket, and he fished it out. *Scott!*

"Why did you hang up?" Nick walked away from the ambulance.

"You gotta believe me. I was bringing Charlie's truck back."

"Take the truck home now and wait for me."

"No, they'll arrest me." Panic filled his voice.

"Then go to your girlfriend's and wait for me."

Silence filled the airway.

"Scott!"

His brother had hung up on him again. Nick jammed his phone in his pocket and hurried toward his car.

"Hey, Sinclair, wait up."

He turned. Sheriff Ben Logan strode toward him. Oh, great. Their earlier conversations about Scott's disappearance had been tense. He waited, dreading the new questions.

"I thought I told you to stay put in case your brother came back to Kate's," Ben said.

"I took that as a suggestion. Besides, Kate and Charlie were there."

"Good thing, I guess." Ben slipped a notepad from his shirt pocket. "You think your brother did this to Taylor?"

"I . . ." War raged in Nick's head. *"You gotta believe me, Nick. I'd never hurt her."* But he had run away. And he had a gun. Not telling Ben that he'd talked to Scott was the same as lying, and it ate at his insides.

Why did he keep holding on to his brother's innocence? Because he knew his brother. But what if it turned out that Nick didn't know him at all? He took a deep breath. "Scott didn't do this. He couldn't. But I think he might know who did. Except, I don't think he realizes he knows."

Gasoline fumes lingered in the air, and he glanced toward the Rav4, where a crew worked to get it loaded on a wrecker.

"It's a wonder the car didn't blow," Ben said.

"Yeah." Nick wanted to punch something, or someone.

"I need your help." The sheriff flipped his pad to a new page. "Taylor couldn't give me a description of the assailant or even the type of vehicle, only that it might've been a truck. Did you meet anyone before you reached the scene?"

The speeding vehicle. "I did. They were flying. High beams, like on a truck."

Ben scribbled in his pad, then looked up. "Start at the beginning."

"I was looking for Taylor. Allison had—" Nick

sucked in a breath. "Has anyone called her?"

"Her line's busy. The storm may have knocked out her power. I'm sending a deputy as soon as I can cut one loose from the scene. You were saying?"

Nick cleared his throat. He didn't like what he saw in Ben's eyes. Not suspicion exactly, more like the sheriff believed Nick was holding something back. Now was the time to tell him about Scott's call. But if he did . . .

"I'd been trying to reach Taylor to let her know Scott had disappeared, but she didn't answer my calls. So I called her mom and found out Taylor was on her way home. Allison told me Ethan and Jonathan had left to look for her. It sounded like a good plan. I never saw either of them."

"How about your brother. Have you seen him?"

Nick hesitated, then shook his head. "I've talked with him, though. Claims he was bringing Charlie's truck home when he saw the accident, so he must have passed by here. I didn't see him and don't have a clue where he is now." A weight lifted from his shoulders.

He turned as the ambulance pulled out onto the road, the siren piercing the air until the night swallowed the red whirling lights. Nick's throat tightened. There'd be no one to meet Taylor at the hospital.

Ben cleared his throat. "Something going on between you two?"

"I, ah . . ." Nick sucked in a breath. "She's a special lady."

"Yeah," Ben said softly. "Go with her. I'll catch you at the ER later."

Nick hesitated. He didn't know if he could walk through those hospital doors and be told Taylor had died.

But neither could he not go.

28

Scott didn't know what to do. Would Ethan even help him after what happened at their last meeting? He grimaced, remembering the blow he'd landed on Ethan's jaw because he wouldn't give him an advance. Another reason he had to quit drinking.

He breathed a sigh of relief when he crossed into Tennessee. He needed to figure out where he was going. Nick's house. At least he could sleep there. Fifteen minutes later, he pulled into Nick's drive and got out. His phone chirped. He let it ring. The front door was locked, and he went to the back. Locked as well. Scott kicked it. "Ow!"

His phone chirped again just as a light flashed from the next-door neighbor's yard.

"Nick, that you?" The question came from the neighbor's yard.

Scott hopped in the truck and backed out of the

drive. *Nosey neighbor*. A few minutes later he pulled onto the Bill Morris Parkway. He didn't know where he was going or what he was going to do . . . maybe he did need to call Ethan. Scott ran his tongue over his dry lips. Maybe Digger was right. Ethan *was* still his lawyer, and attorneys had to help their clients. He remembered reading that somewhere. Scott punched in Ethan's number.

"Trask speaking."

"Uh, Ethan? It's Scott Sinclair. I need a lawyer."

Scott's words seemed to have struck his attorney mute.

Finally, Ethan spoke. "I'm glad you called."

Sirens sounded through the phone. Scott's gut twisted. "I need to see you."

"You're breaking up. Give me a second to step outside."

Scott heard Ethan tell someone he needed to take a call, then the sounds of walking. "Don't hang up," Ethan said, his voice low.

Scott had almost ended the call.

"Where are you?" Ethan spoke normally now.

"In Memphis." Scott had no idea where, then the truck lights caught an exit sign. Hacks Cross Road. That information he'd keep to himself. "Where are you? I need to talk to you."

"Right now, I'm standing in the Bradford County Hospital parking lot. Dr. Martin's been hurt. I'm with her mom while she waits until she can go back and see her daughter."

"Is she going to be okay?"

"The doctors indicate she will be. Scott, do you know what happened to her?"

"It wasn't me."

"Look, I'm going home right now, and I want you to meet me there. We'll talk and figure out a strategy. Okay? You know where I live."

"Yeah." Scott rubbed his forehead.

"Can you be there in half an hour?"

"If I don't show up, I'll see you at your office sometime tomorrow."

"But, Scott—"

Scott hung up. Seconds later the phone vibrated in his hand, and he lowered the window and tossed the phone. That ought to take care of anyone tracing him by the phone. He glanced down at the gas gauge. Less than a quarter of a tank. Had to get gas and something to eat.

Scott wadded the hamburger wrapper in a ball and stuffed the last of the French fries in his mouth. He needed a plan. And going to Ethan's house wasn't it. Too easy for cops to be hiding there.

No, he needed to ditch Charlie's truck and catch a MATA bus. He could transfer a few times in case someone followed him, then catch one going downtown and get off a couple of blocks from Ethan's office so he could stake it out. If cops showed up . . . he'd worry about that when the time came.

It wasn't that he didn't want to talk to the authorities. He just had some questions that needed answering first. Questions only Ethan could answer. Or Digger . . .

Antiseptic smells burned Taylor's nose, but antiseptic beat gasoline every time. She tried to get comfortable in the ER bed and winced at the pain in her rib cage. A dry cough racked her throat, and she reached for the cup of water on the stand beside the bed.

"Here, let me get that," her mom said.

Pain shot through her muscles, and she groaned. At least she didn't have another concussion or a gunshot wound to contend with. The bullet shattered the driver's side window but missed her. She'd let her guard down, told herself her stalker had lost interest, and it almost cost her life. That wouldn't happen again.

She touched the bandage above her right eyebrow where the mirror had sliced her head. She'd never had a cut closed with glue before.

The door opened and she glanced toward it, hoping for a nurse with pain meds. Nope. Only Nick trying to balance three cups of coffee in his hands. Her heart hitched at the worry lines creasing his brow, then at the dark splotches on his shirt. Her blood.

Someone had tried to kill her tonight. The reality hit hard. "Thanks," she said, accepting the cup he held out. She sipped the coffee. Strong. Like the man who brought it.

"It's not Starbucks, but the nurse said it was fresh," he said, handing her mother a coffee. "Which I have my doubts about. But it's hot. I reminded her you needed something for your ribs."

Taylor grimaced over the steam. "Any stronger and it could walk."

Her attempt at humor brought a hollow laugh from her mom, who'd returned to her corner chair. She'd said very little since arriving with Ethan while Taylor was in X-ray.

Mom took one sip of the coffee and dropped it in the wastebasket. "If you can drink that, you don't need to be in the hospital," she said and glanced toward the door. "What's taking the doctor so long to look at your X-rays?"

"I don't know, but I wish he'd come on." Taylor handed Nick the cup and rested her head against the pillow. "Where did you say Ethan went?" she asked.

"Home. He was sorry he couldn't stay, but he received a phone call about an important meeting tomorrow. And I called Chase to let him know you're all right. I don't know where Jonathan is. He's not answering his phone."

"Where's Abby?" Taylor asked.

"Chase took her to spend the night with a friend." Her mom stood and rubbed her arms.

"Taylor, this can't happen again. Promise me you'll stop this profiling nonsense."

"What?" She stared at her mom.

"Go back to teaching and stay there. I can't take this, always worrying that I'll lose you." Her mother's voice broke.

"I'm sorry, Mom, but it's who I am." She spoke to her mother, but her gaze hung on Nick's face. The grimness around his mouth echoed her mother's words.

"Taylor, do you know how hard it was to watch them load you in that ambulance?" Nick rasped the words out.

Was he asking her to make a choice? The door opened and Taylor jumped.

"You're skittish as a street cat," Ben said as he entered the cubicle. He nodded at Nick. "Glad you're here." He pulled a thin book from his pocket and opened it to a bookmarked page. "I knew that poem was familiar. I bought this collection of your short stories last year. You want to tell me why you haven't mentioned this before?" He held the book up for Nick to read.

Death unfolds . . . The words on the page cut Nick's breath off as Taylor snatched the book from Ben's hand.

"I'm waiting." Ben folded his arms across his chest.

Taylor looked up, her face even more ashen.

"You wrote the poem? Did you send it to me as well?"

His insides cringed at the betrayal stamped on her face, in the slump of her shoulders. He had no one to blame. He'd dug this particular hole himself, and it kept getting deeper one shovel at a time. "You know I didn't. The poem is from a short story I wrote years ago. I wanted to tell you the day Scott almost burned my house down. But—"

The glare she shot him cut off his words. "You knew where the poem came from the first day I met you. You could've told me then."

Nick opened his mouth and closed it. *Oh what a tangled web we weave when first we practice to deceive.* If he'd told the truth and trusted God with the outcome, a lot of things might be different.

"I know." He filled his lungs, then exhaled hard. "I was so sure Scott had nothing to do with what happened to you that night. As far as I know, Scott never saw that story, before or after it was published. I convinced myself someone was framing him."

"Stop!" Taylor held her hands up. "So you put your brother right next door. That way, he could reach me anytime he wanted to."

"I'm sorry."

Ben cleared his throat. "You say Scott never saw the poem?"

"I don't think so," Nick said with a shake of his head. "It was in one of the first stories I sold. Scott couldn't have been more than thirteen, and he wasn't exactly interested in my writing. When the story was published in this collection a couple of years ago, Scott was heavy into drugs and alcohol, and he'd disappeared."

"If you're right," Taylor said, "someone's gone to a lot of trouble to frame your brother. Why?"

Nick turned to answer Taylor's question, his heart aching to make things right. "I don't know. Not sure I even buy that theory since he stole Charlie's truck. But he told me he was bringing it back."

"Yet he didn't," Ben said.

Nick turned from the sheriff's intense scrutiny. "He's scared. And I didn't alleviate his fear. More or less told him I held him responsible."

"You don't believe him?" Taylor sounded skeptical.

"I don't know what I believe anymore."

A certainty that he couldn't explain if he tried swept over Nick. Drunk or sober, ten years ago or now, Scott wouldn't hurt anyone. It simply wasn't in him.

"No, I take that back." He turned first to Ben, then to Taylor. "Regardless of how it looks, my brother didn't do these things. I'll help you find him so he can clear his name. But if you're focusing only on him, you're giving the real

370

criminal a free pass and an open invitation to try again."

Ethan parted his drapes and peered into the darkness. Eleven-thirty. Scott wasn't coming. He paced the floor in his den, fingering the small vial in his pocket. Enough GHB to take out a horse. Only a horse wasn't getting it.

Why did the kid have to decide to get sober now? It wasn't that he worried that Scott might put two and two together. As an alcoholic, drugged-out kid, no one would pay any attention to his ramblings. But sober? He couldn't take the chance. Scott could identify Digger. It was only a matter of time before he ran into him in Logan Point. And that would raise too many questions.

He'd told Digger texting Scott to come to Taylor's house that night was a mistake. But the fool had insisted they needed someone to take the blame.

And now Scott had to be taken care of. Why did it always come down to this? He liked the kid, felt sorry for him.

He stopped pacing in front of the mahogany desk in the corner to pick up the first page of the Sunday paper.

Wilson.

Another problem. What did the retired cop know? Or was he just blowing off to the reporter?

He'd driven by his house on the way home from the hospital. Wilson hadn't answered the doorbell, and there was no way to get inside the house the way it was barred up.

Tomorrow. He would take care of Wilson tomorrow. Tonight, he had Scott to worry about. And Taylor. Always Taylor, ever since she'd started looking for James again.

But for not much longer.

29

Taylor groaned as she turned over in bed and groped for the clock. If the red numbers were to be believed, it was only five-thirty. Outside her window, the first gray steaks of dawn lit the sky. Less than eight hours since she'd rolled the Rav4 and four since the hospital released her. A fact her body knew all too well, especially her ribs. If bruised ribs hurt this bad, she'd hate to break one.

She closed her eyes and tried to capture another hour of sleep, but nightmarish images flitted through her head. Headlights. Flashes of gunfire. Her window exploding. Taylor flopped on her back and stared at the ceiling.

Who wanted her dead?

Trying to figure that out was like putting a five-hundred-piece puzzle together without all the pieces. She punched her pillow and tried to find a comfortable spot. But her mind wouldn't shut off. She replayed each event as it happened, from the beginning. The first anonymous gift, the candy that arrived in March, a month later the roses and the photos, followed by the poem in her pocket, the attack, then the bracelet, and now the shooting.

It'd been the black roses that first made her suspect Scott with his Goth attire, and if someone was framing him, what better way? But why?

Her mind spun with the question.

Where did Scott fit in the Coleman case? And that was the problem. He didn't fit anywhere. He was too young and too messed up to plan such an elaborate scheme. One thing was for sure—it took an evil person to play on Ralph Jenkins's hatred just to send Taylor a message.

Thinking made her head hurt along with her ribs and muscles. But if she didn't think about the case, she'd have to think about her feelings for Nick and that he'd written the poem used in the threat. Why hadn't he told her?

That was a no-brainer. He loved his brother, believed in him.

With sleep impossible, she threw back the sheet and sat on the side of the bed, triggering a wave of dizziness and nausea as pain racked her body. The busy day loomed before her like a giant elephant. *How do you eat an elephant? One bite at a time.*

She smiled at Kate's adage. Her head dictated that the first bite she needed was something for her throbbing ribs. The ER doctor wanted to prescribe a pain tablet, but Taylor had nixed that. She planned to drive today and settled for Tylenol. While she was up, she might as well get dressed. Maybe after a shower, she could focus more than two seconds on the intricacies of the case.

A little after nine, Taylor gripped the banister as she took the stairs one step at a time. She'd just spent fifteen minutes explaining to Livy what had happened the night before and another fifteen convincing her friend she was all right. But at least Livy volunteered to make the meeting with Wilson. As for examining her case further, there'd not been any time. Maybe she could bounce ideas off Livy.

Taylor stopped halfway down and took a deep breath. Who would have thought rolling a car would make her so sore. She'd called the rental agency over an hour ago, and hopefully, they'd have a replacement car here before her mother discovered her plan to go out.

"Where do you think you're going?"

Her mom's voice stopped her at the bottom of the steps. Taylor turned as Mom stepped from her office, carrying several envelopes.

"Livy and I have an appointment this morning."

"You most certainly do not, unless it's with a doctor."

"Mom, I'm not a child. I have work to do."

"What if that maniac tries to kill you again?"

"He won't. It's daylight."

"Meaning?"

"Two attacks, both at night. The man's a coward. He won't attack me when there's a possibility he might be seen."

"You didn't hear anything I said last night, did you?"

"Mom." Pain shot through her ribs, and she tried not to show it. "I could get killed walking across the street on a sunny afternoon."

"I don't want you to get killed at all."

Taylor didn't want to worry her mom, but . . . She licked her lips and tried to make her words as final as she knew how. "I have to go."

"Then I'll go with you."

Should have seen that one coming. "Nothing's going to happen to me today. Livy will be with me."

"In other words, I'll be in the way." Her mom eyed her for a few seconds. "Where *did* you get this stubbornness?"

She was not being stubborn. Since last night, priorities had crystallized in her mind, and finding her father had risen to the top. Taylor softened her voice. "I'll be back in three hours. Then I'll take it easy the rest of the day. Promise."

"If you're not, I'll have Ben put out an APB."

"I think it's BOLO now, Mom. *Be on the lookout*."

"You know what I mean."

The doorbell rang.

"That'll be my car," Taylor said. She hugged her mom and winced as pain radiated through her chest. "Thanks for worrying about me, but I'll be all right."

"Wait, these came for you Saturday. With the picnic and then everything that happened yesterday, I've only just now sorted through the mail." She handed Taylor several envelopes.

Taylor glanced at the top envelope and recognized Christine's bold handwriting. She'd told her friend to forward anything that looked halfway important. The doorbell rang again, and she stuffed the mail in her purse. "I'll see you in three hours."

Nick glanced at the clock on the Logan Point library wall. Nine-thirty. He'd gotten the librarian to let him in when she arrived an hour ago and had been researching articles on James Martin ever since. He squelched an impulse to check on Taylor. She would not appreciate it. He wasn't sure if she accepted his explanation about the poem, which had come right on the heels of him agreeing with Allison about her job. Right now he was persona non grata, but at least today, Taylor was home, safe.

Last night when he'd walked through those hospital doors and down the corridor to Taylor's ER cubicle, morbid thoughts had flowed like the blood from the gash on Taylor's head. *What if she dies?* The question kept running through his head. Then to see the dried blood on her face . . . it'd almost been more than he could stand. They had to talk. He couldn't protect her if she wouldn't listen to him, if she kept chasing criminals. One of them would get her, almost had last night.

Just like Angie.

His phone vibrated in his shirt pocket, and he slipped it out. Allison. He answered and couldn't believe what she told him.

"Taylor is doing what?"

"She's keeping some appointment in Memphis today. But she hasn't left yet."

"I'll be right there."

A blue jay fussed overhead as a slight breeze touched Taylor's face. The giant oaks provided shade but didn't let much air through. Taylor winced as she bent over and signed the rental papers. She handed the Gordon's Rent-a-Car agent his copy and accepted the keys to the Civic. "Sorry about the other car," she said.

He waved his hand. "Your insurance company is covering it."

Taylor fanned herself as he and the driver of the second rental car pulled away from the house. At the end of the drive, the car waited as Nick's red Mustang turned in. Seconds later his tires screeched to a halt on the asphalt drive, and Nick got out, his face set for an argument. Overhead, the blue jay screeched at the new intruder.

"What are you doing here?" She continued to fan with the insurance papers. Today promised to be another scorcher.

"I'm going to Memphis. Need a ride?"

"My mom called you."

"She's concerned."

"I'm surprised she didn't call Ben Logan." She opened the door to the Honda and tossed her purse onto the passenger seat. "I can drive myself, and I don't need a babysitter. Besides, I'll be with Livy. We'll be at a retired cop's house."

"I'm not offering babysitting services. Just a ride to Memphis until you meet your friend."

She did not want Nick going with her.

"Come on, Taylor. Let me do this. You rolled your car, and you're bound to be sore. Probably on pain meds. You don't need to be driving."

"I'm only taking Tylenol, and I'm not that sore, at least not too sore to drive."

"Okay, how about the argument that someone tried to kill you last night. Maybe if I'm with you, he won't try anything today. And I want to make up for not telling you about the poem. Let me drive you."

"I wouldn't have a car."

"Then at least let me follow you. When you finish your interview, you can call me and I'll follow you home. I have plenty that needs my attention in Memphis—like checking with Scott's girlfriend to see if she's heard from him."

She couldn't deny she'd feel safer if Nick followed her. She drew in a deep breath and exhaled. "Okay. No rushing me, though."

"Deal."

By the time Taylor pulled to the curb in front of Wilson's house, her body screamed for her bed. Maybe she should rethink this.

Nick tapped on her window, and she lowered it. "You sure you're up to this?"

He had no clue how bad her ribs hurt or her muscles throbbed. She forced a smile. "Don't hover. Don't you have to be somewhere?"

"It can wait until Livy gets here." He nodded toward Wilson's open wooden door. "Looks like your guy is home."

Taylor climbed out of the Civic and limped to a shaded wrought-iron bench in Wilson's front yard. A wave of nausea made her wish she'd eaten. Nick sat beside her on the bench. Down the street, a commercial lawnmower clattered, and the scent of fresh-cut grass wafted through the air. A house wren hopped at their feet. "Looking for crumbs, mama bird? I bet Lieutenant Wilson has been feeding you."

Nick cleared his throat. "What's your thinking about who shot at you last night?"

"Muddled. I can't focus." She uncapped her water bottle and took a sip. "Tell me again why you didn't say anything about the poem the first time I met you."

He shrugged. "Because I didn't believe my brother sent it to you. But you were so sure that Scott was your stalker, I was afraid if I mentioned it, you and the sheriff in Newton would focus on him instead of the real criminal."

"How can you be so sure the real criminal isn't your brother?" After last night, Scott had jumped back on her suspect list. "He could've been my shooter last night—he had the opportunity."

"He didn't do it."

"How do you know?"

He looked away for a second. "My gut tells me it isn't him."

"That could be indigestion. Give me something a little more concrete."

He was quiet for a minute. "You're a psychologist. Do people change their basic personality? Can a person go from being compassionate, gentle, and mild mannered to violent, sadistic, even homicidal? In other words, can a boy who tended to wounded birds turn into a killer?"

Nick was consistent, if nothing else. "Okay, so maybe he isn't the one after me, but he knows something. Scott may not even be aware of what he knows."

"I know . . . but couldn't this whole thing be about a past case? Or even a current one? What were you working on when you started getting the gifts and the photos?"

"That's just it. I hadn't really worked on anything since Christmas. Except . . . I've been trying to find my dad." A cold chill chased over her body. "But that would mean . . ." Her voice faded as Livy pulled to the curb and got out.

Livy walked toward them. "Good to see you again, Nick. I'm glad she had company on the drive over."

"She didn't want me to come."

"Don't talk about me like I'm not here." Taylor searched her purse for Tylenol. It'd been four hours since she had taken anything for pain. She pulled out the letters her mom had handed her, dropping one as she spied the bottle in the bottom of her purse. Livy picked up the letter as Taylor put two pills in her mouth and took a swig of water.

"Thanks." She took the envelope from Livy and glanced at it. No return address. Her heart skipped a beat. Neither had it been forwarded.

"What's wrong?" Nick asked.

Taylor looked at Livy. "Do you have any latex gloves? I think I need a pair."

Silently, Livy pulled gloves from her back pocket and handed them to her. Taylor slipped them on and carefully removed the letter. Bracing herself, she unfolded it.

Dear Taylor, the bold script began. She quickly scanned the words.

"No. No!" Like a jackhammer, her heart thudded against her ribs. She choked back the thick lump that clogged her throat.

Livy pulled on a pair of gloves and took the letter.

It couldn't be. Not after all these years. Taylor blinked back tears. "Read it out loud."

"Dear Taylor," Livy read. "It is with great difficulty that I write you, but you must abandon this search for me. It will only bring heartache. I cannot and will not return to Logan Point. Things have happened that cannot be undone. If you love your mother, please honor this request." Livy's voice faltered. "I'm sorry, pipsqueak. Daddy."

The ground blurred, swimming before her eyes. Her father was alive and knew she was looking for him. He wanted her to stop. She wanted to throw up.

"Is this your dad's handwriting?" Livy asked.

Taylor looked at the letter again. "It looks like the writing on some letters Mom gave me." It would take a handwriting expert to tell for sure. Or Mom or Jonathan. But she'd rather not ask either of them. Or maybe she would. Jonathan, at least. Someone had to have told her father she was looking for him.

"I'm sorry, Taylor." Nick put his arm around her.

"I'm going to find him." She squared her shoulders and started to stuff the letter in her purse.

"Hey, wait. I want to bag that," Livy said.

"What? This is personal."

Livy raised her eyebrows. "Someone's trying to kill you. Anything you receive—"

"Surely you don't believe my dad tried . . ." The thought was too terrible to say out loud.

"I didn't say that. I just think that letter needs to be treated as evidence."

Taylor clamped her mouth shut and handed it to Livy, then glanced toward Wilson's door as she pulled off the gloves. "Are we ready to talk to the lieutenant? Maybe he knows something about my dad."

Nick stood. "Call me when you're ready to go home."

"Nick, there's no need. I'll be fine."

"Call me."

After Nick drove away, they walked toward the porch and Livy rang the bell. "I like Nick," she said.

"Me too." Taylor peered through the glass security door into the dark living room.

"Wood door is open. I'm certain he's here."

Livy rapped on the glass then glanced uneasily at Taylor.

"Maybe he can't hear you. Or maybe he's ill." Taylor remembered the difficulty Wilson had breathing during their phone conversation.

Livy tried the glass door. It was unlocked, and she opened it. "Hello? Anyone here?" she called over the rattling window unit in the living room. "Lieutenant Wilson? It's Detective Reynolds."

"Let's try the kitchen," Taylor said.

"I don't like this." Livy pulled her gun and cautiously pushed open a swinging door that separated the living room from the kitchen. She stepped through it, sweeping the room with her gun.

"Oh no," she said softly.

Taylor looked over Livy's shoulder. An old man lay sprawled in the middle of the kitchen floor, oxygen hissing against his cheek.

Livy pulled more latex gloves from her pocket, handing a pair to Taylor. As Taylor tugged on the gloves, Livy checked for a pulse. "Dead."

As Taylor knelt on the other side of the body, Livy slipped a billfold from his back pocket and looked through it. "It's Wilson. Think he had a heart attack?"

"No. There's a scalp wound on the back of his head. Someone attacked him."

Livy sat back on her heels and scanned his body. "Livor mortis on the legs."

Taylor followed Livy's gaze toward the purplish-red blotches on Wilson's bare calves. The detective pressed her finger against one of the blotches, and the color momentarily faded. "Couldn't have been dead more than twenty minutes." She took out her phone and punched in a number. "Mac, Wilson's dead. Murdered."

Taylor stared at the body. Why would anyone want to murder a harmless old man? And murder it was. Taylor was certain of that. Burglars usually didn't kill unless they felt threatened, and she didn't see how this frail shell of a man could have threatened anyone. As Livy spoke with Mac, Taylor noticed a bruise above his lip. Maybe the blow hadn't killed him.

She stood and scanned the kitchen, mentally cataloging the scene. Mail stacked neatly on the counter. Glass of tea on the table, no dirty dishes. Everything neat and tidy except for the sheets of typed notepaper scattered on the table beside a milk crate filled with folders. She glanced in the sink. Wet. As was the dishcloth.

Her gaze traveled back to the milk crate. Wilson's files. Taylor curbed the impulse to flip through them. She knew the importance of not compromising the crime scene.

Livy closed the cell phone. "The crime scene unit will be here soon. Let's clear out until they're done."

"Have them check for asphyxiation."

"You think he might've been smothered?"

Taylor nodded. "Look at the head wound. The scalp is cut, which would account for all the blood, but there's no noticeable swelling."

Livy pointed to the slight discoloration just below the nose. "Shape he was in, it wouldn't have been hard."

They retraced their way to the front steps to await the technicians. Silence settled between them. Another person connected to her dad's case dead. A letter from her father. Why now? How did he know she was looking for him? Too many questions and too few answers. She broke the quiet. "Does it strike you as odd that both detectives who investigated my dad's case are dead?"

"I was thinking the same thing. When we get back to the Criminal Justice Center, I'll have Allen Yates's records pulled."

"I don't believe Lieutenant Wilson thought his partner committed suicide."

"He may have been right."

Hungry and thirsty, Scott slouched on a shaded bench across from Ethan's building. Office workers filled the sidewalk, barely acknowledging him as they trudged to work. A police cruiser passed by, and Scott tugged the Cardinals cap he'd found in Charlie's pickup lower over his forehead.

During the long night, he'd made a decision. He couldn't live on the run like this, but he didn't want to be captured. He would turn himself in with his lawyer at his side.

By ten o'clock, the shade had fled, and Scott walked up to the next block, keeping an eye out for his attorney. His heartbeat pounded in his temples, and with the sleeve of his T-shirt, he swiped the sweat that beaded his face. Where was Ethan?

Finally, Scott spied his attorney striding down the sidewalk toward his office. Scott crossed the street. Ethan barely broke stride when he saw him.

"I thought you were coming to the house last night," the attorney said. "I tried to call you, but you didn't answer."

"I'm here now."

They rode the elevator to the second floor in silence.

"Good morning, Ms. Leeds," Ethan said as they passed the secretary. "No calls for the next hour, please."

Ms. Leeds's eyes widened, and Scott looked away. She remembered his last visit.

"Yes, sir."

Scott felt her eyes boring into his back as they walked to the end of the hall. He could use one of those nerve pills about now.

Ethan closed the door. "You look shaky. Why don't you sit on the couch?"

"Good idea." Scott sank into the leather couch. "Getting sober isn't all it's cracked up to be."

"I hope you stay sober." Ethan sat behind his desk. "You have enough problems without adding alcohol to the mix."

"I know." Scott leaned forward, rubbing his hands on the top of his thighs. He couldn't keep his body from shaking. "I didn't do any of this stuff they're accusing me of. I didn't stalk Dr. Martin, and I didn't hurt her."

"Slow down, Scott. Take a deep breath."

Scott leaned back into the couch, his insides quivering like a strummed guitar.

"You don't look well." Concern flitted across Ethan's face. "Want a soda? I have one in the fridge."

His parched throat ached for something cold. Perspiration beaded his upper lip, and he wiped it away as he nodded.

Ethan took a canned drink from his mini refrigerator and popped the top. "Ice?" he asked over his shoulder.

"Yeah, that'll be good."

Ice crackled, then Ethan handed him the napkin-wrapped glass.

"I don't have any real food, other than these." The lawyer held out a dish of cashews mixed with almonds.

Starved, Scott popped a handful of nuts into his mouth and washed them down with a swig of the drink. The salty taste burned his tongue. His stomach growled, and he ate another handful, chasing it with the rest of the drink.

"So, let's decide what you're going to do." Ethan took a notepad from his desk.

"I want to turn—" The room moved, and he shook his head. Should have eaten before now. Scott pressed his hands to his temples. Why did his head feel so heavy?

"Would you like more peanuts? Or soda?"

Two Ethans hovered in front of him. Scott squinted and blinked his eyes. For a second the two images merged and Ethan's mouth moved up and down, his words sounding like they came straight from a horror movie. He tried to focus, to understand. Ethan's voice faded. The glass slipped from Scott's hand. He gulped for air. A ton of weight crushed his chest, cutting off his breath. He clawed at his shirt.

Help me . . .

Seconds stretched like hours. Light caught Scott in a tunnel and sucked him downward.

"Scott . . . what's wrong?"

He could barely hear Ethan. *Call 911.* His frozen lips trapped the words. Ethan lifted him from the couch. His body hit the floor hard. *Why doesn't he call 911?*

Minutes ticked by. Scott's breathing finally stopped. Ethan knelt beside him and placed his fingers on the boy's neck. No pulse. He waited to be sure Scott's chest didn't rise and fall again. When it didn't, he released a pent-up breath.

He scooped up the ice that had skittered across the carpet and dumped it in the sink, then scrubbed Scott's glass and returned it to the cabinet. Just in case the police checked, there would not be any lingering trace of the gamma-hydroxybutric acid. Ethan nudged Scott's body before checking again for a pulse in his neck. He took out his cell phone and dialed.

"Nine-one-one. What is your emergency?"

"I need an ambulance. I have a young man in my office, unconscious." Ethan injected the right note of panic, knowing that everything he did from the moment the operator answered would be scrutinized. He gave the dispatcher his name and address. "I'm on the second floor."

"Can you tell if he's breathing?"

"I think so." If he said no, the 911 operator might expect him to administer CPR.

"Is there a pulse?"

He touched Scott's cool arm. No pulse. "Barely."

"I'm dispatching an ambulance. Can you tell me what happened?"

"He was just talking to me and passed out. I can't wake him."

"Okay, sir. Let me relay this to the paramedics."

Cell phone pressed to his ear, Ethan hurried

down the hall to his secretary's desk. "Ms. Leeds, there's an ambulance on its way. Go downstairs and wait for it."

The secretary stood and shot a wild look toward his office. "What's wrong?"

"It's Scott. He's passed out. Go!"

His command scrambled her into action, and she rushed out the door. Ethan hurried back to Scott. The 911 dispatcher came on the line again. "Are you still there?"

He assured her he was.

"Is he sitting up?"

"No, I moved him to the floor."

"Is he blue or cold?"

"A little blue around the mouth."

"Has he taken any alcohol or drugs?"

"I don't know. He has a prior record of alcohol abuse, but he wasn't drinking today." The faint wail of an ambulance reached his ears. "I hear the ambulance."

"Good. I'll stay on the line with you until they arrive."

Before long, two paramedics and a uniformed police officer rushed through the door with Ms. Leeds trailing. Ethan moved out of the way as a medic dropped a large bag to the floor and knelt beside Scott. "Larry" was stitched on his shirt, and an identification card dangled from his belt loop. He shook Scott. "Hey! Wake up!"

Scott didn't respond.

"I don't know what happened. He just collapsed on the couch." Ethan twisted the ring on his right hand. "I laid him on the floor. I hope that was the right thing to do."

The men ignored Ethan and worked in tandem on Scott. The other medic knelt beside his still body and felt for a pulse. "Nothing."

Larry cut away his shirt and set up a cardiac monitor while his partner tilted Scott's head back and threaded a tube down his throat. Once in place, a ventilator breathed for Scott. Ethan hadn't expected this much effort to save someone already dead.

The monitor came to life and a straight line scrolled across the screen. "He's asystole." Larry's voice held urgency. "Inject epinephrine and give him 100 percent oxygen."

The police officer knelt and began compressions as the medic pulled a syringe from the bag and injected the contents into the IV tubing.

The surreal scene unfolded in slow motion. "Scott seemed all right when he arrived," Ethan said. *Why do they keep working on him?* He turned to his secretary, who hovered nearby, wringing her hands. "Did he appear all right to you?"

Ms. Leeds couldn't seem to take her eyes from Scott's still body. Finally, she found her voice. "Yes," she said, hunching her shoulders defensively. "He seemed perfectly fine. Not drunk like the last time."

Thank you, Ms. Leeds.

Larry jerked his head toward the secretary. "He has a problem with alcohol?"

She gulped and nodded, reminding Ethan of a bobblehead doll. "Um, yes sir."

Ethan cleared his throat. "I don't think he's had anything to drink recently. He told me he was getting sober."

"How about drugs?"

"Prior history with that too." Ethan added just the right tone of regret.

Suddenly, a short spike appeared. Ethan's heart almost stopped. He breathed again when the line flattened.

"Come on, son, you can make it." Larry injected two more syringes into the tubing. Another spike, then another. He pressed his fingers to Scott's carotid artery. "We have a pulse here! Let's get him transported!"

Ethan rocked on his heels. *No! This isn't the way it was supposed to be.* The plan was falling apart. What if Scott revived and talked? He knew too much. Ethan forced himself to breathe. *Act glad. Look relieved.* He moistened his lips and tried to sound hopeful. "Is he going to be all right?"

"Your friend isn't out of the woods yet." Larry punched a number on his cell phone as Scott was lifted onto a stretcher. Ethan half listened as Larry rattled off a list of procedures and drugs he didn't understand.

"ETA is twelve minutes." Larry ended the call and turned to Ethan. "We're transporting him. Do you know what drugs he might have ingested?"

Ethan lifted his shoulders in a helpless gesture. "He'd only been here maybe ten minutes when he collapsed."

They rolled the stretcher to the door, and Larry jerked his head toward the policeman. "If you think of anything, tell the officer here. He'll relay it to us."

"Do . . . you think he'll make it?"

"It's a hard one to call." Larry's lips tightened. "Even if he makes it, there may be brain damage."

Brain damage. Ethan calculated how long Scott had been without oxygen. If he lived, he would be a vegetable. The rush of relief made him almost light-headed. The police officer approached, and he cleared his mind of everything but the story he'd rehearsed earlier.

30

Nick paid the Memphis librarian for the use of the copier. He'd found six stories on James Martin. With the articles from the library in Logan Point, he had a total of eight articles. He'd even found one on Jonathan.

Nick hadn't known Taylor's uncle performed as

a clown, but there he was, along with Ethan Trask, on the inside pages of the Memphis *Commercial Appeal*. The photo was taken at a benefit for burned children. He tapped the article with his pen. Was Jonathan the clown in Taylor's dream?

He skimmed over the stories on James Martin. They didn't paint a picture of someone who would walk out on his family. Kiwanis Club Citizen of the Year, Outstanding Citizen Award by the Big Brothers and Big Sisters of Memphis . . . the list went on. So what happened to Taylor's father?

The phone vibrated in his shirt pocket, and he slid it out. Allison? He answered.

"Nick, is Taylor with you?" Panic rode her voice.

"No. Isn't she still with Livy?"

"I don't know. She promised me she'd be back in three hours. That was five hours ago, and now she doesn't answer her phone."

He'd been so focused on searching for the articles, he'd lost track of time. "Have you called Livy?"

"I don't have her cell number, and when I called the police department, they just say she's not in."

"I have Livy's cell. I'll call her and get back to you." Nick scrolled through his contacts. He tapped on Livy's number, and the call went to voice mail. He clenched his jaw, shooting pain down his neck. "Livy, this is Nick Sinclair. If Taylor is still with you when you get this message, please have her call me . . . or her mother. Thanks."

Minutes passed and finally his cell vibrated, and a number he didn't recognize popped up. He punched the green answer button. "Sinclair."

"Nick?"

Taylor. Relief flowed over him like a refreshing rain. "Where are you? Are you all right?"

"Uh, yeah." Her voice trembled, and she sounded almost on the verge of tears. "I forgot to charge my cell phone last night. I'm at the Criminal Justice Center. Wilson is dead. Murdered."

He gripped his cell phone. "What happened?"

"After you left, Livy and I . . ." She took a shuddering breath. "We found him on the floor. He hadn't been dead long."

The murderer could've still been in the house. Fear coiled around his heart like a python, squeezing his lungs. "Stay there. I'm coming to get you."

"No. Don't come. I'm fine."

"Taylor—"

"No, Nick. I can't leave right now. I think his murder is connected to my dad's case. I need answers."

"At least call your mom. She's worried to death about you." His phone beeped in his ear, and he glanced at the caller ID. "Hold on a second.

Ethan Trask is calling. Maybe he's heard from Scott."

"I've got to go. Call me on this number if he knows anything about your brother."

She hung up on him before he could tell her to wait. He switched over to Ethan. "Hello?"

"Nick? Ethan Trask here. I'm afraid something's happened to Scott."

Nick was right. Taylor needed to call her mom. She'd just gotten so caught up in Wilson's murder that it had slipped her mind. Her mom answered on the first ring.

"Why are you not home? You promised you'd be gone three hours, max."

Taylor could almost feel the heat from her mom's voice. "Things didn't go like I thought they would. I'll be home as soon as I can."

Quietness ensued. Taylor imagined her mom counting to ten. "Take care of yourself, Taylor. I worry about you."

The care in her mother's voice almost did her in. She blinked back tears. "I'll be all right. And if you need to call me, use the number on your caller ID."

After telling her mom good-bye, Taylor walked to the interrogation room, where she and Livy had holed up with Mac since returning from the crime scene. The tantalizing aroma of barbeque met her at the door. Evidently, someone had ordered in. Maybe food would revive her. If not, she'd be forced to go home. She eased into a chair across from Livy.

Her friend shoved a Corky's box toward her. "Are you sure you're up to this? You don't look real good."

"Gee, thanks. Makes me feel so much better."

"Seriously, if you're not feeling well, don't stay," Mac said.

Taylor fixed her gaze on the to-go container in front of her. "I'm fine. Or I will be when I get some food in me."

She tore open a ketchup packet and squeezed it over her French fries. "Are the feds still here?"

"Yeah, but after Wilson's death, they released us to work this case."

Taylor's stomach growled, and she picked up her sandwich. "Thanks for getting this."

As she ate, she mulled over what she'd found in Yates's file and how his death might be connected to Wilson's.

The detective had been relieved of duty with extortion charges pending when he was found dead from a bullet wound to the head. The typed suicide note found in the bedroom with the body could've been written by anyone.

The two cases had to be linked. Even with an eighteen-year gap, two cops—partners—dying under questionable circumstances couldn't be a coincidence. She glanced up at Livy. "How many cases did Yates and Wilson investigate together?"

Livy sorted through the papers in front of her. "Ninety, including your father's. Did you see this? Yates had hired Ethan Trask to defend him on the extortion charges."

Mac dipped a French fry into his ketchup. "I'm not sure I buy that the two deaths are connected. If the same person killed them both, why did he wait so long?" He waved a sheet of paper. "Besides, there's been a rash of robberies in Wilson's neighborhood lately."

"This time you're wrong, Mac. There are too many coincidences related to his case. And none of us like coincidences."

"I agree," Taylor said. "Think about it, I make an appointment to talk with Wilson about my dad, and he's killed before I can meet him—right after a newspaper article quotes him as saying the case bothered him and he thought he knew why."

"And his partner supposedly commits suicide," Livy added. "And Taylor hadn't heard from her dad until she starts digging in his case . . . do we need to go on?"

"Okay, okay." Mac picked up the letter. "If this is from your dad, it means he's alive. Maybe Yates found that out during the investigation and tried to blackmail him."

"You're saying eighteen years ago, my dad killed Yates?"

"It's a possibility." Livy cleared her throat. "And maybe he was afraid Wilson knew something as well. The interview with him came out in yesterday's paper. Could your father be the one who took a shot at you last night?"

"No!" That was impossible. Wasn't it?

The conference desk phone rang, and after glancing at the ID, Livy handed it to Taylor. "Nick."

"Maybe he found Scott." Taylor answered. "Hello."

"Scott's in the hospital again."

She gripped the phone tighter. From the sound of Nick's voice, it couldn't be good. "What happened?"

"He collapsed in Ethan Trask's office, maybe from an overdose."

Nick's words caught her off guard. "Did you say Scott overdosed?"

"Yeah," Nick said softly. "He's in ICU. I don't know if he'll make it. He's unresponsive."

31

"Scott, if you can hear me, squeeze my hand."

Nick's voice massaged Scott's consciousness, and he struggled to respond, willing his fingers, his eyes, *anything* to move. Only his chest rose and fell, and Nick's voice faded as Scott slipped into nothingness once more. The next time he woke, Nick's voice mingled with another.

"My brother's going to make it."

"If we could just figure out what he took, but nothing shows on his toxicology screen. I've sent a blood sample to a specialty lab to check for the less common drugs, but that could take twenty-four hours."

A doctor?

Then he heard Nick's voice again. "What do we do?"

"We wait. At least he's breathing on his own now."

"How long will he be like this?"

"I can't tell you without knowing what he ingested. Unfortunately, some of these drugs clear the body so quickly we never identify them, even in an autopsy."

What were they talking about? Autopsy? What happened? Evidently, he was in the hospital again. Did they think he was dying? *Lord, I don't want to die.* How long had it been since he'd talked to God? Too many years, not since he started drinking. *Lord, get me through this and I'll never* . . . No. He remembered enough from his days in church to know he couldn't bargain with God.

But he had to get better. He had to figure out what happened. Urgency coursed through his body as he fought the sleepiness that encroached.

The room was quiet when Scott woke again. Empty.

Come back, Nick. Please come back.

Taylor used the walk from the parking garage to the hospital to compose herself. When the elevator doors opened, she stepped out and followed the arrows to the ICU waiting room.

"Taylor?"

She looked over her shoulder and into cool gray eyes. "Ethan?"

"You should be home resting."

She wished people would stop telling her that, even if it was true. "Do you know how Scott is?"

Ethan reached ahead of her and opened the waiting room door. "No, I just got here. He almost scared me to death when he collapsed."

Taylor stepped through the waiting room doors, glancing around. Nick hurried toward them.

"Thanks for coming." Nick shook Ethan's hand, but his eyes were on her.

The warmth in his hazel eyes sent her heart spiraling.

"How is Scott?" Ethan asked.

"Not good." Nick jammed his hands in his pockets. "He's still in a coma. But at least he's off the ventilator."

She followed him to a corner of the sitting room with Ethan right behind her. A game show played on the muted television on the wall, and an operator's disembodied voice paged a respiratory nurse to room 4210. A half-empty coffee cup sat beside a Gideon Bible. Nick tossed the cup in the garbage before he turned back to Ethan. "Tell me what happened. Why was Scott at your office?"

Taylor sat beside Nick while Ethan took the vinyl chair across from them and crossed his leg over his knee. "To be honest, I really don't know. One minute we're talking about his sobriety, and the next minute he collapsed."

"The doctors said it was an overdose. Did he take anything while he was there?" Nick asked.

"No. Whatever Scott took, he took before he got to my office." Ethan uncrossed his legs and leaned forward. "Have you talked to him yet? What's his prognosis?"

"He doesn't respond, and the doctors are puzzled. He tested negative on the initial drug screen." Nick rubbed his lip with his fingers. "He just lies sleeping. I don't know if he can hear me or not, but I talk to him anyway. When I asked him to squeeze my hand . . . he didn't respond."

Taylor reached for his arm. "Oh, Nick, I'm so sorry."

"The doctors said something about running more tests." He closed his eyes, and his Adam's apple bobbed up and down as he swallowed. "They asked me if he's an organ donor."

Her heart winced. "When can you see him again?"

He glanced at the oversized clock on the wall. "Visitation isn't for two hours. If his vital signs stabilize, they'll let me back sooner."

Ethan puffed out a sigh. "I'm so sorry." Then he stood and glanced at the visiting times posted on the wall. "I have an appointment, but I'll be here for the four-thirty visit."

"Good. He's in room twelve," Nick said and shook the lawyer's hand again. "I'll be with him, but I think they allow him two visitors."

When they were alone, Nick took her hand. "Are you okay?"

She ached all over, but she forced enthusiasm into her voice. "I'm good."

"Yeah, right." He squeezed her fingers. "I'm glad you're here, though."

"I didn't want you to be by yourself." His touch kicked her heart into high gear. She was sure he felt it through her fingertips. "How about you? Are you all right?"

He shrugged. "I've been better."

She stood. "Would you like some coffee?"

"Sure, but let me get it." When he returned, he held out a cup and a small creamer. "I found this."

"You're a good man." Taylor emptied the creamer in the cup.

"Tell me what happened to Detective Wilson."

She sipped the coffee and took Nick through finding Wilson. "We canvassed the neighborhood.

No luck. Actually, Livy did the canvassing while I rested. No one saw anything."

Nick's cell phone rang, and she waited while he answered.

"No, she's right here. Sure." He handed her the phone. "It's your mom."

She grabbed the phone and tried to make her voice upbeat. "Hey, Mom, what's going on?"

"You're not fooling me. Taylor Martin, I expect you to be home within the hour."

Nick's phone was a different model than hers, and somehow Taylor had hit the speaker. Her mom's angry words were loud enough for Nick to hear.

"She's right," he mouthed.

She fumbled with the phone, trying to figure out how to get it off the speaker. Finally, she gave up. "I'm at the hospital with Nick . . . Scott's in ICU."

"Oh no, what happened?"

Taylor told her what she knew, and her mom was quiet for a moment. "Taylor, I know you want to be there, but you need rest. I'm worried about you. Let me come and get you."

"I'm fine. If I decide to come home, I'll come under my own power. I drove from Livy's office to here, I'll drive home."

After she ended the call, Nick said, "Your mom's right. You need to be at home. Call her back and let her come get you." He checked his watch. "It's three-thirty—you need to do it before rush hour starts."

A wave of fatigue hit her. She hated to admit Mom and Nick were right. "Loan me your phone again and I'll call Livy. Maybe she can get me a police escort."

"Great idea."

"I was joking." She dialed Livy and wasn't surprised her friend agreed she needed to go home.

"Give me fifteen minutes to call in a favor," Livy said.

"For what?"

"A black-and-white to follow you to the state line."

Taylor rested her head on her hand, rubbing a spot just over her eyebrow. "I'm in a parking lot near the entrance. Tell him to look for a brown Honda Civic."

"Have Nick walk you down, then the patrolman can call Nick's cell when he gets there."

She looked over the phone at Nick. "Can you go down with me?"

"I had planned to."

"It's all set," she said to Livy. "I'll see you in the morning by nine o'clock."

When she handed Nick his phone back, he said, "I have something for you in my car."

She knit her brows together in a question.

"After I left you at Wilson's house, I went to

the Memphis library and found some articles on your dad and made copies."

His thoughtfulness warmed her. "Thanks. Did I tell you that Livy thinks my father killed Lieutenant Wilson?"

Nick looked stunned. "That really surprises me."

"What do you mean?"

"It'd be hard for me to believe the man I read about could kill anyone."

Ethan rounded a corner in the hallway. Taylor and Nick were coming toward him. He kept his gaze down, not making eye contact, and continued walking. Even if they glanced his way, they'd only see a doctor in green surgical scrubs and a matching cap that hid his silver hair. He counted on the mind accepting what was presented to it.

They passed, and he released the breath trapped in his chest. Now, if he could get by the nurses in ICU as easily and execute his plan. Ethan walked toward the unit, blending with the visitors and doctors and nurses that streamed through the hallway.

His plan was simple. Get into Scott's room and inject enough insulin into his IV to kill him before he started to talk. He couldn't believe the massive dose of GHB he'd put in Scott's drink hadn't killed the boy. Ethan made eye contact with a nurse, and she nodded and spoke. "Doctor."

Bolstered that his theory proved true, he strode

confidently through the ICU doors and oriented himself to the layout he'd studied. Room 12 was to the right. He walked past room 11. Suddenly three high-pitched beeps followed by a continuous drone brayed from the room. His heart crashed against his ribs. The braying continued as a flurry of activity erupted.

Hold steady . . .

He continued walking. The door to room 12 flew open, and a nurse rushed past him. Other nurses swarmed toward 11, one with a crash cart. When he reached 12, he put his hand on the door and peered through the glass window. No doctor, no nurse, only Scott. At least he wouldn't have to wait until his room was empty. He opened the door and slipped in.

32

The parking lot was like a sauna, but for the moment, it felt good as she thawed out. Hospitals were so cold. Nick unlocked the door to his Mustang, retrieved an envelope, and handed it to her.

"You went to a lot of trouble. Thanks."

He touched her cheek, stroking it. "I hope it'll help you find him. Then you can live a normal life, maybe even give up profiling—just teach and write about it."

She tried to ignore how his touch ignited a fire in her. Nick didn't understand. "Finding my father won't change who I am. Sheriff Atkins told me once that I have a cop's heart. I think he was right."

"Come on, Taylor. A cop? I thought you wanted a husband and babies."

"Why can't I have both?"

The color drained from his face. He dropped his hand and stepped back. "You can. Just not with me."

Her hands curled into tight balls. "Don't confuse me with what happened to your wife."

Nick palmed his hands up. "I'm sorry, Taylor, but when I thought you were dead . . . I can't do that again."

It started with a crack, but his words ripped through her chest, shattering her heart like the window of her car the night before. Taylor backed away.

"Wait."

"No, I think I've heard enough."

Scott followed the second hand as it made another sweep around the clock. It'd been his only entertainment since he woke up. Except for the nurse that just shot out of his room. She talked to him even though he couldn't respond, telling him that since he was able to open his eyes, soon he'd probably be able to talk and to move his arms and legs. She didn't tell him what had happened to him, and he couldn't ask.

But at least he could stay awake, and he was breathing on his own now and didn't have to deal with that ventilator tube. Swallowing was next to impossible the way his throat hurt, and the thirst . . . it was worse than after a three-day drinking spree. Ice chips. He'd give anything for ice chips.

If only he could piece together the events that put him in this hospital bed. Something about Ethan, but he couldn't pull it together. He tried again to move his hand, but he couldn't even manage a twitch. He only managed to exhaust himself.

Scott had felt God's presence as he drifted in and out of consciousness. *This sickness is not unto death.* He knew those words were in the Bible . . . somewhere.

In his peripheral vision, the door eased open. Maybe his nurse had come back.

No, a man in green scrubs. Probably another doctor. Hopefully, he'd be more positive than the last one. The doctor approached his bed silently. Odd . . . the way he walked, throwing his foot out. Just like Ethan. The man waved his hand in front of Scott's face.

"Ah, so you can see. Can you hear?"

Ethan? Why was he here dressed like a doctor? The beeps on Scott's heart monitor increased.

Ethan touched where the catheter was inserted

in his right hand, sending a tremor up Scott's arm. Then Ethan slipped a syringe from his pocket and inserted it higher up, near the drip bag.

"Don't worry. It's just a little insulin. You'll simply go to sleep."

The morning came roaring back. Ethan. In his law office. The drink. Ethan standing over him, doing nothing. The paramedics. Every nerve in his body screamed.

"I would like to stay and chat, but I really don't want to be here when the alarms start going crazy," Ethan said. "Besides, Taylor is waiting . . ."

The door closed with a click. Scott strained to see the IV bag. He couldn't tilt his head back, couldn't see the drops releasing into the IV tubing. *Please let it be dripping slow.* The needle . . . had to get it out of his hand.

Scott concentrated his energy on moving his hand, but it would not budge. He riveted his eyes to the IV tubing. The insulin dripped slowly, infiltrating down to the catheter. He shifted his gaze back to his hand. *Move!*

Did his thumb twitch? Maybe. He redoubled his efforts. His left hand moved. Wrong hand! Maybe not. Exhausted, he regrouped and focused on his left hand. Move! Now! Seconds passed. Muscles in his left arm trembled. Sweat drenched his face. Slowly, his hand inched upward and over his chest.

Time was running out. He was so hot, like his

411

blood was on fire. With one last effort, Scott's fingers closed around the IV tubing. He pulled.

Nothing happened. He didn't have enough strength to yank it out.

His chest fell in exhaustion. *Can't give up.* Scott inched his right hand toward the edge of the bed with the left. *Push.* He grasped the tubing in his left fingers.

Once more.

His right hand flopped off the bed. Scott held fast to the tubing.

Alarms howled over his head. The door flew open, and nurses descended on him. Their voices swirled through his head.

"He's pulled out his IV."

"Heart rate's over two hundred. Who's watching the monitors?"

"Must've happened when that other patient coded. Get the IV started again. Prepare to shock him."

Scott fought to keep from losing consciousness. *Gotta tell them about Ethan.*

He felt himself slipping away.

She would not cry.

She. Would. Not. Cry.

Taylor had been doing fine before she met Nick Sinclair. She would do fine again. She turned into the Martin drive, waving to the deputy who had followed her from the state line.

Taylor slammed her car door and climbed the steps to her childhood home. Scarred and bruised by the years, the stairs still held steady. Safety and comfort waited behind the door.

Her mom stood in the foyer. "Three hours. That's what you told me when you left this morning, and now it's been eight. I was worried sick about you."

"I'm sorry. You shouldn't have had to track me down." Taylor's voice cracked, and she choked back the lump in her throat. She hadn't meant to worry her mom. "There were a few unexpected bumps. Like Scott."

Like Nick breaking her heart.

The frustration in her mom's face transformed into concern. "How is he?"

"Not good. The doctors aren't sure he's going to make it." She sighed. "I think I'll go up and rest."

She turned, and the sight of Nick's Bible on the foyer table stopped her. He must have forgotten it yesterday when he came to eat after church. That meal seemed like a month ago. Taylor carried the black leather Bible up the stairs, wishing he had it with him. Maybe she'd drop it off tomorrow on her way to Livy's office.

Why? So her heart could bleed some more?

A tap roused Taylor from a deep sleep, and she glanced at the clock. Nine-thirty? Had she slept five hours?

413

"It's open."

Her mother came in with a tray. "Your light was on, so I thought you were awake. I made you a sandwich and chamomile tea."

Taylor sat up in bed and stretched. She was starved. "Thank you."

"Do you think you could drag yourself away from Livy long enough to spend some time with me at a spa tomorrow? Ethan's treating. He's called and made all the arrangements. He's even going to chauffeur us. It would do you good."

"Oh, Mom, I'm sorry, not tomorrow. Maybe Wednesday?"

"The appointment is for tomorrow."

"Mom, I'm sorry." She hadn't spent nearly enough time with her mother, but she'd told Livy she'd be there early. "I promise, we'll do something later this week."

Mom sighed. "I plan to hold you to that. Now, try to get some more rest."

"I will."

After her mom left, Taylor wolfed down half the sandwich. Maybe since she'd rested, her mind could piece together two thoughts. She unplugged her phone and checked it. Two texts from Livy, the last one sent an hour ago. *Call me.*

Taylor dialed Livy's number as she climbed back in bed.

"I just woke up," she said when her friend answered.

"Good. I'm on my way home—Mac's orders. Almost to my car now. Are you feeling better?"

"Still feel like I've been hit by an eighteen-wheeler." She heard the seat belt warning as Livy started her engine. "Do you . . ."

"Do I what?"

Taylor took a deep breath. "You don't really believe my father could be a murderer, do you?"

Livy answered slowly. "I don't know, Taylor. If he's alive, he's a pretty good suspect. And if he's not alive, then someone is going to a lot of trouble to make you think he is. Mac is going to run that computer-aged photo of your dad on Crime Stoppers. We'll see if anyone recognizes him."

"Thanks for telling me." Taylor needed to warn her family.

"Have you heard from Nick?"

Taylor hesitated. "Not since I left the hospital."

"Scott crashed this afternoon, almost died. Mac found out when he called Nick to see when his brother could answer a couple of questions. The doctors shocked him back."

"I didn't know." Taylor struggled to keep her voice from cracking. Nick didn't call and tell her. He really must not want her around.

"What's going on? I saw the way he looked at you Saturday and the way you light up when you talk about him."

"I don't want to discuss it." She couldn't admit,

not even to Livy, that once again someone had dumped her.

"Come on, this is me, your best friend."

Sniffing, Taylor swiped a tear from her cheek. "Then drop it. Please."

"Are you crying?"

"Of course not." She squared her shoulders. "I'll see you tomorrow."

Taylor stared at her phone long after they'd hung up. *Humpty Dumpty had a great fall . . . and all the king's men couldn't put Humpty together again . . .* She didn't know why the silly little children's poem popped in her head. Yeah, right. Even so, she hated that Nick stood vigil at the hospital alone. She dialed his number but ended the call before it rang. Who was she kidding? She was too high risk for Nick.

Taylor padded to her dresser and found a pair of pajamas. When she crawled back in bed, she took a notepad with her. She couldn't do anything about her love life, but maybe she could figure out who was trying to kill her. And why.

She leaned against the headboard and propped the pad on her bent knees, wishing she'd written down her thoughts this morning. Starting with a time line, she recorded the nightmares about her dad, the "gifts" from her stalker, then the Coleman case, and Lieutenant Wilson's death. She wrote down Allen Yates's name as well because he was connected to Wilson. It was all about connections.

Connections. She went back and added Jonathan's name beside the nightmares since some of them included a clown.

An hour later Taylor didn't know any more than when she'd started. She was missing something. The shadow of a thought nagged at the back of her mind but wouldn't materialize. Sighing, she turned out the light. But it was a long time before sleep came and the nightmares that accompanied it.

33

Quiet settled over the ICU waiting room, leaving Nick alone with his thoughts. His brother had almost died this time, and the doctors had no answers for why, only that his blood sugar had dropped dangerously low. They'd had to shock him back when his heart stopped. No one seemed to know how or why Scott had pulled out his IV.

He'd seen Scott once, but the nurse wouldn't let him stay. Now Nick stared up at the white ceiling and waited, his legs hanging over the arm of the short couch as others around him slept.

What if Scott died? The thought, never far from his mind, slithered down his spine like the cold underbelly of a snake. If he lost Scott . . . Nick's breath caught in his chest, remembering when Angie had died. He didn't want to go through that again. It was why he let Taylor walk away earlier. He couldn't risk his heart with a woman who wouldn't let him protect her, who wouldn't listen.

Nick jumped at a slight touch on his shoulder. Scott's nurse put her finger to her lips and motioned for him to come out to the hall. Scott was dead. He felt it. His feet didn't want to move, but as quietly as he could, he slipped on his shoes and followed her.

When they were in the hall, the nurse turned to him. "Scott came around, and he keeps asking for you."

Nick's knees almost buckled. The adrenaline rush made his head light. "He's able to talk?"

"A little."

In the ICU cubicle, he sat by Scott's bed as his brother slept. He looked so vulnerable, so thin. Nick remembered the sweet kid Scott had been. His gentleness. His concern for others. There had to be a way to help him. He squeezed Scott's hand. No response. He rested his head in hand and waited.

Scott's hand moved, and Nick raised his head. "Hey, buddy. About time you woke up."

A look of panic clouded Scott's face. He gripped Nick's hand and tried to speak, but only groans slipped from his lips.

"Take it easy, Scott. You're going to be all right."

Scott fiercely shook his head. He struggled to speak again. "Mm, mm huh—"

Nick drew closer. "I don't know what you're trying to say."

Scott's eyes closed, and Nick rocked back in the chair. What if Scott had brain damage? He hadn't even considered that possibility.

"He-l-p!" Scott worked his mouth. "Ta—ta—" He sank into the mattress, panting.

"Can you write it?"

Hope flickered in Scott's eyes, and Nick scrambled to find a pen and paper.

The heart monitor screamed. He turned just as Scott's eyes rolled back in his head. The door flew open, and nurses surrounded the bed.

"He's in atrial flutter."

One of the nurses saw Nick. "I need you to clear the room."

"I can't leave. He's trying to tell me something."

"If you don't leave, he may die!"

The glaring fluorescent light cast a ghostly pallor on Scott's face. Nick eyed the monitor. His heart rate had soared over two hundred. Reluctantly, he backed out of the room.

Angie and the memory of screaming monitors sent his heart into a downward spiral.

Nicholas Sinclair. Taylor brushed her finger over the lettering on the black leather-bound Bible in her hands as the pink rays of the dawn etched the

419

sky outside her window. *The Lord is my shepherd. I shall not want* . . . Verses learned so long ago. Nick's peace came from giving God control over his life, trusting him no matter what. The part of her that was tired of fighting her own battles wanted what Nick had, but . . . she'd been burned so many times when it came to trusting.

She placed the Bible on her nightstand beside the picture Abby had colored of David and Goliath, and a memory came flooding back . . .

"I want Jesus in my heart." With trembling legs and a racing heart, she'd spoken those words to her pastor when she was eight. Even now, she remembered the pull on her heart, that hard first step, then almost running down the aisle to warmth and safety.

Accepting Jesus had been real that Sunday. With childlike faith she had placed her trust in him. Then, when her dad left, he took her faith with him. Could she get it back? That was the question. One she needed to answer.

But not today. Today, answers to who wanted to kill her waited to be found, answers that she was almost certain lay in her recent past. She set the Bible on the bedside table and picked up her notepad, wincing at the slight movement. Her body wasn't recovering nearly fast enough.

Taylor read the notes she'd written last night. The sense that she'd missed something worried her brain like a dog worried a bone. She turned to a blank page and started free writing, letting her hand write whatever popped into her mind.

Hurting. Body. Heart. Nick. Why Beth Coleman? Dad alive? Dead? Was he trying to kill me? Why? Clowns nightmares daddy death Wilson why didn't Jonathan and Ethan want me to find dad? Guns. Andy dead Dead Dead DEAD.

With a jolt she paused and looked at the last line. She'd thought the nightmares started when Michael dumped her, but they'd returned earlier, right after the hostage situation that went bad. Had that day of violence triggered the nightmares?

She flinched at the images that bombarded her. Andy Reed, pulling the trigger, his stepfather falling to the ground, a hail of bullets hitting the boy. The memory returned as fresh as the day it'd happened, just before Thanksgiving. And that night she'd had the first nightmare about her dad and the clown chasing her. Everything else happened in sequence afterward.

Taylor glanced at her free writing again. Why did everything start with the Reed shooting? And why didn't Jonathan want her to find her dad? Even Ethan opposed her search. She closed her eyes and let her mind roam.

They didn't want gossip stirred up . . . they were protecting Mom's feelings . . . her feelings . . . they did something wrong that day . . . her dad was dead . . . Yates knew and blackmailed them twenty years ago . . . her father died and they covered it up.

No. *No!* This was her uncle and Ethan she was thinking about. And wouldn't she have known somehow that her father was dead? Besides, she had his letter. She stilled in mid-thought.

Taylor jerked the nightstand drawer open and took out the packet of letters her mom had given her, then found a copy of the letter from her dad in her purse. Side by side, the two appeared to be written by the same person. She peered closer. The *s* was off, and the *t* wasn't quite right. Wait. There was one more letter, the one he'd mailed right after he left. She sorted through her files, found it, and compared it to the one that came yesterday. Maybe . . . no, there was no maybe about it. The handwriting in the last two letters was identical.

"With Ethan's talent for forgery, there's no telling where he could be." Jonathan's words at dinner that night. And if the letter was a forgery, then her dad didn't send it.

She tried to dismiss her suspicion.

And couldn't. Including herself, Ethan was connected to at least four people in the case. Her dad, Scott, Yates. Which meant he probably knew Yates's partner, Lieutenant Wilson. Maybe Yates had been blackmailing Ethan, and her uncle had nothing to do with it.

Stop it! Ethan Trask was a respected lawyer,

recently appointed to a judgeship. *Scott was in Ethan's office when he collapsed.* But there was no way Ethan was her stalker—whoever sent the gifts and photos, whoever hurt Beth Coleman was in Newton. *He could've hired someone. Scott. Or maybe Zeke Thornton.* Zeke had opportunity—both in Newton and here in Logan Point . . . *No, not Zeke.*

Taylor squeezed her eyes shut against the chaos in her head. This was crazy. She pressed her fingers to her face. She needed a break—maybe bounce some ideas off Livy.

The faint aroma of coffee tickled her nose. Mom was up. She slipped out of bed. A cup of coffee, breakfast, and then she'd come back with fresh eyes. Maybe she could even patch up things with her mom about the spa and set a time to go shopping later this week.

She picked up her cell phone, and her yearning to hear Nick's voice blindsided her. She could call . . . just to see how Scott was. Taylor scrolled to his name and clicked on it. While it rang, she sorted through her bag and came across the articles he'd given her before everything went downhill. She pulled out the envelope and laid it on her bed as the call went to Nick's voice mail. Taylor hung up and tossed her phone on the bed.

He most likely saw who was calling and didn't want to talk to her. Not today. Probably not ever.

34

"Mr. Sinclair."

Nick opened his eyes and straightened up. He must have dropped off to sleep after a nurse finally came and told him Scott had stabilized. His eyes focused on the smartly dressed young woman sitting across from him in the waiting room. She smiled and handed him a card.

"I'm so sorry to disturb you. I'm Eileen Crandall, and I work with the hospital as a patient advocate, primarily dealing with insurance issues."

"I don't understand. I gave Scott's card to the admitting clerk."

"Yes, I know. She was supposed to make a copy of it for his file, but I can't find it. Your brother isn't showing up in the insurance company's system. May I see it again?"

"Sure." He opened Scott's clothes bag, dug the billfold out, and handed her the insurance cards.

"I'll be right back with these."

While he waited, Nick glanced at the worn leather wallet. He'd meant to go through it earlier to see if he could find anything that would give him insight into Scott. Nick sorted through the wallet, finding Scott's student ID at Conway and a debit card. No credit card, though. Another ID that said Scott was twenty-one. He slipped it out, and a photo came with it. Scott with someone who looked vaguely familiar. Nick studied the man. Long hair, jeans, a T-shirt, and sunglasses. He turned the photo over. *Digger and me.* So this was Digger.

"Thank you, Mr. Sinclair." Eileen handed him Scott's cards. "Someone had keyed his identification number wrong." She smiled an apology. "And the nurse said you could go back if you'd like."

Nick stuffed the insurance cards and photo in the wallet and hurried down the hall. He tiptoed into Scott's room and sat beside his bed. On the way in, he'd been told he could stay only if Scott's heart rate stayed normal. He couldn't risk asking about Digger. He glanced at the monitor. Pulse beat a steady eighty-two. Good. And his color was better. Nick touched his arm, and Scott's eyes jerked open.

"It's just me," Nick said gently.

Scott grabbed Nick's hand. "Ta—"

"Don't do anything to get me kicked out."

Scott nodded and sagged against the bed. For a minute, he lay with his eyes closed, breathing. He moistened his lips. "E-than," he whispered.

Nick leaned in close. "Do you want Ethan?"

His eyes jerked open again. "No!"

Nick shot a side glance at the monitor. Scott's heart rate was climbing. "Calm down," he urged.

"Remember earlier, we were going to try writing your words? Would you like to do that?"

Scott nodded, and Nick took out the pen and paper he'd brought with him. "I know you're trying to tell me something about Ethan. Start with that."

He held the pad for Scott, and Scott made a few marks, and the pencil slipped from his hand. Nick looked to see what he'd written. Chicken scratches. A frustrated growl erupted from Scott's throat. Disappointment rimmed his eyes.

"Eth—" Scott was trying to talk again.

"Ethan?"

Scott nodded. "Ta—"

"Taylor?"

Scott grabbed Nick's wrist and bobbed his head. "Help . . . her."

"You want me to help Taylor?"

His eyes lit up. "Yes."

His speech was improving. "Go slower."

Scott nodded and relaxed against the mattress. He held up the hand with IV tubing. "E-than," he whispered. "In-su-lin."

Puzzled, Nick frowned.

Frustration welled in Scott's face.

"Put in-su-lin here." He waved his hand again.

Nick gaped at his brother. What he said wasn't possible. He leaned forward. "Ethan was here?"

Scott nodded again.

"In this room?"

Another nod.

"You must have dreamed it, Scott."

"No, no, no! Here!"

"Take it easy." He patted Scott's shoulder.

"Tay-lor," he whispered, his voice dropping off. He bent even closer. "What about Taylor?"

"Danger . . . Ethan . . . he'll . . . hurt Taylor . . ." Scott's eyes drooped shut.

No! Don't go to sleep now. He shook Scott but got no response, and Nick slumped back in the chair. Obviously, his brother had dreamed Ethan tried to kill him. He looked up as a nurse entered the room.

She checked his IV. "Has he drifted off again?"

"Yeah. I was hoping he would stay awake longer."

What if it wasn't a dream? He brushed the absurd thought aside. Things like that didn't happen in real life.

But what if it did? The thought persisted. *Scott's blood sugar dropped for some reason.*

"If you need me, just ring," the nurse said and turned toward the door.

"The doctor said Scott's blood sugar dropped. Is it possible he got too much insulin?"

"I don't think he gets insulin. Let me check." She returned to the bed and punched the intercom button. "See if insulin is on Scott Sinclair's chart."

The reply came quickly. "Not listed."

Nick thanked her. His gaze fell on the IV bag in the trash can beside Scott's bed. What Scott saw, whether a dream or real, caused him to pull his IV out last night. He could get the tubing tested. And if it came back positive for insulin . . . His mind didn't want to go there.

He could get Livy to test it. Taylor trusted her. Wait a minute. He couldn't accuse Ethan Trask of attempted murder, not on what might be no more than a dream.

But what if Scott was right, and Ethan planned to kill Taylor. He couldn't let that happen.

Nick lifted the trash liner from the can and wadded it into a tight bundle and tucked it under his shirt.

In the waiting room, Nick turned his cell phone on again. A call from Taylor. He dialed her number. After five rings the call went to voice mail. Frustrated, he left a message asking her to call him. Then he called Livy on her cell phone.

"I need a favor," he said when she answered.

35

At the Criminal Justice Center, Nick took the IV bag and tubing from the trash bag and handed it to Livy. "My brother thinks Ethan Trask tried to kill him last night by putting insulin in his IV. And that Taylor is next."

"You're kidding, right?" Livy stared from the tubing to Nick's face. "You're not."

"His blood sugar dropped to practically nothing, and he pulled his IV out for some reason." He paced the area in front of her desk. "I don't think Scott was hallucinating, either. Testing the tubing is the only way to know for sure. How fast can you get a test run?"

"I can call in a favor, get it done within the hour."

"I tried to call and warn Taylor, but she doesn't answer." He scrubbed the side of his face. "I hope that's soon enough."

After Livy headed to the lab, Nick tried Taylor's cell phone again. Why didn't she answer? Maybe she'd forgotten to charge her phone again.

"They'll call as soon as they have the results," Livy said when she returned.

"Taylor still isn't answering her cell."

"She may be in the shower. You need to calm down. Scott could've dreamed the whole thing. Think about it . . . Ethan is a respected attorney."

What Livy said was nothing he hadn't already told himself. He took a slow breath and blew it out. He felt Livy's gaze on him.

"I know I'm butting in, but Taylor is my friend, and she was really upset last night about something to do with you. What happened?"

He flinched under her intense scrutiny.

"You told her you didn't want to see her again, didn't you?" Disappointment rang in her voice.

He crossed his arms. "I asked her . . . to choose between me and her police work."

"Why? She lives to solve crimes, and to teach others how to do it."

"The teaching is fine. That's not dangerous. But dealing with criminals . . . she'll get herself killed." His fingers curled into fists. "You don't know what it's like to see someone you love on a cold, wet sidewalk, their lifeblood pouring out of them. I just want to protect her, keep her safe."

"Of all people, you should realize you can't protect her. As hard as you tried, you couldn't protect your wife." Livy's phone rang. "Think about that," she said and excused herself.

Nick rubbed his hand across his mouth. He closed his eyes, thinking how this stubborn, beautiful woman had come into his life and turned it upside down in three short weeks.

Livy returned. "That was Ben Logan. He heard back about the fingerprints on the envelope Taylor received last week. Nada. He's sending them to the Violent Crimes Apprehension Program."

"Good. We need a break, or Taylor might not walk away the next time."

As Taylor descended the stairs, the aroma of fresh-brewed coffee and biscuits baking in the oven drew her to the kitchen.

"Good morning," her mother called brightly. "Are you feeling better?"

She wished. But she knew better than to tell her mom how she really felt. "I think I am."

"Good. Biscuits are coming out in five minutes."

Taylor poured a cup of coffee. Her mother was dressed to go out. "Got a busy day today?" she asked.

"The spa? Ethan's surprise? Remember?"

"Oh . . . yeah." What if her suspicions were true? "Any chance you can change the date? Make it tomorrow, and I'll go with you."

"I'm afraid it's too late." Her mom's eyes twinkled like she had a secret. "When I told Ethan you couldn't come, he decided to take your place."

Taylor's mind raced. Her hunches were rarely wrong, but her mom probably wouldn't believe her. More proof, that's what she needed.

"I still wish you'd wait." Taylor stirred creamer in her coffee. "Have you seen Jonathan?"

"I saw his truck go toward the home place. Why?"

"Oh, just thought I would talk to him a minute before I went to Memphis to see Livy." Taylor didn't know what she would say to her uncle— maybe ask if Allen Yates had blackmailed him twenty years ago. Get him to confess that he and Ethan had killed the cop. She certainly wanted to ask him about that letter from her dad.

"I tell you what." Mom took out the biscuits. "When Ethan gets here, I'll ask him if we can make the spa appointment tomorrow. I'd really like you to come."

"Great." A day's reprieve would make Taylor feel better.

After getting dressed, Taylor checked her cell phone. Nick called. She quickly redialed, but an incoming call flashed, displaying the Bradford County Sheriff Department, and she switched to it. "Hey, Ben." Holding the phone between her ear and shoulder, she picked up the envelope she'd laid on the bed.

"I heard from Jackson. They lifted two sets of prints from that envelope that didn't belong to you or Jonathan or Pete. Nothing on the photos. They're sending all of them on to ViCAP."

"Good. Where are you?" She might run a few of her ideas by him before she went downtown.

"I'm on the other end of the county checking on a reported meth lab. Did you need me?"

"Sort of, but I'm leaving in a few minutes for Memphis." She slid the newspaper articles out as an incoming call buzzed in her ear. Nick again. "Can I call you right back?"

"No need. I just wanted to tell you about the report."

"Thanks." She switched to Nick's call, but he'd hung up. She redialed and it went to voice mail. She left him a message, then slid her phone into her pocket and flipped through the articles. The first was the account of her father's disappearance. Nothing new there. Next was a follow-up article. The following three were clipped together, and Nick had attached a note indicating they were written before his disappearance.

She read the accolades about her father. James Martin was depicted as a man who gave much of his time to helping others. After reading them, Taylor sat absolutely still. The man in the article would never abandon his responsibilities. What happened to change all that? She picked up the last article and gasped.

The clown in her dreams stared at her from the paper. Under the picture the caption read "Ethan Trask and Jonathan Martin perform for sick children." Her gaze froze on Ethan's face.

A wisp of memory curled through her mind. Two clowns. Jonathan and Ethan. Her father, yelling. Ethan raising his arm . . .

Her dad wasn't dancing with another woman.

Her mind released what it had shielded her from for so long.

He had been struggling with Ethan.

Ethan killed her dad.

Taylor jerked the door open and raced down the stairs while she dialed Livy's number. She burst into the kitchen. "Mom! Ethan—"

"Hello, Taylor." Ethan faced her, a .38 Special in his hand.

36

"Taylor! Are you there?" The faint sound of Livy's voice sounded in the kitchen.

Ethan grabbed Taylor's phone and ended the call.

"What are you doing?" Taylor snatched for her phone, but the look on Ethan's face stopped her. "Give me my phone." She glanced around the room. "Where's my mom?"

"Waiting for you." He waved the .38 at her. "Revolvers don't jam."

"You? It was you?" Her mind tried to grasp that it had been Ethan who'd tried to kill her.

Her phone rang again.

"That'll be Livy calling back," she said, not taking her eyes off the gun. "She'll want to know why I hung up. Maybe bad enough to come out here."

"We'll be gone before she can get here."

"Ben can be here in five minutes. That's who she'll call if I don't answer."

He handed the phone to Taylor. "Put it on speaker. I don't have to tell you to watch what you say, not if you want your mother to live."

Taylor almost dropped the phone. With a shaky finger, she pressed the speaker button.

"Did you call me?" Livy's voice sounded hollow in the room.

Ethan shook his head.

"Um, not on purpose."

"Well, where are you? I thought you were coming downtown."

"I, ah, got busy. I'm on my way now."

Taylor heard a voice in the background. "Ask when she'll get here."

Nick was with Livy?

"Hurry up." Livy sounded impatient. "I have some information for you."

"We'll talk about it when I get there, *chère*." Taylor quickly ended the call, and Ethan grabbed the phone, tossing it on the table.

"Let's go," he said.

She narrowed her eyes. "What did you do with my mother?"

"She's waiting for you at Oak Grove. And don't look at me like that. This is entirely your fault. You couldn't leave well enough alone. No, you had to keep digging and digging. 'We need to know the truth.' " He mimicked her voice. "I can't let you ruin my career."

She took a step back. "It's been you from the start. In Newton, you hired Scott to stalk me, but here, you did your own dirty work." Taylor gasped. "*You* gave Scott that overdose."

"You're not as smart as you think." Ethan laughed, and the sound sent chills through her. "I sent him to Newton just to get him out of my hair, and he gets a crush on you."

435

"You can't frame him for this."

"Don't worry your pretty little head about Scott." He jerked his head toward the door. "Let's go."

Taylor swallowed. She had to buy time. It'd take Livy and Nick thirty minutes to get here . . . if Livy understood. And Ben was almost as far away.

"Why didn't you kill me then? When you killed my dad?"

"I didn't know you were in the basement that day. Then you acted weird after your dad didn't come home, and I suspected but could never be sure. There were times I actually considered it, but I knew I had to make it look like an accident. The opportunity never opened up." He shoved her toward the door.

She stumbled, and despair welled up. She should have figured out it was Ethan all the time. And because she hadn't, her mom would pay the price. All of her skill and knowledge wouldn't help now—it wouldn't save her or her mother.

"Move."

The hard steel of the gun pressed into the small of Taylor's back.

Livy put down the receiver. "We have to get to the Martin farm."

"Why?"

"There's only one reason Taylor would call

me *chère* when she hung up—she's in trouble."

Nick hurried behind her, not understanding. But if Livy was going to Taylor, so was he. "Where was she?"

"Still at home. Let's take my car. I'll call Ben and get him to meet us there."

As they pulled from the parking garage, Livy said, "*Chère* was our code for 'I need help, come bail me out.' And it may be nothing more than my overactive imagination—"

Her cell phone rang.

"It's the lab." She put the phone on speaker.

"Got your results. Positive for insulin."

37

Given a choice, Taylor would stage her last stand in the kitchen, but if she failed, it would mean sure death for her mother. Once outside, Ethan forced her into the driver side of his Escalade and instructed her to drive to the old home place. As they inched past Jonathan's travel trailer, she searched for Pete. Where was he when she needed him? And where was Jonathan?

Oak Grove drew closer, its empty windows reminding her of opportunities lost . . . and her nightmares of dying in this desolate house. Adrenaline shot through her veins. Not if she could help it.

"How do you think you're going to get away with this? You can't just kill two people and not be a suspect."

"I'm not stupid, Taylor. The police will have a suspect. A dead one. It's really too bad, you know . . . Jonathan carrying the guilt of killing his brother all those years. Today he just lost it and killed you and your mother before turning the gun on himself."

Ethan directed her to park under the ancient oak. "He's wanted to tell the truth for years, you know. Now I'll tell it for him, or at least my version."

He laughed, the sound so deranged, she shuddered. He pulled the keys from the ignition. "Sit there until I come around."

Taylor thought about making a run for it, but she couldn't outrun a bullet. Instead, she did as he said. Once inside the house, she trudged toward the basement door, her footsteps echoing in the empty hall.

Taylor's heart thumped with each step down the dark stairs. Cold dampness seeped into her bones. She had been here so many times in her dreams. She stepped off the landing into the basement, where a portable lantern lit the room. Her mom's small frame huddled against the brick, her platinum hair plastered to her head, her hands bound in front of her. Jonathan sat on the hearth, his head buried in his hands. He looked up.

"I'm sorry, Taylor. I didn't know Ethan planned . . ." He covered his mouth with his hand.

Her uncle's face framed with fuzzy red hair formed in her mind's eye. "But you knew Ethan killed Dad. You could have told."

"You knew?" Her mom struggled to turn and look at Jonathan. "All these years, you knew?"

Her uncle seemed to shrink before her eyes, then her gaze went to the sealed fireplace behind him. No one had to tell her that the chimney contained her father's body. Dead. Her lips tingled as blood drained from her face. Her fingers curled into fists as shock morphed into anger. Ethan had robbed her of her father. And now he intended to kill the rest of her family.

She could almost hear Ethan explain to everyone how Jonathan broke under the pressure and killed his sister-in-law and niece. He probably already had a story prepared on how Jonathan managed to get them both in the basement.

Ethan prodded Taylor with the gun. "Put your hands behind your back."

"No." She turned around to face him.

He lifted the gun toward her mom. "Would you rather I shoot your mother in her hand or her knee?"

He was evil enough to do it. Which would leave him with four bullets in the revolver. More than enough. She turned around and winced as he jerked tape around her wrists, hope slipping with each wrap. The sealed chimney mocked her. "Why the chimney? Why not the tunnels?"

Ethan jerked his head toward her mom. "Because Allison here roamed those tunnels. Couldn't take a chance on her finding the body."

Mom gasped. "How could you?"

He shrugged. "It really was an accident. I never meant to kill James."

The lack of emotion in his voice sent a shiver through Taylor. She had to buy time and turned to her uncle. "I don't understand why you wanted to sell the land and this house. Weren't you afraid the new owners would find the . . ." Taylor couldn't bring herself to say the word.

Ethan shoved her toward the hearth. "Because I was the one buying the property."

"You? Why would *you* want it?" Taylor braced against the rough fireplace and slid to the floor, the corner bricks digging into her arm. If Livy and Nick didn't arrive soon, they would die. She pressed her back and hands against the rough brick and rubbed up and down, scraping the skin.

"I'm tired of giving your uncle money and never getting anything in return. At least this way I'll have the land and this house."

"What are you talking about?"

Jonathan came to life. "Shut up, Ethan."

How deep was her uncle involved in this? She needed to ask questions. Anything to stall until Livy and Nick got there. If they came. She had to keep them talking. "You won't get away with killing us, Ethan."

"We can't do this." Jonathan stood.

Maybe he hadn't slipped over the edge of no return. "It's not too late, Jonathan. You haven't killed anyone yet." Taylor hoped that was true. "Don't you see? Ethan is going to kill us and pin it on you. It's the only way he can get out of this mess. He told me."

Jonathan shot an anxious glance at Ethan.

"Sit down, Jonathan. You're not going to do anything. You never have."

"Ethan will kill you, just like us," Taylor said. She shifted to face Ethan. "How about the Yates and Wilson murders? Are you going to pin them on him as well?"

"I didn't have anything to do with that!" Sweat poured down Jonathan's face. He paced. "I told you killing Wilson would bring a lot of attention. That the cops would figure out Yates didn't commit suicide."

Ethan turned a cold eye to Jonathan. "You were glad enough you didn't have to pay him any longer."

She'd been right. Allen Yates had figured out they had killed her dad and then blackmailed Ethan and her uncle. "Why kill Rob Wilson? He didn't harm anyone." The tape around her wrists gave a little.

"Shut up," Ethan growled.

"Jonathan." She kept her voice soft, hoping that if it came down to it, he couldn't commit murder. "Help us."

"You're talking to a lost cause, Taylor. Your uncle is in too deep. Like me."

"Did you seal my father's body in the chimney before you used his plane ticket, Ethan? Or after you returned from Houston?"

Was that admiration in his eyes? Taylor hoped so. She knew his type—Ethan needed someone to know how smart he was. For twenty years he'd gotten away with the perfect crime, but he'd been unable to brag about it. Had to be eating him up.

"Security was a joke then. Nobody checked IDs." He cocked his head. "You always were smart. Just not smart enough to leave well enough alone."

"Why? At least tell me why you killed him."

"No, don't answer her!" Jonathan's voice broke.

Ethan glanced toward her uncle, and his lip curled into a sneer. "What's the matter, Jonathan? Don't you want your niece to know that none of this would have happened if it hadn't been for your gambling problem? That even now you wouldn't need to sell the land if you had just quit."

Her mom gasped. "You murdered him for money?"

"I told you, I didn't *murder* him," Ethan said. "It was an accident. James caught me in the act of forging a five hundred dollar check to the company Jonathan and I formed."

"Did you think my husband wouldn't catch you?"

Ethan turned to her mother. "James trusted his brother, the accountant—who better to take care of the farm books? James was going to the police. He didn't care that the money was to bail his brother out of a gambling mess."

"What about the ten thousand dollars in the safe? Which one of you got that?" Taylor asked.

Ethan turned to her uncle. "Jonathan, would you like to explain that?"

Jonathan didn't answer.

"I didn't think so. We split it. I invested my part, Jonathan blew his on the dogs across the river."

"So you killed him." Taylor almost had the tape loose. "And you call that an accident?"

"I wasn't going to jail then." He leveled the gun at Taylor. "And I'm not going to jail now."

"No!" Jonathan lunged at Ethan, knocking the gun out of his hand. It skittered across the basement floor. Taylor broke free of the tape and struggled to her feet. As the two men fought, she pulled her mother up and pushed her toward the stairs. "Hurry!"

They ran for the steps, Taylor urging her mother on. A shot rang out, the bullet splintering the wooden joists above her head. Then three more.

At the top, her mother fumbled with the door. "It won't open!"

Ethan's last bullet blasted a hole in the door over their heads.

She pushed past her mom and threw her weight against the door.

Footsteps pounded the steps behind her. Taylor gave one last push, and the door flew open. She shoved her mother through it. "Run! Get help!"

Ethan grabbed her ankle. She turned and kicked, aiming at his nose.

He screamed again but held on to her leg. They teetered at the top of the steps. Taylor grabbed for the banister, but Ethan's weight pulled her down the steps with him.

Nick clenched his hands as Livy pounded on the Martins' front door. Taylor was in trouble, he felt it. "No one's here." Livy shook the doorknob. "And it's locked. Let's try the back door."

They sprinted around the house. Nick reached the door first. Unlocked. He shoved it open, calling Taylor's name as he entered the kitchen.

"What are you doing?" Livy demanded. "You don't even have a gun. Let me go first." She pushed through the kitchen door. "Taylor, it's me, Livy."

Nick spied her cell phone on the table. "This is why she doesn't answer her phone."

He trailed Livy as she moved cautiously through the dining room, her gun held in front of her.

Empty. At the foot of the stairs, Livy called out again, and again silence answered them.

Nick chafed as they crept up the stairs. He wanted to take them two at a time. Livy paused outside Taylor's bedroom door and then whipped around the corner into the room. "She's not here."

Outside, a siren wailed up the driveway, and Ben got out of his SUV. They met him at the back door.

"No one's here," Livy said.

Ben waved a police report. "Have you seen Pete Connelly?"

Pete! Now he knew why Digger looked familiar. Shave the long hair, and it was the guy Nick ran into at the picnic.

"That's him! Digger." Nick jerked Scott's wallet from his pocket and waved the photo. "He's the one who framed Scott."

"ViCAP says the prints I took from his tea glass match a partial print found at Ralph Jenkins's apartment," Ben said.

"The kidnapper in Seattle?"

The information rocked Nick. "I don't get it. If Pete killed that kidnapper and then tried to kill Taylor, why did Ethan try to kill my brother?"

"I don't know. But Pete works for Ethan sometimes," Livy said. "Ethan must have been involved somehow."

"Have you checked the barn? Or the trailer Pete was staying in?" Ben asked.

"You check the trailer," Livy said. "I'll check the barn. And you," she said to Nick, "come with me."

He followed Livy to the barn. No Taylor, no Ethan, and no Pete.

Livy holstered her gun. "Let's see if Ben's found anything."

At the travel trailer, Ben yelled for them to come in. "You have to see this."

A computer sat on the small table. A photo of Taylor jogging filled the screen, then faded into one of her on a flat rock.

"Pete's obsessed with her," Ben said. He handed Nick three sheets of paper. Meade Funeral Home letterheads. Ben hit the escape button and clicked on another folder. "He has thousands of photos of her, all the way back to high school. And look at this." He opened another folder, and a slide show started.

Livy gasped. "That's those murdered women. The ones with their mouths glued shut. How did I not realize this?" She rubbed her forehead. "I mean, he was always just Pete Connelly, the guy no one ever saw."

"That's how it works," Nick said. "I've researched obsessive love relationships, usually in connection with a serial killer, but it's always the same. The obsessive personality is buried under a normal, nonthreatening persona."

"Well, if he's obsessed, at least he won't kill her," Livy said, her voice sober.

"I don't know." Nick heaved a sigh. "If Pete thinks he can never have Taylor, he might decide no one else can have her either."

"Ohh," Taylor moaned. Cold seeped into her back from the stone floor. She opened her eyes, and her mom's tear-streaked face came into focus. "Mom? What are you doing here? Why did you come back?"

Her mom rocked on her heels. "I couldn't leave you, and when I ran into Pete . . ."

At least her mom's hands were loose, but the look in her eyes . . . Taylor had found a trapped fox once with the same look. "He came to help?"

"Ethan's dead. Pete shot him." Her mom spoke in a monotone.

"Pete?" Taylor struggled to get up. The scent of Old Spice pervaded her senses.

Her mom buried her face in her hands. "I think Jonathan is dead too."

"Having a bit of trouble, Taylor?"

She jerked her head toward Pete's voice and gulped at the .40 mm Glock pointed at her. *Stay calm. Act as if everything is normal.* She lifted her gaze to his face and stared into dead black eyes. The eyes of a psychopath. Ethan had been frightening. Pete terrified her.

"The Old Spice. It was you . . ."

"Nice touch, huh?" Pete's mouth curved into a sneer.

"How did you know?"

"Overheard you tell Livy one time you hated that scent, that it reminded you of your dad."

Taylor lowered her gaze. *Talk to him . . . connect with him.* She sucked in a breath and forced her body to relax, especially her vocal cords. She spoke softly. "Thanks for saving my life."

"He wanted me to kill you in Newton." Pete smiled. A dead man's smile. "Didn't mean to hit you so hard that night, but I had to make Ethan think I tried."

"Why?"

He gave her a puzzled look. "That should be obvious. To stop you from looking for your father."

"But why did he wait until May? I asked Jonathan about my dad at Thanksgiving."

He laughed, the sound dry, humorless. "Jonathan never told him. Ethan found out when your friend on the Memphis Police Department sent a request to the archives."

"How did he know Livy—"

Pete rubbed his thumb and finger together. "Money buys information. All these years, Ethan had someone in the archive department keeping tabs on different cases. Of course, your father's was the only one he was concerned about." He stared at her, his eyes softening. "I've actually been protecting you, Taylor. Now we can be together."

She fought to keep from screaming. Where was Livy? "Did Scott help you?"

"You're better than that, Taylor." He puffed out his chest, tapping it with his free hand. "Or maybe I'm the one who's better—if you actually believed that drunken kid could take those photos without getting caught. And the poem . . . that was a stroke of sheer genius. Scott bragged about his big brother, showed me a story he'd published. And you really should have better security on your email. You made it so easy."

"No, you're just smarter than I am."

His eyes hardened and he grabbed her hair, yanking her face close to his mouth. He laid the gun against her neck.

Her mother screamed.

"Don't try to snow me now." His whisper rasped against her ear. "Ethan believed he was smarter than me too. See where it got him."

She shuddered as he stroked her cheek with the gun.

"Do you remember laughing at me, Taylor? I asked you to go to the school dance—you thought it was so funny, you and your friends."

"Pete, I never . . ." A memory flashed through her mind. She stood in the school cafeteria with Robyn and Livy . . . Pete, red-faced and stammering, asking her to go to the sophomore dance. She *had* laughed in his face. The memory

449

made her sick. "I was a snotty fifteen-year-old. I'm so sorry . . . don't do this—"

"Don't do this." He altered his voice to sound feminine, frightened. "You sound just like Beth Coleman. By the way, I loved the look on your face when you read my note at the crime scene."

Taylor studied his features, and an image floated to her mind. Longer hair, camouflage jacket, and pants . . . the guy with search and rescue. "You were there," she whispered.

The sweet wail of sirens reached her ears, and Pete jerked his head up.

Livy understood!

"Come on! You're coming with me." Pete grabbed her by the arm, yanking her up. "You too, Ms. Martin."

He pulled her toward the tunnel door, past Jonathan's body, where a pool of blood seeped onto the concrete floor. Was he moving?

Pete motioned with the gun for her mother to open the door.

"No! I'm not going in the tunnels." Taylor jerked away from his grasp and shoved him.

Suddenly, Jonathan rose to his knees, bellowing and tackling Pete's legs. He kicked free and turned, firing his gun.

The bullet missed, and Jonathan lunged for Pete, knocking him to the floor.

"Come on!" Taylor pulled her mom toward the stairs.

"No! We'll never make it up the stairs. He'll catch us." Her mom grabbed her arm and tugged her toward the tunnel. "This way."

The tunnel door.

No.

She couldn't.

The darkness would swallow her.

Her mother pushed her through the entrance. "Taylor, trust me. I know the way." She shoved the door shut, cutting off all light. Stagnant air touched Taylor's cheek as darkness shrouded her. Her feet refused to move. Her chest tightened with the rapid-fire beat of her heart. She thought it would explode.

Breathe.

She couldn't. The tunnel smelled like a freshly turned grave.

"Taylor."

She almost jumped out of her skin.

"I'm going to bar the door, and then I'm going to take your hand, and we're going to walk out of here through the caves."

The sound of wood sliding on wood grated against her ears.

"I . . . I can't." Just like Taylor couldn't move the night Sheriff Atkins almost died. Maybe if she touched the wall. She reached out, touching the slimy dirt, and jerked her hand back.

The door rattled.

Taylor sucked in her breath.

"Pete's trying to get it open," Mom whispered.

A bullet thudded into the wood.

Another.

Then quiet . . . until a dull thump shook the door. Pete must have found one of Jonathan's two by fours.

She'd heard the sirens. Where were Livy and Nick? *Nick.* Had he come for her?

"Take my hand." Her mother's fingers locked around Taylor's. "We have to get past where the tunnels cross before he gets the door down. Even if he knows the tunnels, he won't know which way we went. Trust me, Taylor."

If it wasn't so dark . . . if only she could see a spark of light.

"I am the Light of the World. Whoever follows me will never walk in darkness . . ."

God?

Yeah, using her mom's voice.

Her mom squeezed her hand. "I know you thought God didn't care, but Taylor, he protected you from Ethan all these years. He hasn't brought you this far to let you die. Come on. We have to get farther into the tunnels."

She tried, but she couldn't move. It was like chains held her to the floor.

Suddenly her mom grabbed her shoulders and shook her. "You listen to me, Taylor Martin. I want you to take my hand and come with me. Or we will both die right here."

A thud punctuated her mom's words, and Taylor jerked.

"Come on!" Mom tugged her hand.

Taylor licked her parched lips. Then clasping her mother's hand, she took a step in the pitch-black darkness.

38

"That's gunfire!" Nick leaped from the trailer. Livy and Ben followed.

Another shot echoed.

"It's coming from Oak Grove."

Nick ignored the SUV and ran the short distance to the house. Ben and Livy caught up with him as he took the porch steps two at a time.

"Wait," Ben yelled. "You can't go in there."

"The woman I love is here somewhere. You're not keeping me out."

The sheriff eyed him. "Stay out of the way, then."

Nick followed as they went in, sweeping the house. Clean. Livy eased down the basement steps with Ben and Nick on her heels.

"I see a body," Livy said. She knelt beside it. "Ethan. He's dead."

"Jonathan's over here. Looks like he's been shot too." Ben felt for a pulse and spoke into his shoulder mic. "Need an ambulance at Oak Grove."

He looked at Livy. "He's hanging on. Barely."

"They're in the tunnels." Nick pointed to the battered door. "Where do they end?"

"Ben, you know these tunnels," Livy said. "What do we need to do?"

"Only two of the tunnels are still functional. They both end at the caves by the bluffs." Ben held out his hand to Livy. "Nick and I will cover the caves. You take this end. And be careful."

"Taylor!" Pete's voice echoed down the tunnels. "You can't escape me."

He'd gotten through the door. Taylor looked over her shoulder. A thin light glowed behind them. He had a flashlight.

"We should almost be to the cross tunnel."

"How do you know?"

"I know the tunnels like the back of my hand. I always counted how many steps I took—I had a flashlight then, but I was scared it'd go out and I wouldn't be able to get back."

Taylor stumbled and fell forward, losing her mother's hand. Her knee hit the hard dirt. The darkness pressed in like a pillow, smothering her. She clawed the dirt.

"Taylor, where are you?"

The whispered words calmed her racing mind. "On the floor," she whispered back.

A hand touched her shoulder, rubbing it.

"You're okay. Get up. We're almost there."

Taylor's hand raked over something cold and hard and round. "Wait! I found something."

She ignored the faint light as it drew nearer and dug dirt away from the cylinder until she wrapped her fingers around a pipe. She pulled, and it popped out of the ground.

"Come on, Taylor," her mom whispered. "He's getting closer."

She scrambled up, holding the pipe, and grabbed her mom's hand. Her mom pulled her inside another tunnel. "We're safe. We can get to the lake from here."

She hoped her mom knew what she was talking about. Taylor glanced from where they'd come. The faint light grew brighter.

Mom gasped.

Taylor bumped into her mom. "What is it?"

"I hear you . . ." Pete's taunting voice echoed in the darkness.

"The tunnel. It's blocked. We can't go any farther."

Her hope plummeted.

"You can't run, Taylor. I'll find you."

Not without a fight. She pulled her mom close. "When I divert his attention, go!"

"I can't leave you."

"You have to. I can reason with him, but not if I'm afraid he's going to kill you."

Without waiting for an answer, she gripped the

pipe and crept back to the cross path. He was almost there . . .

"Taylor! Are you in here?" Livy's voice echoed through the tunnel.

Pete's light swung around.

Now! Taylor rushed toward the light, swinging the pipe.

She connected.

Pete yelled. The light flew to the floor.

"We're here!" Taylor screamed. "Go, Mom!"

She swung the pipe again.

He grabbed it, pulling her off balance. "I have you now."

Once again she felt the cold steel barrel of his gun against her neck.

39

Nick brushed cobwebs from his face, and using the flashlight he'd found in Ben's pickup, he shined light around the tunnel wall. The sheriff had told him to wait for his deputies, but as soon as Ben disappeared into the tunnels, Nick had followed. Ahead the passage narrowed and became lower. He stooped and crept through the shaft, his ears straining to hear Taylor's voice . . . anything.

A path intersected the one he was on, and Nick hesitated. Keep going or take this path? Ben had said there were half a dozen tunnels criss-crossing to the caves, most of them blocked.

Footsteps. Someone was coming his way. He flicked his light off. The sound grew closer. The figure was so slight, he almost missed it. Certainly wasn't Connelly. "Taylor?" he whispered, his voice carrying in the damp air.

The woman yelped, and Nick shined the light on her. "Allison?"

"Nick!" She fell into his arms, sobbing. "You have to save her."

"Where is she?"

"At the end of this tunnel. At least five minutes away. Is anyone with you?"

"Ben is in one of the other tunnels." He held her at arm's length. "Go on to the cave entrance. Ben's deputies should bc here any minute."

"No! I'm going with you."

"I need you to tell the deputies which way to come. Now go!"

Nick gently shoved her in the direction of the cave. "I'll find her, Allison. Don't worry."

If only he had some way to communicate with Ben. He shined his light on his cell. No service. Nick kept his flashlight on and aimed at the tunnel floor and crept forward until he estimated three minutes had passed, then he flicked it off. He didn't want to give his position away. His progress slowed in the dark as he felt his way along the slick wall.

Voices reached him. A man's voice . . . a woman's . . . didn't sound like Taylor. He stumbled and almost fell, stirring up musty spores on the tunnel floor.

"Let her go, Pete."

Livy. Relief swept over him. At least he didn't have to be the Lone Ranger.

"You come one step closer, and I'll blow her head off."

Not good. Pete sounded panicky. It wouldn't take much for him to follow through on his threat. Nick assessed the situation. Taylor was in another tunnel, one that intersected Nick's. *Be nearby, Ben.* Nick eased toward the voices. Finally, a faint light glowed to his left.

"You do, and you won't leave here alive, Pete."

"Don't make me do it, then. I don't have anything to lose."

Nick dropped to his knees and crawled until the tunnels crossed. He stuck his head around the corner, and his heart leaped in his throat.

Livy's flashlight illuminated Pete and Taylor's silhouette.

Pete held a gun to Taylor's head.

40

Taylor's ankle throbbed where she'd twisted it when she attacked Pete. She shifted her weight, and Pete tightened his choke hold on her. At least with Livy's light, she wasn't trapped in darkness.

"Pete, I have a bottle of water here," Livy yelled.

"Keep your water." He stepped back, pulling Taylor with him. His feet stirred the ground, and the sour odor filled her nostrils. Along with another faint scent . . . fresh, like sunshine. Like Nick.

She didn't breathe. Nick was here. He'd come for her.

"Maybe Taylor would like a drink." Livy's voice had an edge to it.

"Forget the water!" Pete waved the gun, then pressed the barrel against her cheek again. "And get me that helicopter!"

Do it again, Livy. Make him mad. Taylor prepared herself, mentally picturing Pete's most vulnerable spot. If he moved that gun just once more . . .

"Just calm down, Pete."

He slid the gun up the side of her head, then jerked it in the air and fired. "Don't tell me what to do. You got five—"

Taylor rammed her right elbow in his Adam's apple. Pete shrieked and bent over, holding his throat. She jabbed him again, this time aiming for his nose. Something crashed into them from behind, and the gun dropped to the floor.

"Run, Taylor!"

Nick.

Pete scrambled for the gun. Taylor lunged for him as Nick landed on Pete's back.

Livy kicked the gun out of his reach. "You're under arrest, Pete Connelly. On your face, hands behind your back. Now!"

Taylor fell into Nick's arms, and he crushed her against his chest. She felt the pounding beat of his heart as she clung to him.

He kissed the top of her head. "Do you think you're done scaring the life out of me?"

Daylight never looked so good. Taylor braced her back against a post as she and her mother waited on the porch at Oak Grove. Paramedics had wrapped her foot and dressed the scratches she'd gotten in the scuffle. Nick had walked out under the tall trees to call the hospital and check on Scott. Pete sat handcuffed in the backseat of a patrol car, his expression alternating between hatred and resignation.

Her mom slipped her arm around Taylor's waist and heaved a sigh. "It's over."

"Yes. It's over." Taylor leaned into the embrace. Beyond the patrol car, an ambulance carrying Ethan's body drove slowly away. "No more nightmares."

But now they had to deal with the aftermath. Her dad, dead all these years. But for Taylor, and her mother as well, the loss was fresh and painful. She felt her mom shudder.

"Your father . . ." Her voice broke, and she cried silently. Taylor cried with her.

"I always believed he'd walk through the door one day, that he would come back," her mom said through her tears. "But that's never going to happen now."

"I know." Taylor wiped her eyes with the back of her hand. "But at least we can grieve for him."

"I feel so bad for the anger I've harbored. I should have known he would never leave us, but I just never believed he was dead. I thought if he was, I would know it in my heart."

"I know. I did too." Taylor closed her eyes. She'd wasted so many years believing her father had rejected her. At least that weight was gone. "It's in the past. We have to put it behind us and move forward."

Mom smiled through her tears. "Yes. I think we can now."

Taylor wrapped her arms around her mother. Memories of her dad flooded her mind. Memories she could embrace now. She pulled away and wiped her cheek with a tissue from her mom. "Do you think Jonathan will make it?"

Her mom dabbed her eyes as well. "I asked Ben how bad his injuries were while they were wrapping your foot. It doesn't look good. I'm afraid he won't have the will to live. So many mistakes . . . but we'd both be dead if he hadn't . . ."

"I know." Taylor stared at the ground. She'd loved her uncle all her life, and she couldn't imagine their lives without him in it. But after what she'd learned . . . she simply had to focus on the fact that he'd tried to save them. "I hope he makes it."

Her mom squeezed Taylor's hand again. "I'm so proud of you. You're good at this police stuff." She took a deep breath. "You were born to do it. Doesn't mean I won't worry, but I had no right to ask you to stop."

"And I was wrong as well," Nick said.

Taylor looked up. She hadn't heard him approach. His tender smile hooked into her heart, anchoring it. Otherwise, she was sure it would leap out of her chest.

Mom's cell phone rang, and she glanced at it and sighed. "It's your brother. I'd hoped to tell him before he heard about this from someone else."

Her mom walked away from them, her cell phone pressed to her ear. Taylor looked up. Nick's eyes held hers. She wanted so badly to believe what she saw in them was love. But could he really accept her the way she was?

He took her hand. "Want to take a walk with me?"

She nodded, and they strolled toward the grove of oaks. "How is Scott?" Taylor asked.

"Better. The doctor said he's going to be fine, no lasting effect of the insulin that Ethan gave him. But it's not Scott I want to talk about. I want to apologize."

She gave him a curious glance.

He rubbed his hand over his jaw. "In the tunnels . . . I thought . . ." He looked toward the old house. "When Petc held that gun to your head . . . I—"

"I understand, Nick." Taylor wrapped her arms across her stomach and stared at the ground. "After losing your wife like you did, I don't blame you for not wanting to go through that again."

"That's not what I was trying to say. When it was all over, all I could think about was that you were safe and we had another chance." He lifted her chin. "I'm sorry for asking you to give up something you were meant to do. I'd like to start over."

"What . . . what do you mean?"

Nick brushed back a strand of hair, then cupped her face, his fingers sending shock waves through her body.

"I was wrong," he said. "Helping others solve crimes is part of who you are. I don't want to change that about you."

A breeze touched her cheeks, bringing the scent of honeysuckle as hope soared in her heart. She smiled up at Nick through blurry eyes. "You don't?"

"No." His fingers trailed down her neck, sending chills chasing down her spine as he bent toward her and gently kissed hcr lips. She slipped her arms around him, and he pulled her to him.

"I think I'm falling in love with you, Taylor Martin. Would you want to take a chance, see where this relationship takes us?"

She blinked back tears. "I think I would, Nick Sinclair. But are you sure?"

The answer came in the form of a solid, unwavering kiss that melted her like warm butter.

Center Point Large Print
600 Brooks Road / PO Box 1
Thorndike ME 04986-0001 USA

(207) 568-3717

US & Canada:
1 800 929-9108
www.centerpointlargeprint.com

Niles
Public Library District

JUN 1 7 2014

Niles, Illinois 60714